TIDAL WAVE

Mystical Elements Book 1

Meg Lynn

GLOSSARY

People/Things

Elemental: A witch with the ability to control one of the five elements: water, fire, earth, air or spirit. Elemental power is regenerated to each Generation.

Generation: A group of five Elementals, each representing one element, born within five years of one another. A Generation is connected through their powers and are able to feel the other's powers when used.

Seer: An Elemental who has visions of the future and is able to see into the past through memories of other Generations.

Feeler: An empathic Elemental, one who can sense others feelings and cannot be lied to.

Talisman: An object thought to have magic abilities and bring good luck or protection to the wearer.

Archivist: A title passed down to witches that care for old texts and spellbooks, keeping them safe and the stories of the past alive.

Erebus: The legendary leader of the Renati. A powerful witch who lived centuries ago that was banished to the Shadow Realm by the last known Generation of Elementals.

The Renati: A group of witches who believe Elementals are too powerful and therefore corruptible.

Shadows: Carnivorous creatures from the Shadow Realm.

Allurement: A concentration of magic that attracts witches, bringing them to one another and strengthens their powers.

<u>Places</u>

The Dark Star Forest: A massive forest that covers the majority of Western Oregon into the Cascade Mountain Range.

Rifton, Oregon: A small town on the edge of the Dark Star Forest.

Pines Row: A neighborhood outside Rifton city limits where the Dansley siblings live.

Diamond Gate: A gated community by the lake outside of Rifton where the wealthier families live.

Eagle Loop Trail: Hiking trail in the Dark Star Forest that leads around the local lake.

The Corner Cup: A local coffee shop in Rifton where Whitney works.

The Cottage: Whitney's boss, Amilia Burnet's, home.

The Shadow Realm: A dimension of darkness and danger that shares a veil with the modern world.

CONTENT

This book contains death of a parent,
survivor's guilt,
cursing,
blood and off screen torture,
alcohol use,
and an explicit sexual scene (MF).

*Listen to the playlist
for Tidal Wave here
on Spotify!*

For Kerry,
my day one.

CHAPTER ONE

THE WATER NYMPH AND THE PYRO

"We did everything we could. I'm so sorry."

You always assume that when you are faced with death, you become overwhelmed with grief; a pain that weighs you down so low you fall through the floor. But all I could do was count the fluorescent lights. There were eight of them in the hospital waiting room. Long tubes of bright white flickered against the square tile ceiling. The one in the back right corner was out, casting a shadow on the tall fern that stood next to an end table with old magazines. The addresses of their previous owners were marked out in thick, black sharpie. That's kind of what death does when you think about it, crosses people out.

The surgeon placed her hand on my shoulder in comfort, but I couldn't feel it. I couldn't feel anything.

"Whitney? Did you hear me?"

One. Two. Three. I stood stiff, counting fluorescent lighting like I was listening to another drawn-out college lecture. Like I hadn't received the worst news of my life. Like the only mother I'd ever known wasn't gone without warning.

"Whitney, did you hear me?" My younger sister's voice replaced the surgeon's.

I knew I was standing in the kitchen of our new rental brewing a pot of coffee. It had been over ten weeks since I'd been in that hospital waiting room, but mentally, I'd never left. Rayn's warm hand shook my shoulder gently.

"What?" I asked, reaching for the heavy aquamarine pendant that hung around my neck. I held it tightly in my palm, waiting for my pulse to return to normal. The white ink that floated around inside the gem comforted me.

I couldn't explain what the ink was or how it got inside of the gem, but the ink was as much a part of the aquamarine as my heart was to my body. It was like someone had broken a pen inside of the precious stone. The ink always changed from black to white when my sister was near. Seeing the same white ink in the ruby ring sitting snug on her thumb was a constant reminder that no matter what happened, we were in it together.

"Where were you?" Rayn asked, leaning against the tile countertop.

"Lost in thought. When did you get back?"

"Just now. We dropped off the truck and stopped at the grocery store."

"Didn't plan on cooking tonight, did you?" I glanced around at the piles of boxes shoved into every corner of the tiny two-bedroom cabin. I'd gotten as far as unpacking the coffee pot.

"Nah, I grabbed a frozen pizza and some beer. Figured we deserved a drink after that drive and well, everything else."

"I thought your fake ID expired already?" I pulled my straight, black hair into a bun and opened up a moving box, looking for coffee mugs.

"Not yet." Rayn hopped up on the counter. Her long legs swung below her with brown boots tapping against the cabinets. Her thick, scarlet curls were pulled back into a messy ponytail with bangs cut in a perfect line above her blue eyes. An effortless beauty.

"It expires on her birthday." Our little brother, Dmitri, appeared in the entryway between the kitchen and the living room. An oversized t-shirt hung on his long, thin frame. At sixteen, calling him little brother didn't fit him much anymore since he was officially taller than both Rayn and I. In my heart, he would always be a quiet six-year-old with messy hair.

The three of us weren't related by blood, but Dmitri and I looked the most alike. We both had deep brown eyes and naturally tan skin that echoed against Rayn's pale complexion. Genetics or appearances never meant much to my siblings and I. Dmitri may have been her only biological child, but Mom believed the universe had brought us together for a reason; our powers. Mom always used to tell us that like calls to like, as if our magic was a magnet which pulled us to each other. She had always romanticized life, giving divine purpose to everything. It was hard to keep up that mentality without her.

Dmitri set grocery bags down on the counter and pulled out a box of Pop-Tarts.

"Holy shit, tomorrow is the twenty-first already." I whipped around to face my sister. "What do you want to do?"

"Nothing." Rayn's voice went flat, her eyes glued to her feet.

"No, we're not doing that," Dmitri argued, crossing his arms over his chest. "We always make a huge deal out of your birthday."

Rayn huffed. "Well, I don't want to this year. Nineteen isn't a milestone. Besides, tomorrow is the first day of school."

"So?" I moved on to another box in my continued search for coffee cups but settled on a small mixing bowl. I poured myself some coffee and turned back to my siblings.

"Straight black tonight, huh?" Rayn side-eyed my bowl of coffee. "Look, it's my birthday and I want to keep it low key, okay? Hand me a beer, Mit."

Dmitri went back into the cloth grocery bag and handed Rayn a brown glass bottle. Our eyes met as he went back to the bag and slowly pulled out another bottle. He held the cold glass in his hands, looking back and forth between Rayn and me.

I sighed. "Fine, but don't make a habit of it."

With a wave of Dmitri's fingers, the caps of his and Rayn's beer bottles twisted off and fell to the floor with a clink. Of the many things Dmitri inherited from our mother, telekinetic power was probably his favorite. Though his powers were vastly different from the fire and water that Rayn and I wielded, they were still equally as handy.

Rayn held the bottle out toward us. "We fucking did it, guys."

Dmitri tapped his bottle against hers and I held up my small bowl of coffee. We toasted ourselves on successfully packing up our entire lives and leaving our hometown. We left without a single goodbye and every bridge we ever had burned down behind us. Silence fell over us as we all took a drink. Other than getting Rayn and Dmitri out of Hemston, Kansas, there was little to celebrate. We were in a completely foreign place, with little money and no job prospects. Definitely the riskiest move I'd made in my twenty-one years of life, but I had been backed into a corner.

A loud knock on the door made the three of us jump. A chill shot up my spine as I set my bowl of coffee down on the counter hard enough to spill some brown liquid onto the perfectly clean white tile. I shoved my heart back into my chest and went to answer the door.

Janice Roberts, our landlady, stood on the narrow front porch holding a glass casserole dish topped with foil. Her auburn hair was wrapped up in a tight bun and a pair of small square-shaped glasses sat on the tip of her nose.

"Hi, Janice," I greeted, stepping back for her to come through the doorway. "How are you?"

"Very well! I wanted to come see how you were settling in and bring you some dinner. I know whenever I've moved it's been pizza until the kitchen gets unpacked and you can't put a price on a home-cooked meal."

"Oh, wow. Thank you so much. That's incredibly generous of you." I forced a smile.

Guilt washed over me. I knew Janice meant well, but I recognized pity when I saw it. I saw it every day I spent in the foster system before Rayn and I were adopted by our mother and plenty more after the car accident that took her from us. Casseroles and "let us know if you need anything" galore. When I first contacted Janice about the rental home on her property, she asked a million questions.

Why are you moving so far?

Why are you moving somewhere where you don't have a job?

Wow, you're twenty-one with custody of a sixteen-year-old?

How did that happen?

I tried to keep it simple: a dead mother who left me as the sole executor and beneficiary of all she had, including Dmitri. A mortgage I couldn't afford by any stretch of the imagination and credit card debt I didn't know existed. Janice saw a charity case and stepped right in. We got the guest house the Roberts were renting out for cheaper than the listed price and she gave me time to find a job once we moved out here as long as I was able to pay the first month and a cheap deposit. Now she was feeding us.

"It's the least I could do. Enchiladas are my specialty. Pop it in the oven to heat it back up." Janice handed the dish over to Rayn, who had appeared behind me. Rayn smiled and took our dinner into the kitchen.

"How is the job search going?" Janice asked curiously. I knew that question was coming at some point. Of course, the woman who collected our rent would want to know if I had any prospects for income.

I took in a steadying breath, "I put in about six applications already and I'm going into town tomorrow to put in more. I'll have a job within the week, I promise."

"I'm sure you will, honey. In the meantime, Jeff and I want to help you kids out. We own the mini-mart down the street, the one you drive past coming into Pine's Row." Janice wrung her hands together as she spoke. "We don't have anything full-time, but we have been talking about getting some part-time help in the evenings. Is that something either of the kids would be interested in?"

"I'll take it," Dmitri spoke up before Janice could finish her sentence.

"What about me?" Rayn rushed back in from the kitchen.

Janice smiled genuinely at my brother. "The position would be after school and on the weekends. Not quite minimum wage but close and it would be under the table, so more money a week anyway since you wouldn't have to pay taxes on it. Stocking shelves and running the cash register. My son, Abraham, can help teach you how to do everything."

"Sounds perfect," Dmitri replied.

Janice offering my brother a job made me feel worse than I already did. This woman was a saint.

"You only have one opening?" Rayn asked again, louder this time.

"Unfortunately, yes." Janice frowned. "But it'll take some of the financial pressure off you all. You've been through so much already."

"Thank you so much, you have no idea how grateful we are for this." Dmitri reached out to shake her hand as confirmation that he would take the job.

"Am I invisible?" Rayn asked me, anger sparking behind her ice-blue eyes.

"Hey." I reached out and put my hand on her shoulder. "Bringing home money is my problem, remember? I'm going to get a full-time job and neither of you will have to work unless you want to. Your number one concern is your grades, like we talked about."

"It's after school and we need the money," Dmitri replied, sounding more like a parent than a teenager. "I'll keep my grades up."

"Talk it over and let me know. You don't have to make a decision right away." Janice attempted to help ease the tension but Dmitri's mind was made up.

"That's not necessary, I'll take it." Dmitri grinned like a cat who brought home his first bird.

I mustered a smile. "Thank you, Janice, for everything. I can't tell you how much we appreciate your help."

"Oh, of course," Janice nodded. "I'll let you kids get back to settling in. Let me know if you need anything at all."

"Thank you, but we should be fine." I could only take so much charity before I started to feel inept.

Janice gave each of us a big smile showing her age in her laugh lines. "Dmitri, come by the mini-mart tomorrow after school and we will get you all set up, okay?"

"I'll be there," he replied.

Janice gave us a quick wave before she headed back down the dirt driveway to the main house on the property.

"So I won't be contributing at all." Rayn crossed her arms, leaning against the frame of the entryway into the kitchen.

"You'll contribute by finishing out your first year of college and letting me worry about the bills," I told her. "If you're that worried about it, you're the best cook out of the three of us."

Rayn laughed. "So I'll be the housewife."

I stifled my laughter. "Of course not. If you want a part-time job, go get one. But school comes first."

"Yes, we hear you. Stay in school. Don't do drugs." Rayn straightened her posture.

"Don't light anything on fire." Dmitri sent a sideways glance over to our sister.

"Low blow." I snapped at him, sounding harsher than I meant to. "We agreed to move past that."

"Sorry, I'm just messing around," he answered quietly.

Rayn remained silent.

"Don't stay up too late tonight. You have a big day tomorrow," I ordered my brother.

Dmitri huffed. "I still don't understand why I can't be homeschooled."

"Because if we didn't make you go to school you'd never leave this house like an old hermit," Rayn spoke up.

"So what if I'm an old hermit?" Dmitri took a swig from the bottle in his hands. "My introverted ways have never gotten us in any trouble."

I couldn't argue with that.

The next morning, Rayn woke me up with a gentle shake of her warm hand on my arm. My eyelids were heavy as they fluttered open, almost dizzy as the room came into focus. I hadn't made my way to the mattress on my floor until after midnight, determined to unpack as many boxes as possible.

"Good morning." Rayn offered me a mug of coffee.

"What do you want?" My mother's moonstone ring clinked against the ceramic as I took the mug.

"Pardon?" Rayn asked as if I hadn't seen straight through her morning offering.

"Bringing me coffee in bed? What do you want?"

"I can't do something nice for my favorite sister?" Rayn swept her bangs out of her eyes.

"I'm your only sister." Clearing my throat, I checked the time on my phone. The alarm was supposed to go off twenty minutes ago, but I accidentally set it for PM instead of AM. "Shit."

I took a sip of what I assumed would be a warm cup of delicious coffee, but instead, the swig I took was barely lukewarm. "Ugh, shit."

"Oh, sorry. Mit made it when he woke up with the sun." Rayn took the mug from my hands and held it tightly, her black fingernails wrapping around the ceramic.

A tickle of energy ran up my body, making my fingertips tingle as my sister used her magic. Rayn didn't have to concentrate on the mug much as the ceramic warmed and steam wisped up into the air. My sister, the pyro. I had always been able to feel Rayn's magic flow through my body like I did my powers, but never Mom's or Mit's. The matching jewelry hinted that Rayn and I weren't ordinary witches, but the connection of our elemental powers sealed the deal.

I jumped out of bed and nearly stumbled over a moving box, spilling coffee on my leg. I still wasn't used to this small bedroom. I pulled my sweat pants up over my wide hips and stretched out my back.

"Hey, morning." Dmitri appeared in the doorway with a mug sitting snug in his hands. His brown hair stuck up in the back from rubbing against the pillow.

"You ready for school?" I asked, searching a box for some presentable clothing to find a job.

"Ya know, Ray and I were talking, and maybe we can start school tomorrow? We can finish getting the house set up. I mean, what's one day? There are only so many new changes the young mind can process at once." Dmitri persuaded.

"So that's what this is about?" I held up the coffee cup and informed them both, "You're going to school today."

"Whitney, school will still be there tomorrow. And the day after, for that matter." Rayn gave one last attempt to convince me.

"And you will be there today. Dmitri, go comb your hair."

"You're really making us go? We used to ditch all the time together." Rayn huffed as I set the coffee down on my dresser.

"You can take a mental health day, but not today. It's your first day, Rayn. You miss the first day of the semester and they drop you. Dmitri, if you miss too much school, you won't graduate on time. Want to repeat your junior year?" I hated sounding like a nagging mother instead of their sister, but life had forced me to grow up much quicker than I was prepared for.

During my time in foster care, I had grown used to watching out for myself. After meeting Rayn when we were children and realizing we both had elemental powers, my desire to keep us safe only amplified. Then we were sent to live with the Dansleys and everything softened over the years. Audriana Dansley became Mom and her six-year-old son became my little brother. I allowed myself to be taken care of for the first time in my life, but that sense of security crumbled the night my mother was killed. I wasn't prepared to jump into her role at all, let alone as quickly as I did.

Rule number three. Rayn grumbled telepathically.

What does rule number three have to do with anything? I shot back mentally.

Don't be a dick. Rayn's words echoed in my head.

"I'm not being a dick," I defended aloud. "I'm asking for one day. I know you're nervous and you hate new schools, but you're only the new kid for a short time. No one here knows who we are. This is an opportunity to be whoever you want. It should be exciting."

"And if I hate it?" Dmitri asked.

"We'll cross that bridge when we get there, okay?"

"Fine." He grumbled.

I cussed under my breath and turned to face my sister. "Happy birthday, Ray."

"Yeah, thanks," she mumbled as she turned to leave the room.

"I'm sorry. I didn't forget, just distracted. We'll pick you up a cake tonight. Anything you want, okay?"

"I already told you I don't want anything."

"We are celebrating whether you like it or not."

Rayn left my bedroom without another word.

I followed her into the kitchen and took a moment to appreciate that the rest of the house wasn't as hectic as my bedroom. It was officially our first full day in the small cabin that sat on the corner of the Robert's seven-acre property. By the time we got into Rifton, Oregon yesterday, we had enough time to meet our landlords, unpack the moving truck and return it before we were charged for an extra day that we couldn't afford. The house didn't take long to start looking like someone lived there since we didn't bring a whole lot with us. I was more concerned with getting the rest of the house set up and making sure Rayn and Dmitri were settled than organizing the books in my room.

The rental was a tiny two-bedroom cabin with one bathroom and a living room big enough for our old couch. Next to the kitchen was a separate dining area that we hung a curtain across so Dmitri could have his own space. He insisted he didn't mind, but I felt terrible he gave up a bedroom when Rayn and I could have easily shared.

"This way we all get our own space," he had said.

Photos of our mom had been unpacked and hung on the living room walls while my brother and sister slept. After the shit storm of a summer we had, it was comforting to feel like she was still here with us in some small way. The little dark brown house with green gutters wasn't much, but it was exactly what we needed. Safe, cheap, and 1,596 miles away from anyone who knew the truth about us.

I stood on the narrow porch and watched the city bus take my siblings down the road. The bus would drop Dmitri off down the street from the high school and proceed to take Rayn to the community college a few blocks away. Rayn had told me for the third time before they left that they didn't want me to drive them. I knew before I asked that they were going to say no, but it's what Mom used to do on our first day of school. I was still trying to figure out which roles they needed me to step into and which ones needed to remain sacred.

With a sigh, I went into the bathroom and brushed out my hair, weaving it into a braid. After splashing some water on my face, I glanced at myself in the mirror to see if I looked as different as I felt. I sighed at my reflection. The same Whitney from my old life may have been on the other side of the vanity, but I didn't recognize her.

I headed to the living room, contemplating which of the leftover boxes to tackle first. Last night after dinner, Rayn got the kitchen set up and Dmitri organized his bedroom and the living room. All that was left were odds and ends that I didn't know what to do with.

Instead, I hopped on my laptop and opened up the online applications I had book-marked. While most of the businesses in Rifton were family-owned and didn't offer 'apply now' buttons on their website, there were a select few that I decided to check off my list before I ventured into town and attempted to find a job in person.

Hours later, I glanced over at my empty drinking glass. With a wave of my hand, I used my powers to fill the glass, water swirled around until it filled to the top. The same familiar tingle that took over my hands that morning when Rayn warmed my coffee appeared. I felt the water flowing through the pipes of the house, giving me confidence in my abilities. The last time I tried to manifest my powers without being near a water source resulted in a busted pipe and the entire first floor of the old house flooded. That was years ago, but I tried not to push my luck again. Our mother had loved us dearly and reminded us of that daily, but part of me always worried our elemental powers would be too much and she would send us back into foster care.

I took a drink of water and gravitated toward a random box labeled 'Mom'. I ripped the packing tape back and opened the flaps. Papers, binders, and photo albums sat methodically stacked. Neat and tidy Dmitri definitely packed this one. It looked like old curriculum materials and plans from her teaching days. As I closed the flap to move on to the next box, the spine of a merlot-colored notebook screamed out at me. I didn't recognize it, though I had spent countless hours in Mom's home office that sat in the corner of her bedroom. Curiously, I retrieved the notebook and opened the unmarked cover back.

The journal was thick with every page covered in Mom's cursive handwriting. The first page was dated October 17. The first night Audri and Dmitri Dansley welcomed Rayn and I into their home.

I can feel the magic radiating off these two girls as the warmth rises off the pavement during a summer heatwave. They have no idea what they are or what they are capable of. The Shepherds have led them to my doorstep, that I am sure of. The likes of these two haven't been seen in so long and I will do everything in my power to keep them with me, to keep them safe. First, I have to gain their trust and then I will do what I can to help them learn to control their magic. I'm not the most equipped for the task but if it's the task I've been given, I accept it with all my soul. Whatever the future holds, I must keep these girls far away from Rifton. They would never be safe there.

What the fuck.

Mom knew about our powers, but not until Rayn and I told her ourselves... or so we thought. It wasn't until she offered to adopt us that my sister and I shared our biggest secret with her, but apparently it was the reason she decided to adopt us in the first place. I held her moonstone ring up to my lips, the cool metal was a familiar and comforting feeling. A security blanket I had used to ground myself since the day it was taken off her cold body and put in my hands. A bit betrayed, I began flipping through page after page. At least one entry every month or so about Rayn and I. The way our powers developed over the years while comparing us to old stories she was told as a child that she never shared with us. Comparing our magic to her and Dmitri's powers, how different we were from the two of them. None of this made any sense. Why would Mom hide all of this from us? Why did she pretend it was her first time hearing it when we told her our secrets?

My phone began to ring and my heart dropped.

"Oh my god," I muttered, taking the ringing phone out of my back pocket. My heart raced through my body as I answered. "Ray, you'll never guess what I found."

"Come get me." Rayn's voice was shaky and panicked. She wasn't asking, she was telling me to get in the car and drive to her immediately.

"What happened?" I asked, straightening my posture.

"I feel crazy. I'll explain it all when you get here. Just get here. Now." She ordered.

"What's crazy? Are you hurt?" I inquired further, my mind raced with all the possible scenarios.

"Now before it's too late. Hurry." Rayn ended the call before I could ask any more questions.

I left the journal on the floor and rushed to put my shoes on, sprinting out of the house with no sweater and my black leather backpack swung over one shoulder. The crisp mountain air hit me in the face but all I could feel was a race against the clock to get to my sister. I had almost lost her already, I wasn't going to risk it again.

CHAPTER TWO

MOTHER EARTH

I made a valiant effort not to drive eighty miles an hour down the narrow mountain road into Rifton, but it was difficult after hearing the panic in Rayn's voice. Under normal circumstances, I wouldn't have dropped my keys trying to start my Mitsubishi Eclipse. I would have taken the time to soak in the beautiful pine trees that lined the two-lane road. I would have glanced over at the large green sign welcoming me into Rifton city limits and added three more people to the 21,832 population total. But instead, everything was a blur of panic and nausea.

It took me a little longer than twenty minutes to get to the community college, hitting every red light and getting caught behind other drivers who weren't in my hurry. Rayn jogged toward the car as I came to a stop in the front parking lot. She looked okay. There wasn't any blood or broken bones. She was in one piece.

"What's going on?" A whirlwind spun inside of my head. "Is Dmitri okay?"

"Dmitri is fine. No one is hurt." Rayn plopped down into the front seat of the car.

"That bit of information would have been useful when you called."

Winded, she finally filled me in. "Okay. There is this girl in my English class named Rose. I remember it from attendance. I noticed she was looking at me, I thought she was staring at my hair, but she wasn't. She was staring at my ring. I hadn't thought twice about it until I noticed she was wearing a necklace. The chain is exactly like yours, only gold."

"What are you talking about? That doesn't mean anything."

"The ink in my ring was white, Whitney."

My blood ran cold.

Out of everything that happened throughout our lives, the jewelry was the most mysterious. We were in our last foster home before we were sent to live with Mom and

Mit, playing hide and seek when I stumbled upon the jewelry in the bottom of an old desk drawer. The necklace called out to me, changing from a dull gray into an aquamarine, coming to life in my hands. I put it around my neck and never took it off. The ruby ring took a few years for Rayn to grow into and still only fit on her thumb.

I pulled on the long, silver chain and revealed the necklace from its safe place inside my shirt. White ink swirled around inside the light blue gem. That's how we knew the jewelry was somehow tied to our powers. The color of the ink had never changed around anyone else, until now.

"Are you sure?" My heart stopped, sending chills down my spine. "Like, absolutely positive?"

Rayn continued, "I singed a few strands on my jeans under the desk and I think she saw me or felt me, at least."

"You think someone at school saw you use your powers?" I asked her in disbelief.

"But, Whit, she's one of us. I feel it in my bones. The ink was white and it's only been white around you. Don't you believe me?" My sister asked with wide eyes.

"Yeah, but I don't know if I would go as far as saying someone is like us. What if she's like Dmitri or Mom?"

"Whitney, seriously, listen to my words. Did your necklace change around Mom or Mit? No. Did Mom or Mit have elemental powers? No. The jewelry changes around others like it and it will change around this Rose girl. Do you see my ring right now? That ink is white and it's because of you. We came to Rifton for a reason." Rayn held up her hand, shoving her ring in my face.

"We came here because we needed to get the fuck out of Kansas."

The words from Mom's journal shot through my heart. *I must keep these girls far away from Rifton. They would never be safe there.*

"And why do you think this is where we came? It finally makes sense, Whit. I can't imagine Mom knowing that there were other people like us out there and not telling us. She wouldn't lie to us."

I sighed, rubbing my temple. "I'm starting to realize there is a lot that Mom didn't tell us."

"What do you mean?" Rayn tilted her head.

My heart pounded against my chest. This was too much to process all at once. I had to chew on all this new information for a moment.

"Nothing."

"What are we going to do?" Rayn asked me, as we watched a floodgate release eager students from their afternoon classes. They quickly crowded the parking lot to get to their cars.

"I have no idea," I admitted. "What do we say? Hi, we're the Dansley sisters and we can control water and fire, what's your special party trick? It's not that easy."

"It could be. I mean, why not?" Rayn frantically scanned the herd of students, looking for a particular face. Rayn pointed to a girl walking toward the second row of cars in the parking lot. "That's her! That's Rose, right there. The brunette wearing sunglasses."

"You're sure?"

"Watch this." Rayn snapped her fingers, holding the small flame in her half-closed hand.

"What are you doing?" I asked through clenched teeth. I wanted to trust my sister and not panic, but using in public was never a good idea. "Stop lighting fires everywhere."

Once Rose passed our car, she slowed her pace and looked over at us, lifting her sunglasses to her forehead.

"Do you see that? She can feel my powers like you can." Rayn bounced in her seat.

"I think she's wondering the same thing we are. Who the hell are you?" I gripped the steering wheel with white knuckles.

"We need to talk to her," Rayn said, opening the door of the car.

"Wait." I reached out to grab her arm and stop her, but her feet were already on the pavement.

"Excuse me? Rose?" Rayn called out as she approached the girl.

Rose ran her fingers through chocolate brown hair causing bangs to fall against her forehead. Her features could have been drawn by an artist. She had a heart-shaped face with perfect cheekbones and vivid green eyes. The girl wore little makeup, she didn't need it. She was wearing ripped black jeans with a dark gray sweater that hung past her thighs. As Rayn and I approached her, she stepped back.

"Do I know you?" she asked cautiously.

Ambushing her isn't what I had planned. Honestly, I didn't have anything planned. All I knew was if I was this girl, I'd be ready to fight.

"Rose, right? We have English together. My name is Rayn Dansley. I just moved here. This is my sister, Whitney." Each inch Ray moved closer to Rose was matched with a retreating step.

"What do you want?" Rose asked defensively, looking down at my shoes and back up to my eyes. We were invading her personal space.

"Um, yeah. Hi. I'm Whitney." My voice cracked.

"Yes, that's been established." She kept her head low but never broke eye contact. Even with her sunglasses on, I knew she was meeting my gaze.

"We only want to talk. I noticed the chain around your neck and the ink in my ring went white during class. I know it was because of you." Rayn lifted her hand to show Rose her ring. The sunlight glistened against the white swirls inside of her ruby gem.

"What of it?" Rose lifted her sunglasses. She looked at the ring like it had no significance, but her dilated pupils told a different story.

"Is that your necklace? I'm curious where you got it?" I asked, pointing to the small unique chains linked together around her neck. The same as mine, only gold. The pendant itself tucked under her sweater. That was all too familiar.

Could she be hiding her necklace from the world like I did every single day? Keeping it tucked away but always made sure it was with her because she didn't feel safe without it.

"Antique shopping with my mom. Nothing too interesting about that," Rose shrugged.

"What shop did you buy it at, exactly? I need to find out where these came from." My heart raced so fast that I felt like I could topple over.

"Why does it matter, Wendy? It's a necklace. Jewelry is made for all kinds of reasons." Rose looked around the parking lot, waiting for someone to come tell us to leave her alone.

"It's Whitney," I corrected, straight-faced.

"I'm not in the mood to fuck around," Rayn snapped her fingers and lit a small flame in the palm of her hand. She was far too comfortable, not thinking about the consequences of outing ourselves. "I light fires. What's your party trick?"

Rayn Grace, I said to her telepathically. *Put it out.*

"Stop it!" Rose blurted, jumping toward us to wrap her hands around Rayn's, closing my sister's fist around the flame. The tingling faded as quickly as it arrived, letting me know the fire was out. Rose's voice was barely a whisper. "What is wrong with you? Do you know anything about being a witch in this town?"

"We want to know where these gems came from," Rayn repeated.

"No," Rose backed away from us quickly. "No, I'm not doing this. Leave me alone."

"Wait, please."

"I said no." Rose snapped over her shoulder, retreating across the parking lot as quickly as her legs could take her.

"Shit." Tears lined Rayn's eyes as she turned to face me.

"Get in the car," I ordered.

"Where are we going?" She hurried after me as I jogged back to the car.

"To the high school. We need to regroup."

"What is going on?" Dmitri asked, climbing into the back seat after the final bell dismissed him for the day.

Rayn turned to face our brother from the passenger's seat, "A girl in my English class has a necklace."

"So what?" He shrugged.

"We didn't get to see it, but the chain is the same as mine," I explained.

"I tested her, she felt my powers," Rayn said.

Dmitri put his hand up. "Wait, hang on."

I rubbed my temple. "I swear, Rayn if someone outs us again we will have to immigrate to the Netherlands."

"How do you know she felt your powers?" Dmitri leaned onto the center console. "You used at school?"

"I had to know. Obviously asking her wasn't the way to find out."

"But you never actually saw her necklace, so you don't know it's like Whit's," Dmitri pointed out.

"No, she's like us. The ink in my ring went white when I was in class with her," Rayn explained. "That has never happened before, only with Whitney."

"What would someone like us be doing here? We came to Rifton to escape this, not immerse ourselves in it."

"This could be our new beginning, Whit, finding others like us and why we have these powers in the first place. Figuring out where these gems came from and what they mean. We've always wanted to know the truth. That's why Mom sent us here. This could be our chance." Rayn said. All of the little pieces of the puzzle my sister had been building inside of her head began to fall into place. She was romanticizing our situation like Mom would have.

"Mom did not send us here," I clarified, meeting her gaze. "Mom never wanted us to come here. I don't know what made me pick this place."

"Because she grew up here. You don't think that was Mom in your head?"

"No. I need a drink," I mumbled.

"I'm serious. We have to talk to her again."

"You think that girl is letting you within a ten-mile radius of her now? What if she doesn't have powers? What if she tells other people about us? We don't know her at all, Ray." I shook my head, not wanting to risk it.

"What if, what if. Do you know other words? She has a necklace." Rayn reminded me. "The ink in our jewelry went white. She's probably trying to hide from everyone, too. You remember how it was when we found each other. It wasn't planned, or maybe we don't know the plan yet."

"I believe you," Mit announced from the backseat.

I reached for my bag and opened it up, digging for something I could drink to keep myself from getting sick. As my stomach churned, I took some papers out of my bag and retrieved a warm, half-empty, water bottle. I used my powers to cool the water inside and fill the bottle to the top.

It was going to be different now. It wasn't Rayn and I alone anymore. No more sitting up at night when we couldn't sleep going over our different hypotheses of what our elemental powers meant or where the jewelry came from. Wondering who the gems belonged to before us or what the ink inside of them meant. We always questioned if there was anyone else out there wondering if we existed. Of course, we had Mom and Dmitri, but from the beginning, it was obvious our powers were different from theirs. They could never light a fire with their hands or control water like we could.

Did Rose ever sit back, looking at her gem with floating black ink and wonder if there were others out there like her? Maybe not, but now we knew another person like us did exist and we were all living on the edge of the Dark Star Forest.

"So, how did everything else go?" I asked as we pulled in front of the house. "Before English, I mean."

"Same shit, different school," Rayn muttered, biting her fingernails.

"Mit?"

"It was fine," he answered. "I turned in some drawings to the art teacher and he's going to let me take the senior-level class, so that's nice."

"Can we not pretend like everything is normal and our lives haven't changed forever?" Rayn snapped, slamming the car door behind her. Her brown boots echoed heavily against the porch as she stomped her way into the house.

"I'm not pretending anything. I wanted to know how school was," I defended, following her into the house.

Dmitri lingered, taking his time getting through the front door. I wanted a moment of normalcy before I pulled out that red journal and complicated things further.

"You're not taking this seriously," Rayn argued.

"What am I supposed to do, Ray? Chase her down?" I raised my voice. "We scared the shit out of that girl today. We ambushed her and we'll be lucky if she ever talks to us again. Put yourself in her position. If that was me, I'd have done the same thing."

Rayn sighed, avoiding eye contact. "Yeah, I guess so."

"Be patient. I know the ink in your ring changed color but we never saw her necklace. We don't know for sure yet." I took a deep breath. "Besides, there's something else I have to show you."

I probably should have waited. I should have let the initial shock of our interaction with Rose and the overwhelming reality of what we had gone through settle in. We had come to a new place in hopes of regaining our balance only to be knocked on our asses once more.

"What's wrong?" Dmitri asked, sensing the tension.

"Sit down," I told them both, waving toward the couch.

I picked the journal up off the floor where I had dropped it earlier and handed it to Rayn with trembling fingers. My knees were shaky, ready to give out on me as the nerves surfaced.

"What's this?" Rayn asked, looking up at me with the journal in her hands.

"It was Mom's. I found it in a box of her things earlier, right before you called me," I explained. "Read the first page."

Reluctantly, Rayn opened back the cover. Dmitri leaned in, reading over her shoulder. I gave them time to absorb the information, studying how their expressions changed. How the corners of their mouths dropped and their brows furrowed. When Rayn looked back up at me, tears welled in her eyes.

"Wh-what is this?" she asked, the words stuck in her throat.

"I think it was her journal? It's all about you and me. Mom knew about our powers the day we showed up at the house," I answered.

"How could she lie to us like that?" Rayn wiped a stray tear from her face.

I shrugged. "Looking back, I can see it. She never truly acted surprised when we told her, and magic was used so casually around the house after that. She made it all seem so normal."

"She always said home was a safe place, somewhere we could use our powers and not think twice about it," Dmitri added.

"Did you know about this?" Rayn asked our brother.

"No." Dmitri shook his head. "I packed up most of Mom's stuff, but I didn't go through any of it. We packed in such a hurry, I didn't want to throw her things away. I-"

"Mit, it's okay," I reassured him, taking his hand in mine. "No one is accusing you of keeping secrets."

"I would have told you," he said, still panicked.

"I know," Rayn whispered, looking down at the journal. "This is why she kept us, isn't it?"

"Mom loved you guys," Dmitri replied, turning to face Rayn. "She would have kept you either way."

"Would she?" Another tear fell down her cheek. "Because this makes me believe she kept us because she felt obligated, not because she wanted us."

"That's not true!" Dmitri argued. "Mom would never. She-"

"Guys, stop, please..." I put a hand up to each of them. "We don't know what Mom was thinking and we never will. Arguing about it won't change that."

"They would never be safe there." Rayn read the last sentence of the journal entry. "Mit?"

Dmitri shrugged. "Mom didn't tell me much about Rifton, only that she grew up here and didn't leave on good terms. I was little when we left, I don't remember any of it."

The same story Mom had told me. I should have known Dmitri wouldn't know more than Rayn or I, but we had to be sure.

"Maybe there's something else in here." Dmitri hopped off the couch and began rummaging through the box containing the rest of the stuff from Mom's office.

"I can't believe this," Rayn mumbled, closing the journal hard with a thud.

Dmitri sighed, glancing over at Rayn. "I'm sorry you're having such a shitty birthday. We'll make it up to you, I promise."

"Are you kidding? We just found out we aren't the only ones with elemental powers out there. This is the best birthday gift the universe could have given me. I'm upset about Mom, to be honest. One step forward, three steps back."

"No steps back," I rested my hand on her knee. "A lot has happened, we need some time to process and decide what we are going to do next. All you have to worry about right now is what you want for your birthday dinner."

Rayn groaned. "I want burritos and a carrot cake. Now, back to this Rose girl and Mom's secret journal."

"I don't see anything else in the box." Dmitri closed the flaps, defeated. "I have to leave for the mini-mart soon."

I sighed. "Mom knew about our powers before we told her. Not much we can do about that one."

"And Rose?" Dmitri asked.

"I'll try again on Wednesday," Rayn spoke up. "She can't avoid me forever."

I couldn't help but laugh, "I'm pretty sure she can. Try not to ambush her again."

"We're in the dumpster already," Rayn said.

I exhaled. "So much for laying low."

Rayn shrugged. "We've never been very good at staying out of trouble."

Chapter Three

THE CORNER CUP

Four hours in town, two iced coffees, and seven job applications later, I found myself on Amber Street. It was an adorable part of town. The streets were lined with planter boxes filled with brightly colored flowers and little trees with one family-owned business after another. The foliage still clung to the green of summer, but hints of gold foreshadowed a chill that began creeping through the town. I thrived in the cold, it made me feel stronger and braver. My job was on this street, I could feel it.

I found a parking spot in the back of a row of shops. An ice cream place, a bike store, an Italian restaurant, and a coffee shop all nestled together. I looked at myself in the mirror of the sunshade one last time before making my way inside, ensuring I still looked employable in black slacks and a button-up mint-colored top that stood out against my black hair. I kept my makeup simple and clean, opting to leave the dark red lipstick I usually wore at home. As I got out of the car, I smoothed out my shirt. First stop, the coffee shop.

The logo above The Corner Cup was a square cup of coffee with two steam lines coming up from the top. It smelt like warm coffee and cinnamon, and a short line of people waited in front of the counter to order their drinks. Strings of bright lights hung across the ceiling like a blanket of stars. Two girls and a guy wearing black aprons moved back and forth between the coffee machines and blenders. The shop had a relaxing, welcoming vibe that appeared to attract all types of caffeine lovers. College students with books laid out in front of them. Eyes framed in thick-rimmed glasses focused on computer screens. A couple of young women chatting over warm tea.

A chalkboard menu hung above the counter and a selection of bagels sat behind a glass display window next to the cash register. The back walls of the dining area were painted a light cream color with woodland paintings hung in thick, black frames. The walls that faced out onto the street corner were made up of glass panels, allowing customers to sit on the tall stools in front of a wooden bar and people watch.

"Hi, welcome in. What can I get started for you?" A young guy with light blue eyes standing at the cash register asked.

"Oh, yes. Um," I quickly glanced over the chalkboard menu. "Large vanilla iced coffee, please."

"Absolutely. For here or to go?"

"For here."

"Can I get a name for the order?"

"Whitney." I smiled, looking around the dining area. "Are you guys hiring, perchance?"

"Yeah, my boss has been interviewing for a new barista. I'll check and see if she's available, one sec."

"Thanks." I smiled, my knees trembling as I stepped away from the counter. Our survival depended on me bringing home enough money to keep us afloat before I completely drained every last penny from our dwindling savings account. No pressure.

As I waited, I scanned over the community board on the wall advertising various poetry readings and acoustic nights that took place in the Corner Cup. There was a Toyota Tacoma for sale, a missing dog flier, and a tear-off flier for classes at a new yoga studio down the street.

"I have an iced coffee for Whitney." A woman called from the counter, holding a mason jar in her hands.

"Oh, thank you." I took the glass from her.

"Robby said you were asking about the barista opening? I'm Amilia Burnett, the manager."

She looked to be in her early fifties. Her medium-length graying blonde hair framed her round face and her bright blue eyes reminded me of a glacier. She had a short, wider build with a warm smile and an inviting presence. She was wearing five different rings across both hands, all unique and vintage. A metal butterfly hung from her necklace and a purple top flowed down her arms.

"Yes, I'd love to apply. Your place has such a great vibe," I answered.

"Oh, thank you." Amilia smiled, emphasizing laugh lines around her eyes. "Opening this place was a lifelong dream. Rifton needed more places like this when I was growing up here."

She reached behind the counter and grabbed a piece of paper like it had been sitting there waiting for me to show up. "Here we are."

Amilia glanced down as I took the application from her, but her eyes stopped at my neck. Her eyes widened as if she had seen a ghost. She looked at the aquamarine like it was the last thing she imagined seeing in her coffee shop. As if she knew what she was looking at. "Oh, wow, your necklace is unique."

I glanced down at my aquamarine gem that hung around my neck. The top button of my blouse had slipped open, putting my necklace on display. "Th-thank you," I replied, securing the button.

"Where did you get it?" she asked, leaning into the counter.

"Oh, um, a family heirloom," I lied.

"Beautiful. If you're available we can do an interview today. I don't have one scheduled for another hour so I have the time." Amilia gazed into my eyes but I could see her glance down at the chain around my neck.

"I have time."

"Wonderful. Take a few minutes to fill out the application and I'll come check on you in a moment." Amilia disappeared behind an employee's only door that swung closed behind her.

I collapsed into the nearest empty chair. It wasn't until that moment that I realized I was still holding a glass of iced coffee. My head spun as I took a drink, trying to steady myself. I needed to be smart about this. Jumping right into questioning was a disaster with Rose, and I wasn't going to let this fall apart on me. Finding a job was far too important, no matter how badly I wanted to ask Amilia what she knew about my necklace.

I downed my iced coffee and filled out the job application as quickly as my trembling hands would allow. Shaking from anticipation or a caffeine overdose, who knew. It was the sloppiest my handwriting had been in a long time, but focusing was nearly impossible. This woman was a complete stranger but talking to her for five minutes reminded me of my mom. She gave off the same calming energy, the same vibration of assurance that everything would be okay when you didn't believe you'd see sunlight again.

How many people knew more about the jewelry than we did? Rose and her gold chain. Amilia and her knowing gaze, like she was seeing an old friend who she believed to have been gone forever. Since Rayn and I first met, we wondered why we had powers. Why we were both given up to the system by our birth parents, and how we were able to stay together through foster home after foster home simply by willing it. Where did the aquamarine necklace and ruby ring come from and who had them before?

Questioning our existence is human nature. I was in college long enough for a philosophy course but our magical powers certainly added to the uncertainty.

"Ready when you are, Whitney." Amilia appeared next to the table, pulling me back into reality.

I followed her through the employee-only doors into a short hallway. The first door to my left led to the break room. A guy around my age sat at a wooden table on his lunch break with headphones in his ears. The walls had papers pinned upon it with schedules and delivery times.

"Please, have a seat." Amilia waved to the black chair in front of a dark oak desk once we reached her office.

"Thank you." The leather squeaked under me. "Uh, here's my resume." I handed Amilia a piece of paper with little printed on it along with my application. Despite the shake-up over my necklace, I could picture myself at the Corner Cup brewing coffee before I imagined selling clothes at the local boutique or ringing up nails at TJ's Hardware.

"Oh, thank you." She put the resume on top of the existing stack of papers she had in her hands. "Whitney *Dansley*?"

I nodded, studying her expression carefully as she read my full name. Searching for any kind of indication that she knew my mother, or at least recognized the name.

Amilia smiled. "Have you worked as a barista before?"

"No, but I drink a lot of coffee." I smiled.

Amilia laughed, the expression lit up her light eyes. "That makes two of us. This can sometimes be a fast-paced job, would you be able to handle that?"

"Yes, I most recently cashiered at a grocery store that got super busy. I also worked at a food booth at the county fair a few years back home, and it was fairly fast-paced." I laughed realizing what I had said. "No pun intended."

"Where's back home?" Amilia asked, curiously.

"Michigan. I recently moved here so I guess Rifton is home now."

Rayn, Dmitri, and I decided we were going to tell people we were from Michigan in an attempt to keep the people of Hemston, Kansas from finding us.

Amilia smiled again and went on to her next set of questions without missing a beat. She scanned my handwritten application, "What does your availability look like?"

"It's completely open," I answered. "Literally anytime you need me, I'll be here."

As I spoke, my temple began to throb. A stabbing pain concentrated above my eyes, growing stronger with each passing moment. I couldn't focus on anything in Amilia's office, let alone her questions as my stomach began to churn.

"Are you willing to work weekends and closing shifts?" Amilia asked. She noticed there was something wrong with me, but proceeded with the interview.

I nodded with a smile as nausea crept higher and higher up my stomach until the pressure in my throat made me stifle a gag. It pushed against me like a devil on my shoulder pushing me to jump off the edge of a cliff. Chills crawled up my body from my feet, and literal frost formed on my legs underneath my black slacks. Panic sank in when my headache grew to such intensity that my vision went black and I no longer felt the guest chair in Amilia's office underneath me.

Next thing I knew, my stomach dropped as I fell to the ground, opening my eyes to complete darkness.

I sat on a cold concrete floor surrounded by wet air that tasted like sawdust. My legs were bound and my hands were tied behind my back. The tightness of the rope dug into my wrists, cutting my skin. The smell of iron from my blood filled the air as my heart began to beat faster, my head heavy, leaden with confusion. Nothing in the room made any sense.

Panicked, I looked around for a way out as my eyes adjusted to my surroundings. Brick walls enclosed around me. Light from a waxing gibbous moon came in through a round window above a metal shelving unit.

A faint sound of a tune being hummed came up behind me; light-hearted and soft, like a lullaby you would sing to a newborn baby being rocked to sleep in the early morning. The humming grew louder until it was inches away from my back, yet no footsteps accompanied it. I attempted to turn my head to see where the lullaby was coming from but I was bruised and burned, feeling the wounds deep in my bones. The pain was too great to move.

Closing my sore eyes, I tried to remember how I got here when a moment ago I was sitting in the back office of the Corner Cup. Adrenaline rushed through my veins, the air in my lungs thick and hard to breathe. As I opened my eyes once more, something in the darkness shifted in front of me, watching me. My skin crawled as the shadow crept closer until its deep breaths filled my eardrums.

A bloody and wounded pale arm reached out of the darkness toward me, inching its long, skinny fingers as far as they would extend. My heart stopped beating and I opened my mouth to scream but I choked instead.

"Whitney?"

Amilia's concerned voice brought me back to reality, her eyes wild with confusion as to whatever my physical form had done while my mind traveled to a faraway hell. My chest tightened.

"I'm sorry." I gasped, trying to keep my composure, but I was on the verge of hyperventilation.

"Are you all right?"

The headache was gone. The stomach ache was gone. But my mind spun with confusion. I hadn't physically disappeared or Amilia would have freaked out and said something. My body must have stayed in the office. I imagined myself sitting in the chair, staring off into space and drooling on my blouse with my head tilted off to the side. Not my finest hour.

It was only when I looked down that I realized I had vomited on the carpet.

I was not getting this job.

"I am so sorry," I whispered. I got up from my chair and bolted for the door when Amilia's voice stopped me.

"Are you all right?" she asked again, standing up from her chair.

"Yes, I think so. I should go. I'm so sorry." I apologized again as I exited her office.

I had never left a building so quickly in my life, dying of embarrassment. I was going crazy, genuinely losing my mind. I kept thinking about how I would never be able to show my face in the Corner Cup again. A true shame, because they had the best coffee.

The further I walked down the sidewalk, the sadder I became. What an absolute mess I had made of myself. I was overwhelmed with the feeling of grievance and uncertainty growing stronger within me as if I was stuck. Stagnant. Worthless.

Once I reached the back parking lot, I let out a sob of aggression and kicked over a stack of small wooden crates. Pain stung through my foot but I was too frustrated to care.

"You okay?" A deep voice asked from the car parked closest to me.

I jumped like a hammer hitting a nail hearing another person. Wiping a stray tear from my face, I turned to the owner of the voice.

"Everything is fucking great, thanks for asking," I snapped.

He was wearing a white button-up shirt and black dress pants. His strong jaw sported short darker blonde stubble, indicating he hadn't shaved the past few mornings. I looked into eyes so green I could have seen them a mile away.

It wasn't the sight of him leaning against a gray Jeep Cherokee with a book in his slender fingers that brought me to a halt, though he was easily the best-looking man I'd ever seen. It was all the feelings that hit me like a freight train. The feeling of someone else's emotions flooding my core. Though his exterior was calm and collected, his heart pounded slowly in his chest, pumping uncertainty through his blood. I couldn't shake his sadness. I was floored, not knowing what to do. I had never felt someone else like this before. Not Rayn, not anyone.

"Okay then," he mumbled, going back to his book.

I immediately regretted snapping at this beautiful stranger but I hurried off to my car without looking back. I had bigger things going on at the moment.

I ran on autopilot. My hands may have been turning the steering wheel toward the community college, but my mind was nowhere near the car. The scent of wet concrete filled the air around me. My muscles ached from the pressure of the ropes. I ran my tongue over my lip, convinced I'd taste blood instead of chapstick. I had no idea what happened during the interview, but I was certainly going insane. Tears escaped from the corners of my eyes and I let them fall.

I pulled into the front parking lot of the college and parked the car before I sent Rayn a text. I took comfort in the moment of silence. I had more planned for the day, more applications to turn in, and more businesses on my list to submit a resume to but I couldn't go anywhere after what had happened in the Corner Cup. I pinched the skin on my arm to make sure I was awake, to reassure myself that I maintained some sort of control. I took in a breath of relief when I felt the pain.

Movement across the parking lot caught my eye as a familiar brunette rushed toward an older green Ford Taurus. Someone was trying to avoid interaction with her sunglasses on and head down. A girl on a mission to remain unseen.

Before I realized what I was doing, the car door was open and my feet were on the asphalt. Rose didn't see me, she was too preoccupied with getting to her own car, but I had to give it another try. The universe had given me another chance to talk to Rose and I didn't want to waste it. It was time to find out for myself if she was like Rayn and I once and for all. If she had fancy powers to match that hidden necklace.

I knew the puddle in the parking lot was there without looking for it. The stagnant water reflected the white clouds that floated in the sky above it. It called out to me like an old friend. With a discrete wave of my fingers, the water in the puddle began to swirl around in a little whirlpool. My chilled fingertips tingled like they had been dipped into a mountain stream.

Rose stopped dead in her tracks.

Rayn was right, Rose could feel my powers like my sister could. Rose may have been hiding her necklace from us but she couldn't hide this reaction. Rose turned toward me, removing her sunglasses to stare ice-cold daggers into my soul.

"I told you, I'm not doing this." Rose clenched her jaw.

"Why won't you talk to us?" I asked, taking a step toward her to close the gap between us. "My sister and I don't want to cause any trouble. We recently moved into town and we never thought anyone like us existed in the world. It's been her and I. You can imagine we have some questions, and I imagine you have some too."

"What do you want from me?" Rose hissed. "You think I have the witch's handbook or something?"

"We've been trying to figure out where the jewelry came from-"

Rose cut me off. "Please don't tell me you're looking for answers. You'll never find them. I sure haven't." She took an irritated breath. "There are endless questions and possible solutions. A thousand-piece jigsaw. You're going to drive yourself crazy, and personally, I enjoy my sanity."

"All I'm asking is for us to talk and see if we can figure out where these things came from." I put my hand over my chest where my necklace lay against my skin.

"And this is for your own curiosity?" Rose asked defensively.

"You don't think there already is a reason? We need to figure it out. All I want is ten minutes. Please."

"Listen, I really don't want to go through this again." Rose sighed, looking around to make sure no one was paying us any attention.

"I know we ambushed you the other day and I'm sorry for that, but we have never met anyone else who changes the color of the ink inside our gems," I explained. "I'm told Ray and I can be a bit impulsive."

"I'm starting to get used to it, I guess." Rose shook her head. "Like I said, I'm not going down this road again. It doesn't end well. If I were you, I'd go back to trying to blend in as much as possible and quit using in public."

I finally caught on to what Rose had been saying this whole time.

"Wait, are there others?"

"Other what?" Rose tilted her head like she didn't know what I was talking about.

"Other gems like ours. Other people with elemental powers living in Rifton."

"I don't-"

I cut her off, "Tell me the truth."

"I don't owe you shit." Rose backed up. I had pushed too hard and she was retreating again, but her reaction told me all I needed to know.

"Look," I sighed. "This is all my sister and I have ever wanted. We've been dealt some rough hands in life but we always clung to finding the truth about ourselves. We're both adopted, we don't know where we came from or who we were supposed to be. I hoped you were like us, curious and searching for answers. We won't confront you again, I promise. Rayn and I are here when you're ready."

Rose retreated to her car without looking back. I let out a sigh and returned to my car. I sat in the driver's seat for what felt like hours until Rayn showed up. I didn't know how I was going to tell her about my failures that day. Things like this were so much easier when I wasn't the one responsible for our well-being.

"You okay?" Rayn asked. She could see I was a wreck before I said a word.

"It's been a day," I replied, tightening my grip on the steering wheel as we left the parking lot and drove toward the high school a few blocks away.

"For me too." Rayn sighed. "Rose wasn't in English today and they didn't call her name, so I can only assume she switched classes to avoid me. Dmitri was supposed to meet me off campus for lunch, but he ditched me so I had to eat alone until a guy in my class took pity on me."

"Dmitri ditched you at lunch?"

"He sent me a text saying he couldn't make it." Rayn huffed, leaning her head against the seat. "How'd the job search go?"

"It was shit."

"Tom, the guy from my English class, was telling me about this shop his aunt owns downtown that is hiring. I guess it's this cute little witchy store that sells candles and stuff. I'm going to apply."

"A witchy store?" I asked, pulling into the high school.

"I mean, obviously I'm not going to tell them I have personal experience in the subject. But Tom said he would talk to his aunt if I applied and put in a good word. It's practically a done deal." Rayn's demeanor immediately changed as Dmitri got into the car. "What's his name?"

"What?" he asked, confused, dropping his backpack onto the floorboards.

"Whoever you ditched me for today. Hope he's cute."

"I'm not allowed to make friends?" he defended as our eyes met in the rearview.

I loved my brother, but he was not the most social of creatures.

"I'm sorry, friends?" I clarified.

"So, because I'm gay that means every guy I talk to is more than a friend? I know that's your style, Ray, but not exactly mine." Dmitri shot back, defensively.

"Shut up," Rayn muttered, rolling her eyes.

I took a deep breath. "Well, I put out a lot of applications and interviewed at a coffee shop."

"So you got a job?" Rayn asked. "I'm so proud of you, Whit."

Their confidence in me cut deeper than I expected.

"No," I paused. "No, I'm definitely not getting a job there."

"Well, I didn't see Rose today so it looks like we both fell on our faces." Rayn sighed.

"She'll come to us when she's ready," I answered. Pain throbbed in my palm as I relaxed my fingers, not realizing my fist was clenched, leaving crescent moon marks in my palm from my nails.

"You think so?" Rayn asked.

"Yeah, I hope so."

"So, that's it? We're gonna sit stagnant and wait for things to happen for us?" Dmitri inched to the edge of his seat. "That doesn't sound like us."

"I'm going to be honest with you guys," I fixated on the side of the gym that stood next to the front parking lot, counting the number of windows that faced us. One. Two. Three. "I don't know who I am anymore."

"What are you talking about? You're our sister, you're the glue." Rayn put her warm hand on my shoulder.

Four. Five. Six.

"Mom was the glue," I answered, counting the windows again. One. Two. Three.

"We've come too far for you to fall apart now," Dmitri put his hand on the back of our seats. "We'll be okay."

I snapped myself out of it and started the engine. "I don't know."

"What happened to you?" Rayn asked as I drove out of the parking space.

I didn't answer. I got onto the main road and kept driving toward our house in Pines Row. Rayn turned in her seat to face me. "Pull over and talk to us. Is everything finally catching up to you? Are you mad at me for what happened this summer?"

"Ray, no. That's not what this is about."

"Then what is it? Do you regret coming here? You don't think we can start over?" Dmitri asked behind me.

"I think we've already passed the point of no return. This is about me having a shit day and a terrible interview. I'm failing you guys, that's what this is about."

"What happened at your interview?" Rayn asked.

"I really don't want-"

"That bad?" she interrupted again. "So bad you can't tell us? Worse than burning your ex with your bare hands and turning our lives upside down?"

I sighed and pulled into the nearest parking lot. I told them all about the basement, how I mentally checked out of the interview, and ruined my chances of getting hired to work with someone who looked at my necklace like it was something special. How getting closer to our truth slipped through my fingers.

"Shit," Dmitri muttered after I was finished. "You've never had a vision before."

"I'm scared, guys. Everything is falling apart."

"It's not. It's going to take a while to register that this is all happening but we can't give up now." Rayn paused. "You promise you're not mad at me? Not even a little, for what happened with Jon?"

It always circled back to this, back to her guilt.

"I've told you a hundred times, I'm not," I said honestly. "We both fucked up that day."

"You shouldn't have had to..." Rayn hung her head. "I put us in that situation. Having to leave the way we did, it's all on me. It's my fault you're putting all this pressure on yourself."

"Ray, I almost lost you and Mom both in that accident. I'm not going to be mad at you for losing control after everything you went through. Besides, it doesn't matter anymore. After I realized there wasn't anything there worth staying around for, it made leaving a lot easier."

"Even if your fight with Jon never happened, we couldn't stay in Hemston," Dmitri replied. "I couldn't stay, at least."

"We go where you go, Mit, always. Those bigots already had a target on our backs. Our powers being exposed was the tip of the iceberg." I met his brown eyes in the rearview.

"The tip that sank the Titanic," he answered.

"I don't miss that town at all," Rayn muttered, sinking into her seat.

"Then let's try to move forward and stop looking back, yeah?" Dmitri suggested.

"Wise beyond your years, bud," I answered.

Rayn glanced at me sideways before her silent words echoed in my head. *Thank you, for not being mad. You're all I have.*

We have Mit, I reassured her mentally.

I know and I love him, but you know what I mean. You know everything, every ugly detail. You're my day one.

I knew. She was my day one, as well. The person who had been there from the very beginning, weathering every storm. We had somehow managed to keep each other alive while living in foster care, having to hide our powers on our own. We did our best and were only caught once. Not bad for over a decade of risks.

Little did we know the things we could as children were only a fraction of our powers. It's easy to take control of something that was already around, the water in the pipes or the fire of the stove burner. Making it appear in a different spot or bringing the rain from a storm indoors. But materializing it? Making the water come from nothing at all? Those things all required a good amount of concentration and energy. That didn't happen until we were older, after we practiced in secret when no one was looking. After we had Mom to help guide us. The older Rayn and I got, the more powerful we became. In some ways, I couldn't blame people for being afraid of us once they learned the truth.

I jumped as an unexpected ringing filled the car. I'd heard the tune a million times before, but it still took a moment to register that it was my phone.

"Hello?" I answered, not recognizing the phone number with a Rifton area code.

"Whitney, hello, this is Amilia from the Corner Cup. How are you feeling?" The voice came through the other line. She sounded rather pleasant for someone calling to turn me down.

"I'm fine, Amilia, how about yourself?" I looked at my siblings with wide eyes. I told my sister telepathically, *It's the manager from the coffee shop.*

"I'm wonderful, thank you. I'm calling to see if you are still interested in the barista opening we interviewed for today."

Seriously?

"Yes of course!"

"Perfect. Are you available to come in on Saturday morning for some training around nine?"

"I will be there."

"See you then. Thank you, Whitney."

"Thank you so much. Bye." I hung up the phone and announced, "I got the job."

Rayn's lips curved into a smile. "Even after you went blank and threw up right in front of her?"

"Maybe she didn't notice?"

Dmitri laughed. "I highly doubt that."

"I can't believe she hired me after all that," I replied. "There has to be a reason. She has to know something."

"Maybe things aren't as grim as we thought. Had to get a win eventually, right?" Rayn offered.

"Yeah," I answered, my heart still pounding. "I guess so."

CHAPTER FOUR

ENGRAVED DARKNESS

"**H**urry up, Whitney!" Rayn shouted from a few yards ahead of me.

Rayn and Dmitri were treading their way through the dense forest. I wasn't far behind, but apparently taking time to enjoy the scenery wasn't on their agenda. The three of us had been following a main hiking trail up the road from Pines Row called Eagle Loop. We weren't far into the trail when Rayn pointed out an old fork in the path. The side trail was barely noticeable but it was there, whispering for us to find out where it led.

Never in my life had I seen trees this tall. The Dark Star Forest was alive in every sense, towering over us with energy radiating off every leaf. It was calming being away from town after a strange first week in Rifton. A steady reminder that there was so much going on outside of the whirlwind of questions we'd been thrown into. I figured we all needed to step back from it all and go exploring in our new home.

Birds chirped and sang overhead as they chased one another between tree branches. I admired them soaring gracefully through the forest before I followed Rayn and Dmitri further down the trail.

"Woah...Look at this one!" Rayn whispered in awe, walking up to a massive cedar with low-hanging branches. She ran her fingers against the rough bark, introducing herself.

I followed behind her, taking a closer look at the centuries of growth and endurance in front of us, imagining the things this tree had experienced over time. The sun stung my eyes as I gazed up.

"It's huge." Dmitri tilted his head so far back I pictured him falling over. The longer pieces of his hair fell from his brow, allowing him to see properly. "There's something engraved in it."

"Look at this!" Rayn disappeared behind the branches.

We made our way to a meadow hidden behind the tree line. The grass brushed against our ankles and looked like it hadn't been touched by human hands in years. Wildflowers grew in clusters of white, red, purple, and different shades of yellow. It was breathtaking.

Dmitri pulled out his small sketchbook and flipped open to a blank page. "Do you hear that? Absolute silence. It's incredible."

"Can we stay here for a while?" Rayn sat down in the grass and stretched out her long legs.

"Fine by me." Dmitri hopped onto an old log that had fallen on its side and got comfortable.

I loved seeing them like this, happy and content. As if they were able to forget about everything that had been weighing heavily on our shoulders. There had been brief glimmers over the last few months but they had been scarce. So, after Rayn and Dmitri were done with classes for the day, we headed up the mountain.

Rayn and I spent the better part of an hour in the grass playing around with the elements. Gently, Rayn clasped her hands together, like she was holding something precious from escaping, and closed her eyes. I stopped what I was doing and watched her next move carefully. The familiar burning sensation of Rayn's powers tickled my fingertips. Her flame warmed my core like a good cup of coffee, contrasting the icy chill of my own elemental powers.

When she opened her eyes, she wasn't holding her usual flame. In her palm was a perfectly round ball of fire that reminded me of a small sun, like she had reached up into the sky and pulled it through the atmosphere herself. Tiny solar flares escaped from the surface of the fireball.

"That is so cool. I should've brought colors," Dmitri said, turning the page in his notebook quickly to sketch a drawing of the fireball in Rayn's hands. His eyes went back and forth between Rayn and the page, his right hand moving swiftly across the paper.

The ball of fire sparked in Rayn's hands. Startled, she dropped it into the grass. Rayn cursed under her breath and jumped back from the grass that quickly caught on fire.

"What the hell was that?" I asked, holding my hands toward the flames.

The clouds directly above us changed from bright white to a dark gray. Thunder struck and rain began to fall. The other half of the meadow remained green and warm in the sunlight. The energy of my powers ran through me and stopped almost instantly when I pulled my hands back, letting the rain fall on its own.

"You would," Dmitri replied, closing his sketchbook and putting it under his shirt to keep it dry. "A little geyser would have done the trick, you know."

I folded my arms and raised my eyebrows. "What was I supposed to do? Let the forest burn down? We need to be careful."

"I'm so sick of having to be careful," Rayn muttered, kicking a clump of dirt with her boots.

The flames had already begun to smoke and extinguish in the raindrops. The heat crackled against the cold from the clouds before diminishing into nothing.

"Thanks, water nymph." Rayn smiled, slyly.

The falling raindrops thinned out and the clouds turned from dark gray to their original cottonball white, floating around the sky as if nothing had happened.

"What time is it anyway?" I inquired.

"Probably time for us to head back," Dmitri answered. "I'm starving."

Rayn held out her hand to see Dmitri's sketchbook, opening the page to see the pencil sketch of the fireball she had created.

"Mit," she said, almost breathless. "These are fantastic."

Rayn handed his sketchbook to me, so I could see the pictures he had been working on for the past hour. They were good, more than good. They were amazing. He had only looked at that fireball for less than a minute before Rayn dropped it, but the details of the flames were so exact for a quick sketch.

"Thanks. Come on, last one to the main trail has to do the dishes!" Dmitri tucked his sketchbook under his arm and took off sprinting across the meadow toward the tree where we had entered. Rayn ran after as quickly as her long legs could carry her.

"Not fair!" I shouted after them. I wasn't a runner, but I also didn't feel like doing the dishes for the third night in a row either.

I wasn't far behind when Dmitri tripped on a rock. Bracing for impact with the ground, his hands impulsively flew out to break his fall, but as he collided with the ground it wasn't the dirt he hit.

He splashed and vanished from sight.

)·)·●·(·(

"You disappeared." Rayn's voice shook with uncertainty. Her hands trembled as if she was the one who had mysteriously fallen through the ground and into a nearby lake.

"I'm fine," Dmitri muttered, his hair still damp.

"How can you possibly be fine when you don't remember any of it?" I shook my head. Both Rayn and I had been watching him like hawks for the past few hours.

He shrugged, unable to put words together. Words weren't going to convince us anyway and I still felt nauseous from the rush of adrenaline.

Back in the meadow, Rayn had run to the patch of forest floor Dmitri had fallen into. The only reason she didn't go in after him was my tight grip on her arm. The moment my brother disappeared, I felt the lake calling out to me, so I answered. By the time Rayn and I had gotten to the lake, Dmitri had found a small bait and tackle shop on shore and was calling my cell phone to come get him.

He was silent the entire drive home, ignoring the questions Rayn and I offered until we eventually ran out of breath. Upon walking through the front door of the small cabin, he kicked off his soaked shoes and headed straight for the bathroom. Rayn and I sat in silence, listening to the sound of water falling from the showerhead.

Now, the three of us congregated on the living room floor, trying to put the pieces together. Well, Rayn and I were trying. Dmitri was spacing out, staring off into the corner of the couch.

"There has to be something you remember," Rayn pushed for answers.

He closed his eyes and took a deep breath. "Dark eyes."

"Dark eyes?" I repeated.

"Yeah, maybe," He rubbed his temple. "I can't tell if it was a dream or not, honestly."

My head was beginning to throb. At least I was comfortable with a thick blanket wrapped around my shoulders. It was as if the universe was trying to rip my family from my hands.

"What are we going to do?" Rayn asked me quietly like Dmitri wasn't sitting right there next to us.

"I don't know," I admitted. "I don't think there is much we can do, honestly."

"This is a weird time for art, Dmitri." Rayn's head snapped toward our brother. The sketchbook that he had taken into the woods was soaked, but he had picked up a pen and was drawing on his arm.

"What?" His head shot up like he had been caught stealing.

"Is that a symbol?" I leaned forward, analyzing the ink on his smooth skin. I had never seen the symbol before in my life. At least, I didn't think I had.

Scribbled all over Dmitri's arm was a diamond with a circle in the middle. The inside of the circle resembled a cross but the horizontal line was crooked at an angle.

"I didn't realize I was doodling, to be honest," Dmitri muttered, looking closely at his skin.

"The fuck is that?" Rayn stared down at the symbol.

"It kind of looks like what was engraved in the tree. It's different, but the diamond part is the same." Dmitri ran his fingers over the symbol. "The one at the meadow had more circles."

"What?" Rayn said through her teeth. "Why are you just now telling us you found a strange symbol engraved in the tree?"

"I told you when I saw it, you didn't listen." Dmitri leaned against the wall. "You don't listen to half the shit I say. Like I said, it's not the same but it's close."

"Show me the one from the meadow."

Dmitri flipped his arm over for a fresh canvas. It took him less than ten seconds to draw the symbol and hold his arm out to Rayn and I. On his forearm were four linked circles, two on top and two on the bottom. The center links of the four circles reminded me of a flower with a diamond around it.

"Like I said, it's different, but the diamond is the same. Who knows if it means anything." Dmitri let the pen slip from his hand, he waved his fingers and the pen floated across the room to the small desk next to his dresser.

"Something weird happened in that lake." Rayn's eyes locked on mine, tense with worry.

"Ray, I'm fine." Dmitri lied to her.

I could always tell he was lying when he avoided eye contact. He could never lie to me while holding my gaze. He would always crack a smile or fall over his words. "We need to go back to the meadow."

"You want to go back?" Rayn's eyebrows shot up.

"I have to. I can't go on with my life like nothing happened." Dmitri's chocolate brown eyes met mine. "I'm going back with or without you."

"Not if I never give you the car," I answered.

"I'll walk."

"Absolutely not," Rayn snapped.

"You don't sign my permission slips, Rayn," Dmitri shot back. "It doesn't matter what you think."

"Well I do and I don't want you going back," I announced, much to Dmitri's dismay. "We don't know what else is out there."

"Which is why we have to go back," he argued, getting up.

"Fine, we'll go back to the invisible portal. Great idea." Rayn rolled his eyes. "Who knows where it'll spit us up next?"

"That's the point!" Dmitri raised his voice.

"I said no." I hardened my voice.

Dmitri turned on his heel and shot to his bed, waving his hand behind him, using his powers to close the curtain around his makeshift bedroom. The metal rings screamed as they shot across the rod.

Did he metaphorically slam a door in our faces? Rayn asked.

Let him sleep it off.

He's not going back to that meadow, Whit.

I sighed before I answered, *I don't think I can stop him.*

"Good morning." I greeted my brother as the heavy curtains were pulled back from his bedroom.

"What time is it?" he asked sleepily, rubbing his eyes. The back of his hair slicked up from sleeping on it.

"Almost nine." I answered. "Figured you earned that mental health day."

I took a sip of coffee, smiling through my exhaustion as I pretended my eyes weren't heavy from lack of sleep. As if I hadn't stayed up all night worried sick about him, getting up three times throughout the night to peek through his curtain to watch his chest slowly rise and fall with each breath.

"Oh." His eyes wandered down to the coffee cup in my hands, lingering on the moonstone ring on my finger. "I'm sorry I was a dick last night."

"Apology accepted. Are you feeling okay?"

"I think I should be asking you that."

"Me? I'm not the one who fell through the ground and landed in the lake."

"No, but you're the one who blacked out during their interview and had a weird vision. I'd be lying if I said I haven't seen you cracking."

I glared at him sideways.

"Don't give me that look. I know how you get when you're stuck in your head. You've been through some shit, Whitney. I know we all have, but you're carrying it all and it's breaking your back. You aren't sleeping."

"My back isn't breaking. I'm fine."

"Okay, we both have our stories. You're fine, and I assume I have a stomach ache?" He smirked, guessing at the story I'd given the high school when I excused him for the day. "Or the sniffles, maybe?"

"Explosive diarrhea, actually." I smiled.

Dmitri laughed and hopped off his bed, heading for the coffee pot in the kitchen. His blue plaid pajama pants hung loose on his long legs. Now that his bedroom curtain was fully open for the first time since we moved in, I could admire the artwork he had started on the wall.

Mit's art was breathtaking. Above his bed was a massive red, white, and blue shield from his favorite superhero. Currently, he was working on the wall. Painted in the top corner was a full moon amidst the night clouds. Coming up from the floor was a massive black wolf leaning its head up, howling to the moon. The wolf had a white patch on its chest and gigantic paws.

"Are we out of almond milk?" he asked, spinning around to face me.

"Oh, yeah sorry, I used the last of it."

"Is the goal for today to watch over me or torture me?" He shut the fridge door a little harder than usual and took a drink from his black coffee, the bitter taste made his lips curl in disappointment.

"Chill out. Put some pants on and we'll walk down to the corner mart for your milk."

"Ray took the car?" Dmitri asked, setting his mug down on the counter.

"She may never come back." I chuckled.

He threw on jeans, changed into a clean shirt and followed me out the front door. Although I wasn't planning on leaving the house, a walk might help clear our heads. The crisp mountain air was uplifting and the sky above us was a picturesque cloudless blue, stretching for miles. What amazed me the most was the silence that came with Pines Row, the neighborhood we lived in. No car motors, no screaming children, not a single sound filled the void but a few chirping birds and our shoes against the asphalt of the main road.

Before long, we approached the mini-mart gas station owned by our landlords at the edge of Pine's Row. It was a tiny wooden building with an ice container out front and an open sign in the window. Four pumps for gas sat in the middle of the parking lot.

The door jingled when we walked in and Janice stood at the cash register.

"How are you doing today?" She greeted us with a smile.

"Good morning, Janice," I replied.

"No school today, Dmitri?" Janice asked my brother.

"Mental health day," he answered. "I'll still be here this afternoon for my shift."

I turned the corner past rows of candy bars and bags of chips to see someone on their knees stocking shelves. He looked about seventeen with short, curly hair the same copper color as Janice. His eyes were gray and his round face was covered in freckles.

"Finding everything okay?" he asked, looking up at us. A can of baked beans in his white-knuckled hand.

"Oh yeah. I'm just browsing, thanks."

"Hi, Abe." Mit quickly went down the next aisle to the refrigerated doors.

"Hey." The boy said to my brother before he went back to stocking the canned goods.

I walked past Abe, the boy on the floor, to meet Mit in the back of the store. I couldn't help but look over my shoulder and get another look. When I turned my head, the boy was looking at me too. He quickly turned his head when our eyes met and got up from the floor, leaving a few cans behind him.

"Who is that guy?" I asked Dmitri.

"Janice's son, Abe. He works here too." He held a cold carton of almond milk to his chest. His nervous demeanor gave me the impression that he wasn't telling me everything. "We have Biology together."

I grabbed a can of iced tea and a bag of sour gummy worms. Wandering around the small mini-mart, I realized there wasn't much else I wanted. No matter how hard I tried, I couldn't pretend I was fine. I missed my mom terribly. She would have known what to do.

"Hey, Dmitri? While you're here, I cleaned out a spot in the back for your backpack and things during your shift. I'll show you now if you have a moment." Janice appeared around the corner, smiling gently.

"Yeah, of course." Dmitri handed me the almond milk and followed her into the back without giving me so much as a glance.

I took our purchases up to the counter and grabbed a pack of spearmint gum from a small metal rack. When I looked up, Abe was behind the register. He looked so much like his mother.

"No school today?" I asked. I wasn't very good at small talk.

"I have a free period in the morning," Abe replied. "My parents always need extra help."

"That's nice of you." I gazed over the rows of cigarettes and lottery tickets behind him.

"Mhhm. $12.32."

I reached into my bag for my wallet and handed over fifteen dollars. Abe reached out for it, raising the long sleeve of his shirt. Engraved into his wrist was the same symbol Dmitri had subconsciously drawn over and over the night before.

"What's that symbol?" I asked, focusing on the scar.

"Nothing." As he snatched the cash from my hand, his fingers grazed against mine before he pulled away quickly.

"No, not nothing. What does that symbol mean?" My heart raced in my chest.

Abe stood there in front of me frozen, his eyes wide with shock like a dirty secret had been discovered.

"Tell me," I demanded.

"Stay away from me." Abe closed the cash register hard, causing a loud ding, and left the counter. He retreated to the backroom as quick as his legs would take him.

"Wait!" I went after him, but he knew his way around the store better than I did and was behind a closed, locked door before I reached him. "Wait! I want to talk." After a few moments of silence, I asked through the thick door, "Please?"

"If you want to live, stay away from me." Abe's soft warning came from the other side of the door.

Whatever the future holds, I must keep these girls far away from Rifton. They would never be safe there.

"What are you talking about?" I questioned, but silence greeted me. Abe was already gone.

The only thing I could do was walk away. It's not like Abe could hide from me forever. I knew where he worked. I knew where he lived. I rushed out of the mini-mart more confused than when I walked in. So much for clearing my head.

"What the hell was that?" Dmitri appeared behind me, luckily he was alone.

"That guy. He had a brand of that symbol you drew on your arm last night."

Dmitri didn't say a word. His gaze darted to the ground, avoiding eye contact with me like the plague.

"You never noticed that brand on his wrist?"

He remained quiet.

"Dmitri Hawke."

"I wanted to get more information before I told you. Get to know him better and maybe he would give me some answers. Chances of that are slim now after your performance," he answered.

"Did you see it before or after you fell into the lake?"

"Before," he whispered.

So he knew what the symbol was as he drew it on his skin.

"Don't ever keep anything like that from me again, do you understand?" I snapped.

"I'm not a kid anymore," he argued.

"Then quit acting like one."

As I stepped off of the pavement and onto the asphalt, a cold wind blew, hitting me right in the face. It was odd to feel a breeze so cold when it was still late Summer. It chilled down my spine and through my already shaking bones. My knees were so unsettled it made walking difficult.

My attention was pulled to one of the trees where a shadow cast from a branch was much darker than it should have been. I looked closely at the ground and could have sworn something moved. I could feel a pair of eyes on me, watching me closely.

A car honked, making my heart jump. I didn't realize I had moved into the parking lot, toward the shadow. I waved a quick apology to the man sitting in the driver's seat of the red car I was in front of and took off toward the house, Dmitri close on my heels.

Whatever was going on with Abe and his symbol would have to wait. My chest constricted as nightmares of dark creatures hunched in the corner of my various childhood bedrooms resurfaced. I looked back at the shadow, making sure it was still there. They had been gone for so many years, disappearing quickly after we were sent to live with Mom and Dmitri. I had convinced myself they had never existed in the first place. I couldn't accept that the shadows were back.

I spent the rest of the day locked in my bedroom on the internet. I had searched for information on the shadows a million times before and as I had feared, there wasn't anything new that would help me figure out what was going on. My memories took me back to when Rayn and I first started seeing the shadows. When we first felt their eyes on us, waiting to pounce, but they never did. They only lurked and watched, chilling the blood in my veins and haunting my dreams.

"Hey! How was your day?" Rayn called from the kitchen when I mustered the courage to leave my bed.

"I walked to the mini-mart with Mit earlier and the kid next door-" I stopped mid-sentence when I walked further into the kitchen and saw a stranger sitting at the kitchen counter while Rayn dug through the refrigerator.

"How do you feel about pizza?" Rayn asked from the deli drawer.

"Strongly," I answered, analyzing the guy on a barstool. I could smell his cologne from across the kitchen. "Who is this?"

"This is the guy I mentioned from my English class, Tom Campbell. Tom, this is my sister, Whitney. Tom and I were talking about how good homemade pizza would be." I hadn't seen Rayn this happy since we left Kansas. She zipped around the kitchen gladly doing most of the work for their meal.

"Nice to meet you. Rayn talks about you all the time, I feel like I already know you." Tom smiled warmly.

Tom's light brown hair was cut short, framing his oval face. He was handsome, definitely Rayn's type. Though something I'd yet to see in a boy Rayn brought home was a demeanor displaying the epitome of upright politeness.

"You too," I said to Tom after the quick evaluation.

"So, what about the kid Mit works with?" Rayn asked. "What's his name? Theodore?"

"Abraham."

"I knew it was a president. What happened?"

I glanced over at Tom. "Nothing. He's Janice's son, that's all."

"Where does your brother work?" Tom inquired, turning his head to the side.

"The mini-mart down the street," I answered quickly.

"Oh cool, maybe he can get us cheap snacks." Tom smiled at my sister like a puppy who had never seen a pretty girl before. His light hazel eyes echoed against the long sleeve olive shirt he wore.

It took me a moment to realize Tom was referring to him and my sister as if they were a couple. I hadn't realized they were already a 'we' but this wasn't the first time my sister moved quickly into romantic involvements.

"Here Ray, let me help." Tom hopped off of the kitchen stool and took a knife and green bell pepper from my sister's hands. "As talented as you are, you shouldn't have to do all the work."

Rayn and Tom were still sitting a bit too close on the couch by the time Dmitri got home from his shift at the mini-mart. I wanted to have an opinion, but Rayn was an adult and I wasn't going to tell her what to do. I was her sister, not her mother.

"I want to talk to you about Abe." Dmitri led the way to my room, shutting the door behind us.

"And?"

"He isn't a bad guy, Whit. We talked at work," Dmitri explained. He had no idea who this guy was. None of us did. Abe Roberts could be a psycho for all we knew. Why else would I have to stay away from him if I wanted to live?

"And what exactly did you two talk about?" I raised my eyebrows at him.

"Video games. He doesn't seem like he's crazy. He's just a guy." Dmitri answered casually.

"I don't know what you're trying to accomplish by buddying up to him." I took my hair out of a bun and ran my fingers through it. Having it tied up was not helping my headache.

"I'm trying to get some info out of him, find out what these symbols mean. I can't do that if he doesn't trust me. No thanks to you earlier." Dmitri defended himself. "You're always telling me I need friends."

"Yeah, but-"

"Speaking of new friends, what do you think of Rayn's boyfriend?" Dmitri asked, changing the subject.

"Boyfriend?" I raised an eyebrow. "She's barely known him for a week."

"It's only a matter of time, I'm sure. She's acting like he's the greatest guy to walk into her life like she does with all of them."

"He seems nice enough, I guess. Is there actually something wrong with him or are you being overprotective?" I asked with a smirk.

"Hopefully the latter."

"Hey, what are you guys doing hiding in here?" Rayn asked, opening the bedroom door.

"Your friend still here?" I asked.

"No, he left." She stepped further into the room. "What's up?"

"I saw a shadow."

"What?" Rayn froze. "Here at the house?"

"At the mini-mart. That's not even the craziest part."

"The fuck happened?"

Dmitri and I explained the morning's events. Janice's son, Abe, and the brand on his wrist. The shadow in the parking lot that watched me like prey.

"Stay away from me if you want to live?" Rayn sat down on my bed with a heavy thud.

I shrugged, not knowing how to reply. "That's what he said."

"Do you think someone is trying to hurt him?" Dmitri leaned forward, resting his elbows on his knees.

"I don't know what else to think, but why?" I answered, rubbing my temple. "Why would someone want to hurt him if he's such a normal guy?"

"That symbol must have something to do with it. Why else would he run off the moment you saw it on his wrist?" Rayn asked.

"Don't worry, guys, we'll figure this whole thing out." I couldn't tell who I was reassuring more, them or myself.

"I guess. Add it to the list." Rayn shrugged.

Dmitri remained silent.

Chapter Five

GHOST GIRL

My knees trembled as I walked through the main door of Corner Cup for my shift Saturday morning. Whether I was shaking from the insane week I'd had or first day jitters, I hadn't decided. A bell above the door jingled as I entered the building, alerting my new coworkers to my presence.

A line of customers stood at the register for their morning fuel and another handful sat in the dining area. I walked up to a pretty girl with freckles and curly, red hair to ask for Amilia.

"You must be Whitney. I'm Ashley. I'm going to help with your training. Amilia is back in her office, but she asked me to get you started." The redhead smiled and shook my hand. "Whitney, this is Olivia, Robby and Greg. Guys, this is Whitney, our new barista. I'll be in the back if you need me."

"Okay, perfect." I followed her to the storage room behind the counter. Boxes of sugar and cardboard cups lined the shelves next to bottles of flavored syrups and covered bins labeled as different types of bagel. A sink for washing the dishes sat in the corner and a large fridge stood next to it. Ashley opened up a supply closet and handed me a black apron.

"Let me find you a blank name tag and a marker." Ashley rummaged through a cardboard box on a shelving unit.

My first official day of work was turning out to be less nerve-wracking than I anticipated. Excitement began to bubble inside of me, tickling my spine. Once I had my uniform together, I looked at myself in a small mirror and couldn't help but smile. I was finally going to get my family on our feet again.

"Okay, so average day here," Ashley led me behind the counter with a smile. "There should always be someone on register to take orders. Usually, there're two people back here to make drinks and someone keeping the dining area clean. Since I'm training with you today and technically not on the floor, we have extra people to compensate. We're downtown and close to the high school and college so we stay busy. When you need more milk, the fridge is behind us. Make sure to read labels and expiration dates because there's like seven different kinds."

Once she gave me the lay of the land, Ashley took over the register from the girl named Olivia and started showing me how to input drinks. When a customer would come up to the counter, Ashley showed me how to put that specific drink into the computer system at the register. I only messed up a few times, but Ashley was helpful and explained to the customers that I was in training. Hopefully, I would get to work with her often.

"Are you full-time?" I asked Ashley in between orders.

"Yes, I'm one of the supervisors. I live here." She laughed. "I keep a cot in the back office."

"How's everything going with our new member?" Amilia asked, walking up to the counter with a smile. She rested her hands on the counter and leaned forward, her rings clanking against the metal.

"Going great! Whitney's a natural. She is a quick learner on the register." Ashley nudged me playfully with her elbow.

"Keep up the great work, ladies." Amilia went to help another customer who came up to the counter for a coffee refill in their tall, blue mug.

I had no idea how I was going to find out more about Amilia when she was always in her office. With a sigh, I watched people around the dining area. Another calm, average day with average people finding a moment of peace with a caffeinated beverage.

A few hours later, another customer came in. Her long arms filled with a laptop and several textbooks. Her tight jeans showed off her long, slender legs and an oversized beige top exposed her left shoulder. Her light blonde, perfectly curled hair flowed behind her as she floated across the dining room.

I couldn't take my eyes off her. Something about this girl drew me in and called out to me like a song I could have sworn I'd heard before but couldn't remember the lyrics.

"Hi, welcome in! What can we get started for you?" Ashley asked the tall blonde.

"Hi." The blonde smiled. "Can I get a caramel iced coffee with soy milk?"

"Of course." Ashley turned her attention to me. "Got it?"

"Yes," I tapped on the register, inputting the drink. "Got it."

The blonde paid for her drink and made herself comfortable in the far corner of the dining area. She put in her headphones and opened up her laptop like she had come in here to study a million times before.

"Can you do me a quick favor and run that girl's order over to her when it's done? I have to go into the back for a second." Ashley asked.

"Yeah, of course," I answered.

"Awesome, afterwards we'll take a lunch break." Ashley said before turning to one of the other girls. "Can you hop back on register?"

The blonde was the last customer in line and Corner Cup had finally died down from the afternoon rush. Only a few customers lingered in the far corners of the dining area. I took the blonde's iced coffee over to her and set it on the table next to her laptop.

"Oh, thank you." She smiled and took one of the headphones out of her ear.

"Is there anything else I can get for you?" I glanced down at her hand holding an earbud. Her nails were perfectly manicured in beige at the end of her slender fingers. She had a gold ring on her thumb and a simple gold bracelet on her wrist. Tiny chains linked together with tarnish on the edges. Encased in little gold claws was an aged citrine with swirls of unmistakable white ink floating inside.

"Holy shit," I muttered, looking down inside my apron to see the floating ink of my aquamarine had turned white as well.

The blonde saw my eyes on her bracelet and quickly pulled her hand back. Upon seeing the white floating ink for herself, the blonde looked back up at me with dilated pupils. I had no idea who this girl was, but the expression on her face said she knew exactly what the white ink meant.

I reached inside of my apron and pulled on the silver chain, letting my heavy gem fall into sight. In any other situation, I'd never reveal my most sacred possession to a stranger, but my aquamarine called out to her citrine like two lost sisters. I felt the tug inside of my soul. Maybe if I showed her that I had one too, she would be more willing to talk than Rose was. Maybe if I was able to show her I wasn't a threat, I'd actually get somewhere.

Her brown eyes watched me cautiously like I was pulling a gun out of my bra. The moment she saw my necklace, every hair on her body stood up. This girl looked terrified of what was around my neck.

The blonde quickly closed her laptop and threw her still open textbook on top of it. Jumping up from the table, she gathered her belongings as quickly as her arms would move, swinging her white backpack over her shoulder.

"Wait," I said quickly, not wanting to draw attention from other customers or my new coworkers.

"Leave me alone," the blonde hissed through her teeth and beelined to the exit.

As she ran off, the faintest tingle of power washed over my fingertips. Similar to when Rayn used her powers, but on a much smaller scale. A breeze hit my face, blowing my hair past my shoulders. How could there possibly be a breeze inside of a building with no open windows?

I wanted to chase after her. I wanted to demand answers to my questions. Where did you get that bracelet? Why are you so afraid of me? How do you know what the white ink means? Do you have powers and what are they? But I didn't. I let her go not knowing if I would ever see her again.

"What was that all about?" Ashley asked behind me, looking down at the untouched iced coffee the blonde had left sitting on the table.

"I have no idea," I answered honestly. My heart raced behind my rib cage, rattling around my bones like a bird eager to escape.

"Super weird," Ashley grabbed the glass mason jar and nodded toward the employee-only area. "Come on, let's take a break. I'm starving."

Before I followed behind her, I looked back at the entrance on the off chance the blonde had returned. But as I had expected, no one was there. Unlike Rose and her supposed gem, I had actually seen the gold bracelet. I had seen the white floating ink and the same metal links that held my necklace together.

Rayn almost lost it after we found out there was potentially another girl living in Rifton with jewelry that matched ours, someone who may have elemental powers like us. I could picture Rayn's wide eyes when I told her a second one crossed my path, that the magic radiated off of this girl like heat off the pavement in summer. I guess I was finally starting to understand why Mom approached us the way that she did, knowing our elemental powers existed but waiting for us to break the ice. I wished, more than anything, I could sit down with her and ask all these questions. Rayn and I were going to have to figure it out on our own. We needed to get Rose and this blonde girl in the same room as us without them tripping over each other as they ran for the exit.

After my shift, I called Rayn with trembling fingers the moment I got out of earshot from anyone.

"Finally, I've been counting down the minutes until you got off work," Rayn answered the phone after a single ring. "You'll never believe this."

"What?" I asked as my pulse picked up.

"Rose reached out finally. She wants to meet you and I alone tomorrow night at eight in the park by the high school. She's finally ready to talk." I could hear Rayn bouncing in her seat with excitement. "I didn't chase after her or anything. She came to me on her own, like we hoped."

"That's good," I muttered, picking at the plastic of the steering wheel, not sure how to process it all.

"What's wrong? I thought you'd be thrilled. You heard me, right?"

"Yeah, yeah, I did. That's great."

Rayn sighed. "What happened?"

"There's four of us, Ray," I told her. "Another girl in town with a gem like ours. She came into the Corner Cup today. She has a bracelet and her gem was yellow but the white ink was there. My necklace, too."

"Oh," she whispered. "What do we do?"

"Meet with Rose tomorrow and get some damn answers."

"I lied to you," Rose said as Rayn and I approached her the following night.

"Shocker," I muttered, scanning our surroundings.

The sun had set over an hour ago and the sky was dark, giving us the perfect backdrop for secrecy. The trees around us cast long shadows across the pavement from the glow of the streetlights. An eerie silence lingered across the playground. The chain of the swings creaked ever so slightly in the breeze.

Rayn crossed her arms against her chest. "Lied about what?"

"Not knowing about others like us," Rose sighed, running her fingers through her brunette strands. "It's been messy for me. I hope you understand."

"I kind of figured out we weren't the only ones when another girl ran out of my job yesterday after she saw the ink in her citrine turn white," I answered.

"Tall blonde with a permanent scowl?" Rose asked.

"Something like that."

"Oh, good. You met Lauren." Rose said with a dry laugh. "She's a peach. But she's not why I asked you both here tonight."

"Lauren who?" I asked further.

Rose shook her head. "You'll have to deal with *that* on your own. Lauren doesn't speak to us. Besides, there's someone else you need to meet."

A teenage girl appeared behind Rose, stepping out from behind one of the larger trees. I could feel Rayn heat up, preparing for defense, but the girl looked anything but threatening.

"Who the hell are you?" Rayn questioned, taking a step back.

Rose's friend was in her later teenage years with prominent dark brown eyes whose shape showed off her Asian heritage. Her hair was straight and black, cut in layers that fell past her shoulders. The clothes she wore were clean and freshly pressed. A floral print dress that fell above her knee and spotless black boots. Although she was tiny, she intimidated me with the confidence in her stride.

"This is Brooke Evans, she's a senior at the high school. We became friends the day my necklace changed next to her in the lunch line a few years ago." Brooke's eyes darted back and forth between Rayn and I, taking in every inch of us as Rose spoke.

"Do you see things?" The young girl looked me dead in the eyes before she turned her gaze to my sister.

"Excuse you?" I furrowed my brow.

"Can you see things?" Brooke repeated with determination.

"I'm not blind if that's what you're asking," I answered, confused.

"No, like strange things." Brooke tried again.

"Strange things? Like UFOs or pixies?" Rayn jumped in, her head cocked to the side.

"Pixies, Rayn?" I chortled. "Seriously?"

"No, dead people. Ghosts. Spirits." Brooke answered, serious as a heart attack.

"Oh god, of course not." Rayn took a step back.

"Hang on." I held up my hand. "I think we are getting ahead of ourselves, who are you again?"

"I'm Brooke. Brooke Evans." She extended her hand. "Sorry, I'm excited."

"Whitney Dansley," I said quietly, accepting her handshake. "This is my sister, Rayn."

"I heard you're the newest members of the magical jewelry club." Brooke bent down, unclasping something around her ankle. Her hair fell into her eyes.

"Are you armed?" Rayn stepped back, reaching out for my arm.

"Yeah, she's carrying a Glock in her boot." Rose scoffed. "You can trust us."

"You haven't proven trustworthy yet," I told Rose as I watched her friend closely.

Rose's eyes burn into me, "Neither have you, but here we are. I didn't want to entertain you two but Brooke insisted, so be nice."

Brooke didn't say a word. In her open hand was a silver chain with a medium-sized amethyst. My heart stopped beating at the sight of the gem. White ink slowly floated around, trapped inside the walls.

There were five of us with matching gems that all held color-changing ink inside of them. Rayn and I had gone from being the only ones we knew of, to being two of a group. This was unbelievable.

"Where did they come from?" Brooke asked with big eyes full of questions I didn't have answers for.

"We've been trying to figure it out ourselves with little luck," Rayn replied, looking around to make sure no one else was there. "Seems like Rose knows more than any of us."

"I really don't," Rose defended. "All I know is the ink changes color when another is near."

"I can't believe you almost didn't tell me about meeting these two." Brooke's eyes met Rose with a force of fear and rage. She wasn't going to leave until she got some kind of information. I couldn't help but huff in amusement thinking that this was how we looked when we first approached Rose. I admired Brooke's tenacity.

"Can you blame me?" Rose turned away from Brooke and met my gaze. "You asked for ten minutes, so here you go."

"That was before Lauren walked into the Corner Cup. Before I knew there were more of us," I said, my head still spinning.

"Are there others?" Rayn asked, her voice shaky.

"No, not that we know of at least. Just us and Lauren," Brooke answered.

"We need all five of us together."

"Yeah." Rose laughed. "That's not going to happen."

"Why not?" Rayn asked, devastated.

"Because it's not. Lauren was an asshole to me in high school and we don't speak," Rose explained. "We may both have these gems but that's where it stops."

Brooke spoke up. "We can't force Lauren to do something she doesn't want to. I'd love to see your jewelry, if you two are okay with that."

I probably should have asked more questions, but there was too much of myself in Brooke's reflection to not trust her. Rayn held out her hand, showing Brooke the ring on her thumb. I reached for the silver chain and exposed the aquamarine pendant. In the dim light of the street lamps, the white ink inside our gems was clear as day.

"Where did they come from?" Brooke asked, leaning in closer and examining the white swirls.

"I don't know much about them," I confessed. "But we're going to find out. One way or another."

"Then we're going to help you." Brooke looked up at us and nodded. "Whatever you need, we're in."

"B." Rose groaned.

She's a little too eager. Rayn's voice echoed in my head.

She's a kid, I answered. *We could use some enthusiasm.*

"Don't act like you haven't been wanting this as badly as they do," Brooke turned to Rose, her words catching in her throat. "I know you better than that."

Rayn and I looked at each other with the same sympathetic expression.

Rose sighed. "I saw...I saw something a few nights ago. I thought it was a fluke, but then I saw it again the next night."

"What are you talking about?" Rayn asked, suspiciously.

"Have you guys ever seen...shadows?"

My blood ran cold.

"Shadows," I whispered. The most terrifying moments of my childhood that I had locked away in the furthest corner of my brain resurfaced. As much as I had been trying to convince myself otherwise, the darkness I saw at the mini-mart was not a fluke.

"Yeah, it's hard to explain. Like, something is there but not." Rose rubbed her arms with trembling fingers.

"Like it's watching you," Brooke added. "Waiting to rip you apart."

I didn't know what was more terrifying, the fact that the shadows had returned after all these years or the fact that we weren't the only ones to see them. Rose and Brooke seeing them too meant they were real.

"We have," Rayn answered, looking at me sideways. "Whitney saw it recently. We hadn't seen it in so long, we hoped it was gone for good."

"Well, it's back. Whatever it is. I hadn't seen it for years and then you two strolled into town and bam. So, I took it as a sign to stop hiding. To stop pretending to be someone else and finally get to the bottom of everything I've been ignoring over the years."

"Here, let me give you my number." Brooke put her hand out for my phone, which I gave to her instantly.

"So...what did you say earlier?" Rayn asked. "Do we see ghosts?"

"I...I can see spirits. Can't you?" Brooke hesitated for our answer.

"No," Rayn answered, glancing over at me.

Brooke's shoulders fell. "Neither can Rose. I hoped when we learned about you two that it would start to make more sense but..."

I was hoping for more of an explanation that matched closer to Rayn and I. Water and fire.

I don't know about Brooke, Whit. She has a bracelet but she sees dead people? I don't get how she fits in with us. Rayn was skeptical, but no one would have known by looking at her calm and collected demeanor.

"You really won't give me anything?" I asked Rose again.

"I introduced you to Brooke. I told you about the shadows. I gave you a lot," Rose answered. "A lot more than you've given me."

"And your powers?"

"They exist."

"But what can you do?"

"I'm not an all the way on the first date kind of gal."

"You're infuriating is what you are," I mumbled. "Can you at least tell me what color your necklace is?"

"You don't know when to quit, do you?" Rose sighed. "It's green."

My heart skipped around in my chest. "You're earth. You control the earth, don't you?"

"That's a safe assumption," Rose answered, her face difficult to read.

"Mother Earth." Brooke chuckled, nudging Rose with her elbow.

Brooke sees dead people. Dead people, Whit. What if the bracelet isn't meant for her? What if it only changed color because it was near ours? At least Rose being earth makes sense. Rayn questioned telepathically, trying to find every possible reason why Brooke wasn't one of us.

She's one of us, Rayn. I shot back mentally, my patience wearing thin.

"Okay, Ghost Girl," Rayn finally spoke aloud. "Welcome to the team."

"Good. I have to get home, but I'll talk to you soon. Try to actually keep me in the loop this time, Rosie." Brooke trod off, my heart pounding louder with each step she took.

"What now?" Rayn asked Rose.

She shrugged. "I'm not in charge here." Rose glanced over at me. "You tell me."

"We need to retrace our steps. How we got the gems and where they came from. But before we can do any of that, we need Lauren," I replied. "There's five of us for a reason."

"I'm telling you, she won't," Rose answered.

"And if you're wrong?" Rayn asked.

"If you two can get Lauren Thaner on board, then I'm Queen Victoria reincarnated." Rose said. "Luckily for you, Brooke is already on board. She nearly passed out when I told her about you two."

"The jewelry is all linked to our powers somehow. We won't be able to get the full story without all five of us," I insisted.

"Tell you what," Rose nodded. "You get Lauren to agree to meet with us, with *all* of us, and I'll be in a hundred percent."

"You're only saying that because you don't think I can pull it off," I answered.

"Maybe, but if you do, I'll consider you a miracle worker. Maybe you can show me how you walk on water sometime."

"I'll figure it out," I replied confidently. "I always do."

We said goodbye to Rose and headed toward the car.

"Wow, who would have thought this is how life in Rifton would be," Rayn closed the passenger side door and secured her seatbelt. "I got the job, by the way."

"What job?" I asked, confused. I didn't know she had an interview set up anywhere.

"The one at the cute witchy store, remember? Tom's aunt? I told you about it. They hired me, so I will have my own money now and be able to help pay for stuff." Rayn's shoulders fell. She was disappointed I had forgotten.

"Ray, that's amazing. I'm proud of you." I gave her a genuine smile.

"I was thinking I could take over paying for groceries. You and Mit make enough for the rent and utilities. That way we're all contributing and it'll take some pressure off of you, hopefully."

"As long as it doesn't-"

Rayn cut me off. "Interfere with classes. Yeah, I know." She sighed and looked out the window at the moon as I drove us home. "Five lost elemental witches finding their way to one another, kinda poetic when you think about it."

"Yeah." I couldn't help but smile at her optimism. "It kind of is."

Chapter Six

THE TEMPEST

That night, I sat at the foot of a bed that wasn't mine, my hands folded peacefully in my lap. The bedroom was dark but a large window was open, welcoming the brightness of the crescent moon. Abe Roberts knelt on the floor dressed in a dark gray hoodie. Three black candles were lit in front of him in a triangle formation.

His face was hardened and cold. It took a moment to realize he was holding something down. He struggled with his left arm as his right hand glistened in the light of the candles. A blade. His right wrist bore the familiar symbol engraved into his flesh.

I tried to close my eyes, or at least scream, but I couldn't move. No sound came from my lips. I could only sit there with my hands folded in my lap, watching him sacrifice an innocent animal. Red liquid gleamed in the moonlight, covering his fingers as the small rabbit screamed out in pain.

My eyes flashed open. I was back in my bedroom; safe and warm in my bed. What an awful nightmare. It may have been a dream, but it did not feel like one. Nausea permeated through my body as I sat up and hesitantly went to my window. Taking in a breath of courage, I looked outside.

There he was, still kneeling in front of the open window in his bedroom. The moment his figure came into view, I ducked. I didn't want him to know I knew anything. I had no idea what I witnessed or why anyone would ever need to harm an animal like that, but I left my room to wake my sister with trembling hands.

Whoever Abe Roberts was, we needed to stay far away from him.

Even after I told Rayn what I'd seen, she fell asleep next to me quickly. Her red hair fanned out across the pillow. Unable to sleep, I retreated into Mom's journal. It was eye-opening to see Rayn and I from her unfiltered point of view, how she truly felt about our powers rather than the story she gave to our faces. Her determination to help us develop our powers while maintaining the innocence of our childhood, though the system we grew up in had destroyed whatever innocence we had long before. The way Mom knew that buried under Rayn's bold nature was the constant fear that someone would see past her armor and exploit the weakness that she trusted everyone. The way Mom knew that my silent waves meant a storm was brewing on the horizon, that I retreated into myself rather than ask for help or guidance that she gave anyway.

One entry, in particular, made me sit straight up in bed.

Days like these make me miss Mia more than usual. She was always the better teacher, and always knew the right things to say. Whitney and Rayn are getting stronger, accidentally using their powers when they don't intend to. Thank the Shepherds I'm not raising them in Rifton. I can only imagine how they'd be treated there if they were to accidentally use in public there. At least here in Hemston, there is some deniability. Mia isn't the only part of Rifton I miss. I miss the smell of the pines and the mountain peaks that surrounded the city. I couldn't stay there. Not after the fire. Not after Sue threatened to take Dmitri away from me. That place knows too much. Yet, part of me will always long for the time when Mia and I were young and fearless. Brave, naive witches who thought we were invincible. If I am able to accomplish anything with my girls, it'll be helping them understand the target on their backs.

If only she knew that Kansas wasn't any safer than Rifton, or what was going to happen to us when the townspeople did find out the truth about us. I wondered if she would have stayed as long as she did if she knew we weren't truly any safer.

I would have given almost anything to talk to her again, but this journal was better than nothing.

The jingle of the bell hanging above the Corner Cup door had become such a routine sound throughout my shifts that I barely noticed it. It wasn't until a jingle came with a sudden shift in my emotions that I noticed someone had walked in. The stress I had felt all morning melded with a state of contentment that conflicted within my soul. My own uncertainty didn't leave but was joined hand in hand with a joyful glow. I didn't quite understand what was happening, but I knew for damn sure these extra emotions weren't mine.

"Hi-eeee." Ashley waved to the next customer.

"Hi-eee." He sang back, putting a brown paper bag on the counter, and rested his elbows on the glass bagel display case. When his vibrant green eyes met mine, his bright smile slowly faded to a more serious tone. "Hi."

"Hi," I answered, breathless at how strongly my emotions were jumping around.

We stood there for the longest time. His eyes were lily pads, gently floating in a pond. Beautiful on the surface with an uncertain depth you'd have to jump in to find the bottom. My heart thud louder and louder in my chest until I realized that there were two heartbeats I was feeling. The same emotions that invaded my soul after the horrid interview with Amilia.

"Oh, wow. That is some prolonged eye contact," Ashley remarked. "Whitney, this is my best friend, Bryan. Bryan, this is my new barista, Whitney."

"The girl who detests wooden crates." He smiled gently.

"What?" Ashley asked, confused.

"Yeah," I looked away, embarrassed. "Definitely my best first impression thus far." Second only to my interview with Amilia.

Bryan chuckled. "Stuck with me, for sure. You're new here?"

"Yeah, I moved into town a few weeks ago."

"Very new, then. What do you think of Rifton so far?"

It would have been better without portals that dumped my brother in the lake or all the witches in hiding, but I decided to be optimistic.

"It's literally the most beautiful place I've ever been," I replied honestly.

"That is probably Rifton's only redeeming quality." He chuckled. That and those stunning green eyes. "Oh, Ash, here is your burrito."

"You're a gentleman and a scholar, Byn." Ashley took the brown paper bag and hid it behind the counter. "Trade you for some tea?"

"Please, something with caffeine." He smiled.

I was surprised to see Bryan standing in front of me. Unlike our first meeting after my interview, there were calm seas underneath his freckled skin. I honestly didn't think I would see him again.

"Did your day get any better after you took out those crates?" Bryan asked me, his hands deep in his pockets.

"What is up with these crates?" Ashley asked again, pouring some hot water into a to-go cup.

"I thought I bombed my interview here so I kicked over a stack of crates in the back and Bryan was in the parking lot. It was kinda embarrassing, honestly," I mumbled.

Ashley tilted her head to the side. "Why would you think you bombed? As soon as you left, Amilia told me you were the one she was going to hire."

"Seriously?"

Ashley smiled. "Yeah, she likes you. Don't be so hard on yourself."

If only she knew why I was so confused by this.

"Here ya go, my love. Orange spice with cinnamon." Ashley handed the paper cup to Bryan. "Thanks again for the food. I was shriveling away into nothing."

"My girl's gotta eat." Bryan took a sip of the tea.

I had trouble not getting caught up on the pet names they exchanged. I also fixated on how Ashley introduced him as her best friend and not a more intimate title. Not that it mattered. I tried not to stare, but I couldn't help it. Bryan's slender fingers wrapped around the cup, the veins on the back of his hands, the freckles on his arms. His white t-shirt with a list of five black names on them.

I motioned toward his shirt and asked. "Tides of Time?"

Bryan raised his eyebrows. "What?"

"Your shirt. Tides of Time, right?"

"Yeah, it's one of my favorites. The book, not the movie."

"Obviously the book. Sir Anthony's name is on it."

Bryan's eyes lit up.

"I refused to watch the movie after I heard they cut Anthony out, but Tristen is one of my favorite characters of all time. My fictional husband, if you will."

"You aren't missing anything, the movie sucked. They had one of the villagers lead the siege on the castle." Bryan replied, taking a sip of his tea.

"A villager?" I asked, shocked. "But Anthony was the one who led the attack because Prince Gregory killed his brother."

"If you think that's bad, I won't tell you how they changed Emala's origin story. Oh shit. I'm going to be late for work." Bryan glanced up at the clock and then back at me. A smile broke out across his lips. "I, uh...I'll see you soon, I hope."

"Me too." I smiled as he turned and headed to the door. "Bryan!" I called after him and held his tea in the air. "Did you not want this?"

"Oh, uh, thank you." He came back and took it from my hand. His cheeks pink from embarrassment. "Bye, Ash."

"Bye, babe," she said behind me.

I smiled as he left, his heart pounding through my chest.

After I took the next customer's order, Ashley leaped next to me so quickly, she knocked a stack of plastic cups off the counter. "Are you single?"

I blinked. "Yes."

"And you like men?"

"Mostly."

"Good."

"Feel free to elaborate at any time."

Ashley laughed. "I've known Bryan McClintock since high school. I all but fell in love with him sophomore year when he got drunk at a party and performed 'Misery Business' on my parent's dining room table."

"So, you two aren't a thing?" I couldn't help but ask.

"Oh, god no." Ashley shook her head.

"Why not?"

"He's not a woman. Anyway, he's one of my best friends. Great guy, very smart. He likes you."

"I don't think so." I looked back to the glass door though he was long gone.

"You think he gets to nerd out over books with hot girls every day? I'm surprised he didn't pass out." Ashley shook her head and left to retrieve a gallon of milk from the storage room. Halfway there, she rushed back to the counter. "Oh, oh! What are you doing this Saturday night?"

"Working," I answered, grabbing a damp cloth to wipe down the counter.

"I'm talking about after work. My friend, Emma, is having a bonfire. You should come with me."

"Yeah, that sounds great. Can my sister come with us?"

Rayn would never let me go to a bonfire without her and I wouldn't want to. Besides, I figured it would be a good way to get our minds off of everything we had going on. Maybe meet a few new people in town that didn't have a magic gem or secret powers.

"Yeah, that's fine. The more the merrier. Bryan will be there too, by the way." Ashley teased, bumping me with her hip. Now her plan made sense.

"I'm not interested in meeting anyone. I have way too much going on right now to entertain getting involved with someone. Romantically, I mean."

Ashley chortled. "I'm not setting up an arranged marriage, Whitney. You seem like a nice girl. I'm asking you to come meet my friends. You just moved here, I'm welcoming you into town."

"Well, thank you. That's really nice of you." I smiled.

"He is cute though, right? For a guy, I mean."

My face heated. "Yes, Ashley, he is."

"I thought so. Besides, you know about Bryan's nerdy books that none of us can keep up with. We need you around. I'm sure he'll be excited to see you. Probably a bit nauseous, but excited."

"He didn't seem nervous earlier," I replied, playing with a loose string on the damp, white cloth.

Ashley smirked. "Well, come with me this weekend and find out."

Since I worked an earlier shift that day, I was able to drop Rayn and Dmitri off at school on my way in and pick them up afterward. On our way to pick up Dmitri, I filled Rayn in on the bonfire. She was more eager than I had anticipated, bouncing in her seat as she asked a million questions. Who all would be there? How big was the fire going to be? How mad would I be if she played with it?

As Rayn and I pulled into the Rifton High School parking lot, there wasn't a soul in sight. I parked at the far end of the lot and dug around in my bag for my cell phone when I finally spotted Dmitri sitting on a bench next to the main building. He wasn't sitting alone.

Dmitri and Abe Roberts were having a pleasant conversation, or I assumed it was since they were both laughing. They sat close to one another with their knees touching and their backpacks on the ground.

"Oh, hell no." Rayn fumed in her seat.

I honked the horn twice to get Dmitri's attention. When he saw us, he jumped up and grabbed his bag quickly.

"Sorry, I didn't see you at first," Dmitri said when he reached us, climbing behind Rayn into the back seat.

"Well, you were a bit busy to notice, yeah? A bit too friendly?" I asked.

"You have to be friendly to get info, Whit. The more I talk with him, the more he'll trust me. Let me do what I can to get something out of Abe and you guys take care of this jewelry thing." Dmitri defended with a stern tone.

"Mit, I'm serious. I trust you but you are not allowed to get involved with this guy." I repeated. "He's a psycho. I told you about that dream I had."

"I'm not *allowed*?" Dmitri looked at me incredulously. "All because of some dream you had?"

"No, you're not allowed," I said, sterner than before.

"Why were you talking to that Abe Roberts creep again, anyway?" Rayn demanded. "Having lunch with him wasn't enough?"

"I'm handling it," I explained to Rayn but she wasn't listening.

Rayn turned to face Mit in the backseat with fire in her eyes. "Stay away from him. We don't need you to get info from him. We need to have him incarcerated."

"What are you talking about?" Dmitri demanded. His furled eyebrows and clenched jaw didn't hide his aggression.

Rayn's big eyes filled with worry. "I'm serious. I caught him trying to look through our windows from his yard. He's like a fucking horror movie. He didn't move or anything, just stood there like a shadow. Dmitri, you have to stay away from him. We have to move into a different house."

"We can't afford to move into a different house, Ray. We have to show Abe that we aren't to be messed with," I answered.

Rayn's lips broke into a mischievous smile, "So, I set his house on fire?"

"Don't you dare. Janice is a saint." I snapped.

"Leave Abe alone!" Dmitri shouted, causing me to jump. I wasn't used to Mit raising his voice at us. "He isn't what you think he is!"

"Then why the fuck was he watching me change through the bathroom window?" Rayn yelled, her face turning red.

I intervened, "Okay, you two need to calm down right now."

"I can't believe you are choosing this creep over us, Dmitri. We're family and you barely know that guy." Rayn turned her back against the seat hard and crossed her arms.

"I am not choosing anyone over you. I'm simply explaining that you are being judgmental and jumping to conclusions," Dmitri barked. "Our biology teacher showed photos of a dissected frog in class and Abe couldn't look at them. A girl in front of him in the lunch line didn't have enough cash so Abe paid for her food. He's a nice guy."

"Will you two shut the hell up?" It was my turn to fill the small car with my booming voice. "Dmitri, there is something seriously wrong with Abe Roberts, whether you are willing to see it or not. Rayn, the only reason Mit is talking to Abe is to get info for us. The three of us? We are all we have. We are a team, a family. The last thing we need is to take our aggression out on each other, got it?"

"I don't want Mit getting info on Abe Roberts. I don't want anything to do with the freak." Rayn turned to Dmitri again. "Have higher standards."

"That's hilarious coming from you." Dmitri grabbed the back of Rayn's seat and poked his head into the front of the car. "I don't believe he would do anything to hurt either of you."

"Then agree to disagree." I attempted once more to put out the flames of their argument. "Mit, you keep trying to figure out what Abe's symbol is and that is all. Rayn, we need to figure out how to get Lauren, Brooke, and Rose to all show up for a meeting."

"No. I want a break. All I want to think about is the bonfire this weekend and forget about the girl from the coffee shop, that freaky ghost girl, and that liar Rose." Rayn crossed her arms, so I let it go. Nothing I said was going to get through to her when she was in a sour mood anyway.

"Have fun with all that," Dmitri muttered.

I looked into the rearview mirror. "You don't want to come with us?"

"No, I think I'll hang out with Abe Roberts instead."

"You're an idiot," Rayn snapped.

Silence. Thank god they had worn each other out. I was exhausted listening to them. The obstacles in our path were beginning to pile up.

"By the way, the bathroom sink is leaking." Dmitri's voice replied from behind me.

"Are you fucking kidding me?" I groaned.

"I'm going to talk to Janice about it at work tonight."

"No, don't bother her." The last thing I wanted to do was bug Janice after all she had already done for us. Going the opposite direction of our house, I headed toward the local hardware store and turned to Rayn. "Look up a video online to see what we need to fix the sink."

From the moment we walked into TJ's Hardware, I was beyond confused. If we didn't have the video Rayn found, I'd be completely lost. The chill of the air conditioner spiked my senses, uplifting my mood instantly.

"It's like being in a damn freezer." Rayn shivered and wrapped her arms around herself.

She was at her best during the heat of the summer. Her skin glowed and her hair was thick, full of body. I, on the other hand, felt like a wilted flower in the heat waves. This cold concrete building was an environment I thrived in.

"Can I go look at the discounted paints?" Dmitri asked, side-eyeing Rayn, asking to be away from her without wanting to say the words out loud.

"Yeah, get whatever you want. Keep it under fifteen," I told him.

What are we going to do? Rayn asked as we walked past the paint department.

About?

Every damn thing. Rayn shoved her hands in her jean pockets. *Rose knows who this Lauren girl is but she's still keeping things from us. On top of it all our brother is buddying up with Satan.*

What are we supposed to do, Ray? We'll try and find her on our own. Rifton is a small town.

Rayn and I turned down one of the aisles labeled 'pipes and fittings'. I had no idea what anything was for; copper, plastic, and confusing.

Rayn froze in place, staring down the aisle. "Is that her?"

I looked up to see the tall blonde we had been talking about wearing a red employee vest, organizing boxes of pipe fittings. She lifted her head and turned pale when she saw me; her eyes wide like she was about to be sick. Lauren was written on her name tag.

"Are you stalking me?" Lauren asked in a hushed voice, walking up to us. "I'm at work, you have to leave."

"Maybe if you hadn't run out of the Corner Cup when Whitney tried to talk to you, we wouldn't have to stalk you," Rayn answered, keeping her voice low and looking around to make sure there wasn't anyone else around. The aisle was empty.

Jesus, this girl is a model. My sister remarked mentally.

Lauren truly was stunning. Her skin was immaculate and her almond-shaped brown eyes were nicely done with soft-toned make-up.

Lauren took a step back as if we might attack her.

"What do you want from me?" she asked, crossing her arms over her pulsing heart. She was as uneasy as we were. "Who are you?"

"My name is Whitney, and this is my sister, Rayn. We want to talk to you about your bracelet," I said in a calm voice, keeping my hands visible at my sides.

"What bracelet?" Lauren replied monotone and uninterested.

I looked down at her wrists. She was wearing a silver watch, but no gold bracelet. No citrine in sight. My stomach did a flip.

"The one you were wearing at the Corner Cup. You know exactly which one I'm talking about." I met Lauren's attitude with intense eye contact. I wasn't backing down. We weren't walking away from Lauren without some kind of information today.

"I don't know what you're talking about." Lauren shrugged.

"You're joking, right?" Rayn responded. "We already talked to Rose."

Whatever blood was left in Lauren's face drained.

"The ink in my gem went white around you." I replied. "I felt your powers."

"Well, this worked the last time." Rayn lifted her hand and I knew what she was going to do next. She snapped her fingers and lit a small flame in the palm of her hand in freaking public again.

Rayn. I reached out and slapped her hand.

"Stop that!" Lauren hissed with panic.

A tingle erupted in my arms and my stomach rushed like I was falling, only to find myself safely on the ground. A small gust of wind hit Rayn, blowing out her flame and our hair back.

"Stay away from me before I call security," Lauren said, backing away from us.

"You control the wind." I couldn't believe I hadn't made the connection before.

"Air. Fire. Water. Earth." I whispered. "Lauren, you can't tell me there's nothing for us to talk about."

"Water and fire?" Lauren asked, looking at Rayn and then me. After seeing Rayn light her flame, she knew I was water. Lauren turned on her heel and walked off as swiftly as she could. "You're insane."

"Are you kidding me, right now? Look, I don't know what you think we're trying to do, but we only want to find out more about ourselves!" Rayn turned to me, devastated. "Is she seriously not going to turn around?"

I went after Lauren, doing my best to look inconspicuous though my knees were shivering from an adrenaline rush.

"The shadows are back," I warned in a hushed tone.

Lauren froze in place, still as a statue carved from flawless marble.

"Please. Meet us Wednesday night at the Eagle Loop trailhead at nine pm. We can't do this alone, Lauren. We don't want to cause any trouble."

"If you don't want trouble, then leave me the fuck alone." Lauren hissed over her shoulder.

Lauren didn't turn around or slow her pace as she disappeared quickly down another aisle marching into the safety of a group of customers. We knew better than to follow her, it would have only caused a bigger problem. Instead, we watched her go.

We had come so close and were going home empty-handed regardless. Getting any information out of Lauren was going to be like pulling teeth. We were strangers, how can we expect her to trust us right away? Powers aside, Lauren didn't feel like someone who easily opened up and shared pieces of herself with others. This was going to take time. Even Rose took a moment before she came around. Brooke was the only one so far willing to jump off the cliff with us.

"That...that could have been worse. How could she deny having powers right after she used them in front of us?" I put my hand over my sprinting heart and looked at my sister. "She wanted us to know, or else she wouldn't have used her powers. I think she's scared. Maybe she'll show up at the meeting."

"About that. What meeting were you referring to?" Rayn asked. "Do Rose and Brooke know?"

"I'll text Brooke when we get home. Lauren will be there."

"Yeah, I doubt it. I think she's a coward." Rayn ran her fingers through her hair.

"Go find Dmitri," I told her, catching another employee out of the corner of my eye. "Let's get this stupid sink part so we can go home."

CHAPTER SEVEN

FIGURE IN THE SHADOWS

"Do you want a drink?" Ashley reached into an ice chest and handed Rayn and I each a light brown bottle of beer. I took the bottle from her and twisted off the cap.

The bonfire was much bigger than I had imagined. A large group of people stood around the flames while others sat off to the side in smaller groups, talking or playing drinking games. Music played from speakers hanging off the back deck of the three-story colonial-style home. People danced by the fire with drinks in their hands.

It had been a while since I was at a party like this, with the crowd and loud music. Everyone was talking loudly and laughing, a few guests who had too many spilling their drinks into the dirt. Some idiot decided adding more firewood to the already blazing flames was a good idea. I made sure there wasn't any greenery that could get caught in the crossfire of careless actions.

"He's here!" Rayn squealed and clapped her hands together. "How do I look?"

"Who?" I asked, looking around.

"Tom, of course!"

Tom Campbell emerged from the crowd and beelined for Rayn, his face broke out into a giant smile. I didn't expect him to be here but I also wasn't surprised that Rayn had invited him.

"Hey there, beautiful." Tom pulled Rayn into a hug and closed his eyes like he was smelling her hair.

"You remember my sister." Rayn gestured to me once they broke apart.

He nodded. "Whitney, good to see you again."

"You too." At least Ashley was here and I wouldn't have to spend the evening as their third wheel.

"About time you showed up." A girl shorter than Ashley bounced over to us and slid her arm around Ashley's waist. "I haven't seen you in years."

"It's been like twelve hours." Ashley laughed. "But I missed you too, babe. Hey, this is my new friend, Whitney, and her sister, Rayn. Whitney just started at the CC. This is Emma Drake, our host."

Emma's wavy, light brown hair fell above her shoulders, framing her face nicely. She looked me up and down with her dark brown eyes as the edges of her mouth curled up ever so slightly. "Nice to meet you. This is my boyfriend, Troy," Emma replied.

Troy stood as the tallest in the circle. A backward, navy baseball hat hid his hair and echoed against his blue eyes. He had a crooked smile as he wrapped his arm around Emma's shoulders.

Looking between Emma's heart-shaped face and Ashley's freckles, I couldn't help but feel subpar. Shaking my head, I did my best to stop the feelings of inadequacy before they settled in, but it was hard not to notice. I was definitely used to it being Rayn's sister, with her long legs and beautiful, natural curls. As similar as Rayn and I were in personality, we were polar opposite in appearance.

Troy smiled. "So you're Whitney. Nice to put a face to the name. Hope Ash hasn't been driving you too crazy."

"Hey, I am a damn delight." Ashley smacked his arm.

I laughed. "She's great."

"Where's Byn?" Ashley asked nonchalantly, looking at the faces around us.

"I was hoping you'd know. I've been looking for him too." Emma searched the crowd.

I scanned all the unfamiliar faces myself. There were so many people here that I didn't know. Another reminder that there were still so many things about Rifton I was a stranger to. It was like I had shrunk five sizes smaller and everyone else towered over me. Then a sudden rush of messy excitement that wasn't my own took over my body. There was no way I was that tipsy after half a beer.

"There he is." Troy waved his arm in the air. "Byn! You're a wanted man."

"I'm not getting back on the roof." A familiar deep voice came up behind us.

Emma rolled her eyes. "You're such a baby."

"I almost fell off."

"You'd have better balance if you'd let me align your chakras, Bynie."

"I'd have better balance if you would have put your phone down and held the damn ladder."

"Minor details." Emma waved her hand, dismissing him.

Bryan laughed and took another drink from his beer as he finally noticed I was standing next to Ashley. This empathetic connection I felt was clearly one sided. "Hi, Whitney."

"Hey!" My joy bubbled within me as I acted surprised to see him.

"I wasn't expecting you to be here."

"Ashley all but dragged me." I looked over at her and her friends, who watched us like hawks.

Ashley winked at him. "You can pay me back in free pasta."

"All the stuffed shells your heart desires," Bryan replied.

Bryan's eyes sparkled in the light of the flames and a smile curved the edges of his lips. I couldn't help but linger on his mouth as he took another drink. His clean-shaven face made him look younger than the last time I'd seen him. He caught me watching him and cleared his throat, shifting his weight between his feet. I snapped myself out of it.

"Hi," Rayn said loudly, looking between Bryan and I. Her arms crossed as she impatiently tapped her foot against the dirt.

"Sorry. This is my sister, Rayn." I gestured between them. "I met Bryan at the Corner Cup a few days ago."

"Nice to meet you." Rayn smirked and held out her hand to him. "This is my friend, Tom."

"Likewise." He took Rayn's hand in his and nodded at Tom.

I watched Bryan's face carefully as he locked eyes with my sister and politely smiled. I waited for him to look her up and down like the other guys did. I waited for his eyes to linger on her slender build and tight jeans, but the moment he let go of Rayn's hand, his gaze came back to me. His heart skipped a beat in his chest the moment I smiled at him. I went to say something but the music stopped me in my tracks.

The next song that came over the loud speakers triggered a million memories all at once. Rayn and I looked at each other, both of our eyes misting at the opening beat our Mom would play on repeat when she'd clean the house or whenever we'd have a long drive in the car somewhere. My mother's favorite song.

"Fleetwood Mac? Seriously?" Emma threw her hands on her hips. "Who the hell's phone is connected to the speaker? Byn, this is yours isn't it?"

Bryan's only response was to loudly sing the chorus once it started. Troy joined in with him and the two of them swayed to the beat. The louder they sang, the harder Emma rolled her eyes.

"After this, I'm disconnecting you so enjoy," Emma informed him.

"I swear you're the only person I know who doesn't enjoy a little Fleetwood from time to time." Troy put his arm around Emma's shoulders and gave her a quick peck on the top of her head.

"Hey, I love them, but this is a party. Put on your basic bitch playlist if you want your phone to stay connected." Emma frowned at Bryan, who pulled his phone out of his back pocket.

Bryan had no idea what he had done but I took it as a sign from the universe that I was where I was meant to be. It was as if my mother herself reached out from the afterlife and told me it was okay to take a moment for myself. It was okay to be happy and have a life after she was gone. This is what she would have wanted for Rayn and I, to be at a bonfire with cute boys and a cold drink.

"One of the pong tables opened up. Claim it quickly before Chad and his douchebags see it," Ashley announced. "Rayn, how good are you at pong?"

"I've had practice. Tom and I will be on a team." My sister beamed.

"Three on three? Troy can ref." Bryan followed closely behind Ashley as she jogged toward the table before someone else claimed it.

"What I'm not allowed to play?" Troy scoffed, offended.

"Baby, you can play, but you're on the other team. You can't aim worth a shit." Emma chuckled, falling in step next to me as we all migrated behind Ashley and Bryan. "Do you want to play?"

"Sure," I answered. "I have to drive home so I'm not drinking more than this but it sounds like my aim is better than his." I pointed the beer bottle in my hands toward Troy.

Troy plopped down in an empty chair next to the table. "Everyone's a critic."

"Okay, three on three," Ashley announced, setting up the cups and filling them with water. "Rayn and her man with Emma. Whit and Byn with me."

"You don't drink from the cups?" Tom asked, watching Ashley curiously.

Ashley's head shot up at him, playfully offended. "Do we look like a bunch of barbarians? We are adults here. Everyone touches that ball and it falls on the ground."

Tom laughed. "Sophisticated beer pong, I appreciate that. Here, Ray, you go first."

He picked up the ping pong ball and handed it to my sister, their fingers lingering as she took the ball from him.

"So if you make it, you get to pick who drinks," Ashley informed Rayn of the rules as she aimed her shot.

"Get ready, Whit." Rayn released her shot with ease, showing off. A ripple of magic flowed through the air as the ball went into the cup in front of me without touching the rim.

You fucking cheater. I laughed in my head, taking a drink without saying a word aloud.

Okay, clean game, then, Rayn replied silently. That may have been how she and I would have played back in Hemston, but not here. Not after what we had learned about Rifton recently.

"Can I get you something else?" Bryan asked, making note of the face I attempted to hide when I took a drink from the beer.

Ashley took extra time lining up her shot while Bryan and I chatted.

"Oh, no, thanks. I'm fine." I looked down at the bottle. "I'm not much into drinking these days."

"You and Rayn didn't go to any parties where you used to live?" Bryan smiled.

"Uh, we did. I left the person I was back there, you know?"

"I get it. Everyone needs a fresh start at some point. Honestly, I only came tonight because Troy and I rarely get nights off together."

"Your bedrooms share a wall," Emma remarked.

"It's not enough." Bryan put his arm around Troy.

Ashley laughed. "These two say they're like brothers, but I swear they're in love."

"We'd be able to convince people we were actually brothers if Bryan wasn't so short." Troy laughed.

"I'm a respectable five-ten. You are just freakishly tall." Bryan smacked Troy on the arm.

Ashley had already taken her turn and now Tom held the little white ball in his hand, aiming for a cup in the middle but it bounced off the rim and rolled off in the dirt.

"Damn," Tom muttered, chasing down the ping pong ball as it went under a log. He returned with the ball and tossed it across the table to Bryan.

"No one believes Rayn and I are sisters," I replied with a smile. "We were adopted, though."

Rayn sarcastically added in from across the table, "I know that's hard to tell because we look so much alike."

"I read online that Christmas lights and flowers are both beautiful though they look nothing alike, just like you two." Tom smiled at Rayn. She lit up like an early morning sunrise.

Bryan quickly tossed the ball across the table, not bothering to see if he made it into a cup before he turned to face me. "How old were you when you were adopted?"

"Almost eleven," I answered.

"Wow, that must have been a journey."

"Something like that."

"Life is so crazy, how it brings people together," Emma replied, aiming a ping pong ball before she tossed it straight into a cup on our side. "I don't know what I'd do without these guys. Drink up, abandoner."

Bryan took a drink from his beer and rolled the ball across the table, "I did not abandon you. I'll be back in the apartment in January."

"I don't like living alone." Emma took another turn but missed.

"Do you all live together?" Rayn asked.

"Usually I stay with Emma in Falcon Bay during the week, but this semester I'm here in town. I was able to get online classes so I can work more during the holidays. Troy and I live with his dad by the river."

"Where's Falcon Bay?"

"It's on the coast, about an hour and a half away," Tom answered. "The University there is massive. I remember in middle school we did a tour of the campus. Kind of hard to get into, isn't it?"

Emma shrugged. "It can be."

"Not if you're super smart like Byn or super rich like Em," Ashley teased them. "They left Troy and I behind like commoners."

Emma stuck out her hip. "They have coffee shops in the bay. The four of us could have all moved out there together."

"Emma has a two-bedroom apartment out there so we don't have to drive back and forth for classes. She only charges me utilities so it's dirt cheap," Bryan explained.

I wondered how Troy felt about his girlfriend and best friend sharing an apartment during the week. His silence during the conversation was louder than words, but I couldn't tell if it was from missing his girlfriend or something deeper. It was clear that Bryan and his friends didn't exactly agree on their current arrangement. I wouldn't be happy if Rayn or Dmitri lived so far away. I knew the three of us wouldn't be under the same roof forever. Eventually, we'd grow and have our own lives. But in the meantime, having them close kept me sane.

"So you're a, what, sophomore?" I asked Bryan, guessing if we were the same age or not.

"Senior. This is my last year," he answered.

"Oh," I responded, surprised. It was like Bryan and I were a lifetime apart. He was close to graduation and moving into the real world while I was barely hanging on, putting on a mask to pretend like I was capable of being the parent of my house.

"I'm twenty-three," Bryan answered my real question. "And you're not far behind?"

"Twenty-one. So, I've been meaning to ask," I changed the subject. "Byn?"

"Oh, it's a nickname from when I was a kid. My friends picked it up and haven't let it go."

"Bynie is only called Bryan when he's in trouble." Emma took a drink from the cocktail in her hand as I landed the ball into their last cup.

Bryan gave a mischievous smile that made me want to find out what kind of trouble he and I could get into together.

"You're adorable," I whispered, gazing into those perfect lily pads.

"Hmm?" he asked.

Oh god.

"It's adorable, the nickname," I replied awkwardly, looking down at the ground to kick some dirt with the toe of my shoe.

When I glanced back up at him, his eyes had wandered down to my hips. His gaze lingered on my curves and thick thighs before he realized I was watching him. His heart pounded behind his rib cage as our eyes met. Bryan smiled softly, his gaze burning into me.

Whatever this magnetic attraction I felt for him was, it was mutual. It's not like I'd never had a man's interest. Male attention was not difficult to find. Quality male attention that I could empathically feel in my soul and didn't check out my sister? That was new.

"Come on, I'll get you something else to drink. Not everything we have here is alcoholic." Bryan nodded past the massive bonfire to where several ice chests sat in the dirt. Now that the game was finished, I was happy to have a moment alone with him.

"I bet you're an air moon." I revealed a thought I intended to keep to myself as Bryan and I walked away from the table.

"A what?" He chuckled.

"Oh, um...you know, astrology? Like your birth chart? Each zodiac is associated with an element."

"Oh, yeah. Emma is into that. I don't know what a rising sign is but I know I'm a Pisces," he answered.

"Of course you are," My heart swelled in my chest. A water sign. "You'll have to let me do your chart."

"How?"

"Oh, I just need your birth date, time, and location."

He laughed. "Need my social and mother's maiden name too?"

"I mean, if you're willing," I joked.

"I could be swayed by a beautiful face."

Electricity shot through my body. I restrained myself from reaching out to him. I had an undeniable attraction to Bryan, but I had to remind myself that this was the extent of what could be. As much as I could daydream of what his hands would feel like, I knew it was nothing more than a fantasy. I had decided long ago that hidden magic and romance didn't mix.

Bryan's eyes were still on me, not paying attention to what was in front of him when a girl came out of nowhere and ran right into his chest.

The girl looked like Emma, only meaner. Her hair was dark brown and her eyes were even darker. She smiled when she saw Bryan and gazed up into his eyes. I wished Rayn's mind wasn't the only one I could get into because there was a territorial look in her eyes that I didn't like at all, not when she looked at him.

"She was looking for you," the girl said monotone.

"Who?"

"*Her.*"

"Em?" Bryan asked, raising his eyebrows at her. "I was just with her."

"You disappeared earlier, and apparently she's not getting enough male attention." She looked down at her nails, bored. "She needed her other boyfriend."

"Go away, Serenity."

"I live here, unlike the rest of these cretins." Serenity looked around the bonfire.

"Then crawl back into your hole upstairs," Bryan replied, taking my hand. He cupped his palm in mine and wrapped his warm fingers around my skin.

I had to look down and check the dirt to make sure my heart hadn't fallen out of my chest and splattered blood all over my shoes. My skin must have felt freezing against his, but he didn't loosen his grip. Bryan led me past the girl quickly, nearly hitting her with his shoulder as we crossed her path.

I glanced down at her arm, still raised as she picked at her fingernails. The end of her sleeve revealed half of a familiar circle and diamond scar. The same scar on Abe's wrist. Whatever this symbol was, it wasn't just Abe. This was bigger than him and the sick rituals he performed.

I quickly looked away from Serenity's arm, pretending I was oblivious. She and I looked into each other's eyes for only a moment. Her icy glare gave me chills that shot every hair on my body into the air, but I turned my head and kept walking. An odd compulsion to turn around and look at her again came over me, like something was pulling at my heart to go back.

I wanted to ask about the symbol, but I knew better. Whatever the symbol was, it wasn't anything Bryan needed to know about and I wanted to keep him far away from all of it. My magic would stay separate, it was the only way I could ensure everyone's safety.

Once Bryan and I were a few feet away from the girl with the ice glare, he let go of my hand.

"That was Serenity, Emma's sister," Bryan said, noticing my silence.

"Does that make you Emma's other boyfriend?" I asked, trying to understand the dynamics between his group of friends.

"Serenity's being an ass. Emma is my friend. We're more platonic than Ashley and I, and Ash is a lesbian so that's saying a lot. Besides, Emma and Troy have been together for years." Bryan explained. "They're practically married already."

It's not that I was jealous. Whatever Serenity was being, she gave me a nauseous feeling in my stomach.

Whitney, I need you. Rayn's voice echoed inside my skull, taking my attention completely off of Bryan, something no one had been able to do so far. I jumped back with a startle.

"Are you cold?" Bryan asked, assuming I had gotten a chill.

"Yeah, a little bit," I lied and took another step away from him.

"Want my sweatshirt?" He reached for the zipper.

"No, that's okay," I answered, looking around the crowd for my sister.

It was the tone in Rayn's voice that scared me. She sounded small; like she was afraid and trying to mask it with another emotion but fear was all I heard. I had only been away from her for five minutes, what could she have possibly gotten herself into?

What's wrong? I replied. I did my best to hide my inner panic.

Come back, she answered urgently. *Please, I need you.*

"It's getting late. Ray and I should probably get going." I glanced over at Bryan as his shoulders fell slightly.

Bryan did his best to hide his disappointment on the exterior but I could feel it. I was also let down that our time together was cut short but I had to see what was wrong with Rayn.

"Oh, okay. No worries," he replied.

Where are you? I mentally sent out into the air, hoping Rayn was still close enough to hear me.

"I had fun," Bryan said, rubbing the back of his neck. "You're easy to talk to."

I'm over here, by the house in front of the deck. Hurry up. Rayn said inside of my head. I looked around again but I didn't see her anywhere.

Be right there.

"You look like you're having a conversation with someone in your head," Bryan replied with a chuckle, attempting a joke.

I turned around and looked up into his eyes, trying not to give him the 'how did you know' look. I panicked at first, but after a second I laughed. "That would be ridiculous. I, uh, I need to hunt down my sister. I left my little brother at home and I don't like leaving him alone this late."

"Alright," he replied with a warm smile. "Um, I'll see you around?"

"I hope so." I returned his smile and took off toward the deck of the large three-story house.

"Whitney! Wait!" Bryan called, jogging after me. "Hang on a second."

"Yeah?" I turned around to face him.

"Can I," Bryan took in a deep breath of courage and looked me deeply in the eyes. "Could I ask for your number?"

"Only if you give me yours." I blushed.

"Deal." His warm fingers brushed against mine as we exchanged phones.

The moment Bryan's number was saved in my contact list, I gave him a parting smile and quickly made my way over to the deck attached to the house.

Once I found Rayn, I grabbed her arm and whispered, "What the hell is wrong? Do you know that Bryan asked me if I was talking to someone telepathically?"

"Did he really? Watch out, Whit. You might have to tell him about it sooner than you think," Rayn replied, scanning the trees nervously.

"I'm never telling him what we are," I snapped. "Ever."

"Okay, okay. Sorry." She lifted her hands in defense. "But I mean, he's going to find out eventually if you two keep this up. Which I'm assuming you will. You see the way he looks at you?"

I pretended I didn't hear her.

"What was your big emergency? Are you okay?" I asked, changing the subject. She was responsive and I didn't see any bleeding. Nothing appeared to be broken. "Where's Tom?"

"I told him I had to go home. Can we leave?" Rayn was still scared. Whatever she wanted to tell me, she had no idea what we were going to do about it. I hoped this was something I'd be able to handle.

My sister led me toward the street where we had parked. Rayn didn't look at my eyes or at me at all. Her attention was up in the trees, looking around for something. She looked like something might jump out at her at any moment.

Can you please tell me what happened? I asked.

I saw something while you were with Bryan. Something in the shadows.

Here? My hands shook with nerves and anticipation.

Rayn nodded as we got to the car, quickly checking over her shoulder before she got into the passenger's seat. We drove around for a while through the maze of neighborhood houses until I finally found the giant entrance of the gated community.

"It reminded me of the shadows we used to see as kids, but this was different, more lifelike. It felt different, too, but it was there, in a tree in the backyard up on one of the branches. I couldn't make out what it was, but it was something that didn't belong there. It was watching us. It was watching *me.*" Rayn swallowed hard, holding onto her seat belt with white knuckles. "Whitney?"

"I don't know what to say," I answered honestly. "I didn't want to believe Rose but after what I saw at the mini-mart...I don't know."

"It scared me. My blood ran cold the moment I saw it and the only thing that stopped me from screaming was being frozen with fear. I didn't want to say anything at first because you were with Bryan, but I couldn't wait. I didn't want to ruin that for you but this is kind of important." Rayn's voice shook.

"I know. It's going to be okay." I reached out and gripped my sister's arm gently, rubbing her sweatshirt with my thumb. "We'll figure this out."

My phone vibrated in the cupholder between the front seats so softly I almost didn't hear it.

"Is that Mit?" I asked, motioning toward my phone for Rayn to check the message.

Rayn picked up my phone and unlocked the screen with a sheepish grin, "Not Mit."

"Okay," I replied, dragging out the syllables. "What does it say, then?"

"March 8. Flagstaff, Arizona. Around 3 am, I think." Rayn side-eyed me, her smile growing larger. "Since I showed you mine, are you going to show me yours?"

"Shut up. It doesn't say that." I grabbed my phone out of her hands.

"Oh, Whit," Rayn chucked. "He's got it bad. Gave you his birth time on the first date."

I ignored her and turned my head, trying to hide the heat that had spread across my face. As I pulled up to a stop sign, I found myself getting lost in the night sky. The moon and stars outside were bright against the trees of the forest but there was still so much darkness, so much that I couldn't see.

Chapter Eight

CIRCLE OF TRUST

Darkness. If it weren't for our flashlights, there would be nothing but darkness. Now I truly understood the name of the Dark Star Forest. Rayn and I stood with Rose and Brooke awkwardly at the entrance of Eagle Loop Trail, as none of us knew what to say to one another. I had a million questions to ask, but couldn't think of the words. We spoke about the chilly weather and debated if our final guest would arrive. Rose insisted it was wishful thinking but I knew in my heart Lauren was as curious as the rest of us underneath all that fear. Especially after I told her about the shadow's return.

Fifteen minutes later, Lauren's car came to a stop.

"Huh," Rose said quietly and turned to me. "I underestimated you, Whitney."

"Glad you made it," I gave Lauren a genuine smile as she dragged her feet through the dirt and approached us hesitantly. "Lauren, you know my sister, Rayn. This is Brooke Evans. And-"

"Rose." Lauren chuckled, popping out her hip with attitude. "I thought you and I had an agreement."

"I didn't say anything about you to them," Rose replied, crossing her arms.

"I want nothing to do with her. She's evil." Lauren pointed a finger at Rose, taking a deep breath that sent the leaves around her flying.

"We're the same evil, then," Rose said with a subtle smile. "And don't point your finger at me, sweetheart, you might accidentally use your powers."

"You and I are not the same," Lauren whispered, backing away from us.

This is not how I had envisioned our first interaction. This wasn't Rose and Lauren's first real interaction though, and clearly, something had gone terribly wrong.

"So, you two already know one another," Rayn replied, looking for an explanation from one of them.

"It's a small town." Brooke shrugged. "Everyone kind of knows everyone."

Lauren clenched her jaw. "I only showed up tonight because Whitney here said you already told her about me."

"I never said that," I defended myself. "I said we had already spoken to Rose. I didn't specify what we talked about."

Lauren hesitated again. "And the shadows?"

"That's on the agenda too," Rayn said.

"Well, here we are. Witches Anonymous." Rose held out her arms.

"So, you two never told us how you know each other." I reminded Rose and Lauren.

"Lauren and I went to school together. She's only a year older," Rose explained, unenthusiastically. "We found out about each other's magic early on and agreed to coexist. We would stay away from each other and promised never to tell anyone else about our magic."

"Obviously she broke her end of the deal." Lauren bit her bottom lip and looked over at me.

"No," Rose spoke up again in her defense. "These two found you on their own like they found me."

"In class, you looked at me like you knew," Rayn said to Rose. "That's what tripped me up the most, you spoke like you knew what I was."

"Of course I did. I'm not stupid." Rose replied, kicking a clump of dirt.

Brooke jumped in. "The shadows hadn't returned yet and we had reason to keep a low profile. Rifton may seem like a cute little town but it has its demons."

"And who do you think you are?" Lauren asked with crossed arms.

"I'm Brooke Evans and Rose is my best friend."

"I don't get how you knew about each other the whole time, but stayed away." Rayn looked back and forth between Rose and Lauren as she spoke. "You never once wanted to help each other or know more about your powers? You chose to be alone."

Rose took a deep breath as she ran her fingers through her hair. "Brooke and I stick together just fine, thank you. We didn't need Lauren to try and look into where the jewelry came from, but we only found deadends. We decided it was best not to broadcast our powers to be on the safe side, but with the shadows coming back...I don't know if it made a difference."

I tried to understand how Rose and Lauren could ignore each other. Rayn and I had always thought about the rewards of finding out the truth about us while Lauren and Rose were worried about the consequences. I never looked at the unknown and feared it, I was intrigued.

"We're not like you and your sister, Whitney. I don't like her." Lauren announced, shooting an icy glance in Rose's direction.

"No one really cares how you feel. The world doesn't revolve around you," Rose told Lauren. "I think you're a bitch but I'm still here."

At least all five of us are finally together, Rayn replied to me. *One big, happy family.*

"Okay, okay. I get it, you hate each other. Let's try and put our differences aside for tonight, at least, and focus on what we came for. We are here to put all our knowledge together. Our powers are all linked together like the jewelry. We each represent an element." I did my best to ease the tension floating in the air.

Rose chuckled as she shook her head and looked around at the trees. "Lauren controls the air, I remember her six minute mile run."

"My athleticism has nothing to do with it," Lauren justified.

Rose scoffed. "Oh, please, like anyone is naturally that talented. I've seen you angry. You're a fucking tempest. We're Elementals. That much makes sense."

"I can't do any of that." Brooke looked down at her shoes.

"What do you mean?" Lauren asked, looking at her.

"I mean, I can't do any of the things you guys can do," There was a hint of sadness in Brooke's voice.

"Ghost Girl," Rayn muttered under her breath, but Brooke still heard her.

"I don't know *what* I am. I can see spirits and talk to them, but I try not to. I can't manipulate anything, but I have this purple bracelet and it's kept me safe. I've seen a lot of things that I can't explain." Brooke lifted the leg of her jeans to unclasp the gem she wore around her ankle.

"Oh, I'm an idiot. Brooke, I know what you are. It does make sense after all." I counted us out on my left hand. "Water, earth, fire, air, and spirit." My hand dropped. "You can't...you know...animate corpses, can you?"

"Raise the dead?" Brooke asked, the only emotion in her voice was fear. "You don't think I might accidentally..."

"I think if you were a necromancer, we would know it," Rose told her reassuringly.

None of us wanted to think about the possibility.

"Necromancer?" Brooke asked, scrunching her face like she'd tasted cough syrup.

"They raise the dead," Rose explained.

"Why are they called that? There's nothing romantic about that." Brooke looked horrified.

"Who knows, maybe you can and don't know how yet. I doubt we've reached our full potential." Rayn shrugged.

"Don't try to do that, Brooke. Do not attempt to bring anything back to life." Lauren looked up from her manicured fingers.

"Please, you couldn't pay me enough to do that. I started seeing when I was five or six, I'm seventeen now. Don't you think any extra power is a little past due?" Brooke questioned.

I stood in silence, trying to make sense of all the information. We were Elementals. Elementals with no clue. I hoped these girls would have some answers, but apparently it wouldn't be that easy.

"Come on, I want to show you guys the meadow." Rayn waved her hand and took off down the trail. "It's a way in but totally worth it."

"Why do we need to go into the woods?" Lauren crossed her arms.

"Trust me, you guys want to see this." Rayn smiled over her shoulder.

"Let's go." Brooke took off behind Rayn, following her closely.

The rustling of leaves breaking under our shoes echoed into the night as we trekked to the meadow. Lauren kept to the back of the group, following behind us at a distance. Far enough away that if she needed to turn and run she would have a head start. None of us would be able to catch her anyway.

Brooke walked next to Rayn, who led the way through the trees with a flashlight, following the old trail we had before. Rose trailed a few feet behind me, still not sure if she trusted us or not.

"This place is beautiful," Rose breathed in admiration once we reached the meadow.

"How can you tell? It's the middle of the night," Lauren huffed.

It was dark out, but the clearing of the meadow allowed the stars above us to shed some light as our eyes adjusted to the night. The moon was nowhere in sight.

"I can feel it," Rose whispered. She reached down and slipped off her shoes and socks, pressing her bare feet into the wet earth. "I could stay here forever."

"I thought the same thing when we found it," Rayn agreed, gazing around at the wilderness.

Lauren shifted her weight and looked at Brooke. "Can I ask you something?"

"Of course," Brooke said, clearly happy that Lauren was acting interested in our conversation.

"What color was the bracelet when you first found it?" Lauren asked. "The gem, I mean."

"Gray, almost as if there wasn't any color in it at all. Then it turned purple when I took it to my room and opened it," Brooke replied, capturing my attention quickly. "It came to my house in a package."

"Really?" Lauren raised an eyebrow.

"Yeah, but the smoke inside changing color from black to white didn't happen until after I met Rose," Brooke said.

"You said this came to you in the mail?" I asked her, reaching out to take another look at Brooke's amethyst. The metal and stone were cold under my fingers.

"Yes, but there wasn't a return address on the envelope. It had a little note with my name on it."

"What did the note say?" I asked.

"Brooke Sophia Evans," Brooke answered.

I reached inside the collar of my shirt and pulled the long, silver chain into view. The light blue and white gem fell to my chest.

"Did someone send them to you?" Brooke asked, hopeful.

"We found them a long time ago. We were playing hide and seek in a foster home we were living in and we found them in an old drawer with papers and things. The gems were gray until we touched them, too. We felt a connection to them right away," Rayn explained.

"Whoever left it there might be the same person who sent this to me!" exclaimed Brooke hopefully.

"I got my bracelet when I was twelve. It belonged to my mom's great grandmother and when I held it, it came to life in my hands. So she gave it to me as a gift. I didn't think about it having anything to do with...you know. Not until later," Lauren admitted, avoiding eye contact with any of us.

"I never take mine off," Rayn replied, whose thumb had a permanent indent where her ring always sat. I reached for the stone around my neck, remembering how everything felt safer once we started wearing them.

"Didn't your mom think it was weird when she saw the gem change colors?" Brooke questioned Lauren.

"No, we don't believe in magic or anything paranormal. It was strange, but she brushed it off that the gem must have been discolored from age," Lauren explained.

"Well, you should believe in magic because it's real. We're living proof of it." Rose held out her arms, gesturing to all of us.

"Will you help us figure this out?" Rayn asked, turning to Lauren. "It would be so much easier with all of us working together."

"I don't like having these powers," Lauren snapped, looking up to the stars hanging above the clearing.

"Sometimes I don't either," I replied honestly. "But we have them, and there's nothing we can do to change it. You don't have to find the truth, but I think you'll regret never trying."

"You can't leave it alone and try to live your life like a normal person?" Lauren put a hand on her hip.

"You never once wondered why we are this way?" Rayn looked her up and down.

"I do, but I want to survive college, get my degree and move on with my life." Lauren shook her head.

"Lauren," Brooke said. "I don't think we can do this without you. We're obviously all connected."

"Unfortunately," Rose mumbled with an eye roll.

"You still haven't shown them yours," Brooke pointed to Rose's neck.

"I suppose it's only fair at this point." Rose reached for the gold chain and exposed the emerald on the end.

The chain wasn't nearly as long as the one I wore, and the gem hung in a diamond shape against her skin under her sternum. Hints of the white swirls floated around inside the gem.

"Can we look at them all together, side by side?" Brooke questioned, holding her bracelet out in her palm.

Rayn took off her ring and I held the aquamarine out in my hand, the chain long enough that I didn't need to take it off. Rose unclasped her necklace. Lauren stood still as a statue, her eyes wide with stress.

"It's okay, Lauren. No one's going to bite you." I teased in an attempt to comfort her.

Hesitantly, we all held our jewelry out in front of us. The color in my stone became more vibrant than usual, and so did all the others as a bright glow appeared from the jewelry where the stones touched.

Lauren yanked back her golden bracelet, but almost dropped it as soon as she flipped it over. Her face went pale and her eyes widened. "What is this? What did you do?"

An icy chill crawled up my spine as I pulled back my necklace and flipped it over. What was once a smooth, flat metal surface now had a design etched into it. The same symbol Dmitri drew on the underside of his arm. The one he saw carved into that tree. The one that was so similar to the brand on Abe and Serenity's wrists. Four circles all linked together, the middle made a four-petal flower design with a diamond around the edges. I ran my thumb over the engraving, feeling the indentations against my skin.

"What is it?" Lauren demanded again.

"I don't know," I whispered, not knowing if anyone heard me. "But Rayn and I have seen this symbol before."

"Where?" Rose blurted, holding her necklace tight in her fingers.

"That tree over there." I nodded toward the giant fir tree in the corner of the meadow.

"Show me," Rose insisted, wide-eyed.

Rayn led us to the giant tree as if she had been there a million times. As if she had grown up in this forest.

"What does it mean?" Rose ran her fingers over the chunks removed from the bark.

"We don't know. We tried looking online but I couldn't find anything," I answered.

"It has to mean something," Brooke whispered, examining the carving over Rose's shoulder. "I've never seen anything like this on my bracelet before now."

"This changes everything. I knew it had to mean something. Our brother fell through some kind of portal on the other side of the meadow, over there." Rayn spoke so casually about it that the others barely caught her words.

"Excuse you?" Rose raised her brows, her mouth hanging open slightly.

"Did you say 'fell through a portal'?" Lauren backed up to where she must have felt safe, which happened to be over a yard away from us.

"He landed in the lake," I answered, trembling as the fear of almost losing Dmitri washed over me once more.

"I don't believe you. This is insane. I'm leaving." Lauren turned but slowed when she seemed to realize she had no idea how to get out.

"No, stop. Please don't go." Brooke and Rayn nearly lunged at Lauren to prevent her from retreating.

"I would never lie to you, Lauren. I'll show you," I persuaded her.

I retraced my steps from the first day we found the meadow. Even in the dark, I went straight to the rock Dmitri had tripped over. Heartbeat pounding in my ears, I approached the portal. Instead of diving in headfirst, I picked up a rock off the ground and tightened my fingers around it. With a deep breath, I tossed the rock into the portal. When it hit the ground, there was no splash. The rock smacked against the dirt with a soft thud.

"That was anticlimactic," Lauren muttered.

"Something's wrong." I picked up another rock and tried again but got the same results.

"You're sure this is the right place?" Rose asked.

"Positive." I took a bold step onto the earth that Mit had fallen through but I remained on solid ground. Panic took over, wondering if we had hallucinated the whole thing.

Rayn defended me. "She's not lying. I watched the whole thing. We found him at the lake."

"Something happened," I muttered to myself, squatting down to run my fingers through the grass. "It closed somehow."

"Okay," Rose stretched out each syllable. "I'll give you the benefit of the doubt."

"I'm not lying." I snapped in self-defense.

Rose raised her eyebrows at me. "No one said you were, Whitney."

"Add it to the list of shit we have to figure out." Rayn straightened her posture.

"I don't know if I *have* to, maybe want is a better choice of words," Rose replied with a realistic tone.

"No, I have to figure all of this out," Rayn explained wholeheartedly, her voice cracking. "It's all I've ever wanted my whole life, to understand why I'm like this. We all came together for a reason, and I think we owe it to ourselves to find our purpose."

"Well, now that we're all past this awkward stage, where do we go from here?" Rose looked around the meadow. "I told you before, Whitney, this is a thousand-piece jigsaw puzzle."

"And I think we already have five of the biggest pieces. Come on, you know part of you wants to know the truth." Rayn twirled her ring around in her fingers, looking down at the symbol.

I had never thought Rayn and I would ever meet anyone else with elemental powers and the five of us walked right into each other. My sister and I always wondered if we were alone in this life. Mom told me that everything happens for a reason, that was becoming clearer to me each day I spent in Rifton.

"I don't feel like a witch, I can't do any spells." Brooke hung her head.

"Spells aren't the only thing witches are allowed to do." Rose put her necklace back on.

"I am not a witch," Lauren replied sternly with a tense jaw.

Witch. That was nothing new to me. As much as my mother hid from us growing up, the true meaning of that word was not one of them. Mom called herself a witch. She called her children little witches. We knew our powers were magical.

"What have you guys been calling yourselves then?" Rose asked curiously.

"I've been called blessed," Rayn replied, thinking about our mom.

"And I've been called cursed," Lauren mumbled, thinking about someone in her life as well.

"I call myself Brooke. I personally want to see everyone's powers. Am I the only one here who's been dying to watch Rayn blow something up?" Brooke asked, putting her arms up in the air demonstrating an explosion.

"I am always down to blow something up." Rayn smiled. "Let's talk more on that."

"Thank you!" Brooke exclaimed, her fingers curled into excited fists.

"What if the fire gets out of control?" Terror filled Lauren's voice.

"Then I'll extinguish it. Water and fire, get it?" I replied.

"Alright. Who's going first?" Rayn asked, picking at the loose denim strands of her jeans.

"R-right now?" Lauren stuttered.

"Why not? We're already in a secluded part of the forest." Rose replied, gesturing to the tall trees.

"Whit and I have used our powers here. We are completely safe," Rayn reassured them.

"Wasn't that the whole point of the meeting?" Rose nudged Lauren.

"What about you, Brooke?" I asked.

"Oh." She hesitated. "If you want to see my power, I have another place in mind, but first let's see what you four can do."

Chapter Nine

HIDDEN SECRETS

"Are you ready?" Rayn asked eagerly, looking around at the rest of us. "I'll go first."

We all nodded. I had been waiting for this moment, eager to see their powers and what they felt like since I found out the others existed. Surprisingly, I wasn't nervous. I was calm and collected. At peace, even, like this was something we'd done a million times before.

I held my breath as Rayn filled her lungs and held up her hands toward a tiny pine tree growing in the middle of the meadow. It was only a few feet tall with thin branches and barely any needles. Rayn took three steps back from the tree and the rest of us followed. If Rayn was lighting a fire, I didn't want to be standing right next to it.

Rayn focused on the tiny tree and within seconds, flames rose from the trunk, reaching upward and dancing into the sky. Small pine needles shriveled up into ash as the magic tickled my fingertips.

"Woah," Brooke whispered in awe, her hands clasped together in front of her mouth.

I had seen Rayn burn things hundreds of times, but the looks on the other girl's faces were covered with mixed reactions. Brooke's eyes were wide with amazement. Lauren took a few additional steps back from the fire, looking nauseous. Rose stood relatively still, watching the flames burn intently. She didn't look scared or astonished. She was observant and though her face didn't show it, her eyes gleamed as if she was impressed.

I let the flames dance around the branches for a few moments longer before I raised my own hands and drew in a deep breath. I pulled as much energy as I had, focusing on the area of the sky above the flames to create a rain cloud like I had the first time we ventured to the meadow.

I put every ounce of energy and concentration I had into that rain cloud. For a moment, I was convinced I failed until a raindrop hit my forehead. I lowered my tingling hands as thick smoke rose into the sky when the flames began to extinguish.

We watched the rainfall until the last of the flames disappeared. By then, our hair and clothes were misted from the water falling a few yards in front of us. The physical feeling of using my powers had faded, but I could still feel it in my soul that the rain in the sky belonged to me. The rain thinned out quickly as the clouds drifted off into the night.

Once the last of the rain disappeared, Lauren moved in my peripheral vision. She flicked her wrist as if motioning for something to get out of the way. As her hand moved, the same familiar feeling from the day at the Corner Cup jolted deep in my bones.

The wind hit my back before it blew my dark hair into my face. I moved it to the side, looking at where the pine tree had stood. The ashes from the fire swirled up into the sky with the sudden gust of wind that swept through the meadow. All that remained was a circle of burnt grass and charred remains of the small tree. There were only two of us left to show off.

Rose took a few steps toward the burnt greenery and got down on her knees, pressing her fingers into the dirt. I hadn't felt Rose use her powers yet. She didn't reveal herself as quickly as Lauren did. Suddenly, the tingle in my limbs returned.

The dead grass around the small tree grew with ease between Rose's fingers. The vibrant green blades looked much healthier than the other blades of grass around it, and soon any lingering evidence of the fire had vanished. A small, skinny branch grew up from the ground and little pine needles sprouted from it. Once it reached five or six inches tall, Rose stopped and pulled her hands out of the dirt.

"Holy shit!" Brooke shouted with amazement. "You are Mother Earth, Rose, you never fail to amaze me. Plus that fire and the wind. And Whitney...that rainstorm was you? I'm freaking out right now! That is incredible!"

"It's a cycle," Rayn replied, breathing deeply. "Reborn from the ashes."

My heart pounded so fast in my chest that I struggled to breathe. I stared at the pine sapling, unable to take my eyes off it.

"Did you feel that, Brooke? Did you feel our powers?" I asked, turning to face her.

"I did, my arms were tingling," she breathed, excitement still in her voice. "How did you learn to do all of that?"

"It's not something you learn," I replied.

"What about you, Brooke?" Rayn asked. "You said you had somewhere else in mind."

"The cemetery in town. If you want to go…I'll tell you what I can see." Brooke cleared her throat.

"Which one?" Rose was still on her knees, gently running her fingers across the grass. "The old one downtown with the big gates?"

"The old one by the courthouse, yeah." Brooke nodded. "I don't remember the street name, but I've seen ghosts there before."

A chilling breeze picked up, rustling the tree branches that surrounded the meadow as Lauren spoke up. "We shouldn't be playing around in cemeteries."

The wind blew the trees against each other with more ferocity. My hair blew into my face again but I ignored it, not wanting to fight against the wind. The breeze had an icy nip when it hit my skin, causing little hairs on my arms to stand up.

"Calm down before you blow us over, Lauren."

"It's not me," she replied as if we all couldn't feel her power rustle to the tune of her uncertainty.

"It'll be okay," Brooke said. "Nothing bad has ever happened when I see things, sometimes they don't even notice."

"If this is something we have to do, then let's get it over with." Lauren walked toward the trees.

Rayn and I followed, passing her and leading the way back to the cars. By the time we drove out of the forest and into Rifton's downtown area, it was nearly ten o'clock at night. We would be in the cemetery in the middle of the night to see if Brooke could point out any ghosts. Totally fine.

I parked alongside the old curb on Cedar Avenue next to a tall iron fence around the cemetery. Chunks of concrete had been chipped away from the pavement and the cemetery itself didn't look well maintained.

"Shouldn't the gates be locked?" Lauren asked as we walked alongside the fence.

"There aren't any locks here. I think it would be rude to keep people's loved ones from being able to visit their resting place." Brooke opened up one of the side gates and walked into the cemetery like she owned the place.

Rose followed behind her, and then Rayn. I paused, looking back at Lauren, who glued herself to the sidewalk.

"You can wait out here if you want," I told her.

"I think being alone outside a graveyard is a little more terrifying than being in a graveyard with you guys," Lauren replied as she swallowed her fear and walked through the open gate.

"It's actually not a graveyard, there's no church," Brooke replied quietly.

I closed the gate gently behind us, careful not to make too much noise and wake the dead. We passed through numerous rows of headstones before anyone said anything.

"So, Brooke," Rose began. "Do you...see anything?"

"Not yet," Brooke said, her head on a swivel. "Trust me, I'll let you know when I do."

The chilled air blew around us, while scattered dark clouds hung above allowing the stars to peek through. Everything seemed perfectly normal, which made being amongst the dead waiting until Brooke saw a ghost a bit more ominous.

I felt sorry for Brooke, having to see things that no one else could see and try not to go a little crazy. I kept my head down as we walked deeper into the ongoing rows of headstones, only looking up to inspect the inscriptions. 1892. 1904. 1927. So many years ago. I wasn't paying any attention to what was in front of me and ran into Lauren's back.

I stepped around Lauren and looked at Brooke. She was as still as a statue, barely breathing when she was usually so animated. But now, she was frozen as if a landmine might go off below her feet.

"Brooke?" Rose reached for Brooke's shoulder.

After hearing someone's voice, Brooke looked back at us and held a finger up to her lips. A chill ran up my spine causing my blood to turn ice cold. Brooke stepped forward and motioned for us to follow.

"It's okay. It's the same girl I've seen a million times," She whispered, turning back to look at us.

Everything was silent except the sound of our shoes against the grass. Brooke walked in front of us with her hands swinging back and forth at her sides. All I could see were rows of dark gravestones with small trees planted throughout like the groundskeepers were trying to make the cemetery feel less dead.

Soon we came up to an older crypt made of large stones with a statue of an angel in front and a small angel child at its side. Bouquets rested at the angel's feet. The crypt had a dark opening and steps that led down inside. Thinking about being up close and personal in someone's grave sent a shiver up my spine.

Slowly, Brooke approached the crypt, as if contemplating going inside.

"What are you doing?" I asked her. The sound of my voice echoed against the silence lingering around us.

"I think she wants me to go inside," Brooke replied, turning around to face us. "That's where she went and she knows I was following her."

"Does she see the rest of us?" Lauren asked with a shaky voice.

"Of course she can, but you can't see her, so she doesn't pay much attention to you," Brooke explained.

"Who is she?" Rayn asked.

"I don't know," Brooke admitted. "She never talks. I've seen her before though, and she's always been friendly. I'm going inside. Who's coming with me?"

I wasn't surprised when silence fell among us. I didn't want Brooke adventuring into the dark by herself but I didn't necessarily want to go crawling around inside of a tomb where a ghost had led us either. Who knew what else was down there. I looked at the other girls. I expected Lauren to be quiet, but not Rose and Rayn. Both of them looked off in different directions, avoiding eye contact.

I took a deep breath and a small step forward. "Come on, Brooke. Let's get this over with." I looked up at the stars, asking for strength and courage to handle whatever might happen next.

Brooke gave me a subtle smile but I could see the disappointment in her eyes. She couldn't be too hard on the others, who wanted to follow a ghost into a crypt?

Be careful. Rayn's voice echoed softly in my head.

I looked over my shoulder and met her eyes. "Rule number one," I answered aloud.

"What's rule number one?" Rose asked Rayn.

"Stick together," Rayn mumbled as I followed Brooke into the darkness.

Luckily, the entrance into the crypt was large enough for both of us to walk under it, only having to duck our heads as we stepped inside. I couldn't breathe in too deeply without the taste of muggy dirt. I could barely see anything in front of me, having Rayn's flame for light would have been useful, but I settled for the flashlight on my phone.

I counted eight steps before I reached my foot out for the next one and stepped on flat ground instead. Rectangular stones and metal plaques lined the walls of the tomb, each with a name and two dates on them.

"I don't see her anymore," Brooke whispered, looking around. The tomb itself wasn't large, maybe the size of our tiny bathroom in Pines Row.

"Are you sure she wanted us to come in here?" I whispered back, taking a look around like I was in a horror movie and something was going to jump out and kill us at any moment.

"I'm positive." Brooke took the light from my hand and looked around the room. She turned around and her eyes lit up with amazement.

"Whitney," Brooke whispered, pointing to one of the bricks on the wall.

I stepped toward her and turned as Brooke held the light from my phone closer to the brick. Carved into the stone was the symbol that now covered the back of our jewelry.

"She led us here to find this," Brooke said, running her fingers over the carving. "What do you think is behind it?"

The moment Brooke touched the stone, a bright white light illuminated the brick with the symbol on it. A wave of energy washed over the small room, increasing the tension in my shoulders.

"Only one way to find out," I replied.

The grout around the stone crumbled away easily as if the brick had been removed before. I looked over at Brooke to see if she was ready to reveal the secret hidden away for us to find, but she was already reaching forward to pull the brick from the wall with both hands.

I shone the light from my phone into the opening the brick had exposed. Part of me expected a box of ashes or another piece of jewelry, but it was a book.

Slowly, I reached my hand into the compartment, careful of any traps or hidden surprises, but nothing happened. I pulled the book from the darkness.

"What is it?" Brooke asked, looking up at me with wide eyes.

"I don't know," I said, meeting her gaze. "But we should show the others right away."

"What about the symbol?" Brooke asked. "It appeared on our jewelry and now it's shown up in this secret hiding place. It must mean something important."

"You're right. Take a picture of it and put the brick back. We don't need anyone knowing we were here."

As I turned toward the stairs, I froze in place. A familiar weight pressed down on my shoulders as a chill crept up my body like a spider. Eyes burned into me, watching my every move. A predator in the darkness, waiting for its chance to pounce.

"Brooke," I whispered.

"I see it." Fear paralyzed her voice. "In the corner."

My eyes darted to the far corner of the crypt, knowing exactly where to look without needing to ask. Even in the pitch black, I could see its outline; hunched over, head hanging low with hollow eyes peering into my soul. My pulse picked up as the faintest smell of iron-rich blood filled my senses.

"Go!" I ordered, grabbing Brooke's arm and shoving her toward the entrance.

We rushed up the stairs, tripping over the top step and stumbling onto my knees. Brooke turned and grabbed my elbow, helping me up while pulling me away from the crypt.

"Are you okay?" Rayn shot forward.

"Shadow," I muttered, unable to string cohesive words together.

"There's one here? Now?" Lauren backed away quickly.

Rose scanned the cemetery. "I don't see anything."

"It didn't follow us then." Brooke sighed in relief. "I've never seen one here before, but it must have been guarding the book."

"What book?" My sister asked but my reply was interrupted by a high-pitched shriek coming from the entrance of the crypt.

A wispy, taloned claw tapped against the concrete, followed by another. Emerging from the opening of the crypt came a living, breathing shadow. Its back was hunched over as it crawled onto the grass, head low as it stalked us. Its skull had hollowed holes where eyes should have been, but the shadow still knew exactly where we were. I had never seen a shadow this developed, something more than just a darkened figure. This was a fully formed monster, ready to strike.

"Oh, fuck!" Lauren shouted, turning on her heel and taking off across the cemetery.

"Run!" Rayn screamed.

I bolted. My fight or flight instincts kicked in with the other girls hot on my heels, sprinting after Lauren but she was long gone.

My hands slammed down on the car as the momentum of my retreat threw me against the hood. My heart pounded so hard I thought I might throw up. "Did it follow us?" I asked, breathing heavily.

"I don't see anything," Rayn leaned forward, her hands on her knees as she caught her breath. "But we need to leave."

"What are you holding?" Rose asked, noticing the book for the first time. "Is that the book?"

"It was behind one of the plaques," Brooke explained, panting. "This brick on the wall had the symbol from our jewelry engraved on it. Look, I took a picture."

"Are you serious?" Rayn asked with a smile on her face like we hadn't just been chased out of the cemetery by a shadow. "Maybe that book will tell us the truth about who we are!"

"Do you think it would be that easy? This is another piece to the puzzle, but a valuable one, I bet." Rose held out her hands. "May I see it?"

I gently handed the book to Rose and she took it in her arms, carefully opening the cover. "These pages are parchment and the cover is real leather. It looks handwritten. This book is old."

"Is it legible?" Lauren asked, startling me with her sudden interest in anything related to our powers.

"Yes. The first page is a list of names and dates and-" the book began to move in Rose's hands, causing her to fumble it. The pages came alive, flipping themselves as if they were being blown in the wind but there was no breeze. Then it stopped suddenly.

"What the hell was that?" Lauren asked, slowly backing away from us.

Rose froze. Standing with her feet cemented into the sidewalk, her eyes glued to the pages of the book.

"What does it say?" I asked, peering over her shoulder.

"Shadows," Rose whispered. "It's an entry about creatures who grow from the shadows."

"We need to leave," Rayn announced.

We will, I answered my sister telepathically before speaking out loud. "What else does it say, Rose?"

"I think the picture speaks for itself." Rose tilted the book toward me.

The charcoal drawing showed a creature with thick fangs and claws, hunched over like a gargoyle atop an old gothic cathedral.

"Where can we go?" Brooke asked, tightening her arms around her.

Tenderly, Rose closed the book. "I suppose we could go to my house. I'm home alone tonight. My mom is working nights this week and won't be home until like, six in the morning."

"Perfect, let's go." I dropped my keys twice before I successfully unlocked the car.

Chapter Ten

ENCHANTMENT

Soon we were parked out front of 225 Willow Street, Rose's house. My mind was racing and now that I didn't have driving to distract myself, I was forced to face the truth. Shadows. Not a figure in the darkness, but a fully formed monster.

Rose kept the book in her arms, cradling it close to her chest like an infant as she led us up the pathway to her house.

"I can't stay for long," Lauren replied.

"Fine by me." Rose unlocked the front door and turned on the first light switch she could reach. The ceiling light revealed a living room with a tan couch and two matching chairs in front of a television. The wall behind it was covered in various sized family photos.

"I like your house." Rayn smiled, looking around.

"Thanks. Take a seat and we'll get a better look at this book." Rose motioned toward the couch as she set the book down carefully on the glass top of the coffee table. "Would anyone like something to drink?"

"Do you have any coffee?" I asked.

"Uh, sure. I could get a pot going." Rose headed toward the kitchen, leaving the room without a comment about me asking for coffee at ten-thirty at night.

I examined the living room, looking around at the light gray walls with all the pictures. The photo at the end of the mantel halted me dead in my tracks. Two guys with their arms around each other, both of them wearing blue graduation gowns and holding up high school diplomas. Their mouths were full of braces and graduation caps atop messy hair. One had a face I'd been daydreaming about all week.

"Oh my god," I whispered, taking a closer look at the photos on the wall. Nearly half of the photos were of him. He and Rose. Christmas mornings, school yearbook photos, and dying Easter eggs. I didn't let myself accept it at first, that these two people had anything to do with one another, but the closer I paid attention to their vibrant green eyes and similar facial features I kicked myself for not realizing it sooner.

What's wrong? my sister asked.

What is Rose's last name? I replied, staring into the soft lilypad green eyes looking back at me from the photo.

McClintock, I think. Why?

Bryan McClintock.

Rayn shrugged.

I think Bryan is Rose's brother.

"No shit?" Rayn questioned out loud. I think she had the intention of saying her words mentally, but they slipped out.

"What? What is it?" Lauren asked, sitting up in alert.

"Nothing." Rayn shook her head.

"You two were making faces like you were having a conversation with each other in your heads," Brooke said suspiciously, narrowing her eyes.

"That's impossible," Lauren said, crossing her arms in front of her chest.

"What's impossible?" Rose asked, returning from the kitchen with a coffee cup in each hand.

"Whitney and Rayn looked like they were talking in their heads," Brooke repeated. She wasn't going to let this go.

I looked at my sister., *Should we tell them?*

About you wanting to bone Rose's brother?

No, asshole! About us being about to talk like this.

Do you think it would be a good idea? Rayn bit the inside of her cheek. *I mean, it's a lot at once.*

"See? They're doing it again!" Brooke pointed at us. "I can tell."

"Brooke, don't point at people. You can't do that when you have powers, you never know what will happen." Rose set the coffee mugs on the glass table.

"Sorry," Brooke mumbled, lowering her head.

"Well, are you? Telepathic?" Rose asked, looking back and forth between Rayn and I.

My eyes were still on my sister when she nodded hesitantly.

"We always thought we could…I don't know, talk through the powers but we can't communicate with any of you like that, so I guess that's wrong," Rayn said honestly.

"How long have you been able to do that?" Rose asked with a surprisingly interested look on her face. "You can literally hear each other's thoughts?"

"Not exactly…" I looked back to a photo of Bryan on the wall. "We only hear what we want each other to hear. It started the night we met."

Lauren stared at us like she didn't believe a word we were saying. Like we were telling her the earth was flat.

"That's incredible," Brooke smiled.

"It's impressive," Rose replied, nodding.

"So about this mysterious book we found in a grave guarded by shadows," Rayn said, trying to push the spotlight away from her and I.

"We?" I laughed. "You mean me and Brooke?"

Rose sat down on the couch next to Brooke and opened the book slowly. The beating of my heart grew stronger with anticipation as I took one of the coffee cups. The book was all handwritten, almost like a journal. One list of names in the very front stuck out to us.

Thomas Oakes - Stream

William Ansley - Dirt

Josephine Glensworth - Sky

Alexandra Davenport - Flame

Gabriel Hartford - Soul

"Woah." I whispered, staring at the name with 'stream' next to it.

"Who are these people?" Brooke asked.

"They're people like us." Rose smiled, looking up from the book momentarily.

The handwriting on the page talked of this particular generation of Elementals. Page after page of collected thoughts on their magic and different things they were able to do with their powers. Most of the things they listed were powers that we already possessed: burning things down, creating floods, saving crops that had already dried in the summer sun. The ability to take control of their enemy's mind, on the other hand, was not something I was familiar with.

There were maps on the following pages, but I didn't recognize any of the names or locations of the towns.

"Some of the maps are of Europe. This one here is the Irish coastline." Rose pointed her finger to a map on an earlier page.

"This means there were people once like us. Shouldn't there be others besides us?" Rayn asked, looking at me. "We have to find them, Whit, we have to."

"There may have been witches like us years ago but that doesn't mean we aren't the only ones left. This is an old book," Rose replied.

"Maybe they had lesser powers," I suggested, casually.

Like Mom and Mit. Rayn met my eyes again. She knew what I was referring to instantly.

This was exactly what we wanted. Information. There was a reason we found this book. It was intended for us if the same symbol that appeared on our jewelry was on the brick.

"So those rules you mentioned in the cemetery," Rose began. "What was that about?"

"Whit and I have a set of rules. We came up with them before we were adopted, mostly to keep ourselves safe and the powers a secret," Rayn answered.

"How many are there?" Brooke asked.

"Four," I answered. "Number one, stick together. Two, Don't lie or keep secrets."

"Three, don't be a dick," Rayn chimed in. "Four, don't be reckless."

"I like those," Rose said, turning her attention back to the book. "I can go along with that."

"Me too." Brooke turned to the next page. "Lists of ingredients and instructions. These look like recipes."

"Recipes? You mean spells?" Rose asked, flipping to the next page. "My god, how many drawings does one page need?"

"You should be happy there're so many pictures," Lauren mumbled. "Aren't you all about knowing everything? Being a know it all?"

All eyes were on Lauren as she spoke. Lauren seemed to be testing her limits with Rose. If she kept it up, I'm sure it would be a matter of time before Rose strangled her with a vine.

"All the pictures will certainly make things easier for you to understand," Rose shot back with an icy glare.

"Knock it off," I said. "Seriously, this is all hard enough without you going back and forth. We have to trust each other if this is going to work. Rule number one."

"Whitney's right. Can we keep reading through the book, please?" Rayn added in an attempt to soothe the tension.

"Listen to this. Purify a candle and place it in the middle of the cauldron, and fill with water until the candle floats. Light candle and visualize the spell broken." Rose read out loud, running her finger down the page. A smile swept across her face. "I was right, they're spells."

"Spells?" Lauren asked, making a horrified face.

"Yes. Spells. We are witches after all, witches perform spells." Rose rolled her eyes. "Have you never read a book?"

Lauren met her gaze. "It's not what I was expecting, that's all."

There were endless pages of spells and potions. Releasing spells. Sleeping potions. Fertility spells.

"Memories of past generations," Rayn read aloud as she turned the page.

"What's that?" I asked curiously, leaning in across the coffee table to get a better look.

Rayn was silent for a moment as she read down the page. "I guess one Elemental in every generation called a Seer could look into the past through memories of older generations."

"What are past generations?" Brooke asked what I had been thinking aloud.

"According to this, a generation is a grouping of five element witches born within half a decade of one another," Rayn read.

"I guess that makes us a generation," Rose replied. "Good, we are finally getting some answers."

"I don't see how this answers anything," Lauren mumbled, retreating to her coffee cup.

"We want to know what we are. Well, we are an elemental generation. See? Answers." Rose picked up her coffee mug and took a sip as well.

"Are we completely forgetting about the book opening up to a page about shadows?" I asked. As excited as I was to find all these spells and generations, shadows loomed in the back of my mind.

"One thing at a time. Look at these spells. Are we going to try any of them?" Brooke asked with anticipation. "Do we have any of the ingredients?"

"We could get most of these ingredients at the grocery store. Though I have no idea what Fairy's Whisper is." Rose went down the list with her finger, double-checking the current spell we were looking at. "I would be willing to make a potion."

"It's worth a try," I said. "At least see if they work. What do we have to lose?"

Lauren let out a long sigh. "Oh, I don't know, an arm? I won't participate in this. No way."

"Then why are you here? Seriously, there's the door." Rose rolled her eyes and motioned toward the entryway.

"Lauren, this is part of finding out about the truth. You said you would help us," I reminded her, reaching out for my coffee mug, which had already cooled.

"I said I would show up tonight. I didn't say I'd join your little club." Lauren sat on the edge of her seat, digging her fingers into her palms.

"Wow, it's eleven-thirty already." Brooke looked over to the wooden clock on the wall. "My parents must not know I'm gone."

"Is it really?" Lauren asked, alarmed, and dug around in her bag for her cell phone. She turned the screen on and let out a long sigh with her eyes closed tight. "My phone was on silent and my mom has called seven times. I gotta go." Lauren stood up with her bag already around her shoulder. "What am I going to tell her?"

"We were studying late," Rayn said quickly. "Your phone was on silent because you wanted to concentrate without distraction, they can't be mad at you for that."

"Plus, aren't you, like, an adult?" Brooke asked.

"It's more of a courtesy thing." Lauren answered. "There's nothing wrong with her wanting to know I'm okay."

"We'll walk you out. It's time for us to leave anyway." I said, standing up and looking at Rayn, who was right behind me. "Our brother is home alone."

I was absolute trash for leaving Dmitri home all hours of the night like this. He never complained and I know he enjoyed being alone but it still didn't sit well.

"What about the book?" Brooke asked. She looked at it like she didn't want to leave it, afraid a shadow would come for it in the night when none of us were looking.

"I'll keep it here for now, if that's alright with everyone. I'll keep it in a safe place. No one will find it, I promise," Rose said, already holding it against her chest. None of us protested.

"Do you think Rayn and I could take the book when you're done?" I asked, checking my phone to make sure no one had been blowing it up too. "I want to take a closer look at it."

"Yeah, of course," Rose replied.

I picked up my half-full cup of cold coffee and took another swig.

"Here, allow me." Rayn reached out and took the mug in her hands. A faint hint of her powers tickled my skin as she warmed up the mug in her hands long enough to bring it back to life.

"That is a useful skill that I'm severely jealous of." Rose watched Rayn closely with admiration.

"Thanks." I finished off the perfectly heated coffee. "And thank you, Rose, for letting us come over and go through the book. I think we've made a lot of progress tonight."

"We have discovered something huge, that's for sure." Rose nodded and walked us to the door. "The more we get into the book, the more we'll learn."

"We'll see you soon," I said and stepped into the chilly night air. We walked to the car without a sound. I could hear Lauren on the phone with her mom, apologetically explaining she was studying at Vanessa's house and didn't realize it was so late. Whoever Vanessa was.

"Um, Whitney?" Brooke's small voice piped up in the breeze. "Do you think you could take me home? Rose picked me up. I have a car but I didn't want to drive myself in case my parents noticed it was missing from the driveway."

"Of course, get in." I smiled at her and leaned my seat forward, allowing Brooke to get into the back.

"Holy shit this night has been insane." Rayn slumped down into the front seat. "No going back now, not after finding that book."

"I had a feeling once we all got together things would start falling into place," Brooke replied, buckling her seat belt.

"Me too," I whispered with a racing heart. "Any idea who that spirit from the cemetery is? You mentioned that you've seen her before."

"I see her all over town, but I have no clue who she is," Brooke answered. "I tried to find a headstone that looked like it could match her dates, but nothing so far. Whoever she is, she knew the book was there."

Your new boyfriend is definitely not who I expected him to be, either. Rayn's voice entered my head as I pulled away from the curb of Willow Street. I figured she had forgotten about it, but I hadn't stopped thinking about Bryan being related to Rose.

"You know that telepathic thing is kind of rude," Brooke muttered from the backseat.

Rayn turned to look at her. "Sorry, it's about Whitney's boyfriend."

"You have a boyfriend?" Brooke asked, leaning over the center consul in between the two front seats.

"No, I don't. We're friends."

"Yeah. Okay, Whitney," Rayn rolled her eyes. "Tell him that."

Spellbooks hidden in graves. A fully formed shadow demon. The portal in the meadow sealed as if it never existed. As much as it caught me off guard, I had more pressing issues on my agenda than Rose's family tree.

Chapter Eleven

CURSIVE WARNING

The Corner Cup was bustling with the usual morning rush when I walked through the doors. It had been two days since the girls and I met in the forest and things had been eerily calm since. Too calm.

"Hey, Ashley." I greeted as I approached the counter.

"Hey there, sunshine." Ashley's face lit up. "You're on bar again with me today."

"Perfect. I was hoping for a break from the register."

I went through the employee only doors into the back. The small break room had a few tables and a fridge next to the microwave. I was excited to be at the Corner Cup and had grown to love my job. The upcoming paycheck wasn't bad either.

My phone began to ring in my back pocket reminding me that I needed to put it on silent if I was going to sneak it into the dining room. I checked the screen before turning the sound off, and my heart leaped up into my chest. Bryan McClintock.

"Hello?" I answered, not bothering to hide the beaming smile in my voice.

"Whitney, hey. It's Bryan."

"How are you?"

"I'm fine. Is this a good time?"

"I'm clocking into work," I replied, holding the phone in between my chin and shoulder so I could put my bag in my locker.

"I won't keep you. I was wondering if you, uh, if you have plans after work?" Bryan asked. I didn't need to be standing next to him to feel his nerves.

As I reached for my black apron, a small, folded piece of paper fell from the pocket. I stared at it for the longest time on the tile trying to remember when I had put a post-it note in the pocket.

"Whitney?"

"Hm?" I asked, remembering I was on the phone.

"Do you have plans after work? I was hoping to see you, maybe buy you dinner."

"I'm sorry, I can't today. Can I call you later?" Slowly, I knelt down and picked up the folded paper.

"Oh, yeah, no worries. I'll let you go."

"Talk to you soon, promise." I hung up quicker than I wanted to.

I unfolded the note to see big, beautiful cursive describing one of my deepest fears.

Stray from the shadows, for they are always watching.

Shadows.

"Hey, Whitney." My coworker, Robby, passed by the break room on his way out into the dining area. I smiled and gave him a small wave. "You coming?"

"Yeah, yeah let me put on my apron." I shoved the note into my pocket, and with it, the thudding of my heart.

Shadows.

Someone knew about us.

My knees buckled like I would fall over, but there was nothing I could do about it at that moment. All I could do was focus on my job and make some good cups of coffee, or learn to, at least.

I put on my best smile and walked behind the counter. "Okay, ready to make some coffee."

"Perfect. Do you have a marker I can use?" Ashley asked, digging around in her apron but came up empty handed.

I reached into the front pocket of my apron but instead of finding a pen, I grabbed the note. Feeling the rough paper with my fingers gave me a chill. I needed to tell Rayn about this warning immediately.

"Before I forget, I got the cutest picture of your sister playing pong with us at the bonfire." Ashley pulled her phone out of her back pocket and held up the screen. Rayn was beaming, her hair falling gently across her forehead and framing her face. Emma stood next to her, mid-throw and laughing with my sister.

"Can you send this to me?"

"Yeah, of course."

Once I got the message, I forwarded the photo to my sister.

Ashley and I got through the different blended beverages; caramel, mocha, vanilla, and on and on before she took her break. The bell above the front doors went off but I didn't pay much attention at first until I overheard the order our coworker, Olivia, was taking at the register.

"Orange spice tea with cinnamon, please."

My head whipped up to see Rose standing at the register with a dark blue backpack secured on her shoulders. She looked calm and collected, though I assumed she had the spellbook in her bag. Rose paid for her drink and made silent eye contact with me before she gave Olivia a smile of thanks and walked around the corner toward the bathrooms.

"Hey, Olivia, could I use the restroom real quick?" I waited until Rose was in the bathroom for a moment to avoid the obvious.

"No problem."

As I pushed open the doors to the women's bathroom, Rose stood in front of the sinks. Her backpack in front of her, resting on the edge of the porcelain.

"Hey," I said quietly.

"How's work?" Rose asked, pulling a block shape wrapped in a dark green towel from her bag, which I assumed was the spellbook.

"Uh, it's work. Look at this." My hand dove into my apron to retrieve the note I had received earlier.

"What is it?" Rose took it from my hands cautiously.

"It was in my apron when I came in."

Rose unfolded the note and I watched as her face fell. She stared at the cursive warning for a lifetime. "What the hell?"

"I don't know who, but someone knows about us, or me. They know about the shadows."

"Well, I was already planning to stray from the shadows. You don't have to tell me twice." Rose handed the note back to me and directed her attention to the spellbook.

"I don't have anywhere to keep the book, it's too big for my locker. If I give you the keys to my car, can you put it in the trunk?" I asked.

"Yes. I wanted to show you something first though." Rose unfolded the towel and opened the book to a page she'd saved with a bookmark.

"What is it?" I leaned in, looking at the spell before us. An ointment to make scars disappear instantly.

Rose cleared her throat, "A healing spell. It's simple with easy to find ingredients. Most of the other spells have plants with names I don't recognize. I think we should start with these types until I figure out what phoenix dust or holy rope is."

"That sounds great, actually." I thought about a few scars on my body I would love to erase forever. "Rayn and I are in. Let's meet back at the meadow and we will see if this works."

Rose nodded. "Tomorrow."

"Is that enough time to let the other girls know?"

"Brooke would meet us up there tonight if we told her to." Rose tilted her head with a smile.

"And Lauren?"

"I don't have anything to say about her." Rose wrapped the book back up in her towel and slid it into her backpack like it was made of glass.

"What happened between you two anyway?"

"She's insufferable."

"I need to get back to work and I'm sure your tea is done by now."

"You're right, we've been in here long enough. I'll put the book in your trunk and bring your keys back in."

"Thanks, Rose. I'll see you tomorrow. What should we bring for the spell?"

"Nothing, I have the ingredients already. If you can get Lauren to show up again, your work is done."

When I pulled into the driveway at home after work, I was surprisingly optimistic about the note in my locker. It may have been a warning, but I had decided it was a helpful warning and not someone trying to hurt us. I felt okay with the idea of a stranger trying to protect us until I walked into an empty house.

"Mit?" I called into the house, but only my voice echoed back to me. I knew Rayn was out and about with Tom, but Dmitri should have been home. I shouted his name again but nothing.

I peaked out the door in the kitchen that led to the back porch, scanning the tree line for my brother when I spotted two figures leaned against the side of the small tool shed behind our house. They were shielded from the Roberts' house but I could see them crystal clear.

Dmitri stood with his back against the shed, looking up at Abe as he loomed over Mit. I stepped out onto the porch, prepared to bark at Abe to get away from my brother when I saw their fingers intertwined. Abe's touch was gentle, rubbing the back of Dmitri's hand with his thumb. My brother whispered something that made Abe chuckle. I knew I should have gone back inside and given them some privacy but I didn't trust Abe.

Abe reached into his pocket and pulled out a folded piece of paper, handing it over to Dmitri. Mit looked down at the paper in hesitation before he slid it into his own pocket and nodded. They exchanged another soft glance before Abe reached out and traced Dmitri's jawline with his thumb. Dmitri smiled as Abe slipped away, trekking across the field to his own house with his hands in his pockets.

I remained in the doorway, waiting for Dmitri to make his way back into the house. He kept his head down as he came up the steps, halting in his tracks at the sight of me.

"You're home early." Dmitri said, clearing his throat.

"Hmm," I hummed, trying my best to swallow the rage building in my chest.

"Listen-" He began, but I cut him off.

"No, Mit, I don't want to hear it. I want to see what Abe gave you."

Dmitri broke eye contact, scanning the field between the houses to see if Abe was still in view. "I was going to show you, anyway. You don't have to interrogate me."

I held my tongue, knowing damn well my brother didn't care what I had to say on the matter. He had already proven he was going to do as he pleased. Part of me wondered if he would've given Mom the same push back or if this treatment was just for me.

I glanced over at the Roberts' home to see someone in the yard watching from the shadows.

Stray from the shadows, for they are always watching.

Abe leaned against his house, biting at his fingernails. When our eyes met, he leaned further into the siding as if it would give him some camouflage from me. He turned and walked toward his backyard.

"Stay here." I ordered Dmitri, skipping the step off the porch as I rushed across the field. I turned around to the sound of Dmitri scurrying across the porch. "For once in your fucking life, Dmitri Hawke, listen to me."

To my surprise, Dmitri stayed still.

"Hey!" I shouted at Abe's back as I ran after him. "Hey! I'm talking to you!"

Abe turned around slowly, avoiding eye contact.

"What?" He asked quietly, shoving his hands into his pockets.

"What the hell is your problem? You tell me to stay away from you if I want to live and then you watch my sister through the window and put your hands on my brother? I should call the cops on you." My body shook with nerves, but I refused to back down. I took a step toward him, determined to stand my ground and let him know the severity of my threats.

"I happen to think your sister likes the attention." Abe whispered bravely.

"Fucking gross. I saw what you did to that rabbit as if I was inside of your room." I wanted him to know that I saw his horrific spell, that I knew what he truly was under this timid demeanor.

"Did you like it inside of my room?" He raised an eyebrow.

"You listen to me, you little-"

"No, water nymph, you listen to me." Something snapped inside of Abe as he stepped toward me with such quickness I didn't see him move. The next thing I knew, my back was against the wooden siding as Abe pinned me to the wall.

"Get off!" I shouted, but he held me in place. The feeling of his heat against mine sent a spark through my body. I could feel his powers, a small hint of magic permeating from his skin.

"Don't you think I want to tell you everything? I literally can't. You don't understand that, do you? You don't have a clue what is happening around you. You are so terrified of the darkness but you can't see that you've already let it inside. It's in you. It's in me. It's in Mit, your sister and those girls you've become so friendly with." Intensity burned in his dilated pupils. "He will return and there's nothing you can do to stop it."

"Who?"

"You don't know. That's the worst part."

"Why did you kill the rabbit?" I demanded once more, not planning to ask him again so politely.

"A life for a life."

"What does that mean?"

"Not all magic is black and white, Whitney. You are playing with consequences that your worst nightmares would run from. You're clueless. A child with a magician's book."

"Get off of me before I hurt you." I threatened.

"Oh, Whitney," Abe finally let go of my arms. "You can't hurt me when I'm as good as dead."

I shoved him off of me, careful not to let my powers show as my emotions flared, but I only had so much self-control. I cocked my arm back and swung as hard as I could, catching him on the side of his jaw. Abe jumped back with wide eyes, rubbing where I had struck.

"Stay the fuck away from my family." I retreated to the safety of my home with boiling blood and throbbing knuckles.

"You hit him?" Dmitri's voice echoed across the field.

"He had it coming," I answered, stepping onto the porch.

"He absolutely did not!" Dmitri argued.

I turned to my brother. "He put his hands on me, Mit. I saw how he acts when it's just the two of you but he won't push his boundaries with me."

"What did he say?" Dmitri followed me into the house.

As I turned to answer, Rayn came in through the front door. She slowly closed it behind her, watching Dmitri and I storm into the kitchen. "You two okay? I saw you coming back from next door."

"No," I answered, grabbing my bag to retrieve the note left in my locker at work.

"What does it mean?" Rayn asked after I handed it to her.

"I don't know, but someone knows about us." I paced back and forth across the living room, rubbing my sore hand. I was too riled up to sit. "Someone is warning us."

"I wouldn't say they *know* about us." Rayn tilted her head to the side, reading over the note again.

"Rayn, they know about the shadows. They know enough." My pulse coursed through me like a raging river. "Dmitri, you're done with Abe Roberts and I mean it this time."

Rayn furrowed her brow. "What happened over there?"

"I confronted him and he..." I paused. "He told me some confusing things. I punched him in the face."

"Oh shit." Rayn sat on the edge of the couch. "What did he say?"

I took in a deep breath attempting to calm myself. "My head is spinning. Okay, he said that we already let the darkness in and that he will return."

"Why doesn't he enlighten us then?" Rayn asked, picking at her nails. The red paint flaked off around the edges. "Abe will return?"

"No, he was talking about someone else. He said he wants to help us but he can't." Rayn scoffed. "Bullshit."

"He's telling you the same thing he's told me." Dmitri jumped in. "He's been vague so far but I don't think he can go into detail. It's like someone is preventing him from giving us anything useful."

"Like they threatened him?" Rayn asked.

Sadness took over Dmitri's gaze. "Like they put a spell on him."

"When I asked why he killed the rabbit, he said a life for a life but wouldn't explain."

"A life for a life," Dmitri repeated. "He wished he could help but can't."

"Yeah, I heard," Rayn replied, annoyed.

"Shut up. I think he did that ritual to try and protect us. A life for a life." Dmitri explained.

"Give me the paper in your pocket." I ordered, putting out my hand toward Dmitri.

He glared down at my palm like I was holding a pile of shit as he reached into his pocket. He tossed the paper at me. "I already said I wasn't planning to hide this from you."

"Don't be an ass." I picked up the paper off the floor and unfolded it.

The page was ripped out of a book. It was stained on the corner but didn't look nearly as old as the pages from the spellbook the girls and I had found.

"Opening portals?" I looked up at Mit after skimming the page.

"He didn't give any details, just handed it to me and said it was important," Dmitri replied.

"A portal like the one in the meadow?" Rayn jumped up from the couch. "The one Mit fell through?"

Dmitri nodded. "I think so."

"How would he know about the portal in the meadow? Or that we knew anything about it?" I questioned aloud, watching my brother's reaction carefully.

He shrugged. "I don't know what you want me to say, Whit. I don't have the answers, but I do believe Abe's heart is in the right place."

"He may have good intentions but it doesn't make him any less of a creep," I mumbled, trying not to think about how he shoved me against the side of his house.

"Good intentions," Rayn huffed, pulling her phone out of her pocket to check the time. "Did you send me something?"

"Oh yeah," I had nearly forgotten. "Ashley sent me a picture of you and Emma from the bonfire. It's super cute."

"Aw, she's nice. I like Emma." Rayn opened the photo and smiled at the screen. She turned the phone around and showed the picture to Dmitri.

As Dmitri looked at the picture, his face fell and his eyes widened with shock. A faint gasp got caught in my chest and he quickly looked away.

"What's wrong?" Rayn asked, looking at her phone screen again to see if they were looking at the same thing.

"Um..." Dmitri gulped, his voice small. "I don't want you around that girl."

"Emma? How do you know her?" I questioned, tilting my head in confusion.

"Because she was at the lake," he finally admitted. "When I fell in."

"I thought you couldn't remember anything from the lake," Rayn pushed.

"The dark eyes," he whispered. "Her eyes."

"Are you sure it was Emma? She's super sweet." Rayn defended, locking her phone and sliding it back into her pocket.

Dmitri confirmed. "She was there."

"Wait, it couldn't have been Emma." I remembered a conversation from the bonfire. "Bryan told me she lives in Falcon Bay during the week for college, she's only here on the weekends."

"Well I saw her, or someone who looked like her," Dmitri replied.

Someone who looked like her. Chilling dark brown eyes surfaced in my memory and sent a chill up my spine. "Serenity Drake," I announced.

"Who?"

"Emma's twin sister. I saw her at the bonfire when I was with Bryan. She made my skin crawl." I rubbed my arms. "She and Emma have the same eyes but hers are heavy. She has the same brand on her arm that Abe does."

"You must have seen her sister, then." Rayn turned back to Dmitri. "Do you remember anything else?"

Dmitri looked across the room, focusing on a spot on the wall. "No."

"Serenity and Abe must know each other then if they have the same mark. Do you think Abe knows about the spellbook?" Rayn asked.

"He made some comment about how I was a child with a magician's book, so yeah I think so." I rubbed my eyes. The pounding in my head refused to go away. "He's been blatantly stalking us, after all."

"I have homework." Dmitri snapped, heading to his room. "Neither of you are listening to me anyway."

"Mit, I hear you." I kept my voice calm as he stopped at the curtain. "But if Abe has anything to do with Serenity, we need to be careful. She gives off a bad vibe."

"And who introduced you to Serenity in the first place?" Dmitri crossed his arms.

I leaned back. "What are you implying?"

"Just saying I think it's odd that you aren't suspicious of this guy you like having something to do with Serenity but when it's Abe, I have to write him off."

"Dmitri, Bryan doesn't have that brand like Abe does."

"Doesn't mean he's squeaky clean either." Dmitri closed the curtain before I could reply.

"Okay..." Rayn picked up the spellbook and held it to her chest. "Do you want to read with me?"

"In a bit, I have something to do real quick." I reached for my cell phone in my pocket and Rayn saw right through me.

She smiled. "Off to call your boyfriend?"

"He is not my boyfriend."

"Do you think Mit has a point? If Serenity had that brand and was at the lake with him, and her sister is Bryan's best friend...I don't know, Whit. We don't know any of these people very well."

"Bryan isn't involved in all of this," I answered confidently.

"I hope not."

There was no way Bryan was caught up in the mystery of that brand on Serenity and Abe. Not with the way he acted and spoke to Serenity at the bonfire. I liked Bryan, of course, but there was no telling how long this thing between us could last. It was a nice distraction, but a temporary one. One of the many things I learned from my mother was that someone with powers like ours had two options romantically: live a double life or expose themselves and be left. Neither was an option, so I lived without attachment.

I left Rayn and retreated to the privacy of my bedroom. Bryan didn't pick up until I was sure my call would go to voicemail. When he answered he didn't sound as happy to talk to me as he did earlier.

"Hello?" he answered.

"Hey, I'm sorry about earlier. I was distracted but I'm so happy you called."

"Really?" Bryan's voice softened.

"Of course. You're an Aquarius moon by the way. I was right about the air sign."

Bryan chuckled. "So what exactly does that mean?"

"Let me bring up the chart I found, I'll read it to you." I laid down on my bed and took solace in the only normalcy I had felt in months.

Even after a relaxing conversation with Bryan, I still couldn't fall asleep to save my life. Tossing and turning for what felt like hours resulted in going out to the kitchen for a glass of water. I didn't need to go to the kitchen for water, but I figured getting up and walking around might help settle the mess in my head.

I was halfway through a small cup of ice water when the door from the kitchen leading to the back porch opened, sending me into defensive mode. My hand flew up on instinct, preparing to attack whoever was breaking into our home when Dmitri walked into the kitchen.

"You scared the shit out of me, Mit." My hand rested over my chest to still my panicked heart. "What are you doing outside? It's past midnight."

"Oh," Mit hurried into the house and closed the door gently behind him. "I, uh, stepped outside for a minute."

"Why?" I set my cup down on the counter, looking my brother up and down. Even in the darkness of the kitchen, his nose and cheeks were visibly red from the chilly air. The t-shirt he was in earlier was covered by a gray zip-up hoodie I had never seen him wear before.

"Because sometimes I need to be alone, okay, Whitney?" Dmitri huffed and shoved around me, heading toward his makeshift bedroom before I could get in another word, knowing good and well I couldn't shout after him without waking Rayn.

Out of pure curiosity, I slipped out onto the back porch and peered into the darkness, looking for any clues as to what was going on with my brother. Everything outside looked perfectly normal, settling my nerves. Taking one look over at the house next door before I went inside, my gaze stopped at Abe's bedroom window across the field. Dmitri wasn't naive, but I couldn't tell if his faith in Abe was reliable. Either way, Rayn had a point. We didn't truly know who we could trust in this town.

CHAPTER TWELVE
FAILED ATTEMPTS

When I arrived at the meadow the next evening, Rayn, Rose, and Brooke were already waiting, slowly reading over the pages of the spellbook together, analyzing every word.

"Have you been here long?" I asked as I approached them.

"Maybe fifteen minutes," Brooke answered, her eyes glued to the pages in front of her.

"I don't know where Lauren is," I replied, looking around the meadow. The setting sun shone through tree branches in bright rays like it was reaching down to give us a helping hand. We could definitely use it.

"She's slithering her way over." Rose nodded behind me.

I turned my head, and sure enough, there was Lauren dragging her feet. Of course she was the last to show. I honestly didn't care what mood she was in, at least she showed up. Lauren Thaner might be more curious about our abilities than she led on.

"Well, where do we start?" Rayn asked, rubbing her warm hands together in anticipation.

"I found a potion in here that I would like to try first," Rose said, her legs crossed underneath her as she sat on the forest floor. "It's an ointment that is supposed to permanently get rid of scars."

"Scars?" Rayn scrunched her face. "Can't you go pick that up at a pharmacy?"

"This is different. This gets rid of them instantly. It looks simple and I think it would be a good first attempt," Rose explained. "But if you have any suggestions, feel free."

"Did you bring everything we need?" I asked.

"I've got it covered." Rose pulled her backpack to her side and unzipped the large pocket, revealing a pile of various small bottles and vegetables.

"So what do you need me for?" Lauren asked, directing her question to all of us.

"It says right here that a full generation will produce a more powerful brew, plus it'll probably be a lot quicker," Brooke explained, tilting the book toward Lauren.

"Where do we start?" I asked, sitting down in the grass next to Brooke. The ground below me was damp but I didn't mind, I found the moisture comforting. It gave me the confidence to tackle our first potion head on.

"Soak the hazelnut and onion in the base oil until it boils gently. After the mixture has boiled, add small branches of sandalwood and infuse with positive, healing energies. Pour into a vial and apply small amounts of oil to damaged tissue or skin." Brooke looked over at Rayn as she read aloud.

"Positive and healing energies?" Lauren questioned.

"Positive vibes, I guess?" Brooke shrugged her shoulders.

"Thoughts and prayers," I chuckled. "Look, Ray, it has a little drawing of a pyro controlling the heat of a big cauldron."

"You know, the more we use our elemental powers while we're making this, the more powerful it might end up being," Rose suggested, getting up on her knees with excitement. She began to arrange the potion ingredients she pulled from her backpack.

"I could light a small fire, easily." Rayn smiled, kneeling beside me with her hands on her knees.

"How is wood used in po-" Lauren cut herself off. "These recipes, if they're liquid?" She remained standing, towering over all of us as she rubbed her arms.

"Burned to charcoal with herbs, and then the ashes are added into the oil or water. Some of them also have a sweet fragrance. Some potions say to put specific branches into the spell and let it soak overnight," Rose described. "I think it depends on what you're doing."

Someone had done her homework.

"Let's get started, then," I replied, taking in a deep, anticipated breath.

Rose pulled out a small cooking pot from her bag and rested it on the earth in front of us along with a small vial of hazelnut oil and an onion. I was intrigued to see how adding them together could create something that would make a scar disappear.

Anxiety pumped through my body as Brooke set the book down on the grass. Rose handed Rayn the onion and a small knife. My sister peeled the onion and cut it into quarters, quickly handing the pieces to Rose. Rayn squeezed her watering eyes tightly from the sharp aroma of the onion.

"It says to set three candles around the pot while the hazelnut and onion boil together. There's a picture of it, too." Brooke turned the book so we all could look at the page.

The hand-drawn picture showed a small black cauldron with a large spoon and the ingredients inside like a stew. The candles were placed around the cauldron in an inverted triangle.

"This was all I had at my house so it will have to do." Rose lay a white candle alongside two light blue ones.

"I don't think the candle colors matter much," I replied.

"You'd be surprised," Rose answered. "Light the candles from top left to top right and the bottom one last. It says for everyone to circle it and infuse it with positive, healing energies. That must be where it gets the power from, our powers."

Lauren hesitated as usual, dragging her feet across the grass. We arranged ourselves to face the empty pot, and Brooke placed the candles around the saucepan like the book had instructed. My heart pounded intensely behind my rib cage.

"Okay, positive and healing energies into the potion," Rose replied, leaning forward to read over the page of the book. Double-checking. Triple checking that we were actually doing it right before she poured the base oil into the pot.

"For the love of god, stop calling it that," Lauren said, holding onto her stomach.

"Like it or not, this is magic. We are magic users. Witches. Mages. Sorcerers. Whatever you want to call it, that is what we are. That is what you are." Rose huffed in irritation.

"She's right, Lauren," Brooke nodded and reached out to touch Lauren's arm in comfort. "I can think of much worse things than magic."

"And I can think of much better," Lauren mumbled.

"Close your eyes and think about the summer breeze," I told her gently.

Lauren didn't reply, but she closed her eyes and nodded.

"Whenever you're ready, Rayn. Top left, top right, bottom." Rose replied with a nervous tone. "Once the candles are lit, I'll add the hazelnut and onion. Once Rayn gets the mixture boiling, we'll close our eyes and try this positive energy thing."

"And after that?" Brooke asked, leaning forward.

"Let's cross that bridge when we get to it," I mumbled. My nerves were bound up like a triple knotted shoelace.

"How will we know it worked?" Rayn asked, her hands twitching with anticipation.

"It says here that the color of the potion will resemble the sunrise," Rose read from the book.

"Let's do it." My sister said, cracking her knuckles.

Rayn's powers flared as she lit the three candles one by one, the top left, the top right, and finally the bottom candle. The flames danced around the wicks in the light breeze and the presence of Rayn's powers faded quickly. I kept my eyes on the three little fires as Rose poured olive oil into the saucepan, followed by six drops of hazelnut and the large chunks of onion.

Carefully, Rayn lit a small fire underneath the saucepan, flames grew around the bottom. My sister's power didn't fade this time as she kept the fire under control. Brooke took in a deep breath, hypnotized by the mixture as she waited for the brew to bubble.

I did my best to release all the negativity and doubt I had about what we were doing. I tried to focus on the good things. The fact that we had found each other and were beginning to find out the truth about us. This is what Rayn and I had been longing for.

I looked around the circle at the others, all eyes were on the oil waiting to see what would happen next. My heart skipped and a cold chill ran through my body as the first bubble appeared in the pan. It was small, and made a little pop as it disappeared but the ones that followed grew larger and became more frequent. No one had to say a word, we closed our eyes and took a collective deep breath.

Positive and healing energies. I thought about different places around Rifton like the coffee shop or the tall pine trees, but I felt nothing. Not even the beautiful forest and blue waters of that bittersweet lake Dmitri fell into were positive or healing. I let my mind wander. Driving down the curvy route to Pines Row. Bright green lily pads floating in a pond. Waves crashing on the shore. Of course.

I was mentally transported. The ocean breeze blew back my hair, dampening my clothes with mist. The smell of salt overpowered the scent of hazelnut and onion. The sand course against my skin. The majestic waves of the ocean came in toward me and then retreated only to charge forward against the sand once more. Persistent. I needed to be more like those waves. I watched the waves go back and forth in my head, hearing the splash and roaring noise they made. I grew calm and collected, nearly forgetting I was in the forest at all.

As I heard someone take in a sharp breath, my eyes opened, blinking at the simmering hazelnut and onion mixture. Leaning forward, I examined the contents of the pot. The chunks of onion floated and bobbed but the color of the mixture had changed to a shade of dark brown, almost like the contents had turned to mud.

Potions: 1. Elementals: 0.

"That doesn't look like a sunrise," Rayn said, glaring at the pot before she extinguished her fire. "What did we do wrong?"

Brooke's shoulders fell. "I don't get it. We followed the directions verbatim."

"Well, this was a learning experience. Lauren, would you mind blowing out the candles?" Rose asked politely.

Lauren met Rose's gaze but didn't return the pleasantries. Lauren bit the slide of her mouth, but she lifted her hand regardless and barely waved her fingers. The flames extinguished in a single puff.

"What should we do with this?" Rayn motioned toward the sludge in the pot.

"Dump it, I guess. Accept our failure and move on." Rose sighed before she set the book in her lap to try and see where we went wrong.

Rayn carried the contents of the pot to a nearby tree and tipped it over. The thick, brown sludge slid out and splattered in the dirt. The mixture quickly hardened against the air and solidified. She sighed in irritation, clearly frustrated by our failure. We would have been foolish to think everything would have gone perfectly on the first try.

"I got a job at Dragonfly Mystic downtown. They have all kinds of books and herbs and stuff. We should see if there's anything there we could use," Rayn suggested.

"Wait, are you serious?" Rose's back straightened. "You work at Dragonfly Mystic?"

"Yeah. I run the cash register," Rayn answered. "Have you been there?"

"No, I typically avoid it," Rose said.

"Why?" I asked.

"We aren't the only witches in Rifton, and I've made an effort to lay low," Rose explained. "This town has always attracted...an interesting crowd."

"You guys should come visit me next time I'm working. It couldn't hurt to at least see what they have since it's the only place in town like it," Rayn offered.

I glanced over at Brooke, who had remained silent, much to my surprise. She sat with the book in her lap, her eyes wide as she read through one of the pages.

"Find anything interesting, Brooke?" I asked curiously.

"Apparently, for years, witches had to use potions to heal one another, but this spirit user, Gabriel, could heal others with only his magic, without using spells or any kind of plant," Brooke explained, squinting as she read. "Gabriel believed he was powerful enough to mend the soul itself. I wonder if we could learn to do something like that."

"That sounds like it requires a lot of energy and practice," Rose commented, leaning over to see for herself. "We have a long way before we get there."

"Yeah but with all of us maybe it wouldn't be that bad." Brooke smiled optimistically. "This entire section was written by Gabriel Hartford. If he can do this all by himself, I can too."

I could tell that Brooke wanted so badly to find something that connected herself to the rest of us besides the jewelry. Her talent for seeing the dead didn't exactly fit in with what the rest of us could do and I knew she wanted a sense of belonging. The amethyst clipped around her ankle was enough for me.

"We shouldn't be trying to do things like that," Lauren said with her hands in her pockets. "We shouldn't do anything unnatural."

"And lighting a tree on fire and blowing its ashes into the wind with magic wasn't unnatural?" Rose asked, looking at Lauren with a cocked eyebrow.

"And then growing it back again with more magic," Rayn added in with a smirk. "People can't control things like we do."

"But those things end up happening anyway. That's all part of a natural cycle." Lauren argued, glancing behind us quickly.

"Isn't healing people a good thing?" Brooke asked, leaning over the book.

Lauren's teeth clenched in her jaw. "It is, but it should be done by doctors and surgeons, not people who are using some kind of voodoo in an old book they found in a grave. We aren't professionals, we have no training. What if we kill someone instead? Then we'd be murderers *and* freaks."

"You must not know what voodoo is," Rose mumbled.

"What do you think went wrong with the spell?" I asked, changing the subject. "We shouldn't start something new until we know what went wrong this time so we don't repeat the same mistakes."

"We can try again if you want." Brooke flipped to the next page in the book. "I want to look into this healing with your hands. They call it spirit healing. This Gabriel guy was a genius."

"Spirit healing. See, B, you're just as much part of this as the rest of us." Rose smiled and nudged Brooke with her elbow.

"I have a bad feeling." Lauren finally broke her silence as she scanned the meadow.

"Fine, be dead weight," Rose snapped. "But if you're going to bring your negative energy here and ruin our spells then don't come back."

"Rose, knock it off. Lauren, please, you know we need all of us to figure this out," Rayn intervened, turning to face her.

"If she isn't going to try then why does it matter if she's here or not?" Rose threw her hand into the air.

"Because there are five gems for a reason. Five elements for a reason. She's one of us." I argued back sternly.

"Stop talking about me like I'm not here!" Lauren shouted. "You think you have it all figured out, don't you? You think you can corral us all together and everything you want will fall into your lap?"

"We never said that." I defended against Lauren's outburst.

"You don't have to, it's written all over your smug face."

"Stop talking shit to my sister before I hurt you." Rayn threatened through her teeth.

"Knock it off!" Brooke's small voice boomed against the forest. "Whether we like each other or not, we are in this together. We're a generation!"

Lauren bit her bottom lip and looked over her shoulder.

"What a shit," Rose mumbled, shaking her head.

Can we find another air witch? Rayn glared up at Lauren.

I don't think there's a return policy. I sighed in defeat.

Lauren looked nervously over her shoulder for the fifth time.

"What do you keep looking for?" I called her out, my stomach churned watching Lauren survey the forest.

"I...I can feel someone watching us right now, and I can't pinpoint who it is for the life of me." Her face paled as she spoke.

My heart dropped into my stomach.

"And you're just now telling us?" Rose asked sharply.

"I just now sensed it." Lauren defended herself.

"How can you tell?" I raised an eyebrow and looked around myself, but didn't see anyone watching us.

"I...I can tell when someone is following me...or watching me. I can't explain how it happens. I'm not a damn scientist." Lauren rubbed her face. "Call it intuition."

"We need to get out of here," Rose's voice shook as she spoke.

"Don't look so obvious. We'll go home and everything will be okay." Rayn had a skill with talking someone down, especially me. It wasn't the words she was saying, it was the calming look in her eyes. One of the many traits she picked up from our mother.

"I am staying calm. I'm concerned someone followed us here," I replied, my heart rate speeding up.

Snap.

A branch broke in the distance from something much heavier than a squirrel putting its weight on it. My spine turned to ice and spread across my body.

"What was that?" Brooke spun toward the noise.

Leaves rustled, followed by more heavy footsteps. It took a moment to recognize him with a hooded jacket, but the hints of copper hair not covered by fabric gave him away.

The moment I locked eyes with Abe Roberts, fear and panic swept across his face. He had been caught red-handed.

I panicked, but not for my safety. I felt responsible for protecting my group. I had to be persistent like the ocean waves. Without thinking twice, I took off running across the meadow.

"Whitney!" Rayn's voice echoed behind me but I didn't stop. I didn't take my eyes off of Abe. He turned and bolted once he saw me coming and I had to analyze which way he was going to retreat. If this guy had enough nerve to follow us into the middle of the woods, he might as well have the nerve to face us.

"Whitney!"

Abe was running fast, sliding his way past branches and around thick tree trunks. I pushed through the brush to chase after him without a care for the branches that hit me in the face or scratched against my arms. All I cared about was getting to Abe. It may not have been the best approach, but at this point, I was acting purely on impulse.

I realized how much time Abe must have spent in the forest when he knew to take a sharp left back toward the main trail. I followed, attempting to keep sight of him. Abe slowed down as he reached a large trunk of a pine that had fallen in the pathway. There wasn't anywhere else to keep running.

As he turned around, he put his hands up as if he was trying to calm me down. Fear glimmered in his eyes as if I was a wild animal. I pushed myself to speed toward him but each step I took became more difficult. As if the dirt turned to quicksand, sticking to my shoes, enabling me from going on any further.

I put my hands up as well, feeling the energy he emitted toward me.

"Abe, stop!" My voice cracked.

"What the hell is wrong with you?" Rayn exclaimed as she ran up, the others close behind.

Once reinforcements arrived, whatever Abe was doing ended abruptly. I could move my body again but my muscles ached. My legs gave out from underneath me and I hit the ground.

"What do you want?" Rayn called out at Abe.

Abe remained silent with nothing but intensity in his eyes before he turned and leaped over the fallen tree trunk.

"Stop him!" I tried to chase after him but my legs wouldn't carry me. I couldn't understand why my sister and the other girls weren't running after Abe.

"Whit, what the hell," Rayn demanded, reaching down to help me up off the dirt. "Rule number four is there because of this kind of shit! Don't be reckless! Are you trying to get yourself killed?"

"He was following us. He knows about us. We need to go after him!" I didn't mean to raise my voice, but this was urgent. More urgent than my current condition.

"We need to get home, Whit." Rose brushed some dirt from the back of my shirt.

"Don't any of you care that we were being followed?" I shouted.

"Of course," piped Brooke. "And I'd feel a lot better if we left."

"But something is going on with Abe..."

"Whitney...I know. We'll talk about it on the way home, 'kay? Are your legs alright?" Rayn put her arm around my waist to help stabilize me.

They treated me like a child who acted out. I was the oldest one here. I felt responsible for the four souls I brought with me, but here I was on the ground getting picked up by my younger sister with the other girls trying not to look at me like I was mentally insane.

"Sis?"

"I'm fine, really. I'm fine. I'm not broken," I said in frustration.

"The five of us being together like this is going to attract lots of different attention, good and bad," Rose replied, looking at me with heavy eyes. "B, that guy is in your grade, isn't he?"

"He is. We have English together. He's quiet. I honestly never paid him much attention," Brooke answered.

"You never saw the weird brand on his wrist?" I asked.

"No." Brooke shook her head. "He usually wears long sleeve shirts to school. I had no idea he was a witch."

Lauren drove herself home, leaving the forest as quickly as she could. I didn't blame her. I wish I could have done the same to get back home before Abe to wait for his arrival and demand further answers. Rose and Brooke didn't leave until I had given them all the information I had on Abe Roberts. I told them about the interaction at the mini-mart, the symbol similar to ours engraved into his skin, and the dark ritual he performed with the rabbit. All the weird things he said the last time I spoke to him.

"I saw the symbol on someone else," I replied, remembering the night of the bonfire. "Serenity Drake."

"How do you know Serenity Drake?" Rose inquired curiously.

"I don't. A coworker took us to a party and she was there. I only asked about her name when I saw the same symbol on her wrist that Abe has. They're connected somehow."

"We'll figure this out, Whitney. We have to." Rayn smiled softly.

"Wait, you've been hanging out with Ashley outside of work?" Rose wasn't ready to drop the subject.

I hesitated. "Yeah."

"You know Bryan is my brother, right?"

"I said I was hanging out with Ashley." I diverted, but Rose wasn't having it.

"If you've been spending time with Ashley, you've been around my brother."

"And?"

"So don't."

"Don't be friends with Ashley?"

"Whitney, I'm serious. Don't get involved with my brother."

My knees began to tremble with nerves. "Who said I was?"

"I saw you looking at his pictures at my house the night we found the book." Rose bit at her lip as she shifted her weight. "Bryan doesn't know about my powers. He doesn't know any of this exists, and I've worked hard to keep it that way. I'm asking you as a friend, stay away from him."

I tried not to look at Rayn, especially since she had grown extra quiet and started digging into the ground with the toe of her boot. I may not have been seeing Bryan in person but I had been texting him daily and as much as I hated admitting it, reading his messages had become the best part of my day.

"Whitney, I'm serious."

"Okay, Rose, I hear you. I hear you, okay?"

"Thank you."

I sighed and looked up into the darkening night sky. There was a bright ring forming around the rising moon. I knew in my bones that it was a warning of trouble.

Chapter Thirteen
Oils, Incense, and Literature

Dragonfly Mystic was nestled between an old camera store and a little boutique for unique clothing and accessories. There wasn't much traffic on the road, but there were a lot of people walking or riding their bikes.

The sign in front of the shop was all black with silver and purple lettering. A large fairy in a purple dress with a dragonfly on the tip of her finger sat on top of the sign. The words oils, incense, and literature hung from three smaller signs hanging below the store's name. The windows were displayed with various books about inner energy and connecting to nature through meditation and ritual. Rose opened the door as the jingle of a bell echoed through the shop.

The only two customers in the store were both females, dressed in pastel-colored clothing with name brands on their bags. They were particularly interested in the candle section, picking up each candle individually to smell and observe it.

Rayn waved at us from the register, her hand high in the air. She was beaming, excited to show off her new job. As much as I wanted her and Dmitri to focus on school, they both knew my paycheck wasn't going to support all three of us. I hated admitting that I needed their help financially, but maybe it was for the better. Maybe it was good that they had other things to focus on too.

"What do you think?" I asked Rose quietly.

She was in awe, bright-eyed like a child in a toy store. Shelves of various crystals and homemade soaps lined the back walls. A wooden staircase led up to the second story with a big red arrow and a sign that read 'The Library'.

"There's a lot here. Oh, look, eucalyptus oil. We could use some of that for sure." Rose shot off across the store.

I followed her to a wooden shelf with little bottles of oils and a few baskets of dried herbs. I recognized sage and rosemary instantly. Rose went through the small bottles, examining the different labels. She put most of them back but kept five in her hand. At the angle she was holding them, I was able to read labels for eucalyptus, sandalwood, and lavender.

Mom would have loved this store. Whenever we traveled anywhere and she found a place like this, she would pull the car over immediately. You could feel her demeanor lighten, her aura brighten. She knew exactly what every gem was, what they could be used for, and the energies they possessed. No wonder Rayn wanted to work here so badly.

Rose held her emerald pendant in her hand, running her fingers along the edges as she browsed baskets of dried herbs on the neighboring shelf.

"Did you really find it in an antique store?" I asked.

She noticed my eyes on the emerald and dropped it against her chest. "I didn't lie about how I found it."

"Okay." I picked up a bundle of dried sage and inhaled deeply. "We still have to piece together where the jewelry came from."

"I didn't show it to anyone for a long time, especially after the color changed. I put it in my pocket and walked away." Rose added a bunch of rosemary to her pile. "I've never stolen anything before, but I knew it was meant for me."

"Here in town?"

Rose nodded.

"We should go back there. See if they have old records and trace back–"

"Whitney," Rose stopped me. "I already did that. The woman who sold it to the shop was named Laura Smith. Do you have any idea how many Laura Smiths there are?" She sighed in frustration. "Besides, the antique shop is closed now, replaced with a florist."

"Hey!" Rayn came up behind us, practically glowing. "Can I help you find anything?"

"Let's look at the library. There might be something useful up there." Rose nodded upstairs.

"Free from the register?" I asked my sister as we crossed the room.

"Yep, I'm officially clocked out for the day."

We climbed up the rickety wooden stairway through the square hole in the ceiling and emerged into the attic library. There were books from floor to ceiling. Every shelf on the wall was full, with three additional large bookcases that stood in the middle of the room. There were encyclopedias of witchcraft and memoirs and how-to books for meditation and herbs. It smelled incredible, like paper and ink.

"Wow." I breathed, taking it all in.

"I could live up here," Rose replied. She was on her knees in front of the bookshelf with a hardback in her hands, flipping through the pages. "Guys, look at this."

"Find something good?" Rayn asked, kneeling down next to her. Rose tilted the book toward us.

The Shadow Realm.

"Ever heard of this?" Rose asked, running her fingers along the title.

"No, have you?"

Rose shook her head. "I'll buy it. Maybe this will give us some answers."

"Good idea, Rose." I headed down the next row of books, running my fingers along the spines.

"Oh, Whit, before I forget. Can I borrow the car tonight?" Rayn asked.

"Sure. Where are you going?" I inquired.

"Tom is taking me to a movie." Rayn blushed and straightened her slender shoulders.

"And he can't pick you up?"

"Please, Whit."

"Okay, have fun."

"Thank you! You really are the best sister." Rayn squeezed my hand before she lost herself in a shelf dedicated to reading auras.

I scanned the shelves, waiting to see if something would jump out at me as well. As I turned around to look at the shelves behind me, I noticed a little golden star imprinted on the spine of a hardcover book, a few inches thick. Your Soul and the Cosmos. The book was missing its dust jacket, and a golden indentation of the solar system decorated the cover. The binding was rough as I ran my finger over the small golden star. I tucked the book in my arm and kept browsing down the rows.

"Oh...come look at this." Rose's voice came from the other side of the library.

Rayn and I rushed to her side to see what she had found. At first, the shelves in front of us appeared to be another section of books until I took a closer look at the titles. Hexes and curses. Blood magic. Sacrificial rituals. Abe Roberts popped into my head instantly.

"Ew," Rayn muttered under her breath, scrunching her face.

Rose sighed and backed away from the books. "Not everything in magic is auras and crystals."

A while later Rose, Rayn, and I left the library after each of us found at least one book. If I had more money in the bank I would have blown my entire paycheck in this place, but I wanted to be inconspicuous. Rayn was the first one down the stairs, skipping the bottom step when she saw Tom standing at the register speaking with an older woman.

"Tom!" Rayn called him over.

A smile spread across his face. "Hey! Off work already? I came to bring my aunt something but was hoping I'd catch you before you left. Hi, Whitney."

"Hi, Tom." I greeted warmly.

I had reached the bottom of the stairs when Rose gasped behind me.

"Ow." Rose held up her hand.

"You okay?" Rayn asked, turning around on her heel.

"Just a cut." Rose climbed the rest of the way down and tended to her hand. A small gash on the edge of her palm had already started bleeding. Rose reached into her bag for a napkin and put pressure on the cut. The railing leading up to the Library was stained with red droplets.

"Is it bad?" I asked.

"I'm fine, really. I have a band-aid." Rose peeled the red-stained napkin from her hand.

"Let me get something to clean that up." Tom headed toward the counter and returned with a wet towel and a bottle of cleaner. He immediately got to work as Rose secured her bandage. "I'm sorry you got hurt, I'll make sure my aunt knows that this railing needs to be fixed."

"Oh, thanks." Rose wiggled her fingers.

"I'm glad you're okay, Rose. Anything else we need?" I asked, looking around the rest of the shop.

Rose shook her head. "Not today."

Rayn secured a small chain across the entryway of the stairs with a 'closed' sign attached. She turned to Tom. "We were the only ones up there."

"Okay, I'll finish this up since you're already clocked out. Call me later?"

"Of course." Rayn gave him a quick kiss before we took our purchases to the registers. "That was so nice of Tom to help out like that. He's a good one."

I gave her a quick smile before I glanced back at Tom who had finished cleaning up and took the soiled towel to a back room. One of Rayn's coworkers rang us up as I dug around in my bag for some cash. Luckily we were able to use Ray's employee discount.

"I wonder if Mom ever mentioned this place." Rayn said, pulling the journal from her bag once we were back in the car.

Before I could tell her to put it away or ask why she was carrying it around in the first place, Rose spoke up from the backseat. "What's that?"

"Our Mom's journal. We found it when we were unpacking boxes. It's almost like she meant for us to find it." Rayn explained, though I didn't exactly agree with her. "She passed away a few months ago."

I didn't think Mom intended for us to find it at all. I think she died suddenly and didn't think to hide it. I think Dmitri didn't have the heart to shuffle through things when he packed up her desk, so he tossed it all in a box to be dealt with later.

"Oh," Rose's voice fell. "I'm sorry to hear that. Why would Dragonfly be in her journal."

"She grew up in Rifton," Rayn answered. "And since she was a witch too, I'm assuming this place was still around when she was here. She didn't have elemental powers like us, but she could levitate stuff and did little spells around the house all the time."

My sister opened the journal to a random page, much farther back than I had read. Her eyes skimmed over the first few sentences on the page and nearly dropped the book onto the floorboards of the car.

"What?" I asked, my pulse beginning to quicken.

"Uhm," Rayn mumbled, losing the ability to form proper sentences.

Rose leaned forward over the center console. "Read it."

The talisman has been safely delivered to the young girl in Rifton. I knew the moment I saw it. The gray hue of the gem, the chain that matches the jewelry Whitney and Rayn brought with them. I wonder how long it had been singing to her, longing to be reconnected with its owner. It's nothing short of a miracle that Mia and I were able to find her. She's only a child, four years younger than Whitney. She must be the youngest in the generation. I should have known the others would have ended up in Rifton. It makes sense. Those woods are no stranger to magic. I hope she's safe. I hope the Renati have yet to discover her. I know Mia is there and that is what allows me to sleep at night. We may have failed before but we won't make that mistake again.

My vision blurred for a split second and I swore I was going to pass out. Instinctively, I reached for the water bottle I'd left in the cupholder. There was no way.

"No," I muttered aloud. "She wouldn't."

"Hold on, hold on. You're telling me your mother is the one who sent Brooke her amethyst?" Rose tightened her grip on the back of Rayn's seat. "And you had no idea? That's too much of a coincidence."

"Do we look like we knew this was a thing?" Rayn's head snapped over her shoulder. "I feel sick."

"How did-" I paused, taking another drink from my water bottle. "How did Mom find it, let alone know Brooke was the one to send it to?"

"Who's Mia?" Rose asked.

"I don't know, but we're going to find out," Rayn announced. "Hopefully she's still in Rifton."

"You genuinely had no idea?" Rose still didn't believe us. I couldn't say that I blamed her. It seemed like the type of thing Mom would have told us about but the more we read into this journal, the more I realized how little I truly knew the woman who raised me as her own.

"I swear, we had no idea."

Rose looked back and forth between Rayn and I before settling back into her seat. "Brooke deserves to know."

"Absolutely she does." I started the engine and pulled out of the parking space. "And we're going to tell her once we actually have something for her."

"Once you have something?" Rose questioned, fire rising in her voice. "You literally found out who delivered her bracelet to her."

"Yeah, but we don't know who Mia is or how my mom found the bracelet. How they even knew to give it to Brooke. I don't want to keep this from her, I want to have more information before we tell her."

"I disagree."

"Let us at least finish reading through this journal. If that's all the info we have to go off of, then fine but I want to look into this first."

"Mom hid so much from us," Rayn muttered. "It's like she didn't trust us."

I sighed, afraid she was right. "She was trying to protect us."

"From what?" Rayn's head snapped to look at me.

"The Renati apparently. Who are they?" Rose asked.

I shook my head, "I don't know, but we're-"

"Yeah, we'll figure it out." Rayn huffed. "She didn't prepare us for any of this. All she talks about in this stupid book is how she wanted to make sure we were ready. For what? She died and left us alone, completely unprepared. She did nothing but hinder us."

"Ray, we'll-"

"No," My sister held up her hand. "Let me be pissed."

"Okay." Rose's voice filled the silence that had fallen between us. "We'll wait. But hey, look at it this way. We're getting somewhere. We'll keep peeling back the layers until we have the truth."

I nodded. "Keep working on the spellbook, see if we can figure out what we did wrong. Ray, when you're done being pissed, keep reading through that journal. She has to mention Brooke's gem in there again."

"And you?" Rose asked.

"I have some unsettled business with Abe Roberts."

Chapter Fourteen

VANISHED

Each day that I drove to work, I watched the Roberts' home carefully, ready to confront Abe about following us into the meadow. I also wanted to catch a glimpse into his life. What he was trying to accomplish. I guess the two of us were spying on each other. It had been almost a week since the girls and I had gone into the forest and failed our first potion. That was the last any of us, including Dmitri, had seen of Abe, but I knew he was hiding back in the shadows watching. Shadows. I wondered if the two had anything to do with each other.

That Friday afternoon there were two unexpected police cars parked in front of Abe's house. No reds and blues on. No sirens. I slowed down as I passed, but the curtains in all the front windows were closed shut. Odd for the first day of sunshine in an overcast week.

As I pulled into the employee parking lot, there was a gray Jeep with a rather attractive addition sitting in the open trunk waiting for me. A book in one hand and a water bottle in the other.

"Hey, Bryan." I greeted, getting out of my car.

"Hey, you. Are you having a good day?" He smiled genuinely, the sleeves of his white button-up rolled to his elbows. The sight of him made me weak in the knees.

"So far, I just got here, so we'll see how the day goes."

"I start my shift soon, as well." He set the closed book down. "I haven't heard from you in a few days. You doing okay?"

I know, I've missed you so much.

"I know, I'm sorry. My life is complicated right now and I have so much going on." I paused, taking a deep breath. "When I moved out here, it was to get back in touch with myself and to start a new life for Rayn and Dmitri. The whole experience has been a lot heavier than I anticipated. I didn't plan on meeting anyone."

"Oh." Bryan's shoulder fell. Everything inside of him collapsed. "Yeah, of course. I understand. Um, I'm sorry for misinterpreting things." He stood up and turned away from me quickly.

I reached out for him, grabbing his hand. "What I'm trying to say is, I'm a mess and my life is a mess. It's been nice having someone to talk to. I don't have a lot of friends, or any friends for that matter."

"Ashley adores you," Bryan said, his core warming. "And I'm always here."

"You guys are sweet. I like you, but I can't promise anything." I admitted, chewing on my bottom lip. I didn't want to hurt Bryan, that was the absolute last thing I wanted.

"You don't owe me anything, Whitney." His lips curved into a soft smile. "I'm happy being friends. You're easier to talk to than people I've known for years."

I wanted to tell him that he was the best part of my day. That each time my phone vibrated in my pocket I hoped it was a message from him. I wanted to be so much more than friends but after Rose asked me to stay away from him, I had to decide what was more important. The girls and I were finally getting somewhere, digging into the truth behind our powers. I couldn't jeopardize that. Even if Rose wasn't Bryan's sister, I had so much baggage. He didn't deserve to carry it. Instead, I smiled silently and lost myself in his gaze.

He looked down at the watch on his wrist a moment later. "I have to go, my shift starts in a few minutes. Oh! Before I forget." Bryan turned around and rummaged through his navy blue backpack. "I have some books for you to borrow."

"Wait! I have something for you too." I replied, rushing to the car to get Your Soul and the Cosmos from the back seat. My fingers trembled slightly handing it over to him, anxious to see his reaction.

"Wow." He smiled, as he took the book and ran his hand over the cover. "Where'd you find this?"

"Dragonfly Mystic," I answered. "I thought of you when I found it. It's for you to keep, by the way."

"Thank you. You know, I always wanted to be an astronaut when I was a kid."

"Really?"

Bryan nodded and handed me a small stack of books. "Let me know what you think of these. I hate to run off, but I'm going to be late for work."

"Oh, I'm sorry. I'll talk to you soon." I watched him carefully as he closed the trunk of his Jeep.

"Don't apologize. It's time well spent." He caught me by surprise when he pulled me into a hug. Warmth and the aroma of cedarwood and vanilla entrapped me. I rested my head against his chest and closed my eyes. His heartbeat thudded against my cheek as his breath steadied. I couldn't let go, taking a fist full of his shirt. Hesitant, I waited for him to step back but he didn't. His head rested against the top of mine as he tightened his grip on me.

"Bryan! I'm waiting for you to clock in so I can send Nicole on a break." A voice behind us made me jump. Bryan took a step back, but kept one hand on the small of my back.

"Give me a second." He said to his coworker, who remained in the frame of the backdoor leading into Giani's, the Italian restaurant Bryan worked at.

"Talk soon?" I asked softly.

"Yeah, um, text me on your break? Maybe I can come over and get something to drink."

"I will."

I didn't realize how close I had been leaning into him, our faces now only inches apart. I held his gaze for as long as I could, wanting to drink in every second of his presence. No matter how many times the words that I didn't want a relationship left my lips, I couldn't control the gravitational pull I experienced whenever he was around. I knew I had to stop this before it was too far gone but when the moment came to do so, I couldn't bring myself to tell him I was wasting his time. He slowly began to close to space between us, leaning his face into mine.

"Bryan." His co-worker snapped again. "Angela is on a fucking rampage today. Make out with your girlfriend later. For the love of God, I need you to clock in."

"Go," I pushed him away gently. "I'll see you later."

"Okay," he whispered. His mouth was a thin line of irritation and deprivation.

I watched him walk into the back door of the Italian restaurant, admiring him with each step, but I shook myself out of it. I had to get to work myself before I was late. Priorities, Whitney, priorities.

The Corner Cup was busier than I expected, but I was happy to see Ashley behind the counter when I walked in through the front door. She looked up as the bell jingled and gave me a smile.

"Hey!" she greeted me. "I was so happy to see you on the schedule today."

I was glad to have made a genuine friend in Rifton. Someone who wasn't hunting down endless unknown secrets. Someone who wasn't hiding magical powers. Bryan and Ashley had no idea what their friendships had done to help ground me since I arrived in Rifton. I quickly clocked in and headed out onto the floor.

"Two cinnamon raisin bagels and a medium mocha latte, please." A customer ordered at the cash register further into my shift as I daydreamed about whether Bryan and I would have kissed if we had more time.

"Of course, anything else?" I asked.

"Nope." The customer smiled, handing me a ten-dollar bill.

I turned to face Olivia at the espresso bar. "Hey, Olivia. Medium-"

"I heard."

"Oh...okay, thanks."

After I finished toasting the bagels, I reached into the small pocket of my apron for a pen to mark the bags when a folded piece of paper crumpled against my fingertips. My heart jumped into my throat.

"Here you go. Have a great day." I faked a smile and handed the goods off to the customer, who rushed out the door.

"I have to run to the bathroom real quick." My coworkers barely replied to my words but I didn't care. I removed my apron and rushed off, sliding into one of the bathroom stalls for privacy.

I had to find out who was leaving these notes.

Nausea rose in my throat as I held onto the note tightly, willing myself to open it.

Burn every last remnant of your craft and bury it three feet below the ground in the woods, far from your home.

A list of instructions. It looked like a page hand copied out of the book written in the same flowing cursive as the first note. At the bottom of the page was a more personalized touch.

Whitney, if the remnants of the spell are discovered by another, you and the other Elemental's intentions may be easily manipulated. Be mindful of where you bury them. Your mother always kept you safe, and I vow to do the same.

No name. No indication of who was leaving me this information, but they knew me and what I was. There was only one person in Rifton who would have known I was Audri's daughter, a hidden Elemental.

Mia.

The door to the bathroom opened, and I shoved the note back into my pocket quickly. I left the stall and smiled at the customer walking past me, taking a quick glance over my shoulder to make sure my heart wasn't lying on the bathroom floor.

"You don't look happy," Ashley said once I got back behind the counter.

"Oh, I'm fine."

"So, can I please ask about you and Bryan?" Ashley bumped me with her hip as she came up behind me at the register. "He admitted how gorgeous you are, but I have eyes. I can see that for myself. He won't tell me anything else."

"I actually just saw him in the parking lot. I'm borrowing a few books." I smiled, playing with the strings of my apron.

"*And*?" Ashley crossed her arms, unsatisfied with my answer.

"He's smart and kind. He's easy to talk to." My cheeks burned with desire.

"I knew you two would hit it off. I do have to say this though, as one of his protective best friends. If you hurt him, I will be obligated to take necessary action."

"I have no intention of that happening. We're friends."

"Oh, okay. Yeah, good." Ashley took a cappuccino to the counter for whoever Bentley was.

"Excuse me?" A customer skipped the line and came around to the side of the counter to speak with me. It wasn't until I looked up that I realized it was Janice Roberts. Her misty eyes were filled with worry and her voice trembled as she spoke.

"Janice, are you all right?" I asked, meeting her on the other side of the counter.

"Have you seen Abraham?" she asked, eyes red and swollen.

"No, not recently." At least that was one thing I didn't have to lie about.

"He hasn't come home. The police say it's nothing to worry about, teenagers run off and come back home sometimes, but it's almost been a week. Can you hang some of these flyers up for me?"

My heart cracked in half for her. I wanted to hold this poor woman in my arms in a feeble attempt to take away her pain although there was nothing I could do.

"Of course, we'll put up your fliers." I reached out and put my hand on her shoulder. "I'm sure Abe is fine, Janice."

"Thank you." She wiped her nose on a tissue that had seen better days and handed me a small stack of photocopied papers. "I hope so, Whitney. I never thought I could have children. He's my little miracle."

"Is everything okay?" Ashley came up behind me, noticing the mental state of the woman standing before me.

"This is my landlady, Janice," I explained, taking a look at the fliers. "Her son hasn't come home in a few days."

MISSING

Abraham Roberts

Last seen on Saturday, September 23

17 years old. 5'9" 160 pounds

Copper hair and gray eyes

If any info, please call Rifton PD

Abe's most recent yearbook photo was in the center of the page. Smiling brightly but there was something in his eyes that didn't match his grin. A coy darkness that gave me a chill and intrigued me all at the same time.

"We'll put these up right away." Ashley reached out and put her hand on Janice's other arm. "He'll be found, don't worry, ma'am."

Missing person. Abraham Roberts. The image on that flier was burned into my memory for the rest of time. The last day he had been seen by his parents was the day the girls and I went into the forest. The day he followed us to the meadow and used his powers against me.

I was one of the last people to see Abe Roberts before he vanished.

CHAPTER FIFTEEN

CROSSED LINES

I had assembled the girls as soon as I got off work, sending them all texts saying we needed to meet. I didn't tell them why, but I assumed if they knew, they may not come.

"What happened to your arm?" I asked Lauren, eyeing the cut on her forearm. It was bright red and scabbed over, like a deep cat scratch.

"Nothing."

"It doesn't look like nothing."

"Do I comment on every little aspect of your body? I woke up with it a few days ago, okay? Now, what makes you think I'm going to trust the words a total stranger left in your locker?" Lauren folded her arms angrily across her chest, her feet planted firmly into the dirt.

"I could try to heal it for you," Brooke offered, taking a small step forward. "I've read everything in the book about spirit healing."

"No, absolutely not," Lauren snapped.

"I wouldn't be offering if I thought I'd hurt you," Brooke answered calmly.

"I said no."

"Lauren it looks like you should have gotten stitches. What happened?" Rayn jumped in, taking a closer look at Lauren's cut.

"I said I woke up with it. You're not using magic on me." Lauren's decision was final.

Rose sighed. "She's not trying to curse you. B is trying to help you, you self centered-"

"Guys," I cut them off. "It's Lauren's body, let her do what she wants with it."

The girls were clearly annoyed but they dropped it.

Rose bit the side of her mouth and changed the subject. "It pains me to say this, but I think Debbie Downer is onto something. We have no idea who left the notes. It could be a trap."

"What if they're the one who wants to manipulate our intentions?" Brooke handed the note back to me.

"Besides, the experiment didn't work, right? How can this note be relevant when it didn't work?" Lauren pointed out.

"Because it's still infused with our energies," I explained with frustration.

"Hey, my sister has the sharpest intuition of anyone I have ever met. If she thinks this is a good idea, then it is." Rayn came to my defense.

"It's not always that easy, Rayn. What about our intuition?" Rose asked quietly, eyeing the tree line. "We've lived in this town a lot longer than the two of you."

"Think about the first note they left. 'Stray from the shadows.' Whoever this person is, they want to protect us," Rayn rebutted.

Then, a light bulb went off above my head. I pulled the book out of my bag. The others gave me wide-eyed, puzzled looks.

"What are you doing?" Lauren whispered with uncertainty.

I set the book down in the grass, fingers crossed it would do its thing and show us what we needed to see. The book began to rattle as if the ground below it had shifted. The front cover flew open and the pages shuffled past one after another. The five of us sat like statues around the pages coming to life, waiting to see what wisdom the book was preparing to bestow upon us.

"What does it say?" Brooke asked, leaning forward on her knees when the pages stopped.

"Ridding of magical waste," Rayn read aloud. "If not disposed of properly, the remnants of any spell may be manipulated by those wishing to bring harm to the caster."

"We have to do this," I told the other girls. "It's the safest decision for all of us."

Lauren hesitated. "But we still don't know who is leaving these notes."

"I will find that out, but whoever it is, they are trying to help us," I reassured myself. "That much I'm sure of."

"Okay," Brooke nodded. "Let's get this over with before my parents realize I've snuck out." Sometimes I forgot she was seventeen.

I thrust a shovel into the earth. Luckily, I had thought to stop by the house and borrow the shovel from the tool shed in the back of the cabin.

A hole no more than a foot and a half deep lay before me with Rose on the other side. She used her powers and scooped more earth to make the hole deep enough that the remnants of the spell will go unnoticed. The instructions on the note had said it needed to be buried three feet into the ground.

"We need to hurry." Lauren glanced over each of her shoulders over and over again.

Every little snap and sound sent a chill up my spine.

"Is someone else watching us?" Rayn asked, taking a look around herself.

"No," Lauren replied.

"Then feel free to take my shovel," I mumbled.

"You have a lot of trust in this person you don't know." Lauren wasn't backing off.

"What if someone is going to try and hurt us? What if a gamma-ray comes through the galaxy and wipes all life off the face of the earth? What if, what if, what if. You aren't helping." Rose went off, and I didn't blame her. I was getting sick and tired of Lauren's skepticism myself.

Lauren squared her shoulders. "I am so sick of you-"

"Quiet!" Brooke's voice boomed through the meadow. We all shut up instantly. "You're going to get us caught! Dig the hole. Bury the fucking candles. Release our energies and get me home before someone notices I'm gone."

I wasn't expecting the minor to be our keeper for the evening, but Brooke was a force to be reckoned with.

"We're almost done," I muttered and went back to digging.

"I think that's deep enough," Rayn replied a moment later as she gathered up the clumped remnants from our failed spell. There would be no way for us to do this if the spell hadn't solidified, almost as if the magic hardened with the intent for this ritual to be performed.

"Okay, let's get this over with." Brooke brushed dirt off of her pants.

Following the spell in the book, I combined black peppercorns and bay leaves into a half-used bottle of vinegar and swirled the mixture around carefully, wanting to infuse the vinegar with the other ingredients. I took in a deep breath before I poured the vinegar mix over the remnants of our failed attempt.

Rayn lit a black candle and tilted it over the hole, dripping wax onto the mixture.

"I think that's enough," Rayn said, unsure of herself as she looked at Lauren to extinguish the flame, then dropped the black candle into the earth with the rest.

Once Lauren did her small part, Rose waved her hand over the hole we dug, filling it back in with dirt.

"Now what?" Brooke asked.

"Now, we place our hands over the dirt and release our magic." I read over the spell three more times, still not certain what it meant.

"And how do we do that exactly?" Lauren asked, looking over her shoulder.

"I'm not sure," I replied honestly.

"Well, all we can do is try." Rose knelt down and put her hand atop the freshly-placed earth. The rest of us followed suit.

The dirt was damp and soft, like sand next to the water. I pictured myself being detached from the potion we had buried and my magic returning to me. Moments later, a ripple of light shot out from the mound of dirt like a pebble hitting a pond. Once the rings of light passed through us, they dissipated into the air.

"Woah!" Brooke breathed, looking around for the rings of light, but they were gone.

"I guess it worked." Lauren shot up from the ground and wiped dirt from the knees of her coral-colored pants.

"I do have a question, and it is a little off-topic." Brooke straightened her posture. "Who all have you guys told about your powers? I think we all should know who out there knows people like us exist, for all our safety."

"Our little brother," Rayn said.

"When did you tell him?" Brooke asked.

"That's why our mom adopted us, actually, the powers," she answered. "She and our brother both have abilities, too, but nothing to do with the elements."

"Is your family anything like us?" Brooke's eyes widened as she listened intently to my sister.

"No," I answered quickly.

"But your mom has powers?" Lauren's voice was soft.

"She had powers," Rayn corrected. "She died."

Sympathy dwelled in Lauren's gaze. "I'm sorry."

"So you live with your dad?" Brooke asked.

"No, she raised us by herself," I said.

"Then who is your parent now?" Brooke turned to Rayn, not quite reading between the lines.

"I am." My voice was flat. Some time had passed but the sting hadn't diminished any.

Brooke picked at her fingernails nervously. "I told my mom when I was younger that I was seeing dead people. In my room, at school, or on the street corners. She didn't believe me and told me to never tell anyone or they would put me in a mental institution." Brooke looked away from us. "She put me in therapy and they tried to medicate me, so I lied and told her I was making it all up."

"I still can't believe she tried to say you were schizophrenic." Rose's jaw tightened up at the memory. "Communicating with spirits isn't all that uncommon."

"Yeah, where's my TV show?" Brooke chuckled ironically. "Have you ever told anyone besides us? Your family?" She glanced at Lauren.

"My biological mother," Lauren answered. "But I haven't seen her in over a decade, and she was too high to remember. My parents don't know anything and I intend to keep it that way."

"You're adopted too?" Rayn asked as Lauren shifted her weight.

"My dad is technically my uncle, but they are my parents. They've raised me since I was a baby," Lauren replied.

I guess there was a long list of things I didn't know about these girls. We had been spending so much energy on our quest, I hadn't taken the time to get to know them as people.

Rose chewed on her bottom lip. "No one on my end."

"You haven't told a single person outside of this circle about your magic, ever?" Rayn reiterated.

"No," Rose repeated her answer louder. "I meant to tell my family a few times, I actually did the whole 'we need to talk' thing once. My brother thought I was pregnant and almost had a heart attack. No, I'm a witch with magic plant powers. My family knows I have a green thumb, but they don't know the extent of it. If anything they think I'm another introvert."

"Are you ever going to tell your family?" Rayn asked.

"It's not as easy as it sounds," she answered, looking off at the trees.

"I was worried that a bunch of people knew," Brooke sighed.

"Well," I said out loud, looking at my sister. *Should we tell them?*

Probably, Rayn thought back.

"You two think you're going to be able to talk like that around us unnoticed?" Rose asked, leaning forward. "We may not be able to hear you, but I can feel a pull in the magic."

Rayn and I locked eyes. With a silent node, I agreed it was time to share exactly what drove us from our once-claimed home after Mom died.

Rayn and Jon, her boyfriend at the time, had gotten into an argument at our old house after Mom's funeral. I couldn't even remember what they were fighting about. I heard them arguing from the other room but I ignored it at first, until Jon screamed in agony and a warmth bubbled inside my stomach; the feeling of Rayn using her powers. I panicked, and rushed into the room, but by the time I had gotten there the couch was on fire.

I had to put out the fire, pulling in a deep breath and with it the rain from outside. I held my hands out toward the couch and a small dark cloud formed above it, dropping water over the flames. Clouds of smoke rose from the cushions and my hands were still tingling when I realized Jon had seen the entire thing. He looked nothing less than petrified.

"You two are fucking crazy." Without giving either of us a chance to reply, he ran out of the house as fast as he could. It wasn't long before he called everyone we knew and told them Rayn had burnt him with her bare hands while he walked away during their fight. Our phones were blowing up before I could find Dmitri and tell him what happened. We even tried to play it off as a rumor at first, but there were burn marks on Jon's arms in the shape of handprints.

I was terrified something would happen to Ray or Mit and after losing Mom so recently, I had to protect them. Last time something like that happened, people were hung from trees and weighed down with rocks in the river. We were called names, because bitch so nicely rhymed with witch. Our house was vandalized numerous times with spray paint, eggs, and toilet paper. Someone tried to set Rayn's shirt on fire with a pocket lighter in the grocery line to see if she would turn into a human torch.

It got to the point where we couldn't take it anymore. We couldn't afford to stay in our old house anyway, so I sold everything I could and let the house go back to the bank since no one was going to buy a home from abominations. We packed what we could in the moving truck and ran for our lives to a foreign place from our mother's past. The place she ran from so many years ago. The place she feared we would never be safe in.

"How many people found out?" Brooke's brown eyes full of empathy.

"Pretty much everyone we knew heard about it. All of our friends and people who had worked with our Mom. It wasn't pretty." Rayn kicked some dirt with her foot. "People we had known for years said we were possessed."

"I'm so sorry," Rose whispered sympathetically, looking at us like we were abandoned puppies dumped on the side of the road.

"We're over it. Living there was hard enough with how our brother was treated after he came out. It's not somewhere we planned to stay forever anyway, so them running us out of town escalated the inevitable. Those are the only other people who know anything about our powers and they've pretty much left us alone now that we've moved so far away. We've made sure they won't find out where we went," Rayn explained. "We changed our numbers and deleted social media. Everything."

"I had a dream once that everyone found out about what I could do. It was a nightmare." Lauren said.

"Well, I'm glad you decided to come out here," Brooke said with a smile that reached her eyes.

"Thanks," I muttered. It felt good to finally talk about it. I had been burying it all under the surface, convinced if I ignored the past I'd move on. But I realized if we were truly going to have a new life in Rifton, I couldn't pretend our old life never happened.

When Rayn and I took Brooke home that night, I was still in awe of the big houses by the lake. The neighborhood of Diamond Gate was gorgeous. These were definitely not little boxes on the hillside. Each home in the housing development of Diamond Gate was unique. Some were large with extravagant entryways and pillars, others had white shutters on the windows and large front lawns. It looked like it could have been right out of a movie where everyone had unlimited bank accounts to furnish their homes. From what I could remember, Brooke only lived a few streets over from the Drakes. Brooke being that close to Serenity made my stomach churn.

As we approached Brooke's house, the flashing red and blue lights of a police car parked at the end of the street were blinding. Chills surged through my limbs as I fought the urge to make a u-turn and drive away as fast as I could.

"Brooke?" I asked, looking for an explanation.

"Oh no...my parents must have realized I wasn't home," Brooke mumbled, shifting back and forth in her seat. "My dad is a cop."

"Your dad's a cop and you failed to mention it?" Rayn snapped.

"I didn't think it mattered," Brooke replied. "No one else was talking about their parent's occupation."

"Why wouldn't they call you?" I slowed down the car.

"I don't get reception in the meadow."

Of course, Brooke's parents would call in the cavalry when they realized their seventeen-year-old daughter wasn't home. What sort of decent parent wouldn't?

Brooke's house was one of those with a large, fancy entryway. Three stories tall with two large windows on either side of the dark front door. There were brightly colored flowers around the sides of the lawn and a Mercedes in the driveway.

"What do I do?" I parked alongside the curb a few houses down, but it was too late. I could already see a police officer approaching the car with a flashlight held up, shining into the front windows. I wrapped my hands tightly around the top of the steering wheel, keeping them in sight.

"What brings you up here tonight?" The officer interrogated with a stern tone. He flashed the light into the back seat in Brooke's face. "Brooke Evans?"

"Yes?" Brooke barely spoke above a whisper.

He turned back to me. "Please step out of the vehicle."

My heart pounded in my throat, and when I removed my hands from the steering wheel they nearly stuck. Slowly, Rayn and I got out of the car and Brooke leaned the front passenger seat forward to allow her to follow.

"Brooke! Oh, thank god!" A woman with short black hair, who I assumed to be Brooke's mother ran our way and pulled her into her arms. "Who are these girls? Why did you leave the house without telling us? Oh, honey, we feared the worst."

"Mom, it's fine. We were star charting. It's a science project." Brooke explained, her words muffled from her mother's embrace. "For school. I told you, remember?"

"Where were you conducting this science project in the middle of the night?" Another officer standing next to Brooke's mother questioned, not buying the story.

"Dad, I told you we were doing a science project." Brooke began again, but her father cut her off.

"Brooke, I don't care what you were doing. I care that you snuck out of the house and scared the hell out of your mother and I." Brooke's father turned to me and Rayn. "And who are you two taking my daughter into the woods?"

"Are we in some sort of trouble here? Because if so, I don't feel comfortable speaking to you without legal representation." Rayn spoke up but the first cop showed his light at me, nearly blinding me.

"May I see your driver's license?" he questioned.

"It's in the car, in my purse," I informed him.

"Get it."

"Are we in trouble?" Rayn asked again.

"Not yet but I'd like to know why my seventeen year old daughter is sneaking out to meet with you." Brooke's father replied.

I took a deep breath and retrieved my wallet from the car, handing over my license to the intrusive cop. The shiny name tag on his dark blue uniform read J. Grady. He looked over my license, making a questioning face. Thankfully, I had already received my new Oregon license or else there would have been a lot more questions.

"Miss Dansley, you're twenty-one years old, is that correct?" The officer asked, handing back my license after he scribbled a few things down in his notebook.

"Yes, sir," I answered. *Shit, I'm going to jail.*

"You were dangerously close to contributing to the delinquency of a minor if you had brought Miss Evans home any later."

"I understand. I was giving our friend a ride home from their experiment. She goes to school with my little brother." My voice was small and I felt even smaller. Officer Grady could have stepped on me and crushed me like a bug with those shiny black boots of his.

"Next time, I would think twice before you take a teenage girl from her home without her parents' permission. It's borderline kidnapping."

"I had no idea that her parents were not informed." I looked at Brooke and apologized to her with my eyes. I didn't mean to throw her under the bus but I also didn't want to get arrested. She nodded when our eyes met, she understood.

Brooke's father turned to her in disbelief. "We are going to have a serious discussion inside."

"And this young lady's parents?" The officer waved his flashlight toward Rayn.

"I'm nineteen," Rayn answered, keeping her cool.

"Don't let this happen again. Drive safely." Officer Grady dismissed Rayn and I as he turned on his heel and walked back to his squad car.

Brooke's mother tightened her grip around her daughter and walked her back to their mansion by the lake. I stood with my feet planted into the concrete, unable to move.

Holy shit that was terrifying. I can't believe Brooke's parents called the fucking cops. Rayn wiped a bead of sweat from her brow and opened the passenger door. *Whit?*

"Huh?" I asked aloud, my head spinning.

Get in, I'll drive us home. I want to get the hell out of here.

I nodded and got into the car quickly, keeping my eyes on Officer Grady, who was standing close to his squad car writing in his notebook again. He looked up from his scribbles to watch Rayn and I pull away from the curb and leave Diamond Gate. One thing I knew for sure, I never wanted to see that man again.

Chapter Sixteen

BITTERSWEET

"This is not what I ordered." An older woman slammed a ceramic mug down on the glass countertop so hard, I was amazed neither of them shattered. Coffee sloshed over the side, spilling onto the counter.

"Oh, I'm sorry about that. What did you order?" I asked.

The woman furrowed her brow. "Not this."

"I understand that, but I can't fix your drink unless I know what you ordered."

"Well for starters, this is not oat milk and I am highly allergic to dairy. Second, the coffee tastes stale. Third-"

"Ma'am, I can assure you the coffee is brewed fresh every half hour, but I'll put in a new order for oat milk. That was a regular black coffee?"

"No, you're not listening. How hard is it to brew coffee? This is your job. This is all you have to do all day long is press buttons and you can't do that? I need to speak to someone competent who knows what they're talking about."

"I'm still fairly new."

"I said get me someone else."

Before I could turn around, Ashley was at my shoulder attempting to pacify the angry woman, but there was no pleasing her. I took the coffee cup from the counter and turned toward the sink at the back of the bar. Before I knew what had happened, an elbow jabbed into my chest and warm coffee ran down the front of my shirt and into my jeans. The mug fell from my hands and shattered on the floor.

"Oh no. Whitney, I'm so sorry." Robby set the blender he was holding down on the counter and grabbed a towel but the damage had already been done.

"See?" the customer spat, "Utter incompetence."

"Get out of my store," Ashley snapped, pointing to the front door.

"Excuse you? Where's the manager?"

"I am the manager on duty. Get out of my store."

Slowly, I took the towel from Robby's hands but I didn't bother cleaning myself up. I squatted down and picked up the broken pieces of coffee mug. Clenching my jaw, I swallowed my emotions, but a tear still escaped from the corner of my eye and fell down my cheek before I could wipe it away.

"Please don't cry. I'm so sorry." Robby put his hand on my shoulder. "I have an extra shirt in my locker you can have. God, I feel like such a dick."

"It's not you." I fell to my knees and covered my eyes, unable to hold the tears back.

"It's okay. Customers make me cry sometimes, too. Come on, babe." Ashley held out her hand and helped me off the floor. "Your shift is almost over anyway, head home when you're done."

I cleaned myself up in the bathroom, blotching my shirt with paper towels as best as I could but the stain wasn't coming out. Trails of eyeliner and mascara trickled down from red eyes. What an idiot. My face was flush with embarrassment. Wadding up another paper towel, I did my best to clean the smeared makeup from my face but only dark circles remained. Maybe that customer was right. Maybe I was in over my head.

The last week and a half had been uneventful. Eerily quiet since Brooke's parents thought she was missing and called the police. The girls and I had stayed in vague touch but it felt like limbo, waiting for something to happen. Rose and Rayn had taken it upon themselves to study the book as often as possible but it only offered so much information. As much as I wanted to stay in the bathroom and wallow, I wanted to get the hell out of there.

I bundled my apron over the stain and took out my phone to let Rayn know I was ready to be picked up. When I came through the door, Ashley wasn't the only one standing at the counter waiting for me.

"Hey, you okay?" Bryan asked, his arms folded across his chest. He was still in his work clothes.

"Uh, yeah," I answered, turning to Ashley. "Is Amilia going to be upset that you kicked that lady out?"

"Nah," she answered. "Boss lady doesn't tolerate people making us cry like that."

"She made you cry?" Bryan's heart sunk in his chest.

"I'm fine," I answered quickly. "I need to get home and change my clothes, and probably take a shower."

A quiet vibration went off in my hands and I eagerly checked the message from Rayn. *Up at the lake. I can be there in like 30.*

"Are you fucking kidding me?" I muttered. "Rayn took my car to the lake."

"Do you need a ride home?" Bryan offered. "I'm off work."

"You sure? I'm up in Pines Row so it's out of town."

"I came in here to see you and Ash, anyway." After taking a look at my coffee stained clothes, Bryan continued. "But if you need a ride, I'll drop you off. Either way, I have time to kill."

"Okay. Yeah, that would be great. Thank you." I texted Rayn not to worry about it and slid my phone into my back pocket.

The interior of Bryan's Jeep was much cleaner than I kept my car. There were no empty water bottles in the back seat and no wrappers on the floorboards. A stack of books and his backpack sat in the seat.

"How was your day?" I asked, not wanting to allow him to ask anything else about my bitch customer or why I was covered in coffee. I imagined Ashley filled him in on it anyway.

"Slow." He pulled out of the parking lot as he answered. "Opening shifts during the week usually are. So, how did you end up in Pines Row?"

"Honestly, it was the cheapest place I could find. We're renting a guest house on our landlord's property."

"You and your family?"

"My brother and sister, yeah."

"Oh." His voice raised an octave in surprise, but he didn't push the topic. "I've only been up there a few times. We've been invited to a couple of gatherings around here, but the stories always get into Troy's head so he refused to be in that part of the forest."

"What stories?" I asked, turning to face him. My blood pressure elevated a notch in curiosity.

"The ones about the old witch coven?" Bryan answered. "It's a scary story people made up to keep their kids from wandering off the older hiking trails."

"Tell me the story."

"Well, I'm no expert on the topic. I've only heard it a few times."

"Tell me anyway."

"Well, apparently there was this old coven of witches that founded Rifton. As the years progressed and more non-magic people moved in, everyone began to fear them until they finally drove them out of town. The witches disappeared into the forest. Over the years, people and pets have gone missing around Pines Row. People in town always whisper about the witches but it's probably bears. I mean, we're in the woods, after all."

Witches founded Rifton. Old magic. This had to be connected to my mother in one way or another.

"What kind of witches?" I asked.

"Whit," Bryan chuckled, using my nickname for the first time. "It's an old ghost story. It isn't real."

"It's interesting though, isn't it?"

"Sure, if you're into that sort of thing."

"Totally."

We pulled into the dirt driveway and Bryan slowed to a stop in front of my little house.

"I hope your day gets better." Bryan put his Jeep in park but left the engine running, waiting for me to decide what I wanted.

I had decided before we left the Corner Cup.

"You can come in if you want, but I'd like to clean up. I have coffee on my jeans."

He smiled. "Yeah, take your time."

After a quick shower and some clean clothes, I came out of my bedroom to find Bryan in the living room. His hands were nestled in his pockets as his eyes wandered between photos on the wall like he was at an art gallery. The glow of the setting sun illuminated the living room, bathing him in a golden hue that blended into his blonde hair like a halo.

"Hey." I greeted, getting his attention.

"Hi." He stepped back from the wall, but his gaze returned to the photo in front of him.

I sighed and took my place next to him, looking into a pair of brown eyes I knew all too well staring back at me from behind the glass. "That's my mom," I explained.

"She's beautiful," Bryan replied softly.

"Thank you." I took in another deep breath. "Do you want to sit outside? The sky looks really pretty."

"Yeah, of course." He put out his hand, motioning for me to lead the way through the kitchen door that led to the back porch.

We didn't have any patio furniture. Honestly, I hadn't been out here much since we'd moved into the house since the porch faced Abe's bedroom window. The back field was stunning. The orange and reds of the setting sun bounced off the bright green pines scattered throughout the property. An endless view of grass, wildflowers, and trees. Bryan and I sat down on the two steps that connected the porch to the backyard.

"It's peaceful up here in Pines Row," Bryan remarked. "Makes you forget there's anyone else around."

"Yeah," I agreed. "I love it here. It's nice to come back to this after being in town all day at work."

"How do you like working at CC?" Bryan asked, breaking the brief silence that had fallen between us. "Other than today, of course. Ash has been there for years. She loves the boss. Amilia's a nice lady."

"So far, so good. The Corner Cup has good energy. It's helping Rifton feel like home, which is a feeling that took me years to get before, so that's something." I said, catching his vibrant eyes. I nearly forgot about the whirlwind of events that happened this year when I gazed into those gentle lily pads.

"I hated this place when we first moved here but it grew on me. There's something about this forest that almost feels healing. I always said I was going out of state for college, but I didn't want to leave when the time came." Bryan looked around at the scenery. "All of my people are here, all my friends and family."

"What brought you here in the first place?"

"Uh..." He paused, his heel tapping against the wooden porch. "My mom wanted to run away. I think she threw a dart at a map and it landed here, to be honest."

"That's why my mom left Rifton. She wanted to run away."

"Never seems to solve anything, does it? About a year before we left Arizona, my grandma passed away after a long fight with cancer. Then my parents finally separated, and I think my mom needed a do-over. I was so mad when she moved us here, but I was thirteen and couldn't see past wanting to stay in the place I knew. Now that I'm older, I understand her reasoning better."

"Is your father still in Arizona?"

"Yeah." Bryan shifted his weight. "We're not on great terms."

"Oh, I'm sorry."

"It's okay. We never have been. I, uh, I had actually gotten off the phone with him when you and I first saw each other. When you kicked over those crates. It was exactly what I had been wanting to do since he called."

The sadness. The frustration. The feeling of stagnation. Bryan's father must have been a real asshole to dim the bright light in this beautiful person.

"Anyway, I thought about running away but I realized I would be taking my problems with me. So, I stayed and I'm glad I did." Our eyes met with a soft smile.

"I'm jealous." I crossed my arms against my chest, doing my best to keep my hands to myself. "Part of me wishes I could have finished school."

"Why aren't you?"

During our conversations, I had been avoiding the topic of my move to Rifton and the events that led to it like the plague. Mostly because I didn't want to think about all of it. I wanted to live like there weren't any skeletons in my closet, but I could only keep the facade up for so long.

"I had a rough summer," I said softly, picking at my fingernails.

"Do you want to talk about it?"

As fun as this had been, I knew there was an expiration date. Rose made her feelings on that matter clear. This had to be the last time I spent time with Bryan like this if I wanted Rose's help. If I lost Rose's trust, surely I'd lose Brooke's as well. I wouldn't let it go that far.

"I lost my mom in a car accident in June. My brother is still in high school so I got custody. Rayn was already eighteen, which was a blessing because I don't think the court would have given me both of them, though that's what my mom had in her will. I was in college but I dropped out to work full time and take care of them. We had a hard time afterward coping with all of it. I couldn't afford to stay in our old house anyway, so I moved them here for a fresh start. We came to Rifton because this is where my mom grew up, but that's opened up a bunch of old wounds. It's been an 'out of the frying pan, into the fire' type of thing."

Bryan was quiet for a moment. I couldn't blame him, there was only so much baggage that a person was willing to take on. I felt his heart sink, then he looked over at me with admiration in his eyes. For the first time since the accident, someone didn't look at me with pity.

"I'm so sorry about your mom," he finally said. "I can tell you're taking good care of your siblings."

"It's the least I could do," I paused, catching my breath before I continued. "She asked me to pick up Rayn from a friend's house the night she died, but I said I was busy when I could have, so my mom went instead. A truck ran a red light and hit the driver's side on their way home. It was supposed to be me."

"You can't blame yourself like that, Whitney. There's no way you could have known." Bryan attempted to ease my guilt but nothing could strip away the weight I'd been carrying for the past few months.

"How could I not? Rayn and Dmitri are shattered, homesick for a place that doesn't exist anymore, and I'm barely holding it all together. This whole situation would have been easier on them if it had been me." I surprised myself hearing those words out loud. I had said them in my head a million times but they didn't taste any less sour. "It should have been me."

Bryan fell silent again, his eyes scanning the tree line in the distance. I expected him to fake an emergency and head out at any moment. Nothing ruins the mood like the girl you're watching the sunset with telling you she wished she had died instead of her departed mother. To my surprise, he didn't flinch. Without a word, he reached over and gently set his warm hand on my knee. Impulsively, my fingers inched toward him but I stopped myself. I watched the wheels turn in his head from a side glance, but instead of running away, he stayed.

"I think you're doing the best you can with what you've been given." Bryan's gentle voice soothed my fears. "With everything you've been through, you're holding it together better than most people would. Look at the home you've made for them here. Look at everything you've accomplished on your own. You're resilient and your mom would be proud of you."

His words tugged at my heart so hard that I felt the pull in my chest muscles. My vision blurred and my cheeks were wet before I realized what was happening. I wiped the tears away as soon as they fell, blinking quickly in an attempt to stop them.

Sniffling, I reached for his hand still resting on my knee, and laid my head on his shoulder. The space between us closed in as we both scooted closer to each other, our sides fitting together like two pieces of the same puzzle. His fingers laced into mine, radiating heat into my cold hand. Hugging his arm to my chest, I let out a sigh. The tears faded, but the fact that I had given into temptation and betrayed my word to Rose was not lost on me.

"Thank you," I whispered into the fabric of his sweatshirt.

"Yeah, of course." He spoke softly into my hair.

"Besides," I sniffled, changing the topic while I still could. "College was quickly becoming stagnant anyway. I don't know what I want to do with my life. I don't know what to major in. I don't know what profession to get into. I don't know what I want to do about anything right now. I'm kinda stuck."

It was like a broken faucet. When I tried to turn it off, I couldn't. I couldn't stop the feelings I'd buried from surfacing around him. I guess all it took was a warm hand to hold and pretty eyes to get lost in.

"We all feel rushed into making a decision but I think it's better to take your time and get into something you care about rather than hating your job for thirty years," Bryan said.

"That's the problem, there are plenty of things that I like but not many career opportunities. I like coffee, books, the stars...your eyes."

I could feel the smile spreading through his body. "Maybe optometry?"

We both laughed. His thumb gently traced the lines in my skin.

"Don't worry, Whitney. You are far from the only person who hasn't a clue what they're doing with their lives." He encouraged. "We're young. We have time."

"Says the guy who has his career path figured out."

"I have a couple years on you. Besides, they wouldn't let me into FBU with an undeclared major, so I had to figure something out. I figured since I read so much, English would be a safe bet."

"I can see you as an English teacher."

"I've escaped into books my entire life, might as well get paid for it."

"Your students are going to crush on you so hard."

He groaned. "Ugh, I hope not."

"I forgot what this was like."

"What's that?"

"Having a friend," I said quietly. "Rayn and Dmitri are so supportive and I know I could talk to them about anything. Anything except this. I couldn't put this on them."

Bryan put his free hand over mine, the one I had wrapped around his bicep. His thumb gently grazed across the moonstone ring on my finger.

"That was my mom's ring. She never took it off. Neither have I since the hospital." I watched his soft touch. Bryan pulled his hand back at my words.

"I'm so sorry," he apologized. "I don't know why I can't keep my hands to myself."

I reached out for his free hand and brought it back. "I don't want you to."

I didn't think it was necessary to tell him that not even Rayn or Dmitri had touched that ring since it came into my possession.

"Tell me about her," Bryan whispered. "Your mom."

Tears welled up in my eyes once more but I pushed through the pain. For the first time since the accident, I actually wanted to talk about it.

"She was a fifth-grade teacher. She would wake up early to do yoga on the weekends and burnt nearly everything she cooked." I chuckled, reminiscing about the happy memories. "She kept books in the cabinets and would listen to music really loud when she'd vacuum. She would put a mattress on the back porch in the summer so we could all sleep under the stars. She was everything I used to dream a mother would be when I was in foster care."

"Sounds like she was a wonderful woman."

"She was," I whispered, nuzzling my face into his arm. "She truly was."

We sat there for nearly an hour, long after the sun disappeared behind the mountains and the night sky set in. He complained about his job at Giani's Italian Kitchen where he had started washing dishes at sixteen and eventually got promoted to one of the head waiters. Bryan talked about the stars and how he always dreamed about going into space when he was a kid. He told me about the dry heat of Arizona he grew up in after his family moved from Flagstaff to Tucson. I shared the lightning bugs of Kansas and how I always dreamed of owning a house with a porch swing. Bryan spoke fondly of his mother. He beamed with pride when he spoke about Rose, as if he raised her himself. He revealed his love for cheesy Sci-Fi movies from the nineties and listened intently when I told him how much I loved punk rock and hated having a summer birthday.

"You hate your birthday?" Bryan asked, lifting his head from mine for the first time.

"It's July fifth, so it sort of gets overshadowed by the holiday."

"Cancer?"

"I thought you didn't know anything about astrology." I raised my head off his shoulder to look at him, instantly feeling the loss of warmth from my face. Our fingers stayed tightly clasped.

"Emma's birthday is July ninth, so that's why I know Cancer. So if I have an air moon, what do you have?"

"Pisces, so water moon and sun for me."

"So you have a Pisces moon but I don't? Even though I'm also a Pisces. I don't understand," he admitted.

"Pisces is your sun, your main zodiac that most people focus on. Your moon sign reflects your emotions and how you portray them. Air signs are typically intelligent and social, but they hide their sadness. You have strong emotions that you don't express, like, all the time."

"Like, all the time?" His voice purred, teasing me.

"Mmhmm." I smiled up at him.

Our eyes met and locked into a gentle gaze that warmed every inch of me. His smile was gentle, his lips barely moved but his eyes reflected all I felt from him. I didn't think either of us had been this happy in a while.

"Whit, are you home?" Rayn's voice boomed through the house. "You better be because you aren't answering your phone."

"I'm out here!" I answered, finally moving away from Bryan. I quickly let go of his hand and allowed the air to fill the space between us once more. He nodded with understanding; the intimacy we shared was meant for moments of privacy.

"Why weren't you-" Rayn froze in the doorway. "Oh, hi Bryan."

"Hi, Rayn," he answered.

"I didn't know we had company," she replied. "Are you staying for dinner?"

"Oh, I'd love to but I should probably get home." Bryan checked his phone for the time. "I have dinner plans."

A shot of jealousy pinged through me. After I told him I didn't know what I could give him, did he move on to someone else? Was he really sitting on the porch holding me while I cried over my dead mother before a date with another woman? I couldn't be upset. Bryan had expressed nothing but interest and I had done nothing but panic. It was my own damn fault.

"With my mom," Bryan answered quietly as if he'd seen the sudden change in my eyes. "I'm having dinner with my mom and sister."

Oh.

"Thanks for staying. I really needed that." I watched his every move as he stood from the stairs and stretched his back. The curve of his spine, the way his sweatshirt lifted enough for a quick peek of skin above his jeans.

"Me too." Bryan put out his hand and helped me onto my feet. Giving my fingers a quick squeeze before he let go and headed toward the front yard. "Text me later."

"Drive safe," I answered, counting his steps until he disappeared around the house.

"You love him," Rayn announced once Bryan was out of earshot.

"Love him? We haven't known each other that long." I defended, fearing the truth in her words.

"Since when does love have a time frame?"

"Ray, I'm not falling in love with Rose's brother."

"Does he know that? Because he's falling for you pretty quick. He's a water sign, yeah?"

"Pisces," I answered. "Aquarius moon."

"Oh no." Rayn laughed. "He's already in love, then."

If that was the case, I definitely hadn't helped things crossing the line of physical touch. Clinging to him in parking lots and interlocking our fingers. I could still feel his thumb gently gliding across my skin in a comforting sweep. Nothing I could do about it now.

"What's for dinner?" I asked, changing the subject.

"Oh, I'm not cooking tonight. Tom is picking up a pizza on his way over."

"And you were giving me shit about boys," I mumbled.

"I like Tom, I'm not in denial about it," Rayn stated matter-of-factly. "He's a good one, Whit. This time feels different."

"I get that."

Being around Bryan felt different. I didn't think about magic or anyone who possessed its power. For a moment, I forgot I was a witch. Being around him that night was the most relaxed I had been since we moved to the forest. For the first time in my life, I wasn't nervous around someone I found attractive. I didn't second guess every move or worry about the words falling from my lips. Underneath those bright green eyes and handsome face wasn't anything to be nervous about. It felt like home.

"Speaking of Tom, I want to show you something before he gets here." Rayn reached into her bag and pulled out Mom's journal. A bookmark was sticking out from the top. "Read this."

I opened the journal at the saved place and steadied my pulse before I let my brain process the words on the page.

I found Rayn snooping around my closet, looking for a scarf to wear to school. Something so innocent, but she nearly found the books I brought with me. It would have opened too many doors that I'm not prepared for. Too many questions from my girls that I don't have answers to. I had no choice but to package them up and mail them back to Mia. Rayn broke the protection spell I placed over them without trying. If that doesn't tell you the potential of their true powers, I don't know what will. The books will be safer with Mia. I only brought them with me for sentimental purposes anyway. I wonder how many of those old books are floating around the world, sitting in old libraries or second-hand stores waiting for someone who can read the text to stumble upon them. I hope they're out there. I can't bear the thought that they're all gone, up in flames. I suppose it would make sense if they were, everything else from that period of our lives went up in flames, too.

"There are more books?" My head snapped up, meeting my sister's wide gaze.

She nodded. "Here in Rifton."

"Any luck finding out who Mia is?"

"No." Rayn sighed. "I can't find anyone in this town with that name."

"It has to be a nickname, then."

"Has to be." Rayn went to say something else, but the doorbell cut her off. "And there's Tommy. We'll figure this out, okay?"

"Sure." I forced a smile that didn't convince either of us.

CHAPTER SEVENTEEN

DARK ATTRACTION

"Looks like you need this more than me." My coworker, Robby, handed me the warm drink he was preparing for himself. The extra espresso he added masked the sweetened syrup but I didn't mind. If I hadn't been holding myself up against the countertop, I wouldn't be standing.

"Thanks," I said in between sips. "I haven't been getting a lot of sleep the past few days."

"I know how that goes." Robby nodded. "Why haven't you been sleeping?"

I retreated back to the coffee, hoping it would compensate for the shadows that plagued my dreams. "There's a lot on my mind."

Abe Roberts, for one. The other girls didn't seem as upset about it as I did. They had the same reaction as Rayn, relief. Dmitri, on the other hand, was worried sick. Each day that passed without news on Abe only drove my brother deeper into himself.

The bell above the front door chimed and I turned to greet the new customers. But it wasn't any ordinary customer standing at the register. It was Rose, pale as a ghost with bloodshot eyes and hair tied up in a messy bun.

"Hey, are you okay?" I glanced down at her shaking hands.

She shivered as if she had been standing out in a snowstorm with her arms crossed tight against her chest. There were dark circles under her eyes that made them look sunken into her skull.

"I need to talk to you." Rose's hushed voice cracked as she spoke, like she had been screaming all night. Rose looked over her shoulder, then back to me. "Now."

"Robby, could-"

"Yeah, sure. I'll grab someone to cover." Robby replied.

"Can I make you some coffee?" I asked Rose. She didn't respond. And I thought I was a wreck that morning. "Rose?"

The doorbell jingled again, causing Rose to jump with terror. My own heart skipped a beat.

"I don't think coffee will help." Rose finally spoke after she realized the intruder was only a paying customer.

"Tea?" I tried again.

Rose accepted the drink with a nod. I made the tea as quickly as I could, offering her a seat at one of the tables next to the windows. She crumbled into a chair against the wall as I took a seat across from her, accepting the mug from me without a word and scanned the store one last time.

"Rose, who are you looking for? You're starting to-"

"Something is following me, but not here. Not yet."

"A shadow?" My tone barely a whisper.

"No...I-I think it's an entity."

"A ghost?"

"It has a face and a body. It started last night after my mom left for work. I could feel something crawling under my skin so I went to bed early and..." Her voice trailed off. Slowly, Rose raised up the sleeve of her heavy sweater.

My pulse quickened, thudding against my throat. There were deep bruises in the shape of hands wrapped around her arms. Dark blue and purple against her milky cream skin. She covered herself in an instant. "I was trapped. I don't know how I left my house. I don't know what to do." Tears welled in the bottom of her eyes and fell to her trembling lips. I reached across the small table and took her cold hand in mine.

"There has to be something in the book about this. I'm going to get ahold of Rayn and she'll bring it to us." I put on my bravest exterior, not wanting to show Rose how utterly terrified I was. I had no idea what to do. I didn't know how to keep her safe, or any of the other girls.

Rose nodded and took a sip of tea. Her face relaxed ever so slightly at the familiar comfort the flavor brought her. She held my hand tightly. I glanced over to the counter, checking on my coworkers but there was only one customer in the store. It wasn't until I made eye contact with Amilia that I noticed she made an appearance on the floor. Her gaze focused on Rose and I, making me nervous that I was going to get in trouble with my boss, but the vivid image of those hand marks on Rose's skin came back to me. I pulled my phone from my pocket and sent Rayn a message.

911 come to the Corner Cup ASAP with the book. Rose is hurt.

It took a second for Rayn to respond. *On my way.*

Ray had dropped me off at work that morning, begging to keep the car so she could go see her friends on her day off. It didn't take much convincing, I wanted her to enjoy her Saturdays. I just hoped she wasn't too far away.

Amilia went back to her office and I breathed easier. One of the downsides to living in hiding was the feeling that someone already knew your secret. That someone was always paying a little too much attention to your every move.

I shivered as an icy chill crept up my spine, causing me to stir in my seat. I dared not breathe out, assuming that if I did the air would smoke from the cold. The only warmth was from the feeling of eyes burning two holes into the side of my head. Someone was watching us.

Slowly, I turned my head to the window, and jumped when I came face to face with cold, black eyes.

Serenity Drake stood like a statue on the sidewalk as she glared into the Corner Cup, her eyes glued on Rose and I. While her face was completely void of any emotion, her eyes smiled cruelly.

I slid my chair out to stand as Serenity turned on her heel and headed down the sidewalk. I frowned. Apparently, she didn't want a confrontation, but if Serenity Drake had anything to do with what was happening to Rose, I would make her pay for it. No one fucked with my generation.

"Rayn will be here soon," I replied, turning my attention back to Rose. She didn't seem to notice Serenity outside and I didn't want to alarm her. I pushed Serenity out of my mind and focused on Rose again.

Rose was still on edge, scanning the room before she pressed herself against the window, as if that might help her feel some sort of stability.

"Rose, please tell me what happened," I said quietly.

"I already did."

"Not exactly...We're in this together, remember? Isn't that why you came here, of all places?"

She took another sip of tea before she spoke. "At first, I thought I was dreaming. I dreamt we were all at Dragonfly and then the floor began to deteriorate. You, Rayn, Brooke, even Lauren, you all fell into the darkness leaving me alone, clinging to the edge. I began to pull myself up, but I was sucked in. I fell onto my bed, but it wasn't my bedroom. It was twisted and that...thing was hovering over me before it attacked." Rose was crying now and buried her face into her hands, letting go of my palm for the first time since I offered it to her.

The bell jingled once more, and Rose and I both jumped. But it was only Rayn, her backpack slung over her shoulder. My sister spotted us and rushed to the table.

"You're hurt?" she asked Rose in a hushed voice once she reached us. When Rose raised her sweater sleeve, Rayn threw her hand over her gasping mouth. "Oh my god, Rose. What happened? Who did this? I'll kill 'em."

"She was attacked," I whispered. "Last night by some entity. A ghost maybe. I thought there may be something in the book to help."

"A ghost? Shouldn't we call Ghost Girl?" Rayn asked.

"I called her seventeen times this morning," Rose muttered. "She didn't answer."

"I hope she's okay." Rayn took a quick scan of the Corner Cup as Rose had been doing every few seconds since she walked in. "Is it here? The thing that attacked you?"

"No. It followed me here but didn't come inside. I'm starting to think it can't."

"Whitney, may I see you and your friends in my office, please?" A voice spoke behind us, making me jump. Amilia.

"Amilia, I'm so sorry. I was only taking a quick break. I was about to get back behind the counter when-"

"Whitney, please, there is little time. Bring Rose and Rayn to my office immediately." Amilia was off as quickly as she appeared through the employee's only door.

How did she know their names?

Amilia was already behind her desk when the three of us entered her office. With a quick flick of her wrist in the air, Amilia closed and locked the door without touching it.

Rayn, Rose, and I all snapped to attention, not knowing what to expect. Rayn's power began to build inside of her, preparing to unleash a flame when Amilia spoke.

"I'm here to help," Amelia insisted, holding out her hands. "My intentions have been sincere since the moment each of you walked through my doors. You need to trust me if we are to overcome this darkness."

"What did you say?" Rayn's jaw dropped but she stood solid, still ready to fight.

"I've cast a perimeter charm around the property. Spirits cannot cross the boundary. You're safe inside of these walls, for now. I can help you get rid of this darkness, but we must act quickly." Amilia disregarded Rayn puffing up in defense.

"Amilia, I don't understand," I blinked in confusion, trying to make sense of her words.

"Whitney, there isn't much time," Amilia replied.

"How long have you known?" I wasn't sure what to say.

"That you're a witch? I suspected it when you first walked in but was only sure of it at your interview."

"You asked about my necklace. The first time I came in here, you commented on my necklace."

Rose perked up at my words. "You know about the jewelry?"

"I know there is a violent spirit stalking Rose, feeding on her fear, and it will not stop until it has taken her life." Amilia grabbed her bag from the desk and a sweater from the coat rack.

"Who did this to Rose?" I balled my shaking hands into fists at my sides to steady myself.

"I'm not sure, but I have an idea who the Renati living in the forest may be," Amilia explained. "If anyone is behind this, it must be them."

"Renati?"

"I will explain everything when Rose is safe, but right now, Whitney, you have to learn to listen." Amilia's eyes locked into mine.

"Why should we trust you?" Rayn crossed her arms. "You've been watching us for a while now, why did you wait until now to tell us anything?"

"You of all people should know the consequences of revealing your magic to others, Rayn Dansley," Amilia answered.

"Her intentions are good," Rose turned to Rayn and I. "I can tell."

"How?" Rayn inquired.

"You two mentally communicate. B sees ghosts. Lauren can feel stalkers. I'm an empath. We all have our thing."

"An empath?" I turned to her. "Since when?"

"A feeler," Amilia spoke. "One who endures the emotions of those around them. One who cannot be lied to."

"How do you know so much about us?" I moved toward the desk.

"I am an archivist." Amilia spoke as if we should have understood her words. As if she wasn't confusing as hell.

"An aardvark?" Rayn misheard.

Amilia wasn't amused. "Rose, has the spirit laid their hands on you?"

Rose nodded, tears welling in her eyes once more. She lifted her sleeves, allowing Amilia into the circle of trust.

"Oh, my dear." Amilia went to one of the cabinets on the wall.

Where I expected there to be stacks of business files and paperwork lay bottles of liquids and dried herbs, small stone mixing bowls, and thick books. An apothecary.

"Amilia, what are you making?" I asked for an explanation.

"For the pain," she replied. "We can't perform the spell here. It requires vanquishing the spirit, and they do not go down quietly. My cottage is not a far drive." Amilia mixed up ingredients in a small bowl that I couldn't see. "Rose, drink this." She put a hand on Rose's shoulder and gave her the tonic to drink.

Rose did as Amilia instructed, trusting her much more than I would have.

"What did you give her?" Rayn and I both asked.

"It's a mixture of olive oil with fae root and white willow bark. Completely medicinal," Amilia answered. "Please, you have to trust me if we are going to save Rose's life."

It wasn't the powers Amilia had exposed to us or her words that made me trust her, it was the look of care and comfort in her eyes. The look my Mom used to give me when I would have nightmares.

"We'll follow you in my car," I replied after a moment.

"Stay close. You must be on high alert." Amilia took out a pen and paper. "This is the address to the cottage, just in case."

"We're going to blindly follow her to her house and do magic with her? Whitney, we don't know what we're doing." Rayn still wasn't convinced.

I trust her, Ray. She's been good to me so far. I paused briefly, meeting her eyes. *She reminds me of Mom.*

Amilia handed me the paper with her address. 3837 Maple Drive. I didn't recognize the place, but I knew the handwriting.

"Mia?" I looked up at Amilia. "You left the notes in my locker."

Her smile was soft as she slowly nodded. "I was only presenting options, you girls made it happen."

"Wait, you're Mia? You knew our Mom?" Rayn asked with wide eyes. "She wrote about you in her journal. What kind of witch are you?"

"One who vowed to serve the generations," Amilia said, proudly. "One who loved your mother dearly."

"But how–"

Rose stifled a scream. She fell forward, clutching her stomach. Rayn and I reached out for her, helping her rest on the ground. Rose trembled, collapsing into herself. I wrapped my arms around her, pulling Rose against me in an attempt to shield her from whatever was happening.

"I feel the crawling again," Rose muttered, tears streaming down her face.

"It's what I feared," Amilia whispered.

"What is the crawling feeling? Why does she hurt like this?" I demanded more answers from the experienced witch in the room.

"Witches are able to put curses on each other through small hosts and blood rituals." Amilia explained. " Somehow, someone was able to get ahold of Rose's blood and used a small host, usually an insect. This curse seems to include a vengeful entity. I haven't seen anything like it."

"If you've never seen anything like this, how can you get rid of it?" Rayn questioned.

"I have vanquished spirits before. I have unbound curses. Doing them both at once will require much energy on all our parts but it is possible. We are leaving now." Amilia opened the door leading out of her office.

Rose cried, but never a full sob although I imagined the pain was agonizing. I was beginning to realize that Rose had the tolerance of a mighty oak, but it still cracked through the surface.

"Okay," Rayn finally agreed. "For Rose."

The drive was a blur. Rayn stayed in the backseat with Rose, who didn't want to look out any windows. Rose rested her head in Rayn's lap with her eyes shut, her teeth grinding together the entire fifteen minutes it took to drive from the Corner Cup to Amilia's cottage. Rayn ran gentle fingers through Rose's hair.

Amilia's cottage was a small, white, two-story home. Out front was a magnificent, colorful flower bed, with a white wooden fence covered in ivy lining the perimeter. Enough foliage for the privacy required of a practicing witch while remaining inviting enough to be discreet. Amilia had been doing this for a while.

Amilia waited for us out front. "Come inside quickly."

Amilia opened the door and shuffled us in before stepping inside herself. She secured all three of the door locks behind her. One on the doorknob and two more latches above that.

The front door of the cottage led into the living and dining room, separated only by two large throw rugs atop the wood flooring. A large, cream-colored couch faced away from the kitchen and toward two smaller armchairs. Blankets and pillows were thrown across them. A staircase sat in the corner leading up to a loft above the kitchen, which oversaw the living room.

"What do we need to do?" Rose asked, holding her stomach tightly.

Rayn pulled out the nearest chair in the dining room set and motioned for Rose to sit down.

"She's getting worse," my sister replied, feeling Rose's forehead with the back of her hand.

Rose's complexion had grown even paler since we left the Corner Cup, and her body temperature increased, causing sweat to trickle down from her forehead.

"We must remove the curse host from Rose's body and destroy the insect. Then, we must draw the spirit to us before we can get rid of it for good." Amilia opened a large, antiqued hutch in the dining room, revealing three rows of thick, leather-bound books that reminded me of a certain leather-bound book the girls and I had in our possession.

"Ah! This is the one." Amilia pulled out a book from the middle shelf and carefully laid it on the dining room table.

"Aaahhhh..." Rose groaned in pain, still holding her stomach. "I feel sick."

"There's a bathroom at the end of the hallway to the left. Wash rags in the cupboard. I think some cool water will help." Amilia flipped through the leather-bound book in front of her, using her powers to shuffle through the various spells until she found the one she was looking for.

Rayn helped Rose down the hallway, while I stayed behind and approached Amilia at the table. My head spun. How Mia could have been right in front of me this whole time. I should have known the moment she hired me after my vision during the interview. Part of me suspected it, but I never thought she would be that easy to find.

"You said someone used her blood to do this?" I asked, thinking back over everything Amilia had said about the curse.

Amilia went over the page with her finger. "Yes."

"Yes to the spell or yes to me?"

"To both," she clarified. "Did Rose tell you anything about how this happened? Where was she before this began?"

"She said it began with a dream. We were all at Dragonfly, the three of us and the other two girls."

"Dragonfly Mystic?" Amilia's head shot up from the spellbook.

"Yes, Rayn works there," I muttered. "We went in a few days ago and Rose cut herself on the staircase, but it was cleaned up. We-"

"Have you contacted the other girls about this?" Amilia inquired, interrupting me.

"Rose said she called Brooke, but she didn't answer. I don't think Lauren would care about Rose being in trouble."

"Whitney, I thought you understood the connection within your generation. If one of you is in trouble, all of you are in trouble. Magic is all connected."

I clenched my fist, digging my nails in my palm. "I don't know anything. I have no idea what an archivist is or why I have this necklace. I don't understand why we each only have one power but they all have to do with elements. You're the one with all the answers, but you're barely telling me anything! As if you assume we all grew up knowing we weren't alone in the world."

Amilia remained silent.

"Whitney!" Rayn's shaky voice called from down the hallway. Amilia and I rushed to her.

Rose was on the bathroom floor, barely holding herself up as Rayn held a washcloth to the back of Rose's neck.

"She's getting worse," Rayn replied, panic in her eyes.

I knelt next to Rose and put my hand against her forehead. She sighed in relief at the feel of my cold skin.

"Tell me more about Rose's dream, as much as you can remember," Amilia said from the bathroom doorway.

I told Amilia everything I remembered. The floor collapsing and all of us falling through. Her bed and the spirit being above her, attacking her.

"The insect must have entered her body while she slept." Amilia sighed. "Bring her into the dining room, onto the table. We must find and remove this parasite as quickly as possible. Rose can only hold back the spirit from joining for so long."

"The spirit from joining?" Rayn and I asked in unison.

"The longer the parasite eats away at Rose's power, the quicker the spirit can overcome her physical form. It's dangerous for a witch when her magical barrier is down like this. It is a vulnerable time for you all. Quickly, on the dining room table," Amilia ordered.

I helped Rayn pull Rose off the floor and move her toward the table. Rose had little strength to hold her arms around our necks, so we carried her down the hallway. The back of Rose's shirt was damp with sweat.

"Is the parasite easy to find?" I asked Amilia as she cleared the dining room table.

"I'm going to draw it out into the open. It must be killed immediately before it finds a new way into Rose, or into one of us." Amilia took a small bowl from the bottom of the hutch and lit three dark green incense cones inside it. "Whitney, in the kitchen next to the fridge there is a rosemary plant. I need three sprigs. Garlic from the pantry, and three candles, dark green."

Although I had never been inside her kitchen before, I navigated through it as if I had grown up in this house. The cupboards had panels for windows but no glass, so I could see and reach for things without opening doors. Inside the pantry, garlic hung in bunches by their long, dried-out sprigs. I took the ingredients back into the dining room.

"Anything else?" I asked, my heart pushing against my rib cage with each terrified beat.

"Rayn, put the candles in those holders behind you and light them one by one. Afterward, I'll need each of you on Rose's sides, holding her down. Drawing the parasite from her will be painful, and she will fight it." Amilia was already mixing the ingredients I'd brought her together in a separate bowl next to the burning incense cones. The scent of sage and pine filled the room.

Rayn lit the candles in their holders and looked to me for strength before she reached down and grabbed hold of Rose with both hands, one on Rose's shoulder and the other on her hip.

"Don't be afraid. You two must be strong for Rose. Focus on extracting the evil that is inside her. It will fight, and it will wear you down, but you must remember you are stronger than it is. You are much stronger than anything that dares to challenge you." Amilia spoke as if she was preparing us for battle. As if she stood in front of us as we fought against a force oppressing our freedom.

Amilia mixed her concoction one more time before there was a tear in some fabric. I opened my eyes to see Amilia spreading the green salve across Rose's abdomen.

"Close your eyes and concentrate, Whitney," Amilia ordered.

I cleared my mind, focusing only on Rose. The way she was before this morning. Clever, bright, strong, at a normal body temperature.

Rose screamed in agony and her body thrust forward, causing Rayn and I to both throw all our weight against her to keep her on the table.

"It's working! Stay focused!" Amilia shouted.

I closed my eyes once more and pictured the entity that had attacked Rose. I pictured it standing before us, weak and vulnerable. I thought about Rose standing tall and healthy against it, using the strength of a mighty oak to overcome this.

Rose cried out in pain and I couldn't keep my eyes closed. She coughed heavily, struggling against the grip Rayn and I had on her. A moment later, Rose gagged as a long, black centipede crawled out from her lips. My stomach churned as Rose coughed the centipede out. It fell onto the dining room table and scurried back to Rose in an eager attempt to get back to her.

A force came through the room that hit me like a freight train. I flew across the room, my back slamming against the wall as something heavy hit my chest and knocked the air from my lungs. A ringing in my ears permeated throughout my entire body.

I struggled to breathe as I opened my eyes to see the table on its side, blocking my view of Amilia and Rayn. Rose lay limp in my arms. I shook her to see if she was conscious, but her eyes remained closed.

A black figure rose up above the dining room, hovering in the air. Dark smoke wisped around it as it turned toward Rose. The figure was shaped like a human, though it was anything but. There was no face but it knew where she was, like the shadows. A chill ran through my body as I tightened my grip around Rose.

"Leave this place!" Amilia's voice rang throughout the dining room. "Leave this place, in the name of the Elementals and all they stand for!"

The figure remained unbothered, ignoring Amilia's demand as it started to float toward Rose and I. I tried to get up, but fell back to the hardwood once I put pressure on my right arm.

"It's not working!" Rayn's voice called out.

"We cannot vanquish the spirit until the host insect is killed." Amilia's voice cracked as she shouted. "Quickly!"

I scanned my side of the dining room, searching every corner as my heartbeat drummed in my ears. Rose stirred in my lap, groaning. A light tapping echoed in my ears, a scurrying sound across the hardwood floor. I shot up onto my knees as Rose slid off my leg, coming face to face with the long black centipede. The centipede's dozens of legs hurried toward Rose at full speed, desperate to crawl its way back inside her.

I grabbed the salt shaker, which had flown off the table during the spell. The ceramic blue and white chicken had broken in half, a sharp edge down its back from where the two pieces had split. With all of my strength, I thrust the sharp ceramic at the centipede. I stabbed the floor instead but quickly aimed again, striking the insect right in the middle of its body. The black figure hovering above the dining room shrieked, folding in half from the strike on the insect host.

"Kill it!" Rayn screamed as the spirit lunged at Amilia.

I twisted the shard of ceramic deeper, trying to cut the centipede in half, but the ceramic chicken wasn't sharp enough to break through the exoskeleton. As it began to wiggle away, I wrapped my free hand around it. Squeezing as tightly as I could, the insect fought against my grip but quickly hardened to my touch. Frost grew across its long body as the centipede slowly turned to solid ice.

"It's dead!" I screamed over the cries of the spirit.

"Leave this place!" Amilia repeated her previous words to the now-vulnerable spirit. "Leave this place in the name of the Elementals and all they stand for!"

The spirit lost altitude, falling to the hardwood. I peeked over the top of the table as Amilia threw her hands out in front of her, hitting the spirit with her power. I glanced down at the frozen centipede still gripped in my fingers, terrified to let it go.

"It's working." Rayn was on her ass, lifting herself up as she watched Amilia intently.

"Raaaaahh!" Amilia's deep battle cry rang throughout the cottage.

Without the centipede, the weakened spirit's attempt to attack Amilia failed. One final blow from Amilia and the spirit crumbled into itself. Energy erupted through the room once more and my back hit the floor as it blew me over. With a blink of the eye, the black, wispy spirit vanished, only thin clouds of smoke and dust remained as it slowly fell and settled on the hardwood.

Amilia let out a sigh of relief, looking between Rayn and I to make sure we were okay. She spotted the frozen centipede in my hand and nodded her approval. I unwrapped my icy fingers as parts of the insect stuck to my skin. Rayn got on her feet and hurried over to me, placing her warm hand over mine. Finally, I was able to flex my frozen fingers. The ice didn't seem to bother my skin as circulation returned to my fingers like nothing happened.

"Rose." Her name flew from my lips and I turned around and hurried to her side. She was still on the floor, half-awake and rubbing her temple. "Are you okay?"

"Mmhmm," she muttered, letting Rayn and I pick her up. With one of Rose's arms around each of our shoulders, we carried her to the couch and laid her down gently.

Amilia grabbed a blanket to lay over Rose as her eyelids fluttered closed.

"Come," Amilia placed her hand on my shoulders. "Now that Rose is comfortable, let's clean up this mess."

CHAPTER EIGHTEEN

THE COTTAGE

R ose slept for hours on Amilia's cream-colored couch with a red and orange crochet blanket draped over her. Rayn and I sat in the two armchairs in silence. Even if I knew what to say, I was too exhausted to say a word or dare to close my eyes. Instead, I counted the wooden slats of the dining room chairs.

The sun sunk down over the mountains casting a shadow across the trees, slowly darkening the woods outside. We should have gone home already, but after what we had been through I was hesitant to leave the Cottage. What if the spirit that attacked Rose was not truly banished and waiting for us outside these wooden walls. I was afraid that if I didn't stay and push Amilia for answers, she would disappear like Abe. Night was quickly approaching and I knew my time was running out. It was now or never.

"Is this where my magic comes from?" I turned to Amilia, holding the aquamarine of my necklace tightly in the palm of my hand.

"The talismans? No, your magic is your own," Amilia answered. "But what you wear around your neck is valuable. It should be kept close to you at all times."

"We never take them off," Rayn replied.

"Good." Amilia seemed relieved. "Keep it that way."

"What are they, then?" I pressed, unsatisfied with her answer.

"Talismans," Amilia replied as if we knew what that entailed.

"But what does that mean?"

I felt like a three-year-old. What's this? What's that? Why? Why? Why?

"Talismans are meant to protect those who wear them. A good luck charm, if you will." Amilia left to the kitchen as a tea kettle on the stove began to scream. She returned with a tray of light brown teacups.

"Your powers…" Rayn began, but she seemed unable to come up with the words she wanted. "Your magic. When did you get it?"

"I've always had my abilities, as you have always had yours." Amilia poured us each a cup of tea.

I sighed and scanned my surroundings. Amilia's living room had no television or family photos hanging from the walls, only paintings and photographs of wildlife. One of a bear in a stream catching a fish in its mouth, and another of a herd of horses running through a field, dust rising up around their hooves. Three large bookshelves rested against the walls not taken up by old furniture, each one filled to the brim. The books were leather-bound and ancient, many of them were unmarked. The ones that did have words on the spine were hand-carved into the cover in the same swirling handwriting as the notes left in my work locker.

Healing Herbs

Potions and Brews

Spells of Old

Myth and Legend of Generations Past

"Where did you get all of these old books?" I asked, getting up from the armchair for a closer look at her collection.

"Travels. Some I sought after, and others came to me through other witches." Amilia explained. "I even wrote some myself."

"You write your own spellbooks?" Rayn asked from the edge of her seat.

"Amongst other things. I am an archivist." Amilia's relaxed tone unsettled me.

"You keep saying that like it means something to us."

Amilia smiled at our impatience. "An archivist is a witch who cares for old texts, to ensure that our history is preserved. That our *true* history is preserved."

"What other history would there be?" I asked, leaning toward the bookshelf as if the books would tell me their secrets.

"Tales of the past are always skewed one way or another," Amilia answered, sipping her tea.

"I don't understand," Rayn admitted. "There is so much you aren't telling us. All Whitney and I want…all *any* of us want is the truth about who we are." My sister looked over at Rose asleep on the couch.

"That, my dear girls, is a rocky path. I can't give you all the answers because I don't have them. Who you are can only be found within yourself, in your hearts." Amilia spun us a riddle.

"I don't mean who we are as individuals. I mean where our powers came from. Are there others like us? Others who can create fire and grow plants back from ashes? What is this floating ink inside of our jewelry and what is the symbol that appeared on them the first night we were all together? Why are we all in Rifton?" Rayn counted her questions out on her fingers as she asked them.

"Well, that is quite the list of demands, Rayn." Amilia couldn't help but smile.

"You won't tell us any of it?" Rayn rested her elbows on her knees.

"Your powers come from within yourselves. The magic you wield is older than I understand. It has been passed down to you." Amilia offered the teapot for a refill but I shook my head. "Magic is energy, energy in its purest form. The magic chose you."

"That doesn't make any sense." My sister huffed in frustration, accepting more tea from Amilia.

"What does this symbol mean?" I turned the gem of my necklace around, allowing Amilia to see the circles and diamond.

"That is the symbol of the Elementals. The generations."

"What about a symbol with one circle and a diamond with a crooked cross?"

"You refer to the Renati." Amilia set her tea cup down on a side table. "They're a group of witches who believe the Elementals, that *you*, are corrupt."

"So, the bad guys," Rayn replied, taking a drink from her teacup.

"I suppose that depends who you ask." Amilia said.

"Who are the Renati exactly? What do they get out of hurting Rose or any of us? Mom wrote about them in her journal."

"The followers of Erebus."

"Who?"

With a graceful wave of Amilia's hand, the thick book titled *Myth and Legend of Generations Past* slid out from its place on the bookshelf and floated toward me.

"Why aren't we able to move things like that?" I asked, grabbing the book.

"Of course you can."

"I can't move anything around with my mind." I insisted. "I can only control water."

"Have you ever tried?" Amilia asked.

"Yes," I admitted. "A few times, actually, but nothing."

"You doubt yourself, Whitney. You will never unlock your full potential if you continue to drown in such doubt." Amilia sat on the edge of her seat. "You must trust yourself."

"You mean what we can already do is not our full potential?" Rayn raised a brow curiously.

"That is entirely up to you." Amilia took a sip of her tea before standing up, stretching her back as she headed into the kitchen. "You girls must be starved."

"I'm not hungry," I answered.

"Yes, you are." Apparently there was no lying to Amilia.

"Amilia…" I pondered. "There's something I've been wanting to ask you. During my interview…When I blacked out and came to again, you hardly looked surprised."

"I knew you had a vision," Amilia admitted. "There is one Seer per Elemental generation. The Seer can look into the past and the present. They are the only one who has these visions, but they can be rather metaphoric. You must take whatever you see with a grain of salt." Amilia paused, and a sad smile took over her face. "And to be honest, once I found out you were one of Audri's girls, I knew I had to do my part in making sure you were taken care of."

"So how exactly did you know our mom?" Rayn turned to Amilia.

Amilia's smile faded. "She was a dear friend. I was devastated to hear of her passing. I knew the moment I saw Whitney. Audri sent me many pictures of you girls over the years."

"You should have told me instead of leaving encrypted notes in my locker." I shook my head.

"I was trying to handle things delicately, I didn't know how you'd react," Amilia admitted.

"How did you know her?" Rayn asked again eagerly.

"We grew up together, staying in touch over the years after she decided to move to Hemston. We wrote often, but we never saw each other again. She wanted to stay hidden and it was safer that way. Life took your mother on her own journey. She wanted Kansas to be home, so that's where she stayed."

I sat in silence, absorbing Amilia's words. I watched her every move; how her lips curled into a nostalgic smile when she spoke about my mother. How she played with the rings on her fingers. One ring, in particular, she spun around on her thumb. A thick silver band with a round moonstone in the middle. The exact twin of the moonstone that I wore.

My mother's ring.

"You really are Mia." My head spun thinking back to the entries in Mom's journal I had read a million times the last few weeks.

"I am," Amilia gave a soft smile. "You girls have to eat something."

"Wait." I tried to stop her, but she was already on her way into the kitchen. "Why did you change your name?"

"I didn't. Mia is a nickname from when your mother and I were young."

"We found our mom's journal recently. She wrote that Ray and I would never be safe in Rifton."

Amilia nodded. "The Renati. Your mother also didn't leave on good terms with her family. I think she was afraid to face them again. Your grandmother passed away a few years ago, but your aunt is still in the area. She and your mother didn't get along."

I blinked. "Is she the one who threatened to take custody of Dmitri? Sue?"

Amilia nodded again.

"Prove it," Rayn demanded, her back straight as an arrow. "Prove you're the Mia our mom wrote about."

"That's a fair request." Amilia went up the stairs into the bedroom loft.

After a few moments of rustling, she returned with a small cardboard box. She handed it to Rayn, and I rushed over to examine her evidence. Rayn opened the lid and pulled out stacks of letters, all in Mom's handwriting. Envelopes addressed to Amilia Burnett with the return address as our home in Hemston. Underneath the letters were thick, leather-bound books similar to the ones on Amilia's shelves.

"Were these Moms?" I asked, retrieving the first book in the pile. "She wrote about sending her spellbooks back to you in her journal."

"The very same." Amilia smiled. "They're yours now. I know Audri never intended for me to keep them forever. Jam with your toast?"

The crumbs of information I was being fed didn't satisfy me in the least. I had waited too many years, asked too many questions. Rose almost died right in front of us because we had been left in the dark, it wasn't going to happen again.

"Amilia, I need to know why Mom kept all of this from us." I pleaded.

"Audri wanted you to live normal childhoods, to be safe and cared for. She wanted to wait until you were ready. Right now, you need to eat." She pointed to the book she'd pulled from the shelf. "Look through that book I gave you."

I opened the cover of the old, leather-bound book as Rayn leaned in, resting her head against my shoulder. The pages were thick parchment like the spellbook from the cemetery. The first page we turned to was handwritten.

The Heralds. The first Great Generation of the Elementals established the colony of Paradisus and the first of the Magisters.

The Martyrs. The Magisters of the last Great Generation of the Elementals, murdered by Erebus in the Great Uprising.

The Shepherds. The last Great Generation of the Elementals sacrificed themselves to banish Erebus to the Shadow Realm.

Erebus. Whoever this leader of the Renati was, they did a great deal of damage before they were banished. If the Elementals were supposed to be the most powerful witches, who was this person that murdered an entire generation and forced another to sacrifice themselves?

Moments later, Amilia emerged from the kitchen with a loaf of homemade rosemary bread. The loaf smelt heavenly, fresh out of the oven.

"Shadow Realm, we've read about that." I looked up from the book. "Who is Erebus?"

"He was a witch, a powerful one that used forbidden magic. He turned his followers against the way of the Elementals and destroyed everything. He is the reason we are in hiding, the reason your mother kept you in the dark. The Renati believe Elementals are corrupt, that they must be eradicated."

"But why?"

"Lust for power. The Shepherds sacrificed themselves to banish Erebus from our world, but the Renati have been attempting to bring him back for centuries. They've been running Rifton for a long time. Generations help us if they do, but as long as the Renati remain unsuccessful in bringing him back to power, Erebus is not someone you need to worry about. I know you must be starving, Rose. Would you like butter and jam on your bread?" Amilia asked.

I turned at Rose's name to see her sitting up on the couch, rubbing her forehead with a pained look on her face. "Yes, please," Rose answered quietly.

I left the leather-bound book in my sister's hands and rushed to Rose's side. "Are you okay?" I sat down next to her and reached out to rest my hand on her still trembling shoulder.

"I will be," she whispered. Dark circles had formed under her eyes, and her skin was still pale.

"It's over now, you're safe here," Amilia reassured, offering Rose a plate of food. "Eat."

"I'm still so tired. How long was I asleep for?" Rose's eyelids were heavy as she took the plate of bread with a small smile.

"A few hours," Rayn answered, her eyes still glued to the book in her lap.

"The spell you endured took most of your willpower." Amilia explained. "You will need to stay here for the rest of the night so I can keep an eye on you while you recover."

"All night?" Rayn cocked an eyebrow.

"I would like to. I have questions." Rose's voice was soft, yet determined.

"Your friends have asked many, but I don't have all the answers." Amilia's warm smile reached her eyes.

"Of course not." Rose ripped off a piece of bread as she looked over and met my eyes. "Thousand piece jigsaw. What do you mean Renati run the town?" Rose asked.

"Many of the Renati elders hold positions of power in Rifton. Local government, industry, city council. Hiding in plain sight. They took over nearly twenty years ago." Amilia looked away, though I could still see the sadness in her eyes. "Not all witches in the Renati flaunt their magic around like the younger members. Those who hold the real power stay in the shadows."

"Why Rifton though? How did all these witches end up in town?" Rose asked Amilia.

"The Dark Star Forest has always been a place of magic, an Allurement. Witches have always been drawn to these woods."

"A what?"

"An Allurement is a concentration of magic, calling out to witches through our energy. Renati and the Elementals are two sides of the same coin, using the same energy that flows through all living things for different purposes. Certain magic is forbidden, such as blood magic and necromancy. Under no circumstances should the magic the Renati wield be performed; it's the Elemental Code and it exists to protect us. Before the split, all witches followed the guidance of the Elementals."

"So the Elementals were like the leaders?"

"You were, yes."

"*We?*"

"Elemental magic is reincarnated from one generation to the next. You are very much yourself and at the same time those who came before you." Amilia explained everything like she was reading a children's bedtime story. "I think that's enough for one night, there is plenty of time for questions later."

"But-"

"You girls need some rest. I'm not going anywhere. Finish your bread."

As much as I wanted to push Mia for more, I couldn't keep my eyes open.

I dreamt I was in the crypt of the cemetery where the girls and I found the book, only everything was distorted. The walls kept shifting and morphing into a place I didn't recognize. Brooke's screams echoed off the concrete walls, making my body tremble. I tried to crawl to her, but I was too late. Blood splattered across the walls of the crypt as ear-shattering cries for help filled my entire being, then silence. Claws tore down my back before I realized what was happening, ripping my skin apart. Burning overwhelmed my body as warm liquid ran down my legs. I pleaded for help as the shadow's teeth sunk into the curve of my neck.

When I awoke the next morning, I was alone in the living room of the cottage. Startled, I jumped up from the couch, tossing the heavy quilt off of me. I grabbed my neck where the shadow had bitten me in my dream, but all was as it should be. Nausea stirred in my stomach as the memory of Brooke's screams vibrated through my skull. My heart pounded deep in my chest not knowing where my sister or Rose were.

"Rayn?" I called loudly. "Rose?"

No one answered.

I went straight to the kitchen and called their names again. As I turned the corner from the living room, the wide-open kitchen door greeted me. It led outside to a small, cherrywood-stained deck and the back garden. From the front of the house, I had not realized that the rest of the property was so lavished with flowers and herbs, fruits and vegetables.

Stepping off the deck into the dirt I saw three figures through the tall shrubbery and rose bushes that surrounded the railing.

"Rayn? Rose?"

"Over here! Come on, I want you to see this!" Rayn called out.

I sighed in relief and made my way through the maze that was the Cottage's impressive garden. I had never seen such a collection of greenery in my life.

"Isn't this place amazing? It's better than the meadow!" Rose exclaimed. Her eyes lit up with excitement. I smiled in relief seeing Rose back to normal.

"The meadow?" Amilia inquired curiously.

I didn't answer, as if the meadow was nowhere special. "These flowers are gorgeous." I reached out and gently touched the light purple petals.

"We should get home," Rayn replied as she closed her eyes to soak up a few more rays of sunshine. "Dmitri's been by himself all night."

"My mom thinks I was at your house." Rose laughed, looking at Rayn. "I need to get home too, though. I have homework."

"You girls are welcome at the cottage any time, day or night." Amilia reached out and put her hand on Rayn's shoulder. "Stay safe and keep your wits about you, and I promise next time we will talk more about your mother." Amilia gave a kind smile, which slowly faded as the wheels of her mind turned. "I've been wanting to ask but-"

"What?" Rayn shifted her weight between her feet.

"Dmitri. How is he? What is he like?" Amilia asked, tears welling in her eyes. "He was barely three last time I saw him in person."

"He's okay," I answered slowly, not realizing this woman had loved my brother. That she had held him as a baby and maybe cared for him like her own. "Losing Mom has been hard on him but he's holding it together. He's a sweet guy. Dmitri is kind and talented, he can paint and draw pretty much anything he wants."

Amilia's eyes warmed as a wide smile spread across her face. "I'm so glad. He's lucky to have you two watching over him."

"Thank you, for everything." I reached for Amilia's hand, overwhelmed by all she had done for me and the girls. She had not only employed me but she had saved Rose's life, and for that, I would be forever grateful.

"I'll see you at work." Amilia smiled.

When we got back home, Rayn fell asleep the moment her face hit the pillow. We had gotten some sleep at the Cottage, but nothing compared to the comfort of your own bed, and not being in the same room where a vengeful spirit had been expelled from someone's body. As exhausted as I was, I couldn't sleep. I had experienced too much and learned too much to clear my mind and drift off.

Instead of turning to the internet for research like I usually did when I was questioning my own existence, I picked up a book. Reading was one of the few activities that actually relaxed me and helped me get out of my own head. Bryan had supplied me with several options. The top book in the stack was a collection of short stories. The second, a novel by Michael Crichton. The third had no title or author. It was thick with a black and gray striped pattern on the cover. I turned back the first few pages curiously to a full handwritten page. Every page was handwritten, margins and all. The first few pages were notes on a Hemingway novel, analyzing theme and character development. But the page after was definitely not homework.

It's astonishing how one can be surrounded by so many faces day after day but loneliness still echoes in their soul. The sun shines brightly amidst the clouds yet offers no warmth, no comfort. This hollow pit grows deeper with each passing hour, but recovery is a struggle I wish no part in. I've grown accustomed to despair, like a badge of honor received from a battle wound. Nevertheless, I cannot ignore the longing to feel the rays of the sun once more. I am much too young to feel this tattered.

Wow. What sorrow. What beautifully written words. I had always been jealous of those who could write well. I flipped to the next page.

I worry about Rosie. She pretends she prefers to be left alone but I know her better than that. Pretending the outside world doesn't matter. Pretending I am blind as she lays awake at night, terrified of sleep, for the night only holds demons of self-reflection. I wish I knew what words to string together to make her see that it is unnecessary to face these trials of life in solitary confinement. We all suffer, but we don't have to suffer alone.

It wasn't until I finished the paragraph that I realized this handwriting belonged to Bryan. Never had I read something that set my soul on fire as these words. Bryan's words.

I should have closed the notebook right then and there. I knew I shouldn't have been reading such private feelings, but I couldn't help myself. This was a window into Bryan's soul and I was dying to know more, to see the dark corners and depths of his heart.

Three pages later, Dmitri knocked on my door. I slammed Bryan's notebook shut as if the police were at my door asking about stolen property in my possession.

"Hey," My brother said entering my bedroom. "Where the hell were you two last night? Rayn texted and said you slept at your boss's house?"

"Sit down, I have some stuff to tell you," I answered. "We met Mia."

Chapter Nineteen

INTANGIBLE

*B*oom. *Boom. Boom.*

I stopped cold in the living room. That was no regular knock on the front door at 7:45 in the morning. Rayn, who was closest to the door putting her shoes on to leave for class, answered.

"Can I help you, officers?" She kept the door closed far enough that I couldn't see. *Whitney, it's the cops from Brooke's house,* she warned.

"Is Whitney Dansley home?" a male voice asked from the other side of the door.

"Yes. What's going on?" Rayn shifted her weight, blocking their view inside.

"We would like to ask her a few questions regarding the disappearance of Abraham Roberts."

My heart sank and my knees turned to gelatin.

"And why do you need to ask my sister about that?" Rayn held her ground firmly in front of the door as if to let the police know they had no business in our home.

"We want to ask her a few questions. It's a standard formality," the cop replied reassuringly.

My sister stepped back and allowed the two police officers to enter. They stayed in the entryway, pens and small notebooks grasped firmly in their hands. I approached them, nearly tripping over myself.

"Do you know Abraham Roberts?" the taller of the two police officers asked with a stern face. His badge read R. Higgins.

I recognized the dark brown haired officer at his right all too well from the night we were caught taking Brooke home. Officer J. Grady.

"His parents are our landlords," I replied. "They live next door."

"What's going on?" Dmitri asked, opening back the curtain from his bedroom.

"Do any of you have any idea where he might have gone?" Grady questioned.

"No," Rayn answered quickly. Almost too quickly. Anyone with any kind of interrogation experience would be able to tell that Rayn and I were panicked beyond recognition.

"So it's a coincidence that you were both out nearly past curfew in the same area where Mr. Roberts went missing?" Officer Grady peered up from his notebook with a smirk.

"What exactly are you insinuating?" I took a step toward the intruders in dark blue uniforms. "We're both adults, we don't have a curfew."

"The station has received anonymous tips that you two have been seen numerous times at the exact spot off Eagle Loop where Mr. Roberts was last seen. Including the night you were with Brooke Evans. Star gazing, was it?"

"Anonymous tips? That sounds fabricated." I crossed my arms. "Everything you have is speculation. Technically, we haven't done anything wrong."

"We're asking questions regarding-"

"It sounds like you are accusing us of having something to do with that boy's disappearance. The Roberts are good people and they have been nothing but great landlords to us. Officers, you're wasting your time and you are unwelcome in this home interrogating me and frightening my kids while there are real criminals out there who require your attention," I snapped.

"Ma'am, please calm down." Officer Higgins held out his hand, but his tactics were pointless. "Maybe we should take this down to the station."

"Is there a law against stargazing on public hiking trails?" I asked.

"No ma'am," Higgens answered.

"Am I under arrest?"

"No ma'am."

"Well then, you two have a wonderful rest of your morning." I reached around them and aggressively opened the door, showing Higgins and Grady out.

"We'll be in touch," Grady said, looking back and forth between Rayn and I the same way he had the night he spoke with us outside of Brooke's home.

I closed the front door behind them and slid down the wood until I was sitting on the floor.

"Holy shit, Whitney, you went full mama bear." Dmitri stood in the middle of the living room, engulfed in worry. His eyes glossed over. "Why were they asking you guys about

Abe? They're acting like something bad happened. I'm worried something happened to him."

"Good." Rayn scoffed, crossing her arms.

I intercepted before Dmitri blew a fuse. "Rayn, enough. Mit, don't fall down a rabbit hole of potential scenarios. They're following leads because they legally have to but we aren't one. Abe will show up, okay?"

Dmitri stood in silence for a moment. "Janice said she doesn't know where Abe went after he left their house."

"I know," I replied.

"If the cops had anonymous tips that he was last seen at Eagle Loop, why wouldn't they tell Janice?"

"Probably to keep her from driving herself crazy like you are." I sighed and checked the time on my phone. "You two better get going."

"If those douchebags come back, text me. They need to charge us with something or leave us the hell alone." Rayn grabbed her bag and opened the front door.

I gave her a fake smile. "It'll be fine. They can't prove anything."

Once Rayn and Dmitri left for school, I called Lauren. We had tried calling her when Rose was attacked but she was ignoring us. Surprisingly, she answered on the third ring.

"I'm at work, Whitney," Lauren answered. No hello, no pleasant greeting.

"Well, it's nice to know you're alive." I collapsed onto the couch in relief.

"Why wouldn't I be?" Lauren asked, her voice hushed.

"Rose was attacked. You could have at least answered my texts." I sighed. "She's okay, if you give a fuck."

I could almost hear the scowl in Lauren's voice. "I figured you'd let me know if she wasn't okay."

"I'm quickly approaching the point where I don't care why you and Rose hate each other, but we are a generation. You don't get to choose your family, Lauren, but we still have to look out for one another. Any one of us could be the next target."

Lauren was silent for a moment and then took in a deep breath, "It's a lot to process."

"I get that," I answered. "But we need you."

"Hey." Lauren's tone went soft, a moment of vulnerability that I had yet to see from her. "I'm at work, I have to go, but...I'm glad Rose isn't dead. And I'm sorry I've pulled back. I needed a moment to pretend all of this wasn't happening. I need some space."

"I don't know if you're going to get that luxury, Lauren," I said.

"I'll talk to you later." The call ended.

I spent the rest of the day on the couch, reading Bryan's notebook. It wasn't all as sad as the first entry, but it was all equally beautiful and a welcomed distraction from our morning visitors.

A little past three in the afternoon, Rayn and Dmitri got home but three people walked through my front door.

"Hey!" I jumped up and greeted them by the door, pulling Brooke into a hug. "Your parents let you leave the house?"

"Finally. Ray caught me up on the cops showing up," Brooke said. "I think Abe is like us."

"I don't think so, Brooke." I pursed my lips. "He has powers but he isn't an Elemental."

"What if he is and he hid it? Or what if he's like Dmitri?"

I shrugged and let out a sigh. "That would make sense, but we can't exactly ask him."

"There's only one way to find out. We need to go through his things." Brooke said nonchalantly.

"Break into his house and go through his room?" I almost laughed. "Brooke, you can't be serious."

"Yeah, whenever his parents leave, we go in there and see what we can find." Brooke spoke like this would be an easy operation.

"Brooke, his parents have done a lot for me. I don't feel right breaking and entering on them."

"I thought we were in this to find answers," Brooke argued.

"I know, but-"

"I think we should," Dmitri agreed. "Especially if it'll give us some idea of where he's gone."

"You think his parents haven't already gone through his room looking for that? What are we supposed to do if Janice finds out we were in their house?" I asked.

"Tell me you aren't the least bit curious about Abe. He knows so much more than we do and I am sick and tired of having no idea what is happening around me. It's worth a try." Brooke pushed. "Whitney, we're going with or without you."

I huffed. Of course they were. "Fine."

"What do we do if someone comes home and we're still in there?" Dmitri asked reluctantly.

Rayn turned to him. "You and I will stay behind at our house and keep a lookout. If they do, stall them so Whit and B can get out of there. We're going to be next door, not across town."

Brooke and I going into the unknown again, like the cemetery. This wasn't a recurrence I was growing fond of.

"But I want to go," Dmitri argued.

I shook my head. "Mit, I don't think that's a good idea."

Dmitri was already teetering on the edge of stability with Abe's disappearance and being in his bedroom could push my brother right over. He didn't argue.

The back door of the Roberts' home was unlocked. When we first moved in, Janice had told us that this was one of the safest neighborhoods they had ever seen, hardly anyone locked their doors. Luckily for us, that was true.

The inside of their house looked like it had been decorated by someone's grandmother. The couches were neat and tidy with doilies on the arms. Crochet blankets draped over a rocking chair in the corner of the living room, and photos of a small copped-hair boy covered the walls.

"Come on." Brooke led the way to the staircase. "You said his bedroom was upstairs, right?"

The two of us tiptoed, but any creek or noise still put us on edge. Who knew when Janice or her husband would be pulling into the driveway.

Abe's bedroom was exactly as I remembered from my nightmare. My blood ran cold as I took it all in, hearing the rabbit scream in my head. There were posters on the wall of cars, and one from a video game I'd seen Dmitri play before.

Brooke wasted no time, going to Abe's dresser. She pulled open the drawers and began sifting through his clothing, looking for anything that would give us some kind of answer. When she didn't find anything there, she slid back the door to his closet.

I stood frozen in the doorway, unable to move as I had a staring contest with his bed.

"Whitney? What's the matter?" Brooke asked over her shoulder.

"The nightmare I was telling you guys about...the one about Abe. Everything looks exactly the same." I was afraid to touch anything, as if Abe was going to return one day and see all his things rummaged through. He would know we had been here.

Abe Roberts did strange things to my intuition. One moment I was ready to strike, to defend myself against him at all cost. The next, I almost felt sorry for him. The last conversation we had buzzed around my head like wasps. I still couldn't figure out what his words meant.

Slowly, I knelt down beside Abe's bed. I could only imagine a dark creature with fangs and talons lurking as it waited for me to come into sight and attack, but there were no shadows hiding under the bed. Only some lost socks, a pair of jeans, and a box.

I slid the wooden box out from under his bed and a chill ran through my veins. The design burnt into the cover was the same that Abe wore carved into his skin.

"Brooke...come look at this." I left the box sitting there, glaring up at us while she came to my side.

"Bingo." Brooke reached down and opened the lid attached with two small brass hinges. At the top rested a small, black spiral notebook with the same design on the cover of the box doodled all over it in silver ink.

Brooke picked it up, but I stopped her before she could open it. "Be careful, we don't know what any of these things are or what Abe used them for."

She nodded in acknowledgment and opened the notebook as my attention went back to the box. There were a few dark colored candles and a box of matches. A vile of dark red liquid that I convinced myself was not blood. What drew my attention was the small dagger with a red gem on the handle. The same dagger I distinctly remembered from the nightmare, the one Abe used to kill the rabbit. At least now I knew for certain it wasn't all in my head.

"What does it say?" I asked Brooke, who was still flipping through Abe's notebook.

"Some really weird drawings. He writes about you and Rayn, especially you."

"What does he say about me?"

Bang.

A door closed downstairs, and the soft sound of low murmurs alerted us that we were not alone in the house.

"Fuck," I whispered. "His parents are home. We need to get out of here now."

Brooke's eyes widened in fear. "You suggest we go out the second story window?"

I searched the room in a panic, attempting to think of some way we could sneak past them, but it was too risky. It's not like we would be able to sneak down the stairs and slide past his parents as they did dishes or sat on the couch watching television.

This was a mistake. The Roberts were going to find us, realize we had broken into their home, and kick us out of their rental. Officer Grady would be back up here in a heartbeat. I could see in his eyes that the cop was looking for anything to connect Rayn and I to Abe's disappearance and we had given him the perfect evidence. How was I supposed to defend myself? Oh, it's no big deal, Officer, we are only witches who are looking for what these symbols mean. But we are good witches, I swear.

"Whitney!" Brooke snapped in a hushed tone. "What are you doing?"

"Thinking." I crept to Abe's door and peeked around the frame.

I couldn't see either of his parents or hear them for that matter. They could have been anywhere in the house. Taking a deep breath and doing my best to feel what to do with my intuition, I grabbed Brooke's elbow and led her out into the hallway.

Ray, they're home. Where are you?

No reply.

"Whitney, they're going to see us," Brooke whispered but I didn't answer, trying to formulate a plan.

"Janice, you can't keep torturing yourself going into Abraham's room every day. He will come home soon, darling." A man's voice echoed from downstairs followed by footsteps up the staircase directly in front of us.

I began to panic, reaching out to put Brooke behind me. The last thing I wanted was to get her into more trouble with her parents or associate her with the investigation going on by Rifton Police. I wanted to keep Brooke and the other girls safe, and so far, I wasn't doing a great job.

"I'll go into my son's room whenever I please. I'm his mother." I could see the top of Janice's red hair as she climbed the staircase.

I closed my eyes, preparing myself for Janice's confused demands of, 'what are you doing in my house'? But instead, Brooke's hands gripped onto my shoulders and yanked me against the wall. Only we didn't hit the wall, we went through it.

When I opened my eyes, Brooke and I were no longer in the hallway. I was no longer looking at the staircase or the photos on the wall, I was staring at two-by-four studs and insulation.

"Brooke?" I asked quietly. "What the hell happened?"

"I don't know," she whimpered, a silent tear rolling down her cheek. "I think I did this."

"I sure as Hell didn't," I whispered.

Footsteps on the other side of the wall passed us as Janice walked down the hallway and into Abe's room.

"Jeff!" Janice Roberts shouted, her voice frantic and uncertain. "Jeff! Come quick!"

"What happened? Are you hurt?" More footsteps up the staircase were followed by the sound of jogging down the hall.

"He was here! Abe was home!" Janice cried.

Oh shit. We didn't put the box away. We didn't close the dresser drawers.

"Can you get us out of here?" I asked Brooke quickly. Now that both of Abe's parents were preoccupied in his room, it was our chance to get out undetected.

"I don't know…"

"B…" I said through my teeth.

Brooke closed her eyes tight and grabbed my arm, throwing us both at the studs and drywall before us. I barely felt the wall as we went through it again.

"I don't understand," Brooke whispered, but I grabbed her hand and sprinted toward the staircase.

We didn't have time to try and analyze what had happened. There would be an opportunity for that once we were safe and sound back in my house and out of the Roberts'. Brooke and I blew through the back door and ran as fast as we could across the lawn. Even when we got to the side yard next to our rental, I still couldn't breathe. I collapsed onto the grass and put my hand over my chest in an effort to keep my heart from pounding out of my skin.

Rayn came charging down the porch steps and knelt down beside us. "Oh my god, what happened?"

"What happened? Are you fucking kidding me, Ray? Where were you?" I glared at my sister. "They came home! They came home and we were still in the hallway and Brooke pulled us through the damn wall!"

"I'm sorry, Tom called and I went inside for a minute. What do you mean you guys went through the wall?" Rayn leaned back on her feet.

"I don't know what happened," Brooke breathed, tears welling in her eyes. "Nothing like that has ever happened before."

"I guess seeing ghosts isn't your only power, B. Don't cry, it's okay. You guys got out of there and everything's okay." Rayn reached out and took Brooke's hand in comfort.

"What's happening to me?" Brooke asked, more tears flowing down her red cheeks.

"I know it's scary." I sat up and rested a hand on Brooke's knee. "But you aren't alone in this."

Brooke pulled the small, black spiral notebook from her back pocket and flipped to a back page before she handed it over to me. "You need to see what Abe wrote about you, Whitney. He's nothing like we thought he was."

I took the notebook from Brooke with a shaky hand and breathed deeply to settle my nerves before I read over the sloppy handwriting.

She charged at me today, the girl next door. I can't protect her. Not from the Renati and their plans. It's only a matter of time before they come for her. If it wasn't for Dmitri, I'd be dead. I knew it was coming and I had accepted it, but he gave me another chance. I want to share everything with him. I want to help his sisters, but I can't. Ren made sure of that. I'm so scared he will get caught in the crossfire. The sacrificial spell will only keep him safe for so long, it's only a matter of time before they go after him, too. I don't think I can handle that. He's too good. He means too much. Whitney wants to know more. Those girls think they want answers. I tried to scare her off but that girl doesn't scare easily. That'll be her downfall. However this all ends, he should have let me drown. It may have saved all their lives.

The dark ritual I had seen Abe performing was to keep my brother safe. A life for a life. Amilia warned us that the dark magic of the Renati was forbidden by the Elemental Code, but how could this magic be so evil if it was performed out of love to keep my brother safe?

CHAPTER TWENTY

TRANSPARENCY

Friday evening at the Corner Cup was much busier than usual for Acoustic Night. Ashley told me the store would be packed but I didn't actually think we would have so many people show up.

Two sets had already been played, one solo artist with his acoustic guitar sang about recovering from heartache followed by a younger girl who read a few original poems. They were both so talented, it amazed me that they had the courage to put their hearts out for the entire shop to see. The initial surge of business died down as the majority of guests took their seats in anticipation of the rest of the night's performances.

Ashley let out an exhausted sigh and rested her weight against the back counter next to one of the espresso machines. She grabbed a clean towel and began to clean the counter of coffee and milk. "Whoo. Acoustic Nights are always so busy."

"If I knew it was going to be this bad, I would have brought more food," I answered, acknowledging the rumble in my stomach. "I'm starving."

"Me too." Ashley pulled out her phone and answered a quick text message. "Do you want an espresso shot? I'm exhausted and it's going to be a long night."

"Sure." I could use caffeine. My body was slowing down from lack of sleep and the night had barely begun.

While Ashley set up two shot glasses under the espresso machine, I went to the water dispenser and got myself a glass. It was lukewarm, but I chilled the glass in my hands discreetly. I made sure to do it quickly while Ashley had her back turned and the dining room full of customers were focused on their phones or coffee mugs. I was always hesitant to use my powers in front of this many people but I was only changing the water's temperature, not creating a rainstorm.

"Ready?" Ashley smiled and handed me a small shot of warm espresso.

"Oh," I laughed. "I didn't think you meant an actual shot."

"Cheers."

I took the small glass from her and we clinked them together. I had a deep love affair with coffee, but the bitter taste of pure espresso made my nose crinkle. Ashley took her shot and waved toward the front door.

Troy and Emma made their way to the side counter and sat down at two of the empty bar stools Ashley had been saving.

"Ladies," Troy greeted us. "Are there any cookies left?"

"I set some aside for you." Ashley reached under the counter and set three chocolate chip cookies in front of Troy.

"Oh, you beautiful woman." Troy took a bite from one of the cookies and handed me a ten-dollar bill. "Put the rest in the tip jar, please."

"Did you just get in?" Ashley asked, leaning against the counter.

"Yeah. You think the drive would feel shorter the more I do it, but it never does." Emma set her bag down on the counter and stretched her arms over her head. "It's easier when Byn is with me. I can't wait until next semester."

"Hello, hello! Thank you all again for joining us tonight! Up next we have the talented duo who have graced us with their tune many times before. Please welcome, The Sky and I!" Amilia introduced the next act from the microphone. The room erupted in applause and whistling. I stood at the register watching her, unable to look at Amilia the same.

"Hey, stranger." A familiar voice warmed my heart from the side counter. Bryan took a seat on the empty barstool next to Troy. He set a round, aluminum to-go container on the counter with two plastic forks on top.

"You came!" I exclaimed as the musical duet took the stage and thanked the audience for joining them.

"I just got off work," he replied, still in his ironed black pants and white button-up shirt, the sleeves rolled up to his elbows. "I come bearing alfredo."

Ashley shot me a smile and I realized Bryan was the one she sent the text to earlier.

"Whit and I are starving." Ashley handed me one of the forks and took the top off the container. Steam rose up from the fettuccine alfredo, fresh from the kitchen. Thick pieces of grilled chicken tucked into the swirls of pasta.

"Shit, I didn't realize this was dinner. Em and I would have put in our order too." Troy laughed, side-eyeing Bryan.

"Snooze you lose," Ashley answered, twirling up a fork full of fettuccine.

"You didn't have to bring food. How much was it?" I asked, my stomach releasing another growl as the aroma of cheese and butter took over my senses.

Bryan chuckled. "It's free. I've been trying to buy you dinner for a few weeks."

"Oh. I'm third-wheeling aren't I?" Ashley said with her cheek full of food.

"No," I answered, picking up the fork and taking a bite.

As delicious as the alfredo was, it tasted like guilt. Not because Bryan insisted on paying, but because of Rose's request to stay away from him. Bryan had been asking me out since the bonfire but I had an excuse every time. I convinced myself that the parking lot chats between our shifts or late-night phone calls were innocent. I wanted to apologize but Bryan wasn't upset. He didn't make me feel like I had anything to apologize for, not to him at least.

"So, how's it going over here?" Bryan asked, changing the subject.

"A lot of fun. It's great to see all the talent in Rifton." I smiled, leaning against the counter. "Can I get you guys anything to drink?"

"It's an interesting place, that's for sure." Bryan smiled. "Tea would be great, whatever you have."

"Coffee. Lots of coffee." Emma stretched out on the countertop and rested her head in her open hand.

"Ash saved us cookies." Troy slid the last treat in front of Bryan who tore off a piece eagerly.

"Excuse me, could I get a refill?" A teenage girl on the other side of the cash register pulled my attention away.

"Do we have to take her order out?" I asked Ashley after I handed the customer her receipt.

"Nah." Ashley shook her head. "Olivia and Robby are in the dining room. You and I are on bar and register tonight so we get to stand back here the whole night." That was the best news I'd heard all evening.

"How was work?" I asked Bryan, leaning against the counter. I wanted to soak up every second I could until someone else ordered a cup of coffee.

"I feel like I live there sometimes. I smell like tomato sauce." Bryan unbuttoned his shirt as he spoke. Underneath he wore a white t-shirt with a UFO on it and a tiny green alien waving from the front window of their spaceship.

"There are worse things to smell like," Troy said in between bites of his cookie. "Remember Meridian?"

"What's what?" I asked.

"A music festival in Seattle. Three days with five of us in tents and no showers," Troy explained. "Great music though. Poor Byn doesn't remember half the weekend."

"He got too drunk and fractured his elbow." Ashley reached across the counter and smacked his arm. "Remember when we thought adulting would be fun? No one would be able to tell us what to do anymore."

"That's why I moved out." Bryan smiled.

"Yeah, Pops is easier to manage than your mom," Troy said.

I smiled, remembering my daydreams of what adulthood would be like. It certainly didn't go as I had planned either. With a sigh, I turned to Bryan. "Hey before I forget, I was wondering if I could ask a favor. Rayn is out with her friends tonight and she has my car. If you have the time, could I maybe get a ride home after this? If not I can ask Ashley, it's not a big deal."

"Absolutely." Bryan nodded, taking a drink of his tea. "I've been thinking about that sunset on your back porch."

"Me too." My cheeks heated as I avoided the questioning gaze of his friends.

Rayn had been borrowing the car much more than usual lately. Going to the movies with Tom, going to the park with Tom, going to get ice cream with Tom. It seemed like every moment she spent away from our time with the girls, she was with Tom.

"Bynie," Emma said, leaning against the counter to see him around Troy. "You brought my textbooks, right?"

Bryan nodded. "Did I leave my notebook in your car? I can't find it anywhere."

"The gray one? Nope."

Oh.

"Can I get something from my locker?" I whispered to Ashley.

"Sure," She answered.

My knees trembled with every step to my locker, unsure if Bryan would be upset that I had his journal for this long without saying anything. My thumb drummed on the gray cover nervously before I took a deep breath and went back onto the floor.

"I think you gave me this by mistake when I borrowed those books." I handed it back to him. "You're an amazing writer."

"Oh shit," Bryan's face fell. "I didn't realize that was in there. I'm sorry, I should check before I hand things out like that." He took the notebook back from my hands quickly.

Emma and Ashley looked at one another like I was handing Bryan a bomb.

"The way that you put your thoughts into words is so unique. You're very talented." I attempted to ease his nerves.

"Well, umm...thanks...I never intended for anyone to read it."

"Is that your diary?" Troy teased, nudging Bryan with his elbow. "You still keep one of those?"

"Shut up," Bryan shot back. "You sleep with a night light."

"It's a fucking salt lamp and Emma bought it for me." Troy defended himself, putting his arm around his girlfriend. "It's supposed to help you sleep."

"I'm sorry, I read the first page because I didn't know what it was." I glanced up into his eyes full of uncertainty and quickly realized Bryan McClintock was not the type of person that revealed his soul often. "I wanted to let you know how captivated I am by you...your words, I mean." I added.

His lips curled into a subtle half-smile. "You're the only person to ever read that, so thank you."

"I'd like to read more of your writing if that's okay with you."

"Uh, maybe," Bryan answered, his gaze wandered.

I sighed and dropped the subject, running my fingers through my thick ponytail, pulling my hair up when it yanked on the chain of my necklace. A couple strands of hair had gotten caught in the clasp, and pulled against my scalp. The clasp on the chain always caught in my hair, but the gem wouldn't come off to be put on a new chain and I didn't want to force it. I untangled the strands from the clasp and rubbed my scalp.

"I like your necklace," Troy said, leaning in closer to take a look at it. I hadn't realized it had been pulled to the outside of my shirt when I was fighting with my ponytail. "Bryan's sister has a similar one."

"Huh?" I asked, hoping that I had misheard him.

"My sister, Rose, has a necklace kinda like this one." Bryan pointed at the gem of my necklace. "Only hers is green and gold."

"Oh...uh, well, it may not be exactly like this one. This one is old." The panic rose up in me and I failed miserably to contain it. I didn't know what Rose had told him about her gem or if he noticed the mysterious floating ink inside, but if he got close enough, he would notice it moving around. The ink was more obvious in my aquamarine than the dark green of Rose's emerald.

"Maybe they're from the same collection, then. Either way, it's beautiful. Yours reminds me of the ocean." He leaned back on the barstool and took another drink from his tea.

"Thank you." I breathed and tucked the gem back under the protection of my sweater. "Do you guys go to the ocean a lot with how close you are?"

"One of the many perks of Em's apartment in the bay." Ashley smiled.

"When I'm there for school I'm at the beach a lot, yeah," Bryan said. "I haven't been since summer though."

"I've only been once," I replied, looking at his hands wrapped around the orange mug.

"While you've been in Rifton or in general?" Surprise fluttered over Bryan's face.

"I've been landlocked for most of my life, you know." I reminded him with a smile. "My mom took us to the Gulf once when we were younger."

"That's not the coast," Bryan informed me. "There is nothing like the Pacific Ocean. We can go whenever you want to. It's my favorite place in the world." He had no idea how much I thought about being at the coast, especially after I actually tasted the tranquility of the waves for the first time.

"It's a deal," I told him before I had to take another order at the register.

After I took a dark haired girl's order for two cappuccinos, I did a quick scan around the dining room to see how Olivia and Robby were doing when a familiar face jumped out at me.

Serenity Drake sat in a chair against the wall with her feet up on the side of the empty chair next to her. She wore all black with dark, thick makeup around her ebony eyes. Serenity looked at me instantly, like she knew my eyes were on her. She gave me a half-smirk that sent a chill up my spine.

"Hey, Ashley, you know her, right?" I asked, taking another glance at Serenity before turning my back against the counter.

"Serenity? Yeah, I know her. She's Emma's twin. She used to be part of our group, but I try to stay away from her as much as possible."

"How come?" I asked curiously.

Emma sighed. "Serenity and I had a big fight years ago that we never recovered from. So many people think having a twin is like having a built-in best friend but that's not my experience."

"We all chose Emma's side, obviously. Serenity is a total bitch to us now. She's a self proclaimed witch or something." Ashley explained.

A chill shot down my spine at how fluid the words were coming from Ashley's mouth. "What do you mean?"

"I mean she thinks she's a witch." Ashley chuckled as if she was saying Serenity thought she had wings. As if it was the most absurd thing a person could say.

"My mom raised us Pagan, so that really isn't that strange."

"Yeah but it's more than that with Serenity. She thinks she has real power, like the powers you see in movies. She isn't the only one either. There's a group of them that walks around like they own the town. Like they could literally turn us to stone if they wanted."

"Hmm." I leaned against the counter, hoping no one could see my fingers trembling as I gripped the side of the register.

"Some people think it's all part of Rifton's charm," Troy added. "They think it's cute. It's fucking spooky."

Emma's tone was soothing and calm. "My family has been in Rifton since day one. It's a bunch of bullshit people created to make this boring little town seem interesting. My sister got wrapped up in the facade. She lives on a different planet."

"Bryan was telling me about how people say the town was founded by witches," I replied.

Emma gave Bryan a sideways glance, glaring at him through Troy.

"It's a story, Whit." Bryan didn't look at Emma, though his heart sped up. It was discrete, but enough to let me know that Emma wasn't happy.

"Why would you be talking about that?" Emma asked.

"I'm curious to learn more about the town." I defended quickly. "I thought it was all kind of interesting."

"There's more to Rifton than old ghost stories." Emma huffed.

"It's more than stories. Weird stuff always happens in this place. People go missing or die young. An entire group of people all disappeared like fifteen years ago. People try to say they moved away, but fifteen people moved away all at once, abruptly? Never to be heard from again? The witches in the forest drag people off." Troy went on a tangent.

"That's absurd." Bryan furrowed his brow. "You believe that shit?"

"Bro, I've lived here my entire life. It's always been like this," Troy argued back.

"That doesn't mean the town was founded by an old witch coven that drags people off to eat them in the forest," Emma argued.

"Baby, I know your dad is on the city council and your family was part of the town founders, but it's not a personal attack on the Drakes." Troy turned to Emma. "I know your dad runs a tight ship to help keep the town afloat."

"I never said it was." Emma shifted in her seat, picking up the coffee Ashley had made for her.

"Then don't get so defensive whenever it's brought up." Troy leaned over and kissed her cheek.

"See?" Ashley chuckled and nodded toward her friends. "Charming as ever."

My pulse picked up and my eye began to twitch. I pushed on my eyelid with my finger, attempting to calm my nerves listening to them talk. Emma's dad was on the city council helping run the town. The Drakes were one of the founding families of Rifton. Amilia's warning of the Renati rang in my ears. The people who wanted my generation dead, the ones who had put an end to Elemental magic years ago. I loosened my clenched jaw and took a deep breath.

Emma had been nothing but welcoming and kind to me, but I didn't want her to discover that I was putting puzzle pieces together. Emma's sweater prevented me from seeing if she had the same brand as Serenity and Abe. I didn't notice anything at the bonfire either but she was wearing a hoodie that night. My stomach churned as the gravity of the situation sank in. Emma didn't give off the same darkness that Serenity did. I had a hard time wrapping my head around the idea that she could be part the Renati. Taking a quick scan of the room, my anxiety peaked. Who else in this room were members of the Renati? Who else besides the Drakes would try to kill me the moment they discovered who I was?

"You said your mom was a witch?" Robby asked, joining into the conversation without an invite, bringing me out of my head.

"You dropping eaves?" Ashley teased him, tossing a white cloth at him.

"Not intentionally." Robby laughed, setting the rag down on the counter.

I nodded slightly, seeming uninterested. I wanted to steer the conversation back to Serenity and her mysterious powers without seeming desperate, though I could have smelt my desperation from a mile away. If I was going to keep our cover and prevent another witch hunt, I needed to approach the topic carefully.

"Are you a witch, Whitney?"

"What do you think a witch is, Robby?" I asked, crossing my arms.

"You know, they fly around changing the weather and shit."

I couldn't help but laugh, holding my hand up over my mouth. "No, Robby. I don't fly around changing the weather and shit. Neither did my mom. She collected rocks and memorized moon cycles."

The mundane turn of the conversation lost Robby's interest and he went back to the stockroom.

"I'm sorry, Whit, I wasn't trying to belittle your faith. I meant Serenity takes it way too far, acting like she lives in a fantasy novel." Ashley turned around to face me with worried, wide eyes.

"Oh, don't worry about it." I offered a warm smile.

As if she could hear us talking about her, Serenity got up from her table and slithered over to the register.

"Can I get another latte?" She set a black coffee mug down on the counter with a clang. "The last one wasn't made right."

"Okay. $2." Ashley began punching buttons on the register angrily.

"Um, why would I pay when I told you the last one wasn't made right?"

"Because you drank it anyway?" Ashley crossed her arms. "You have to pay for refills."

Serenity rolled her eyes and handed Ashley a few dollar bills before casually glancing over to Bryan, Troy, and Emma.

"Looks like the whole gang's here." Serenity's eyes iced over when she looked at her sister.

Emma held Serenity's gaze and replied. "I'm surprised you left the house, Ren, figured you'd be too busy kissing dad's ass."

"We'll bring the latte out to you," Ashley told Serenity sternly, making it clear that she wasn't welcomed in our space.

"Thank you so much for doing your unskilled job correctly this time." Serenity smiled and winked at me before she left the counter. "Guess you aren't completely incompetent."

"What a bitch." Ashley turned to face us. "The fuck was that?"

"Who knows anymore." Bryan shrugged.

Troy set his drink down. "She's changed so much, I don't recognize her."

"I swear, if I didn't love you so much I'd beat her ass." Ashley shuddered, turning to Emma.

"She's not worth it." Emma brushed it off.

"Serenity hasn't always been so slimy?" I asked.

Emma shook her head. She tried to mask it, but the pain in her eyes was clear as day. "No. We all used to be really close but not anymore."

My heart ached for Emma. It would destroy me if that kind of rift ever grew between Rayn and I.

"Serenity's been like this the last few years," Ashley agreed. "But she's one of many kooks in this small town."

I needed to confirm my recent suspicion with Amilia and the girls that the Drakes were members of the Renati. How Emma played into all of this was still a mystery, but regardless, I avoided eye contact with her for the rest of the night.

When Acoustic Night ended, there was more cleaning up than usual on a closing shift. Everyone vacated the Corner Cup at the same time which left the tables covered with coffee mugs and dirty plates.

"I have no idea how long it'll take to close up," I said to Bryan after most of the crowd had shuffled out.

"I don't have anywhere to be. Besides, I don't mind waiting. I understand how nights like this are. I'll be outside." Bryan reached out, putting his hand on top of mine before he grabbed his notebook and headed to the front door.

It wasn't long before I headed out to meet Bryan in the back parking lot with anticipation. It was raining when I walked outside, but I knew that before my hand touched the back door handle. I could already feel the drops falling from the sky against my skin like I had been standing under the storm clouds for hours.

I walked to Bryan's Jeep slowly, taking in the healing power of the rain and letting it wash away the nerves I still felt from all I'd been through the past few months.

"That was quick." Bryan smiled as I opened the passenger door to his Jeep. He was sitting behind the steering wheel with his notebook in front of him and a pen in his hand. He closed the book the moment I showed up.

"I guess there wasn't as much to do as I thought." I looked down at his hands, wondering what he was scribbling away about.

"Are you okay?" Bryan asked softly. "You're getting soaked."

"Yeah, yeah I'm fine," I replied.

"Get in, it's pouring rain." Bryan nodded toward the sky.

I had honestly forgotten I was standing in the rain.

"No." I smiled and set my damp bag down on the floor of the Jeep. "Come on, get out."

"Get out of the car?" Bryan laughed nervously.

"If you're up for it, of course," I teased and closed the passenger door.

Reluctantly, Bryan followed me and pulled his jacket tighter around his body. His eyes squinted through the thick rain. "Whitney, what are we doing?"

I closed my eyes and threw my arms out, tilting back my head to embrace the rain clouds. I could already feel the uncertainty washing away and down the sewer drains.

"Don't you ever dance in the rain?" I asked, spinning around slowly. Safe and secure in my element with a certain green-eyed boy.

"Not since I was a kid. Aren't you freezing?"

"Bryan," I reached out and took his hands in mind. "Humor me."

"Okay," he mumbled and let me take the lead. Although he was reluctant at first, I could feel him begin to relax in the downpour.

A moment later, Bryan took hold of me and lifted me off the ground. The puddles beneath us splashed as he spun me around. I couldn't tell if the heartbeat in my ears was mine or his, but they beat strongly together as one. My laugh echoed across the parking lot as he finally set me down, pulling me close to his chest. I rested my forehead against his sopping sweatshirt. As he tightened his arms around me, the rain thickened and my skin tingled with magic.

Bryan had picked me up and flung me around like I didn't weigh more than him. He ran his hands down my curves like I was something to be desired, something to be cherished. His chest constricted as his fingers found my hips. His heart pounded and his stomach did a flip as his hand bravely moved further back, further down into unchartered territory. I wasn't going to stop him from grabbing my ass. I wanted his hands on every inch of my skin.

A strong crackle of thunder boomed above our heads as lightning illuminated the sky. Bryan pulled away quickly, startled. The absence of his warmth was heavier than my soaking wet clothes. He squinted up through the rain with worry in his eyes. I couldn't tell him the rain thickened because my knees were shaking and my heart ached for more of his touch. He couldn't know that I was to blame for his soaked clothes or the strands of wet blonde hair that fell perfectly into those lily pad eyes.

I reached for his hand to bring him back when I felt a familiar chill crawl up my spine. The feeling that something was lurking in the darkness. Peaking around Bryan's shoulder, I scanned the base of the buildings. I couldn't see through the thick rain, but I knew something was there, waiting for my guard to fall.

"We should get back in the car," I said, my voice echoing against the patter of heavy raindrops.

Slowly, Bryan reached out and grazed his cold fingers along my jawline. "I should probably get you home before the storm gets worse."

I caught the shadow in the corner of my eye a moment later. It had shifted its weight, giving away its position like a lion rustling in the grass. I laced my fingers in with Bryan's and tugged him toward the Jeep. I didn't know how shadows reacted to people without powers, if they had any bias toward witches or if they had enough consciousness to care, but I wasn't going to stick around and find out. Not when Bryan was with me.

"You're freezing," Bryan said, his arm snaking around my waist, pulling me against the side of his warm body.

I leaned into him, allowing myself to be vulnerable. The rain didn't let up, pouring down heavily with my emotions tangled up in it. As we climbed back into his Jeep, it took every fiber of restraint I had not to lean in and whisper in his ear, to tell him to take me back to his place and get him out of those wet clothes. Instead, I stayed firmly in my seat. Best display of self-control I'd performed in years, though I knew it was only a matter of time before I gave into it.

Chapter Twenty-One

BAD BLOOD

You're on my mind, just wanted you to know. A text from Bryan read, making my heart flutter in my chest. If it wasn't trapped by my ribcage, my heart would have flown around the room like a sparrow in spring.

You haven't left mine. I wrote back.

"Still with us, Whitney?" Brooke's voice brought me back to the living room.

"What's up?" I glanced up to see her, Rose, and my sister all watching me.

"The cops showed up asking about that kid from the woods?" Rose sat on the edge of our couch fidgeting with her fingernails. The emerald gem that hung around her neck was out in the open, lying gently against her hooded sweatshirt. Seeing her necklace out in the open made me realize mine was still hidden away. I guess it was a habit to keep it out of sight, to keep it locked away from the outside world. It was easier that way. I took a sip from Mom's favorite coffee mug, checking myself back into the conversation with my phone face down on the armrest of the couch.

"Why would the cops come here?" Rose asked.

"It was the same cop from the night at B's house," Rayn told Rose. "Grady thinks we have something to do with Abe disappearing."

"We were the last people to see him," I muttered.

"That we know of," Rose reminded me. "Who knows what happened when he left the meadow. We didn't do anything wrong."

"No, but it still makes me nervous having them bang on my door first thing in the morning," I said.

"Whit scared them off though, went full mama bear on their asses," Rayn said.

Brooke smiled. "I can imagine. Anything from Lauren?"

Rayn looked up from Mom's journal, "Of course not. She'll show up if we're doing potions in the woods but won't come to the house."

"Neutral ground, I guess. It's too bad there isn't anything in that journal telling us where the jewelry came from. I guess that would be too easy, huh?"

I felt Rose's eyes on me before I looked up and met her gaze. I took a deep breath, turning to Brooke. "Actually, my mom did write something about the jewelry. I hadn't brought it up because I was hoping to get more info before we shared, but that was the only entry."

Brooke looked around the room, her eyes the only ones wide with surprise. "Am I the last to know? Tell me."

"Here." Rayn flipped to the page about the amethyst and handed Mom's journal to Brooke. "It's about your bracelet."

Brooke eagerly took the journal and sat silently, taking in every word. She tapped the cover in thought before setting it down in her lap. She looked over at me with a furrowed brow. "How did she know what it was?"

"It was after Ray and I were adopted, so she had already seen our jewelry. She knew what they were."

"How did she know to send it to me?"

"We're not sure," I answered. "But I'll ask Mia about it next time I have the chance to talk to her alone. The first time we were at the Cottage was too hectic."

"I want to ask her myself." Brooke said, handing Mom's journal back to Rayn. "I don't want to be left out again."

"We should have told you sooner. I'm sorry, B." Rose added.

Brooke sighed, looking down at the floor. "You two really had no idea before you found this entry?"

"I didn't postpone telling you because I wanted to deceive you, Brooke. I didn't want to drop this bomb on you without figuring out where my mom got it from. I assumed there would be more about it in the journal." I explained.

"Finding out who sent my amethyst to me is huge," Brooke replied. "But I have to be part of it."

"Of course." I nodded. "I'm sorry."

Rayn played with the corner of the back cover of the journal that had ripped from years of use. Her fingers froze for a split second before she peeled open the last page that had stuck to what we thought was the last page. None of us spoke, but every eye in the room was glued to her hands.

"Tell me it's a missing entry about the jewelry," I said, studying my sister's furrowed brow and dilated pupils. She didn't answer, blue eyes skimming the page. "Rayn."

"It's not," she muttered. "It's about the shadows."

The girls told me about the Shadows today. I hoped that since they'd yet to tell me, that meant they hadn't been followed, but that was naive of me. Apparently, they have been seeing them periodically since they were young children. Now they're grown and still terrified of the demons, as they absolutely should be. I have done what I can to protect the house but I can only do so much. Luckily, none of them have fully formed. Remnants of Erebus, weak and feeble as they should be. Unfortunately, I have a strong feeling it won't stay this way for long. I will have to tell Whitney and Rayn the truth about everything sooner than I'd hoped, but Whitney is twenty now. She's a woman and Rayn is close behind. They're both mature enough to wrap their heads around it all. I should have told them years ago but I'm their mother and I wanted to protect them.

"Well, they're fully formed now," Brooke said after Rayn had finished reading the passage aloud.

That was it, the last page. Rayn and I had sped through the journal but I wanted to cling onto her a bit longer. The journal was the last little bit of Mom we had left. Knowing we had actually finished the journal was like losing her all over again.

Rayn cleared her throat. "Well, at least we know she was planning to tell us."

"What's the date on that last one?" I asked.

"June 13."

"Figured."

The day of the accident.

"I'm so sorry, you guys." Rose looked over at Rayn as well. "I don't know what else to say."

"There's nothing else to say." My voice sounded foreign, calm and collected while I was drowning on the inside. "We'll be fine."

I tried my best to hide it, but they knew by now I was a terrible liar.

"I think the shadows are tied to witches, I just haven't figured out how yet." Rose reached into her bag and pulled out the book she'd purchased from Dragonfly Mystic.

"This book presents it almost as fiction, like an old myth, but I think there's more to it." Rose flipped open to a page she'd bookmarked. "The shadow realm sounds like a purgatory. It said very few have ever gone and come back, but demons have leaked through the veil between the realm and our world. Demons that look an awful lot like the shadows we've come across. They start off weak, blending in with the environment until it gains enough strength to return to its initial form."

"So it's like hell?" Rayn asked, crossing her arms.

Rose shook her head. "More like a void in reality. Apparently it's been so long since anyone has traveled there, it's all speculation now. The author isn't even sure it truly exists."

"Who is the author?" Brooke asked.

"Margaret Daniels. I looked her up online. She's written a few other self published witchy books but this was the only one Dragonfly carried."

"If it's been that long since anyone has traveled to this shadow realm, how are the shadows getting out into our world?" I wondered aloud.

Rose chewed on her bottom lip. "There's either a tear in the veil somewhere or someone opened a portal, according to Margaret Daniels."

"Again with the portals. Abe Roberts gave Mit a page out of some book about a spell to open portals." Rayn replied.

"There is definitely a pattern, but the one in the meadow led to the lake, not a different dimension." I pointed out.

Rose shrugged. "Maybe there are different types? It doesn't seem like a portal is open. Daniels writes about how it was sealed off centuries ago, but witches have been trying to open it back up."

"Do you guys think Abe is trying to open the portal to the Shadow Realm?" I wondered aloud.

"I sure as hell hope not," Brooke shuttered. "I can't imagine what that would look like."

A loud boom filled the room, rumbling through the entire house. A sharp chill crept up my spine as the thunder outside caught me off guard. I knew it was going to rain, but I wasn't ready for the sky to start yelling at us.

"Fitting," Rayn replied, looking outside at the gray clouds covering the sun.

Brooke got up off the couch and walked over to the window, leaning against the sill to get a better look at the oncoming storm. "You sure this isn't you, Whit?"

"Do you feel my powers?" I asked, my eyes wandering back to Mom's journal.

"No, but I can tell you're sad. Interesting coincidence with the rain," Brooke answered.

"I'm sad too. You don't see fireballs falling from the sky, do you?" Rayn looked up.

Rose's eyes widened as she tried not to laugh. "Can you imagine?"

"I like to think we've gotten a better handle on our emotions affecting our powers like that over the years. We rarely use without intending to." I glanced over at Brooke, who was still staring out the window.

She could have been a photograph of herself, silent and still. Her shoulders barely moved with each breath as she stared out the window like a cat mesmerized by a flock of birds.

"B?" I asked, bringing everyone's attention to her. "You okay?"

When she didn't answer me, I scrambled to my feet and joined her at the window. Tightening my grip around my coffee cup to keep myself grounded. I scanned the empty fields behind the property, but not a blade of grass was out of place. Rain had begun to trickle down the window glass but there wasn't anything out of the ordinary.

"Brooke."

She finally heard me, glancing over at me side-eyed without moving her head. She indiscreetly nodded her head towards the Roberts' home where two police cars were parked out front. "Nothing good is going on over there."

I exhaled, not sure what to say. Before I could put words together, the front door flew open. Dmitri stormed into the house, fallen leaves from the porch tumbling in behind him. Dmitri panted, out of breath as he leaned forward with his hands on his knees.

"Jeff closed the mini-mart early." Dmitri joined us at the window. "I heard about the cops and ran home. What happened?"

"Do you think they finally tracked that kid down?" Rose asked.

"His name is Abe," Dmitri corrected, turning to face her. "And I haven't heard from him in a month."

"I'm sorry."

"Come on." I left the window and headed towards the back door. "I see an open window on the first floor. Let's see if we can overhear anything."

The five of us trekked across the field in between the houses. We were soaked from the rain by the time we made it to the open window on the Roberts' house. I crouched down beneath the windowpane, listening closely to hear the voices over the sound of the oncoming storm.

"And you're certain?" Jeff Roberts' shaky voice asked.

"We ran a DNA test upon finding the garment," Another male voice replied. "I know this is unsettling but this is still an ongoing investigation and nothing has been determined yet. We will keep you updated on any further findings."

"Thank you, Officers." Jeff sighed.

Heavy footsteps echoed across the floor as the police officers left the house. We remained statues as they got into their cars and left the driveway. I glanced over at Dmitri, but he stared at the ground. His eyes glossed over but remained unreadable. I reached out and placed my hand on his knee. Dmitri looked down as Janice's sob filled the house.

"Jan-" Jeff began.

"No!" Janice's painful cry cut him off. "They found his sweater drenched in blood, Jeff!"

"You saw the same photo I did, Janice. It wasn't drenched. We can't let our imaginations get the best of us."

"My imagination? My baby has been gone for a month and the first trace we find of him is a bloody sweater?" Janice's voice cracked. "I'm scared, Jeff. I can't lose him."

Dmitri left my side and took off sprinting across the field into the trees.

I glanced over my shoulder to Rayn. *Get back to the house without Janice or Jeff seeing you.*

Without a word, I left the girls and went after Dmitri. I didn't see him at first, but eventually, I found him leaning against a tree trunk, sitting in the dirt with his face in his hands. Raindrops fell down on us through the pine branches.

"Mit?" I stepped toward him slowly. His shoulders bobbed as he cried. "Dmitri."

"Go back to the house," he sobbed, wiping his runny nose on his sleeve.

"Mit, I am not leaving you out here alone like this. Are you okay?"

He glared up at me like I was stupid for asking a question I already knew the obvious answer to. Dmitri was anything but okay.

"I've been having nightmares that something terrible happened to him. He has a good heart. He doesn't deserve to be brought into any of this. He tried to be one of them, but his heart wasn't black, Whitney. He's a good person."

"I believe you," I took a seat on the wet dirt next to my grieving brother. "Abe admitted that he wanted to help us but couldn't. I know he cared about you."

"There's something I haven't told you," Dmitri muttered, avoiding eye contact.

My throat began to tighten. "Okay."

"I lied about not remembering what happened at the lake." He picked at the skin around his fingernails to keep his hands busy.

"Why would you lie?"

"To protect him."

I put my hand on his shoulder. "Start at the beginning."

"I-I don't know if I can." Tears continued and his chest heaved.

I pulled him close, cradling him in my arms. I smoothed his messy hair with my fingers when that same tug I felt at my interview overwhelmed me and I was no longer sitting on the ground.

Dmitri was under the water and Abe was right in front of him, floating. It was too dark to see what was holding him down, but it was clear he had been under long enough to run out of fight. Long enough that he'd come to terms with his fate.

Reaching out to him, Dmitri wrapped his arms around Abe's waist and pulled. They moved only slightly toward the surface before they were yanked back down. Something was pulling on the boy's feet. They weren't alone in the water.

Dmitri focused all of his energy on the boy in his arms and kicked toward the surface. Toward oxygen.

There was one last tug on Abe's feet, one last attempt to steal his life away. Dmitri closed his eyes and gave everything he could muster and the energies around him began to bend to his powers. Finally, whatever was holding Abe let go, allowing them to glide to the surface.

The moment he broke the surface, Dmitri gasped. Air filled his lungs and he coughed, gagging from going so long without it before he looked down at the body in his arms. Abe wasn't choking and gasping for air, he wasn't breathing at all. Mit got him to the empty shore as quickly as possible.

"Can you hear me?" Dmitri asked, gently shaking Abe's body. The sun reflected against the droplets in his copper hair.

Dmitri leaned forward and held his ear to Abe's nose and mouth, looking at his chest to see if he was breathing. Keeping his right hand flat, Dmitri laced his fingers on Abe's chest. Dmitri went through the CPR steps one by one, stopping to check if Abe was breathing before he went back to chest compressions. Mit didn't stop until Abe opened his eyes and began to cough, spitting up lake water. Relieved, Dmitri looked up to see dark eyes filled with anger and hate staring him down.

"Who are you?" he asked, leaning back onto his heels.

"Seems I should be asking you that question." Serenity lifted her hands and shoved an energy wave at Dmitri and Abe.

The spell hit Dmitri hard, knocking him onto his back. Abe groaned in pain, holding onto his stomach with both arms. Panicked, Dmitri scrambled to Abe and threw himself on top of the defenseless boy. The next spell Serenity threw their way deflected off them. Frustrated, she tried again but her magic bounced off an invisible shield once more.

Dimitri looked up at her, teeth clenched. "I won't let you hurt him."

As quickly as I had arrived at the lake, I was sucked back into my own mind. I was back in the trees behind the house, holding Dmitri in my arms. My brother looked at me with dilated pupils.

"Are you okay?" he whispered, his eyes not leaving mine. "Your eyes turned white."

"I saw you and Abe at the lake," I answered, rubbing my throbbing temple. "Like that vision I had at the Corner Cup. You saved his life."

Dmitri was quiet for a moment before he spoke. "I think my adrenaline was so intense I was able to protect us. Serenity finally ran off after a few more tries to break the shield. I think she was going for help so we ran. The island is connected by a strip of sand so we used it to get back to shore. When we reached the dock, Abe ran off without a word. That's when I went to the bait and tackle shop at the docks to call you."

I didn't know what to say. I didn't know if I had anything *to* say. Dmitri could have gotten himself killed, but there were no words to discipline him with. He had been through enough. Besides, it wasn't like he chose to put himself in harm's way. He didn't go through the portal intentionally. He didn't fall into Abe's mess on purpose.

"Abe meant more to me than anyone realized." Dmitri continued, covering his face again. "I know you forbade it, but I couldn't stay away from him. That night you caught me sneaking back in? I was with him. I've been sneaking out to see him a lot."

"I assumed." I pulled him closer in a comforting embrace as tears began to well in my eyes. "I've been so preoccupied with the girls, I've been ignoring what's right in front of me. I've been overlooking you when you needed me. Dmitri, I'm so sorry this happened."

He only cried harder in my arms and I did my best to comfort him, but I had no idea how to soothe his fears that Abe wasn't coming home. Dmitri and I sat there in the dirt until he finally caught his breath.

"Abe's notebook entry makes a lot more sense now. Why didn't you tell me?" I asked.

"You would have been furious. It was easier to keep it a secret."

"Dmitri, I know the dynamic between us changed when I became your guardian but we're still us. You can still talk to me."

"The dynamic only changed because you treat me like I'm ten again."

"I'm sorry..." I sighed, pulling him in closer. "I'm trying to protect you."

"So was Abe," Dmitri whispered, nuzzling his face into the dip of my shoulder.

Surprisingly, we got Lauren to meet us in the meadow that evening. I all but dragged Dmitri into the forest with us, there was no way I was leaving him home alone. Dmitri was growing up but he was still only sixteen, and no teenager was equipped to deal with this level of stress on their own.

"We need to come up with a plan. It's only a matter of time before the search party finds something else and the cops will be back at our door," I announced. I chose my words carefully, not wanting to be insensitive to Dmitri.

"Janice and Jeff deserve to have their son back." My brother avoided eye contact.

"Of course they do," Rose agreed softly. "But we don't know what happened after Abe left the meadow."

"Wouldn't it be a good thing if he was dead? I thought he was part of the Renati, you know, the people who want to kill us?" Lauren crossed her arms tightly against her chest.

"He was trying to get out," Rayn explained. "Plus, he loved my brother and did everything he could to protect him."

"Oh..." Lauren paused, glancing slowly in Dmitri's direction. "I'm sorry, I had no idea."

"Maybe if you showed up half the time and were mentally present the other half, you would have found out when we did," Rose muttered, glaring at Lauren.

Lauren scoffed. "With you here, you're lucky I showed up at all. Contrary to the narrative you made up, Rose, I actually do give a fuck about all of this. I don't like running headfirst into the unknown. This isn't a game."

"No, it's not a game but you haven't been taking it seriously. You've been holding us back the entire time and it's starting to wear on me."

"You have no right to talk shit to me after what you've done. You're lucky I keep my cool when all I want is to beat your face in every time I'm forced to see you," Lauren snapped, taking a step into Rose's personal space. The wind rustled through the pines and blew Rose's hair back.

Rose blinked in confusion, her brow furrowed as her voice echoed against the trees. "After what I've done? What are you talking about?"

"You know damn well what you did." Lauren tightened her arms around herself.

"Remind me," Rose demanded, stepping closer to her.

Lauren turned away, looking anywhere but at Rose as tears filled her eyes. Her words caught in her throat as the harsh wind died down into a breeze. "You told everyone."

"What?" Rose asked, still confused.

"You spread the rumors in high school. You were the only one who saw us, I know it was you. No one else knew." Tears left wet streaks down Lauren's cheeks as the rest of us stood dumbfounded. "You know exactly what I'm talking about."

I glanced over at my sister wide-eyed, completely lost as Lauren and Rose screamed at each other. Magic radiated off the two of them as their emotions took advantage of their senses.

"Lauren," Rose breathed, her shoulders falling in disbelief. "I didn't."

"Don't try to fucking deny it. I know it was you," Lauren snapped back.

"What the hell are you two talking about?" Brooke stepped in as we turned to look at her.

"Please, as if Rose hasn't already told you." Lauren huffed.

Rose turned to Lauren. "It's yours to tell the others, but I never said a word about it to anyone. I'd never do that to you, or anyone else."

Lauren choked as she cried. "When Rose and I were still in high school she saw me with someone, someone that no one else knew about and after she walked in on us rumors started to spread about me."

"I didn't start them," Rose repeated, adamant that she was innocent.

"They wrote 'dyke' on my locker, Rose!" Lauren screamed. "My mom couldn't look me in the eyes for a week! Layla had to leave school. You outed me before I was ever ready to tell anyone or figure out who I am. You took that away from me."

"Wait, what?" I snapped, turning to Rose. Disbelief washed over me, hanging heavy on my shoulders. I knew whatever happened between Rose and Lauren was substantial, but I never imagined it would be something like this.

"Do you honestly believe that's the kind of person I am?" Rose looked at me with heavy eyes.

"No," I breathed. "But Lauren clearly isn't making this up. Someone did this."

"I'm sorry it happened, but I never told anyone about you and Layla. I'd never do that to you." Tears glossed over Rose's eyes as she defended herself, arguing with a brick wall. "Is that why your friends bullied me so badly? Are you the ones who egged my house? I know you dumped trash all over my car for the rest of the year. The mustard ruined the paint, by the way."

"And the rumors you started almost ruined my life," Lauren snarled.

Brooke stepped forward. "If Rose said she didn't do it, then she's telling the truth. What did she have to gain by spreading your business all over school?"

This was so much heavier than I could have imagined. I wanted to wrap Lauren in my arms and hunt down whoever caused her this kind of pain. When Dmitri came out, he received some backlash at school, but he was in control of who he told and how he told them. I remembered how important that was for him, and I couldn't imagine how detrimental it would have been if someone had hijacked that moment in his life. Catching this glimpse into Lauren's life made me wish I had been gentler with her over the last few months.

"Lauren," Dmitri's voice caught me off guard. "I know what it's like to be an outcast for your sexuality, to have other people make you feel like there's something wrong with your authentic self." He rested a gentle hand on her elbow. "I'm sorry that happened but look at Rose's face. You can see it in her eyes that she isn't the one who did that to you."

Lauren's bloodshot eyes glanced up, finally turning to Rose. "If it wasn't you, then who was it? I never told anyone."

"I don't know," Rose admitted. "But it wasn't just you in the empty classroom that day."

"Layla wouldn't."

"Well I didn't, but if you don't want to believe me there's nothing I can do about it. Whatever issues you have with me don't excuse you taking it out on the rest of our generation. Whit, Rayn, and Brooke haven't done anything wrong yet you sabotaged our potion and dragged your feet every step of the way over something you *assumed* I did. This is literally the first you've ever confronted me, you decided what kind of person I am." The tall grasses around Rose's feet began to grow, slowly at first but the louder her voice boomed the higher they went until they touched her knees.

"I can't do this." Lauren swung her bag over her shoulder and turned on her heel.

"Lauren, wait," I said, my words finally returning after the initial shock of their argument began to wear off.

"Everyone is taking Rose's side, so why should I stand here and have you look at me like I'm the asshole."

"No one is saying you don't have the right to be angry," I answered. "But if Rose swears it wasn't her, then she deserves to be heard."

"Don't call me." Lauren was already heading toward the tree line.

"I believe you." I put my hand up to stop Rose from leaving as well. "Stay here."

I hurried after Lauren. She was faster than me, but I caught up to her before she reached the parking lot at the trailhead. I called out after her, "Lauren, it's just me. Talk to me."

"You don't believe me, why should I?" Lauren finally stopped walking and turned to face me.

"I think this has been a massive, hurtful misunderstanding," I replied, reaching out to put a hand on her shoulder. Surprisingly, Lauren didn't pull away, she leaned into it. "I'm here for you."

I wrapped my arms around her back and pulled her in close. Lauren trembled as tears took over her again, leaving a wet mark on my shoulder.

"I'm so sorry someone outed you," I whispered. "You didn't deserve that and you have every right to be hurt and angry about it. I'm angry for you. If someone did that to my brother, I'd kill them."

"I still like guys," Lauren muttered in my sweatshirt. "I started seeing this guy afterward so the rumors would die off, but I've never forgiven her. I never will."

"Whoever did this deserves that, but what if it wasn't Rose?" I asked. "I'm not saying you're lying or that I'm not on your side, but for a second, what if it was someone else?"

"I don't know," Lauren whispered. "I need to get out of here."

"Okay." I let go of her and took a step back. "We'll give you some space."

Lauren didn't say goodbye but I let her walk away, not knowing if this was the last time I'd see her. I didn't know what to say or do to make the situation better, if there was anything I could do in the first place. Lauren's behavior since the first day we all met in the meadow together made perfect sense now. She had spent years believing that Rose had done something unforgivable. I hadn't known either of them for long and there was still so much about my generation left to learn. One thing I knew in my bones to be true was that Lauren's justifiable anger was targeted at the wrong person.

Chapter Twenty-Two

PERIMETER OF DEFENSE

"Whitney!" My name echoed from up the dirt driveway as I got out of the car. Janice made her way toward me from her house, a heavy sweater wrapped around her body. But even hidden behind the fabric, she looked smaller. The bones in her hands were more prominent and her face was slimmer, giving her chin a sharper point.

"Hi, Janice," I replied, leaving the car to meet her.

"How are you kids doing?" A cool breeze rustled through the trees, blowing her graying hair into her face.

"I feel like I should be asking you that question," I answered, tightening my grip on the strap of my bag. "How are you holding up?"

Janice sighed. The dark circles under her eyes told me before she could respond. "I'm trying to have faith. I wanted to apologize for the police coming to the house. They said they were going to be interviewing those close to us but I didn't think...If I knew, I would have given you some warning."

"Oh, that's not your fault. We live on your property and Dmitri works for you guys, I understand why we would be on the list." I tried to keep my voice calm as the knot in my stomach tightened.

Funny how the cops didn't mention any of that as reasons why they were dropping by, but Janice didn't need to know that Officer Grady was convinced we were suspicious. At least now I knew Janice wasn't the one who sent them our way.

"Your brother has been a godsend during all of this. I don't think Jeff and I would be able to keep the store open without him. He's a wonderful young man." Janice paused, her breath catching in her throat. "I was so happy to see him and Abraham becoming friends. It was always so hard for Abe to connect with people, especially as a child."

My heart grew heavy in my chest seeing the pain in Janice's eyes. "Mit, too."

"Dmitri hasn't heard from him at all, has he? The other day some things in Abraham's room were moved around like someone had been in there. If he had come back, maybe he would have tried to reach out to Dmitri."

"No, Mit would have said something. He's been so worried about Abe, he would have told us if he had heard anything." Tears welled in my eyes as I tried to blink them away. "Dmitri wants Abe home more than anything."

"I figured, but there is no harm in asking. Our church is hosting a group prayer at Oak Park for Abraham tomorrow night, everyone is invited. It would mean a lot if you and the kids could come. In times like these, we find our strength from our community and loved ones."

"Of course. I'll talk to Rayn and make sure she doesn't have to work but we would love to come and support you and Jeff."

"Thank you, dear." Janice reached out and placed her hand on my elbow. The sleeve of her sweater lifted up her arm and I glanced down at Janice's wrist. There was no brand, no marking to indicate she knew anything about Abe's affiliation with the Renati.

I hated this. I hated pretending to Janice's face that everything was going to be okay when I had no proof it would. I wondered if Abe was the only one in his family to be born with magic. If he hid in his room and practiced late into the night, feeling alone and scared. I guess there wasn't much difference between Abe and us after all. Maybe he was desperate for answers, for a community, and the Renati were all he had access to. Maybe he didn't know who they truly were until it was too late, and that's why Serenity had tried to drown him in the lake.

"Whitney?" Janice asked softly. I blinked back to reality, meeting her sad eyes.

"Sorry. Um, I'm so sorry about all of this Janice. I wish there was something I could do to help. You've been so kind to us and I don't know what to do in return."

"We do not love our neighbor because we expect anything in return, dear. We do it because it's the right thing to do." Janice's hand slid down my arm and took my hand in hers, giving it a gentle squeeze.

I tried to smile back at her but it felt dishonest. "We will be at the park tomorrow night. It's the least we can do."

The next night Rayn, Dmitri, and I drove to Oak Park for the community event for Abe. Rayn was hesitant to attend, but I wanted Dmitri to see he wasn't the only one who cared about Abe's disappearance.

The words Abe spoke to me in between our homes echoed in my brain over and over again as we approached the gathering crowd.

The darkness has already been let in.

My heart raced with fear as to what he meant.

Rose and Brooke agreed to meet us at the gathering. Surprisingly Lauren said she would meet us there as well, though I was skeptical after her tainted history with Rose had finally come to a head. I wanted to give her space and understanding, but this wasn't the time to be alone. If the five of us were in the same place, at least I knew we could keep each other safe.

A sea of people packed into Oak Park like sardines, waiting in silence. I had no idea so many people were touched by the missing teenager's story but I guess this is what happens in small towns. Even those who had never spent any time with Abe or given him a second glance all came out to show support because they wondered what if. What if it was them, or their child, or their best friend?

What if.

People handed out candles with little paper cups at the bottom to collect wax. Rayn, Dmitri, and I each took one and slowly made our way through the dense crowd looking for familiar faces. Rose found us within a few minutes.

"Hey," she greeted. "Did you bring the book?"

"It's in the car," Rayn replied.

"And Amilia knows we are coming over after this?" Rose asked.

"Yes, she said she has what we need," Rayn answered.

"What are you talking about?" Dmitri asked Rayn, who clearly had an earlier conversation with Rose that she didn't share with us.

"We are going to set something up to protect ourselves, to protect our families," Rayn answered vaguely.

"What do you two have planned?" I asked, furrowing my brow.

"There's a perimeter protection spell in the book, and Amilia has what we need to perform it. We make an oil and put it in the doorways of our houses and on our person. It's supposed to keep us safe from unwanted guests," Rayn explained.

"Can we not lose sight of why we're here in the first place?" Dmitri snapped, his voice thick with pain.

"We're trying to prevent whatever happened to Abe from happening to one of us, Mit." Rayn defended herself.

"Let's find Brooke and Lauren and focus on this right now," I replied, looking around to see if I could spot our other two missing members.

What is going on with Dmitri? Rayn asked between the two of us.

Are you serious right now? I answered mentally.

"I see Brooke." Rose broke the tension and took off through the crowd of people holding their unlit candles close to their chests.

"Whitney." Dmitri grabbed my wrist and pulled me aside as Rayn and Rose went ahead. "What are you guys doing?"

"I don't know what they have planned, to be honest. I told you about my boss, Amilia, and if we can do something to protect ourselves, I think we need to do it. Especially after seeing those shadows."

"You're a hundred percent sure this Amilia is the Mia that Mom wrote about?" Dmitri asked quietly. Moments like this made me wish I could telepathically communicate with my brother as well.

I grabbed the side of his face, forcing him to meet my gaze. "I'm sure, Mit. A hundred percent. She showed us letters Mom had written to her from Kansas and the spellbooks that Mom had sent her. She asked about you."

"Oh," he answered, his face a blank page.

"Come with us. I think she'd like to see you."

"I don't know." Dmitri's voice was a whisper.

"Mit, I'm not leaving you alone right now."

"Okay, fine."

"Hey," I put my hands on his shoulders. "I couldn't get through any of this without you. I love you."

"I know." Dmitri attempted a smirk as Rose and Rayn came back with Brooke trailing behind them.

Brooke went to say something, but she was interrupted by a woman in a blue sweater and a megaphone. The sun had already begun to sink behind the mountains, turning the red and pink sunset-streaked sky into dark blue and purple

"I wanted to thank everyone for coming out tonight in support of the Roberts family as we rally behind them during this difficult time. Lean on us and we will carry you through this hardship until your sweet son has returned home safe and sound. Let us fill this uncertainty with the combined light of our candles, representing the strength and solidity of our community." The woman preached from her megaphone with a hopeful tone. She held her hand over her heart as she addressed the crowd.

Everyone around us began to light their candles with lighters, and I realized that I didn't bring anything with me to illuminate the wicks. "Do you have a lighter?" I asked Rose who shook her head.

"I always have one with me." Rayn smiled, and it wasn't until her power bubbled inside me that I realized what she meant.

With the slight wave of her fingertips, the wicks on each of our candles were engulfed in tiny flames that danced up into the darkness and lit our faces.

Rose's eyes widened as Dmitri quickly reached out to turn Rayn toward him. "What has gotten into you?"

"Rayn that was stupid," I added.

"Oh, please. No one is paying any attention to us." Rayn tucked her hair behind her ear as she justified her decision.

"He is." Brooke's voice shook as she tightened her grip, crumpling the small paper cup at the bottom of her candle.

"Who?" Rose looked around at the sea of people.

"Joseph Grady, that cop who works with my dad." Brooke nodded to her right. "I'm sure you recognize him, Ray?"

Sure enough, Officer Grady stood with his boots cemented into the sidewalk, his eyes burning holes into the side of my head. Grady looked like he had seen a ghost. No, he had only seen the five candles light up all at once without a lighter in sight.

"We need to go," I said quickly. "He already thinks we have something to do with this."

"No, don't move." Rose's voice halted me. "That'll only make us look more suspicious. Carry on like nothing happened. Maybe he'll think it was only his mind playing tricks on him."

"I'm sorry," Rayn whispered. "I didn't think anyone was paying attention."

"No, you were the only one not paying attention," I muttered.

I didn't enjoy giving my sister a hard time for her mistakes but how many times could Rayn use her powers in public without consequence?

"Rayn!" A voice from behind had all of us jumping.

"Tommy! There you are. You never texted me back, I wasn't sure you'd come." Rayn put out her arms and gave Tom a kiss on the lips.

"Of course I'm here." Tom reached out and tucked a loose strand of hair behind Rayn's ear. The long sleeves of his shirt were pinched between his fingertips and his palm. Rayn closed her eyes, taking comfort in his touch.

"Please, we ask for a moment of silence in prayer to ask our Heavenly Father to bring Abraham Roberts home to his parents safely." The woman spoke into her megaphone again. I had no idea who she was, but she was obviously the one who organized this gathering.

I reached out and took Dmitri's hand in comfort, giving it a slight squeeze to remind him that he wasn't going through this alone.

Everyone around us lowered their heads in prayer and I followed suit. I bowed my head but didn't close my eyes. I didn't want to let my guard down, not with Officer Grady watching us like a hawk. Not when I didn't know who might be a member of the Renati hiding in plain sight. I could still feel eyes on me. It eerily reminded me of a shadow.

Once the event came to an end, we did our best to blend in with the crowd as people dispersed. Luckily, we didn't see Officer Grady anywhere. Rayn said goodbye to Tom which took a bit longer than we had time for. We searched for Lauren for as long as we could before we left for Amilia's cottage. Brooke attempted to call Lauren three times, getting nothing but voicemail. I know Lauren had asked for space and I didn't want to push her after the big fight with Rose.

I was glad Rose and Rayn called Amilia. I didn't know who else we could turn to. All I knew was Amilia should know the truth about Abe and his power. So far, Amilia had been the only one with any sort of answers to our questions. Without her, Rose would be dead and I'm sure the rest of us would have been close behind.

Dmitri and I drove the Eclipse with the girls following us in Rose's car. Amilia came outside when she saw us pull up. She wrapped a heavy brown cardigan around her body and opened the front gate with a relieved smile.

"Come inside where it's warm." She mustered a smile and closed the wooden gate behind us. "You must be Brooke. It's wonderful to meet you. My name is Amilia Burnett."

"Hello." Brooke smiled and offered out her hand to Amilia.

Warmth filled the cottage, and a fire burned strong in the brick fireplace. A cast iron pot hung from a hook above the flame, reminding me of something you'd see in a colonial setting.

"Lauren didn't show," Rayn informed her. "She's not answering her phone either."

"She's scared. She needs you girls to rally around her, remind her that you five are in this fight together." Amilia offered us a seat in the living room next to the fire. When her eyes wandered over to Dmitri, her smile fell to the ground.

Amilia and Dmitri stood there, staring at each other. Dmitri's eyes wandered down to his shoes, and he cleared his throat awkwardly. Amilia's eyes glossed over as she broke the silence.

"Dmitri." His name fell from her lips like a prayer.

"Hi." Mit's voice was quiet and unsteady.

"You've gotten so tall." Amilia wrung her hands together. "It's wonderful to see you."

"You too," Dmitri muttered, finally looking back up at Amilia.

She took a step toward him and held out her hand. "May I?"

Dmitri hesitated, but approached her, filling in the space between them. Once he was close enough, Amilia pulled him to her chest and engulfed him in a tender embrace. Dmitri moved his hands up to her back slowly, hugging her.

Amilia took a step back, wiping a stray tear from her face. "It's hard to believe you're in Rifton."

"Yeah," Dmitri said, his voice still quiet. "I always wondered what things would have been like if we never left."

"Me too." Amilia smiled at him, giving his shoulders a quick squeeze before she turned to the rest of us.

I pretended not to hear him since that was something Dmitri had never admitted aloud to either Rayn or I. What if he and Mom never left. What if they never found us. This was a tender moment meant for Dmitri and Amilia. We were imposing enough witnessing it, let alone giving an opinion.

"Did you bring the spellbook?" Amilia asked, wiping another tear from her face before she brought herself back to why we were there.

I nodded, and looked down at the book wrapped in a sweatshirt on my lap. I was hesitant to hand it over to not just Amilia, but to anyone. It was the only link we had between us and the generations that came before us. Looking at the bookshelf of old texts Amilia had in her possession brought comfort. If she was telling the truth, people like Amilia were the only reason books like these were preserved. This was a woman my mother loved, someone she trusted. That was enough for me.

"Good. I should have everything you need to create the tonic." Amilia took a wicker basket off of the dining room table with a vile of salt, bay leaves, white candles, and a large chunk of black onyx.

"Will it still work without Lauren?" I asked. "I know that a generation is supposed to be strongest when all five of us are together."

"I was worried about that, too. We tried something out of the book already, but it didn't work and all five of us were there," Rayn explained to Amilia.

"Probably because Lauren wasn't trying," Rose muttered under her breath.

I glanced over at Rose. "Cut her some slack."

"We could have saved each other a lot of bullshit if she had come to me in the first place," Rose said. "We could have sorted it out years ago."

"What would you have done in her position?"

Rose sighed. "I wouldn't have done the things Lauren and her friends did to me."

Amilia sat down in one of the armchairs pulling our attention to her. "The protection potion won't be as strong without a complete generation but those without elemental ability have performed this spell. It will still be successful. Unwanted guests won't be able to enter your homes."

"Where do we start?" I asked.

Amilia laughed. "You have the spellbook and the abilities. You are entirely capable of doing this yourselves. I am merely here to provide ingredients." Amilia smiled and reached for a novel from the table next to her.

"Okay," I breathed. "Let's do this."

The four of us sat around the wicker basket in front of the fireplace. I laid the book out in front of us carefully. The book began to tremble and shake like it had before, the pages flying one after another before the book settled on the instructions to create the tonic to keep out unwanted guests.

"Woah," Dmitri breathed, sitting on the edge of the couch. "That's a new one."

Amilia sat on the edge of her seat, the novel dangling from her fingertips.

"How peculiar," she mumbled, leaning forward to get a closer look at the book.

"Is it uncommon for a spellbook to do that?" I asked.

Amilia nodded. "Yes. Carry on. There is little time to waste."

"First things first." Rayn smiled, lighting the three white candles surrounding the wooden bowl between us. The wicks flickered in anticipation. A thin line of smoke ran into the air from the candles, reminding me of Lauren's absence.

Rose got to work quickly with her finger sliding down the instructions in the book with each step. She waved her hand over the bay leaves, and tiny bits of the plant fell to the floor. The word 'safety' appeared on each leaf. I picked one up and looked through the tiny letters that had been etched into the greenery.

"Whitney, can you fill the bowl with water? About three-quarters of the way." Rose ground the salt into a fine powder as she spoke as I waved my hand above the bowl.

"What can I do?" Brooke asked, sitting on her knees anxiously.

"Take the onyx," Rose replied, adding some salt to the bay leaves and water.

"And do what with it?" Brooke's eyes were wide.

"Trust your gut, B. Being a witch isn't about following directions properly, it's about using your abilities and intuition." Rose smiled at Brooke with encouragement.

"Okay," Brooke whispered. She picked up the onyx and held it close to her chest with her eyes closed.

Dmitri watched in awe as the four of us worked together. He had seen Rayn and I use our powers a million times but this was his first experience witnessing us with other Elementals. I glanced over at him and smiled as our eyes met. He sat on the sidelines, but I felt safer knowing he was here with us. Dmitri was an anchor, keeping me steady. His presence alone was the comfort I needed to carry on.

"When you're ready, put the onyx in the water," I told Brooke, reading the book over Rose's shoulder.

Brooke slowly reached forward and placed the onyx in the bowl, her fingers dripping with water as she pulled away. The four of us sat in silence, infusing the spell with our intent and energies until the contents of the bowl began to sparkle.

"Okay...I think it worked." Rose muttered as a smile emerged on her face.

The tonic we poured into five small vials glowed a beautiful light blue color as the book said it would.

"I would agree so." Amilia smiled and stood up, admiring our handywork.

"Here." Brooke handed a vial to Amilia.

Amilia put up her hand. "Oh, no dear. Do not worry about protecting me. I established a perimeter of defense along my property lines long ago. No witch can cross it with any ill intent."

I hoped our potion would have the same effect.

"Your books look a lot like ours." Brooke's attention diverted to the oak bookcases against the wall. "Are these the ones about the generations? Rose was telling me about them."

"Yes," Amilia answered, watching Brooke run her fingers along the spine of a thick leather book. "There aren't as many left as there used to be but luckily I am able to keep these secured."

"Do you know anything about the generation our book talks about?" Rose picked up our spellbook and turned to the first few pages that listed the groups of Elementals.

As Amilia glanced over Rose's shoulders, her eyes widened.

"Do you recognize them?" I asked.

Amilia nodded. "I do. All of the great generations were given a name, the one from your book included. They are the Martyrs."

"The book has some blank pages in the back like it isn't finished. It leaves off with Gabriel's spirit healing spells but nothing after that," Brooke replied. "Did something happen to them?"

Amilia was quiet for a moment before she answered, "They were killed by Erebus in the great uprising of the Renati. That is why we call them the Martyrs."

"Erebus murdered them? The entire generation?" Rose clarified. "How?"

"Yes. Erebus and the Renati used forbidden magic. Those who survived documented that the Elementals were caught off guard. The death of the Martyrs and the self-sacrifice of the Shepherds brought an end to the Generations for centuries. Elemental magic lay dormant for so long that many believed it was gone for good." Amilia glanced between us, her voice gentle.

"Until us," I whispered, the weight of our past heavy on my shoulders. "Mia, what do you know about the Drake family?"

My gaze remained on Amilia but I felt Rose's eyes on me.

"They're old money. One of the founding families," Amilia answered. "Henry Drake is on the city council, has been for years."

"They're Renati," I stated, not a question.

Rose crossed her arms. "What makes you say that?"

I turned to her. "I'm putting two and two together. I heard Rifton was founded by old witch families and that the Drakes still help run things. Serenity all but admits it. It's obvious."

Amilia gave a slight nod. "Yes."

"What about Emma?" Rayn asked.

"No." Rose shook her head. "I've known Emma for years. She's not one of them."

"I don't think she is either," I agreed. "But I've also never seen her wrists to check for a brand."

"Well I have and she doesn't have one," Rose confirmed.

"When witches have children there is a higher chance they will have powers, but it's no guarantee. Many children born to witches do not have magic." Amilia announced. "Jumping to conclusions will not serve you girls well. It's best you stick together and be mindful of who you trust outside of this room."

"Why are you so interested in the Drakes?" Rose asked me.

"Serenity has been lingering around Corner Cup, and I saw her brand like I told you. I saw her at the CC when you were attacked, Rose. I think she had something to do with it."

Rose was quiet for a moment, chewing on her bottom lip. Then she nodded and stood up from the floor. "You're probably right. I'm going to get home and get this oil down as soon as possible. Do you need a ride, B?"

Brooke nodded and turned to Amilia. "Before we go, Whit and Rayn's mom wrote about my amethyst in her journal. I know you helped her get it to me. I need an explanation."

Amilia raised her eyebrow in surprise. "Straight to the point, then. Um," she sat down on the edge of the couch. "Shortly after Audri met her girls, she went to an estate sale. She told me that she felt a pull towards the house because normally she would have driven past, but that day she stopped. She found the bracelet and sent it to me."

"But how did you know to give it to me?"

Amilia was silent for a moment, letting out a sigh before she continued. "Knowing Rifton is an Allurement, I've been searching for Elementals for years. Hoping that one day I'd be able to serve a higher purpose than collecting old books."

"Did you know about Lauren and I?" Rose asked, crossing her arms.

"I had suspicion, but was only certain of Brooke."

"But how? I'm so confused how you knew I was an Elemental, let alone the one that this specific bracelet belonged to." Brooke held out her arm, the amethyst bracelet now on her wrist instead of hidden on her ankle.

Amilia tapped her finger tips against her knee. "I have family buried in the cemetery and I used to go quite often. Whenever I'd go, I saw a young girl sitting at different graves talking to herself and one day I realized you were not talking to yourself. Ordinary witches do not have the ability to communicate with the dead, so there was only one explanation."

Brooke nodded. "Thank you. I finally feel like we're getting somewhere."

Amilia smiled at her. "It's my pleasure, dear."

Rose and Brooke left, but I stayed planted on the floor. Rayn and Dmitri were talking but I didn't hear their words. My head spun at how much life could change in a matter of months.

"Whitney?" Amilia sat down on the rug next to me. "Something else on your mind?"

"Is there only one empath per generation, like there's only one Seer?" I asked, turning to face her.

"Not necessarily. Magic is the manipulation of energies, so it varies from witch to witch. Why do you ask?"

"What would it mean if a witch could feel someone else's emotions, but only that one person. Hypothetically."

"Well, hypothetically, I've never experienced anything like that first hand. But I have read when two witches' energies are sensitive to one another, they will have a stronger connection through their powers. If that answers your question?"

"And if the other person doesn't have powers?"

Amilia's gaze locked into mine. "I've never heard of anything like that."

Chapter Twenty-Three

NIGHT TERRORS

"I like your room," I said, gazing around Bryan's bedroom.

"Oh, thanks," he replied. "It's nothing special."

The walls were painted the same light tan as the rest of the house he shared with Troy and his father, but Bryan had decorated them with his own personal touch. A poster of the Milky Way galaxy was surrounded by drawings and pieces of paper torn from notebooks with scribbles and writing. Behind his wooden bedframe sat a large window and wide sill with a stack of books and a small fern atop it.

You could tell a lot about a person based on their room. Whether their laundry was strewn around or if their bed was made. Bryan's room was tidy for sure, but part of me knew after he invited me over during our earlier phone call he dashed around speed cleaning. I could tell by the unorganized pile of books on his dresser and the sweatshirt sleeve sticking out from the bottom of the partially opened closet door. I had allowed myself to daydream about what it would be like the first time I was in Bryan's room. If there ever would be a first time.

It was intriguing to see him at home, more so than his bedroom. Bryan was barefoot, wearing a pair of gray sweatpants and a Jurassic Park t-shirt. His hair was messy and he was sporting a pair of black-framed glasses I hadn't seen before.

"So, how was your day?" Bryan inquired, sitting down at the edge of his bed, watching me carefully as I examined his bedroom walls.

My day. What was I supposed to tell him?

How could I tell him that the night before I woke up with a start, unheard whispers calling me to the window. When I finally got the courage to pull back the curtains, a black figure sat on the grass, crouched on all fours, as real as the dirt it sat on. Smokey talons were visible on the ends of its paws, but the edges of them blurred like a mirage. Black voids looked right through me, seeing everything that I was and used to be. It bent its head to the side, studying me. It felt wrong to be intrigued by something so sinister-looking but I couldn't help feeling drawn to it.

Did I tell Bryan about the awkward mix of relief and disappointment that washed over me when I looked away for a split second and it was gone? How I went through my shift at the Corner Cup in a daze? How every darkened corner of the room had given me chills? I knew I shouldn't be in his bedroom. I knew this was crossing a line I had promised not to cross and if Bryan still lived at home, I wouldn't be here. But he was the only place I truly felt safe.

"Oh, it wasn't all that great, to be honest. I'd rather hear about yours." I sat next to him on the dark gray blanket.

"It was boring, honestly." He shrugged. "I was on the computer most of the day. I had a paper due in British lit and I banged my head against the wall doing econ."

"That doesn't sound boring at all. You work hard, that's not nothing. What were you watching?" I asked, glancing over at his television. It was paused on a spectacular shot of a cluster of stars that matched closely to a photo up on his wall.

"Oh, you're going to laugh at me. It's a documentary about space. Troy gives me heartburn about it all the time." Bryan looked away sheepishly.

"Can we finish watching it?"

A smile swept across Bryan's face and he relaxed. "Of course."

He stretched out across the bed, reaching for the controller to his gaming console that sat on his pillow. He remained sprawled out across the blanket and turned back to look at me over his shoulder.

"You don't have to stay on the edge. It's a queen-sized bed." Bryan shifted himself to the far side of his bed, sitting up with his back against the headboard. "Unless you want to."

"I could definitely lay down after working all day." My voice didn't match the day that I had. It was flirtatious and calm, the polar opposite of the bundle of nerves I had been throughout my shift.

"Come here," he said softly. I gladly obliged, longing to be close to him. It was sad how much I'd daydreamed about his arms around me, the way his breathing steadied as we clung to each other.

I set my bag on the floor and kicked off my shoes before I climbed across Bryan's bed and lay down next to him, resting my head on one of the pillows. Bryan's shoulders relaxed as he nestled against the headboard. Our hearts beat loudly to the same rhythm. The anxiety and uncertainty trapped inside of me withered away into nothing, quickly replaced by a flame burning in my soul too brightly to ignore.

"Are you cold?" he asked nervously, fidgeting with his hands.

"No, I'm fine." I smiled, turning my attention to the documentary. It changed the subject to a distant black hole.

"Are you sure?" His voice was shaky. Bryan grabbed a blanket from the foot of the bed and draped it over me. "The heater has been acting up so it's been rather cold in the house."

"Thank you." I grabbed the edge of the blanket and pulled it up to my chin. "So what else do you do in your free time besides reading and watching nerdy documentaries?"

"Nerdy documentaries." Bryan laughed. "Um, I don't have time for much else. I play video games sometimes. I listen to a lot of music when I have to drive back and forth from FBU."

"What do you listen to?" I asked, looking up at him. He looked like a statue from the angle I was at. His strong jaw turned ever so slightly.

"Whatever is on the radio, honestly. The bay has a good pop station."

"Ugh," I groaned. "Almost perfect."

"What?" He chuckled, nudging me with his elbow.

"You were almost perfect. Pop music, Bryan? Seriously? There's so much better stuff out there."

"Hey, nobody's perfect. There's some good popular music out there. I have rock bands on my playlists too. Not everyone can be all punk rock all the time. Only you're that cool."

"You remember that?" I had only mentioned the type of music I liked once, the evening we watched the sunset together on my back porch. He got so wrapped up in the fact that I hated my birthday I didn't think he remembered.

"Of course. What you have to say is important."

"Sometimes I feel like you're the only one who listens to me."

Bryan shifted and slid down the bed, resting on his side facing me. Lying next to me. The pillow slightly skewed his glasses to the side. Our hands were only inches apart. Close enough I could feel the heat radiating off his fingers. All I'd have to do is reach out my pinky and we'd touch. He took in a breath like he was about to say something but stopped, his thumb drummed against the bedding.

Bryan. His name echoed in my head, and his eyes locked into mine as if he heard me. His lips curled at the end into a soft smile and he relaxed.

"I was reading about gravitational waves the other day, and it got me thinking about all the energy flowing through space, through everything, really." Bryan's eyes poured into mine as he spoke. "Makes it difficult to believe in coincidence or chance. Every decision we make, there's that energy that is pulling and pushing us in one direction or another. So, do we have free will or is destiny guiding us? Like there's these magnetic pulls that lead us on the route we're meant to take. Like both of us ending up in this town."

"Wow, that's deep," I said. Bryan's sudden rush of nerves washed over me, making my skin tingle.

"Do you ever feel it? That pull toward something...or someone."

That familiar tug on my heart gave me the answer, sending goosebumps across my skin.

"I feel it right now," I whispered, my eyes locked into his. Locked into his soul.

"Me too." he breathed, barely a whisper. "You've been through so much yet you've weathered the storm regardless of what life throws at you. You make me look at the world differently. You make me want to be better, to be more resilient. Whitney, I know you want friendship and I want to give you that. I enjoy being your friend and if that's all we ever are, I'm happy as long as I get to have you in my life but..." he paused, unsure if he should continue.

"Say it." I urged him on, my heart racing in anticipation. Each hair on my body stood on end, dying to hear the words that had been echoing through my own head when I thought about him.

"I'm okay with being friends, I am. I don't want to mess up what we have or be disrespectful to what you've already expressed. But if you ever wanted it...I could give you so much more."

"Like what?"

"All of it." His body pressed against mine before I realized I had inched myself closer, filling in the gap between us. The soft scent of cedarwood and vanilla filled my senses. "All of me."

Bryan's fingers grazed my chin, lifting my head up to meet those stunning lily pads. His eyes wandered down to my lips briefly before they darted back up to meet mine, asking permission for something he didn't think he deserved. The thud of his heart echoed in my head like a drum. Bryan looked nervous, as if he was waiting for me to wake up and find something better. As if he wasn't the best thing I'd had the privilege of being close to. I leaned my face toward him, gazing up into his eyes to let him know that this was the moment I chose to cross the line into uncharted territory. Bryan met me halfway, taking my face in his warm hands as his lips crashed down onto mine.

I couldn't help but smile against his mouth when I finally felt the scratch of his facial stubble against my fingertips. His hand left the side of my face as he wrapped his fingers in my hair, pulling me deeper into the kiss. There were no fireworks or dramatic signs and if there were, I didn't notice them. My heart beat loudly in my chest, but I couldn't hear it. I couldn't hear anything. The noises of the television in the background had disappeared. Nothing else in the world existed.

I leaned into him, pressing against his body in all the right places. His hand wandered down my back searching for bare skin but much to my dismay he broke the kiss, slowly pulling away from me. The tip of his nose swept against mine as he sighed. I reached up and removed his glasses, carefully folding the arms. I leaned over him and set them on the nightstand.

"Can you still see?" I asked, wondering if what I'd done was okay.

Bryan smiled, moving a loose strand of ebony hair from my forehead. "I'm nearsighted. I see you perfectly."

"You're special," I whispered.

"I'm not, but I'm glad you think so."

"Yes, you are. You don't get it, Bryan. Even after I was adopted, I couldn't bring myself to trust anyone or let them in. Then you come along and walk right into my life like the door was never locked in the first place. I didn't feel much of anything before, not with anyone else. This short time I've lived in Rifton has been a tidal wave but you are the only thing that makes sense. I've held back how badly I want you because I know it'll actually mean something and that's terrifying." I breathed the words, more vulnerable and naked than I'd ever been.

He remained silent for a moment, collecting his thoughts as he ran his fingers through my hair. "The day I first saw you was an awful day and then you showed up. The most beautiful and frustrated woman I had ever seen. A force to be reckoned with, shining so brightly. You're the sun, Whitney, and I'm some rock floating through space with no choice but to be pulled into your orbit. I did so without a second thought."

Woah, this man was a poet.

"I want you."

"Come get me."

Bryan met my lips again, this time with more force and hunger. My leg hooked over his waist as we lost ourselves in one another's embrace. His fingers dug under my thigh as he pulled me on top of him. His touch burned into my skin after he let go, making the flame inside me stronger. His arm wrapped tightly around my back. His fingers tangled in my hair. His teeth against my bottom lip.

Every detail mesmerized me.

My hand wandered to the waistband of his sweatpants and lifted his shirt. I grazed bare skin with my fingertips, finally indulging in an impulse I'd had a million times before. Bryan sat us up and grabbed the back of his t-shirt, breaking our kiss only to pull it over his head. I tried to admire him but he reached out and pulled my mouth to his like he needed the kiss to breathe. His arms tightened around me and I was on my back before I realized he had flipped us, his weight pressed me into the soft sheets. We were a tangled mess of hands and tongue, tossing clothes onto the floor as quickly as we could get them off, giggling as he fumbled with the button of my jeans.

Bryan gently lifted the aquamarine that lay against my bare skin, running his thumb across the gem. He studied it carefully, watching the black ink swirl around inside the blue walls. I had been in bed with other men, but this was the most intimate moment I'd ever experienced. Touching someone's body was one thing but that necklace was an extension of my soul and he currently held it in his hand. His eyes trailed up to meet mine. I waited for him to say something but he remained silent.

I slowly leaned forward and reached for the back of the silver chain, lifting the necklace over my head. Bryan watched as I carefully took off my aquamarine for the first time in over a decade and placed it on his bedside table next to his glasses. There was no way for him to know what kind of trust I displayed at that moment but the way his eyes lingered on the necklace made me think he had an idea. I ran my fingertips along the line of his jaw and pulled him into another deep kiss.

His hands explored my body, lingering in sensitive spots, taking cues from the way my breathing quickened at his touch. He took in every inch. Every curve and stretch mark I was self-conscious of came to life against him. Bryan peppered kisses down my body, kissing the side of my breast before he wrapped his lips around my alert nipple. I groaned as he nipped his teeth against my flesh, arching my back into his mouth as a glimmer of pain shot through my body. He bit down harder, causing me to hiss.

"Too hard?" He pulled away as if he was worried that he'd hurt me. I welcomed the pain, it was just enough to bring my soul to life and remind me that I was alive.

"Don't stop," I breathed, pulling his head back to my chest.

Bryan went to my other breast, gently massaging the one he'd left as he swirled his tongue around the neglected nipple. His hands slipped to my sides and ran down my body as he kissed the skin between my breasts and moved further down, lingering at my hips. The anticipation drove me mad with desire. All I wanted was to grab a fist full of his hair and guide him, but he wanted to take his time so I let him have a few moments before I whimpered.

"Bryan, please."

"Please what?" he asked, gently pressing his lips into my inner thigh.

"I am not a patient person." My hips shifted against the mattress.

His eyes met mine and he hummed with satisfaction against my skin before finally giving in to me. "Whatever you want, baby."

I gasped as he slid his tongue against me, gripping a fist full of blankets so hard my knuckles turned white. Bryan didn't hold back, gripping hard onto my thighs as he dove in with enthusiasm, knowing exactly what he was doing. The heavier I breathed, the louder I gasped, his excitement rose in my blood. Our emotions wrapped together into one entity.

It was overwhelming to be so stimulated, to experience so much at once. Both heartbeats pounding beneath my skin racing with desire and serotonin as I tethered close to the edge. Climbing higher and higher toward the peak until finally, it all came crashing down, washing over me all-encompassing. He tightened his grip, holding me into place as I writhed, unable to stay still. I cried out louder than I intended, and I knew we weren't in the house alone but I didn't care. Bryan didn't either, riding out the waves with me until I completely melted into the mattress.

"Holy shit," I muttered out of breath as his lips trailed back up my body.

He planted a soft kiss on my neck and pressed himself against me, hard on my thigh, "We're just getting started."

Grabbing a hold of his shoulders, I shoved him down onto his back, eager to feel him underneath me. The fire in my heart was too strong to be calmed. In the past, intimacy had been something I used as an escape to forget or desperation to feel anything, not caring who it was with as long as I was out of my head. But with Bryan, it was something for both of us; the two of us equal halves to a whole being.

I grasped the waistband of his sweats and slowly pulled them down, watching where the trail of blonde hair from under his belly button led. He reached down and took the rest of his clothes off, eyeing me carefully. I placed a hand on his warm chest and eased him back onto the bed. Bryan laid back with ease, letting me take complete control.

Without a second thought, I wrapped my hand around his erection. Bryan's breath caught in his throat as I took a hold of him, his body tensed as I slowly moved my hand up and down. I began to lean into him, eager to take him in my mouth when he shifted, rolling onto his side as he opened the drawer of his nightstand. He dug around, cursing under his breath until he found what he was searching for.

When Bryan rolled back over, he grabbed my face and pulled me into a quick, tender kiss. His other hand met mine, placing a wrapped condom on my palm.

"Whenever you're ready." He whispered. It would be completely my choice to stop now or finally give into each other. I already knew what I wanted. Part of me knew the moment I sat down on his bed.

I unwrapped the condom and rolled it down his shaft, squeezing him gently. Bryan groaned softly, lifting his hips into my touch. I swung my leg over him, straddling his body. His body heat radiated into me, wrapping me in comfort and safety. The moment I had him lined up, he froze.

"Wait." He stopped me, grabbing my hips to keep me steady. "Look at me."

I gazed down to meet those devastatingly perfect green eyes beaming back at me. Once our eyes locked into one another, he thrust up into me. I tilted my head back and cried out, fully indulging in how he awakened all my senses.

"I've fantasized what your face would look like at this exact moment," he confessed, withdrawing slowly before he inched back in. "Fuck, you feel amazing."

My hips rolled against his, falling into a steady rhythm. Bryan cupped my cheek in his palm and ran his thumb across my lips, pulling me in for a deep kiss. I opened my mouth, inviting in his tongue, longing to be joined with him in every way possible. I tightened my pelvic muscles around him and a low growl fell from his lips, turning that steady burn into a full-blown forest fire.

He rolled us onto my back, slamming into me with such force my nails dug deep into his shoulders. Bryan grabbed my right hand and laced his fingers tightly into mine, holding it down against the mattress above my head.

His heart race picked up and his skin tingled with mine until he found his release, his muscles tensed as he buried himself deep inside of me. He let out a final groan as he collapsed onto my chest, his body damp with sweat. I rubbed his back gently as his labored breath steadied. Bryan sighed, nuzzling his face into my neck.

When I came to Bryan's house that night, I hadn't planned on shedding clothes as quickly as we could or entangling my soul with his, but I was tired of holding back. I had spent my entire life cautiously treading through the day, convincing myself that I had what I needed. I couldn't pretend I hadn't completely fallen for Bryan McClintock.

"So, you've fantasized about this?" I asked, breaking the silence that had consumed us as we came back down from the high.

"I shouldn't have said that. I got caught up in the moment," he mumbled against my skin.

"Is it true though?"

He lifted his head slightly to look at me. "Would that be wrong if it was?"

"No," I breathed, running my fingers through his hair, slicking it back from his forehead. "I've done the same thing."

"I should have kissed you in that rainstorm." His voice was soft, gently running his fingers up and down my arm, covering me in goosebumps.

"You should have kissed me at the bonfire." I pressed my lips to his forehead.

A soft laugh vibrated in his chest. "I wanted to."

"I have a confession," I whispered, shifting my weight.

He finally withdrew and laid down next to me, resting his head on the pillow. "What's that?"

"Please don't be angry, but when you accidentally gave me your notebook, I didn't read the first few pages." My heart pounded in my throat, waiting for his reaction.

"Oh?" His face was unreadable, but embarrassment flooded his chest.

"I read all of it. It was so good, Byn. All of it was so beautifully written that I wanted to see what it was like inside of your head. I'm sorry, I shouldn't have done that to you. I understand it was an invasion of privacy but your words set my soul on fire." The confession spilled from my lips quicker than I could comprehend what I was doing.

"Well," Bryan finally spoke after a few moments. "I guess this isn't your first time seeing me naked, in a way."

"And I love all of it."

He grinned, flashing white teeth as he covered his eyes with the crook of his arm. Love was a heavy word to drop during pillow talk but it felt so natural, I didn't think twice about it.

Bryan wrapped his arms around me and pulled me to his chest. As he ran his fingers through my hair, he pressed a soft kiss to my forehead. The steady thud of his heart was a lullaby that sang me into a tranquility I hadn't experienced in years.

"Come on." He sat up and grabbed my hand. "Let's get cleaned up."

I jolted awake with a gasp, as if it was the first breath of air I had taken all day. It took me a moment to remember where I was or how I had gotten there. My dreams would forever be haunted by dark, sightless creatures that wanted nothing more than to tear my beating heart from my chest. It appeared that I couldn't escape those shadows no matter where I went.

"You all right?" Bryan shifted next to me.

"Yeah," I took a deep breath, realizing I was still naked in his bed. "I'm sorry. I, um…I've been having a problem with night terrors recently."

"Don't apologize. We all have nightmares." Bryan rubbed my back.

"I've had one every night this week," I whispered, feeling tears build up in my throat.

Bryan reached out and pulled me back onto him, resting my head on his chest. He wrapped his arms around me and engulfed me in comfort. "I'd never let anything hurt you."

He slowly tickled my bare back with his fingertips as I listened to his steady heartbeat. Everything was perfect, tangled up in him until the screen of my cell phone illuminated and my blood ran cold.

Taking one look at my phone, I knew something was wrong. Eight missed calls from Rayn. Three missed calls from Rose. Eleven missed calls from Brooke. And to top it all off, a text message from my sister read: *911! Where the fuck are you?*

"Shit." I sat straight up in Bryan's bed, unlocking my phone to see the three of them had been trying to get a hold of me for over an hour.

"What?" He propped himself up on his elbows.

"I literally have a million missed calls from my sister." I quickly tapped her name on my recent call list.

"Whitney, what the fuck? Where are you?" Rayn answered the phone in a rage I hadn't encountered in a while.

"I'm sorry, my phone was on silent from work. What happened? What's wrong?" I intentionally skipped over my answer to 'where are you?'

"The girls and I are at the cottage. We-"

"Is that Whitney? I need to talk with her!" Brooke's voice echoed in the background before she came on the phone. "Where are you?"

"What happened?" I dodged the question again.

"You need to come to the cottage. Oh, god, I'm so glad Rose came to get me. Whitney, you have no idea how terrified I was."

"Tell me what is going on." I tightened the blanket around my body with white knuckles and a knot in my stomach.

"I was attacked by a shadow." Brooke began to cry.

"I'm on my way." I jumped up, frantically searching for my clothes. I had to get to the cottage as quickly as I could before I attracted a shadow to Bryan's place.

"What's going on?" Bryan turned on the light on his nightstand, his pulse elevated with concern.

"I'm sorry, but I have to go. It's an emergency, a family emergency. I, um, I'll explain later." I turned around to look into his eyes. "I don't want to leave you."

He looked back at me with understanding but the weight of his disappointment hung on my shoulders. "It's okay."

"Thank you," I whispered. "I can't find my shirt."

Bryan slipped on his sweatpants and put his glasses back on as I clasped my bra into place. I had already hastily put on my jeans and got down on my hands and knees to look for my shirt under the bed.

"Here, take one of mine." Bryan opened up one of his dresser drawers.

"Are you sure?"

"Of course. Besides, this gives you a reason to come back." His words broke my heart.

"Oh, Byn," I dashed to him and wrapped my arms around his bare back. "You're what I want to come back for."

Bryan pulled me into a tight hug and kissed the top of my head as my phone began to vibrate in my back pocket.

"Better get going." He handed me a long sleeve dark green shirt with a line of silhouette pine trees across the front. "Don't forget your necklace."

"Shit," I mumbled as I retrieved the aquamarine from the table. I finished dressing quickly, and threw my coat on with a heavy heart.

"My clothes look good on you." He hid his sadness well. If we didn't have this one-way empathic connection, I wouldn't have been able to tell. He didn't want to make me feel bad for having to leave.

Bryan opened the front door and held it back as I stepped onto the porch. Moths and small bugs flew around the porch light and a half moon lit the sky above us. As I turned back around to face him, he pulled me into his arms and held me against his bare chest. He leaned in like he was going to kiss me, but instead of my lips, he went for my forehead, sending chills through my entire body.

"Drive safe," Bryan whispered. His deep voice made my knees weak and I leaned into him, not wanting to leave and face what was ahead of me. I wanted to postpone it a little bit longer, but I couldn't. I knew the girls wouldn't linger if I was in trouble.

"Bye, Bryan," I mumbled into his chest before I pulled away.

"See you soon." He touched my face before he stepped back inside.

"Finally!" Brooke cried as I flew through the front door of the cottage.

"I'm so sorry, I got here as quickly as I could. I'm so glad you're alright." I pulled Brooke into a hug and checked her over. "What happened?"

Surprisingly, Lauren stood there with Rose and my sister. Despite all the bad blood that had built up between Lauren and Rose over the years, the large bandaid on Brooke's arm had finally gotten us all in the same room again.

"Are you hurt?"

"It cut me," Brooke answered with wet eyes. "I went back to the cemetery to see if that spirit who showed us the spellbook would finally talk to me. The shadow came out of nowhere, I didn't even hear it coming."

"Come, dear, I have your tea." Amilia put her hand on Brooke's shoulder and led her to the fireplace to warm her up.

Brooke wiped the tears from her face and sat down with Amilia.

"Where were you?" My sister inquired sternly.

"You always answer when I call." Brooke furthered the interrogation.

I looked away from them. "I had my phone on silent when I was at work and forgot to turn my ringer back on. I'm sorry. I got here as quickly as I could."

"At least we're all safe and together now." Rayn sat down in one of Amilia's armchairs and let out a deep sigh.

Rose stood frozen in place, shooting me an icy glare that nearly suffocated me. "Whitney..."

"What?" I asked, confused as to why she was acting so cold toward me.

"Where were you?" She annunciated each word carefully to ensure I heard her.

"I don't know why that matters."

Rose slowly nodded with a pissed off smile. I didn't know someone could smile and be so infuriated. "It matters because you're wearing my brother's shirt."

Shit.

When I made eye contact with her, I could feel daggers pierce through my skin. For the first time, I actually felt bad for feeling the way I did about Bryan, that what I was doing was wrong.

"W-What?" I stammered.

"Don't play dumb with me," Rose snapped, balling her hands into fists.

"Did you sleep with him?" My sister blurted out a question I would have much preferred she asked telepathically.

"Oh, god." Rose made a disgusted face.

"I...Rose, I can explain." I began, but she had no problem cutting me off again.

"You damn well better. You show up here in the middle of the night wearing his clothes, thinking I wouldn't notice? I bought him that shirt!" Rose kept her eyes locked on me. "You made a promise as my friend that you'd keep him out of this."

"I wasn't trying to hide this from you, I swear," I said with shaky hands and voice. It didn't help how quiet Rayn got as Rose spoke, shrinking down into her chair.

"You're lying to my face." Rose crossed her arms, hurt and disappointment pouring out of her.

"Rose-"

"Rule number two, Whitney. Don't lie or keep secrets, remember? It's your fucking rule after all. Bryan is the most important person in the world to me and I'm going to need you to back off. He can't get involved with someone like us, especially you." Her words cut me like a knife.

"Especially me? The fuck is that supposed to mean?"

"You know damn well what I mean. You're reckless and you're going to get him killed. There are people and shadows out there trying to kill us. We are drawing attention to ourselves with every spell and I won't let anything happen to my family." When I didn't reply, Rose continued on, "He would be in that much more danger if we attract anything. If someone wanted to hurt us in any way, he'd be the first one to get hit."

"He's in danger either way then, and so is everyone in our families," I said in defense. "I'm not going to stop seeing Bryan because of something that would already happen." I crossed my arms across my chest.

"Well, look at you," Rose spoke in a tone she'd only used with Lauren.

"Rose, you can't exactly march in here and start telling people who they can and can't sleep with. We're all adults." Lauren defended me. Of course she was, I was against Rose. The enemy of your enemy is your friend. I didn't want to be any of their enemies.

Rose looked over at her, raising her eyebrows as she spoke harsher than she had to me. "I don't remember anyone asking you."

Lauren looked away from us toward the wall, resting her cheek in her hand.

"A while back he went to this music festival with his friends and came back with a broken arm and no memory of what happened. After that, Serenity Drake went to the dark side and I always felt the two events were connected. Like she had something to do with it."

"That doesn't mean anything."

"Bryan and Serenity were inseparable and all I know is the last time he was close to someone like us, he got hurt. I don't know what happened but I do know it could have been much worse. That wasn't the first time weird shit happened to Bryan around Serenity and I'm not willing to risk that theory on you. Stop seeing him or I'm out. I won't help you with anything ever again and I'll burn the book on my way out."

"What?" I stared at Rose in disbelief, my jaw hitting the floor.

How could I choose between Bryan and the truth about the magic? I suppose I always knew that choice would come up eventually, but not like this.

"I won't help you piece together this puzzle anymore. I told you not to play games and you are playing a dangerous one. If this is going to be about all of us, then I have a say too and I say you delete my brother's number from your phone and forget you ever met him," Rose spoke sternly.

"You're serious?" I asked, overwhelmed.

"As a 9.5 earthquake," Rose said through her teeth. "If you still want me on your little team then leave my brother out of it."

"Rose," My blood began to boil as I made a conscious decision that throwing an end table at her was not the best option. "I don't want him to know about the magic either,

I'm not going to tell him. We can keep him safe. Besides, I work with Ashley. She's my only friend in this fucking town. I'd have to quit my job if you wanted me to never see Bryan again."

"I don't care!" Rose pulled in a deep breath of air and with it a foreign magic slithered down my arms. I'd never felt it so strongly before.

On reflex, I put my hands up, pushing all my energy toward Rose before she could hit me first. I didn't physically touch her, but my powers hit her like a tidal wave.

Rose flew back and hit the living room wall. She slammed into the wood, but remained on her feet. The front of her was soaked, along with a large area of the wood floor. Droplets fell from her damp hair down her face. I didn't quite realize what I had done, but it startled everyone in the room, including me.

"Rose, I'm sorry," I said immediately. "I didn't mean to do that."

I didn't intend to hurt her, once I looked into those green eyes I remembered she was Bryan's, someone he loved. Someone I had grown to care for deeply. My chest constricted as I realized I had used my powers against one of my own.

Rose didn't say anything out loud, but I knew she was deciding what to do. She looked down at the ground and kept her eyes low as she walked out of the cottage. She waved her hand behind her, slamming the door shut. The plants sitting on the end table wilted instantly in sadness and frustration.

"What did you do?" Brooke bellowed angrily. "You used your magic against Rose!"

"That was awesome." Lauren laughed.

"No, it wasn't!" Brooke shouted, her hands flying up in the air.

"Are you kidding? Did you see the look on her face? She finally got what was coming to her." Lauren sat on the edge of her seat, bright eyed.

Brooke's voice boomed against the walls, "I can't believe you two! Rose has done everything you've asked and you hurt her over some stupid fling with her brother? Weren't you the one who wanted answers so badly?"

"Stop yelling at me!" I said through my teeth.

"You're the most selfish person I know!" Brooke stood up and ran out the front door after Rose.

I sat on the couch and covered my face with my hands, taking a deep breath.

"They're being so immature," Lauren replied, grabbing her bag off the floor. "I don't see why this is such a big deal. Besides, she was ready to throw at you first, I felt it. I know you did too."

"That could have gone...better." Rayn took a seat next to me. "She'll be back. They'll both be back."

"What makes you so sure?" I asked, leaving my face hidden.

"Because we aren't the only ones who want answers," Rayn reassured. "The real question is, what are you going to do about Bryan?"

I let out a hopeless sigh. "I have no idea."

"Did you sleep with him?"

"Yeah."

Rayn raised her eyebrows. "Was it good?"

"I think I have a beard burn on my inner thighs." I lowered my voice.

Lauren nodded in approval. "Good for you."

"Damn." Rayn leaned back. "Well, you have two options, sister. You can finally fulfill our lifelong dream of learning the truth behind our powers or you can get laid. I want you to be happy but not at the expense of everything we've worked for."

"It was bound to implode eventually," Lauren added. "Honestly I'm surprised it took this long."

"May I offer a word of advice?" Amilia broke her silence and took a step forward. She reached out to put her hand on my shoulder in comfort. "Lovers come and go, but your generation shares a bond that lasts forever. No one else on this earth understands what you are going through better than these girls."

I nodded as Amilia pulled me into a motherly embrace. I rested my head against her shoulder and shut my eyes tightly.

"Mia," I muttered into her shoulder. "Remember when I asked you about empathic connections?"

"Yes," She said, gently.

I glanced over at Rayn. "Could I talk to Amilia for a second?"

Rayn nodded and turned to Lauren. "I'll show you the garden."

After they left the room, I shifted back to Amilia. "I think I have an empathic connection. It's only one way. He hasn't said anything about it and he isn't a witch so, I'm pretty sure it's only one way."

Amilia listened intently before she responded, "Rose's brother?"

"Yes," I answered. "I've never experienced anything like it. I can feel both of our hearts beating sometimes. I'm not just fooling around, Amilia. This is...I'm not playing a game."

"Hm," Amilia hummed. "I understand, Whitney, but I stand by what I said. Your generation must come first, especially now that you're all together and the Renati knows it."

"But," I paused. "This empathic connection to someone without powers has never happened before? I don't believe that."

"I don't know everything, Whitney," Amilia admitted. "But no, I'm not familiar with it. Please listen to me. I had my coven and since I lost them, there has forever been a hole in my heart. Think long and hard about what is important to you."

I let out a sigh, realizing that if Amilia truly had more information she wasn't going to share it with me. One thing I knew for sure, no matter what I decided, there was going to be a hole in my heart.

Chapter Twenty-Four

CAUGHT OFF GUARD

I didn't sleep much the next three nights. I tried, but my mind raced, preventing me from getting any rest. I was a zombie throughout my shifts at the Corner Cup. Fitting that I felt like the walking dead considering it was Halloween day.

Rayn hadn't spoken to me much since the incident at the cottage. I hadn't heard a word from Rose or Brooke either. I felt bad for using my powers against Rose but she'd be lying if she said she wasn't ready to use hers first. I wasn't going to apologize for caring about Bryan. Still, Rose's threat worried me enough that I hadn't answered any of his texts.

"Whitney?" Amilia asked from the employee hallway. "May I speak with you for a moment?"

Olivia raised her eyebrows and turned her head to the side like I was a child getting called to the principal's office, but I knew whatever Amilia wanted to talk about had nothing to do with coffee.

"How are you feeling?" Amilia asked as I closed the door to her office behind me.

"I haven't heard from Rose or Brooke...Rayn isn't speaking to me either. I haven't returned Bryan's messages. I feel like I'm in limbo."

Purgatory was more like it.

"Give them time. Now, regarding Abraham Roberts, it does appear he was trying to leave the Renati. Though, it's not something you're allowed to leave alive."

"Yeah, I know. The first time we went to the forest, my brother fell through this portal and into the lake." Amilia's interest instantly peaked at my words. "Abe was being held underwater and Dmitri pulled him out. After he went missing, I found his notebook and

I'm pretty sure he wrote about Serenity Drake and the Renati. He said they were trying to kill him."

Amilia took in a deep breath and leaned back in her chair. "Whitney, I need you to understand the severity of this battle between the Elementals and Renati, in Rifton and beyond. It is more than a feud, it is an old and bitter war that has taken many lives, some innocent and some not. Though you and the other girls have your differences at the moment, it's imperative you stay alert and stay together."

Rule number one.

"Amilia, they aren't speaking to me and I don't see that changing any time soon," I replied with frustration.

"You know in your heart what you need to do." Amilia dismissed me from her office. "Your shift is almost over. Go home and set things straight with your generation, Whitney. Go clean up your mess."

I tried calling Rayn on the way home but her phone went straight to voicemail, which was bizarre. Her battery must have died. I called Rose and big surprise, she didn't answer. I tried Brooke next but no such luck. Lauren, on the other hand, answered my call on the second ring.

"I don't know how to fix this," I admitted a few minutes into our conversation.

Lauren sighed. "I don't know if we should. We've stirred up a lot of shit, maybe this is our sign to call it quits. I can go on with my life, you can keep screwing Rose's brother and we all move on."

"That's not an option, Lauren. Abe could be dead."

"Yeah, which is why we need to stop before the next ghost Brooke sees is one of us." Maybe Lauren had a point.

On the drive home, the street lights I passed under flickered one by one. I tried to brush it off as faulty wiring but the moment I pulled into the dirt driveway, I knew something was wrong. I could feel the imbalance of the universe in my bones.

I rushed to the front door, but it was already cracked open.

"Rayn! Dmitri!" I called, pushing into the house. Everything looked to be in its proper place but the house sounded empty and hollow as a shell.

"Rayn! Dmitri!" I shouted again as I rushed to the bedrooms.

Rayn's room was trashed. Her bedding was all over the floor. Her bookcase was flipped over with paper strewn everywhere. The string of Christmas lights she had lining a large tapestry behind her headboard were all torn apart. The floor lamp that stood in the corner now laid atop the carpet as if someone had thrown it across the room.

"Dmitri!"

I threw back the curtain to his bedroom. Dmitri's things weren't nearly as torn up as Rayn's but there was clearly a struggle.

"Whit..." He groaned from the floor. I rushed to his side and helped him sit up.

"Mit, what happened? Where's Rayn?" My airway constricted. I couldn't feel my heart pounding in my chest or the ringing in my ears. I couldn't feel anything.

"I...I don't remember." Dmitri rubbed his temple and looked around with confusion. "Where's Rayn?"

Oh god.

"Rayn?" I screamed again. I left Dmitri's side and ran through the house onto the back porch. No one else was home. No one was there.

My sister was gone.

I grabbed my phone from my pocket but my hands were shaking so bad I dropped it against the tile floor of the kitchen. I retrieved it and sent a message to the other girls, the only message I knew would get their attention and convince them to finally speak to me again.

Rayn is missing.

I collapsed onto the kitchen floor. The tears were already trickling down my face and I could feel myself losing control. I bit down on my lip hard, trying to keep myself from crying but that's all I could do. I imploded.

The water fell from the faucet in the kitchen, flowing through my veins like the pipes under the sink. Water began to pour from the fridge and onto the floor. The pipes under the sink began to leak.

"Whitney, stop." Dmitri's voice rang as he looked at the ground like poison spilled onto the floor. "Whitney, you need to stop."

I don't know how long I was out of it, but the next voice I heard shouting my name wasn't Dmitri.

"Whitney!" Rose's voice shouted close to my head. "What are you doing?"

I blinked and looked around the kitchen, stopping the water that had flooded the house. Rose wasn't the only one standing in the living room. Brooke and Lauren were behind her with worried looks in their eyes.

I had to snap out of this. I had to be strong and persistent like the ocean waves.

I had to find my sister.

"Where was the last place you saw her?" Rose knelt down next to me. She didn't seem to care that her jeans were soaked.

I took a deep breath. "Here. I went to work and came home and she was gone. Her room is a disaster."

"Her phone is in her room." Dmitri stood by the entrance into the kitchen, rubbing the back of his head. "It's broken."

"You don't remember anything?" Brooke asked him with wide eyes.

"No." Dmitri looked defeated like he had failed his family. "I have a headache. I think I got knocked out."

"That's not a good sign," Rose said, biting her lip. "Who goes somewhere without their phone? Where would she go?"

"What about the meadow?" Lauren asked.

"I don't think Rayn is alone," Dmitri admitted, helping me up off of the floor.

Brooke took a few steps toward the bedrooms but stopped herself. "Something bad happened here."

"Like what?" Rose walked to Brooke's side.

"Someone who wasn't supposed to be here." Brooke went into Rayn's room and looked at her open window. "Did she have anyone with her?"

"Obviously, look at the state of her bedroom," I said, shaking.

"We have to go look for her, Whitney. Nothing feels right about this." Brooke turned back to us.

"I agree," Rose replied.

"Where should we look first?" Dmitri asked.

I thought of all the different possible locations my sister could have gone. Various coffee shops and swings at the park came to my mind, but I knew I wasn't thinking broadly enough. She hadn't gone for a casual outing. She was missing. She had been taken somewhere that she wouldn't usually go, but where?

"Anything?" Lauren asked with concern.

"We're going to look for her." I turned to face Rose. "I'm so sorry about what happened, about using my powers against you and for lying to you."

Rose nodded. "Don't ever do it again, but I forgive you."

"Thank you."

I followed Rose out of the kitchen. "Let's find Rayn."

I slowed down for another sharp turn as we drove into town. It was hard not to drive as fast as I could looking for a sign, a feeling, anything. In an attempt to signal Rayn, I used my powers, feeling the water inside of the dirt and the small puddles on the side of the road. Simple things that allowed me to keep most of my focus on the road, but it was enough that the girls in the back seat could tell what I was doing.

I didn't know how close Rayn and I had to be to each other to detect it. I had been mentally calling for her since the moment I got home, but she had yet to reply. That meant she wasn't within hearing distance. It had to have been that, any other alternative was out of the question.

The leaves in the trees had already begun to fall from their branches, blowing behind the tires as I drove down the narrow road into Rifton. It was hard to imagine such darkness lived in this beautiful forest.

"Where exactly are you planning on going?" Dmitri asked.

"I don't know," I slowed down as we came to a stop at the first traffic light in town. "I don't feel like we're getting any closer to her. There has to be a sign somewhere."

"What kind of sign?" Brooke leaned forward in her seat. "Maybe we're looking for the wrong things."

"To feel her magic, or hear her. Something..." I tightened my grip on the steering wheel.

"Maybe she isn't able to do that right now," Brooke hesitated. "What if..."

"What if what?" I looked at her in the rearview mirror.

"I'm trying to think." She took a deep breath and looked me in the eyes. "She has to be somewhere in town."

Suddenly I felt it, that burning feeling in the pit of my stomach. I took a deep breath and looked around, trying to figure out where it was coming from, but I didn't see anything. Instinctively, I turned right and stopped by a row of storefronts. I barely had time to kill the engine before I leaped out of the car.

"Whitney!" Dmitri called after me, unbuckling and opening his door.

The feeling of Rayn's power slowly faded away. I looked at a puddle of rainwater in the dirt on the other side of the road. I raised my hand and moved it like I was running my fingers through the water, making waves and ripples. I didn't use my powers for long, only long enough for Rayn to notice.

"Anything?" Brooke asked.

"Not yet, but I felt the burning," I said.

"Me too," Rose replied.

I glanced over to see that Lauren was also out of the car, looking around at the trees lining the street. "Lauren?"

She turned her head and looked at me. "Shhh. I hear something."

"What?" I asked, walking around the car to stand next to her.

"It's a whisper. I can't make out any of the words, but it's coming from over here." Lauren pointed to the other side of the road.

I had been to this part of town before. We were close to the camera shop and the toy store. We were close to Dragonfly Mystic.

"Do you think Rayn is over there?" Brooke asked.

"I think she might be," Lauren replied. "It's hard to tell whose voice it is, but it sounds like a girl."

"It has to be Rayn," Brooke said. "Who else would it be? Let's go."

Rayn! I screamed inside my head and aloud.

I ran aimlessly across the street. I had no idea where I was going. No one else knew where we were going. Rayn wasn't answering. I couldn't feel her power and I was beginning to believe what I had felt earlier was a delusion until the burning sensation surfaced again ever so slightly. A glimmer amidst all the chaos surrounding us.

"Whitney!" Brooke shouted.

"I felt it," I breathed.

We went into the alleyway behind the businesses as I searched frantically, praying the burning feeling of Rayn's powers would return. It was a trail of breadcrumbs that had disintegrated in the rain, but I remained determined.

I scanned our surroundings and stopped dead in my tracks at a familiar round window at the bottom of one of the buildings. It was above the pavement where a basement would be.

The basement of Dragonfly Mystic.

I froze. "Oh my god."

"What? What happened?" Brooke rushed to my side.

"I've seen that window before," I muttered, the words coming from my throat like bile. I remembered all too well what happened inside of that basement.

"Where?" Rose asked from behind me.

"The round one over there. I had a vision. I was in a room, tied up and beaten. Someone was trying to kill me." I hadn't told the girls about my vision. But now, I couldn't shake the feeling that my vision was important, that I needed to remember every detail.

"A vision?" Lauren demanded. "You have visions? Can you fly, too?"

"Now isn't the time for jokes, Lauren," Rose snapped.

"Whitney," Dmitri stepped forward. "Maybe you weren't seeing things from your perspective in that vision."

"What are you talking about?" I couldn't think straight and I didn't have time to decode his riddles.

"You're the Seer, Whit. You were seeing the future. What if you saw that room through Rayn's eyes? What if she's in there?"

"Dmitri you genius! I'm going in." I stormed toward the round window when a hand caught my arm. I jumped, turning to Brooke holding me back.

"Whitney, hang on a minute, we can't-"

"I can't what? I can't find Rayn? The four of you can stay here. I'm going to get my sister." I pulled my arm out of Brooke's grip and strode forward, but a voice stopped me in my tracks.

Whitney.

"Whit! Listen to me," Rose called out behind me. "Whitney, I can't let you go by yourself."

"I'll be fine. I've taken care of myself for this long," I argued, charging at the building again.

"Don't be reckless. You don't have to do this alone, not anymore."

"Then stop slowing me down," I ordered.

"You guys go get Amilia," Rose said over her shoulder. "Get back here as fast as you can."

I took off toward the building, my heart pounding in my chest. Each step I took caused a tighter knot in my stomach. I had never been this terrified in my life. My entire body shook as adrenaline pumped through my veins.

Rose came after me again. "Whitney, we can't charge in there with guns blazing. If someone took Rayn, they are dangerous, and trust me, they will be expecting you to come after her. Anyone with a brain would know you'd come after her. You have to trust me."

"I don't know who to trust anymore," I admitted, choking back tears with every pound of my petrified heart.

"Us. You trust us," Rose cupped my cheek in her palm. "You trust me, and Rayn and Brooke. And Dmitri. And yeah, I guess, Lauren, too. Rule number one, remember? We stick together."

I nodded as Rose smiled. "Good. Let's go get our girl."

I froze the lock on the door in the back of the building. Rose and I were able to shatter it and snuck to the basement as quietly as possible.

Rayn! I shouted mentally, bolting down the stairs and further into the basement. *Ray!*

My sister was on the concrete floor lying on her side with her hands tied behind her back. Rope marks dug deep into her wrists underneath links of chains, which told me she had been able to burn the ropes. Rayn's right eye was black and her cheek was bruised as if she had been punched in the face, more than once. Her bottom lip was cut and bleeding.

"Oh god, Rayn, who did this to you." Rose knelt down next to us and waved her hand over the padlock, it unlocked with a click. A glimmer of hope rose through me, until a familiar humming filled the basement. The same lullaby I had heard in my vision.

Rose began to choke and cough on thin air, her hands ripping at her neck as if something tightened around her throat but I couldn't see anything.

"Rose? Rose, breathe." I put my hand on her shoulder as her face turned red.

The humming grew louder, followed by a pair of footsteps.

"Look what we have here. Just in time, ladies." A familiar voice sang as Serenity Drake came into view from the shadows. Her hand balled into a tight fist.

"Ren, we can't kill them. Not yet." A male voice replied, still shielded in the darkness. I recognized that voice.

"You ruin all my fun." Serenity eased her hand and Rose gasped for air. She fell forward on all fours and coughed hoarsely.

"Are you okay?" I asked Rose, who nodded slightly. She glared up at Serenity with a look that could kill. Unfortunately, Serenity Drake stood alive and well.

"Ren, you know the ritual must be completed with live blood." The figure stepped out from the darkness and stood proudly next to Serenity. "Now, if you're done playing cat and mouse, we have some business to attend to."

"Tom." I gasped. "What's going on?"

Tom smiled. The boy who Rayn had been so sure of began to laugh. The look in his eyes had changed entirely from warm and welcoming to malicious and sadistic.

"I told you they were gullible," Tom replied to Serenity before he stepped toward us. "Are you shocked? Are you overcome with surprise and fear?"

"Don't patronize me," I snapped. "You two are together...you acted like you cared for Rayn."

How did I not see that Tom was part of the Renati? The pieces fell together now that I saw him standing next to Serenity. Tom always wore long sleeve shirts. Tom was the one who suggested Rayn get the job at Dragonfly. He had weaseled his way into her trust so he could betray her.

Tom laughed again. "Do you actually think someone could love an Elemental? No. The moment I saw Rayn's fire on the first day of classes trying to get Rose's attention, I knew. I knew this was our chance to bring Erebus back once and for all."

How could we have been so careless?

"But the protection oil…it worked. It was supposed to ward off unwanted guests. We did the spell right." I turned to Rose, trying to understand. I thought it had worked. I thought we had kept ourselves safe.

Tom chuckled. "I was not an unwanted guest."

Rayn whimpered next to me, rubbing the marks on her wrists. Tom had taken advantage of Rayn's ability to see the good in everyone, in her desire for companionship and love. Tom and Serenity's plan to lure us here had been methodical and conniving. I could only imagine what Serenity had done to lure Abe to the lake.

I turned to Serenity. "Where is Abe Roberts?"

"If I knew, he'd be dead." Serenity grinned. "I wish I had finished what I started in the lake but next time I get my hands on that slimy traitor, he won't leave my grips alive. Neither will you."

"You can't kill me," Rose breathed. "What about Bryan?"

"What about him?" Serenity shrugged.

"Byn and Emma were everything to you, I don't believe anyone changes that much. You wouldn't hurt him like this."

"You think either of them are off limits? Everyone is expendable."

"You won't touch him." I snarled, not a question but a warning.

"Fuck around and find out." Tom matched my tone. "I wonder who will be the next to disappear? My money is on your little brother."

"You're a snake!" I shouted, grabbing ahold of Rayn. I wrapped her in my arms and pulled her close. I was going to get her and Rose out of this Hellhole if it was the last thing I did. Right after I strangled the life from Tom and Serenity.

"Whitney, run!" Rose shouted as she shot to her feet.

Rose threw her hands in the air and thick vines broke through the cement below us, wrapping around Serenity and Tom's ankles before knocking them both on their backs.

I grabbed Rayn and pulled her to her feet, carrying the brunt of her weight as I dragged her toward the staircase.

"You little bitch!" Serenity screamed and threw her own hands up.

Rose shrieked as she was thrust into the air, her arms thrashing around in an attempt to catch some kind of balance. Serenity shoved her arms forward, and with it, Rose went flying across the room against the brick wall. She fell to the concrete unconscious. Fear pulsed through my body.

"Rose!" I screamed, gripping Rayn's waist tighter.

I had to get my sister out of here but I wouldn't leave Rose behind. My legs felt like they were about to turn to gelatin. Then I remembered what Amilia said when I told her I couldn't move objects with my power.

Have you ever truly tried?

Still holding onto Rayn, I lifted my left hand and pushed forward with all of my strength. I mustered my fear and harnessed it to knock Serenity onto the floor, her head bounced off of the concrete with a cry of pain.

"Get off your ass and grab the unconscious one. I'll deal with the sisters," Tom ordered Serenity as he charged toward us.

I attempted to push my powers at him as well, but Tom flew across the room with such speed that I blinked and he was already in my face. I tried to let out a scream for help as Tom's hand gripped around my throat tightly, squeezing the air from my lungs. On his wrist was a familiar carving of a symbol I had grown to hate.

Rayn threw herself forward and wrapped her bleeding hands around Tom's ankle as she bit down into his skin through his pant leg.

"Arg!" Tom let out a painful wince before he kicked my sister in the face. Rayn's head flew back with such force I feared her neck would snap.

"No!" I screamed with the last bit of air left in my lungs.

Serenity rushed over and grabbed Rayn by the hair, dragging her back across the floor to where Rose lay, still unconscious. I finally noticed the circle drawn in the concrete that I hoped wasn't blood, but the red liquid could be nothing else.

I had no idea how long I had been without air, but Tom's tight grip around my throat finally loosened and I stumbled to the ground. My vision went spotty and then black, but I could still feel myself being dragged across the floor.

I was the only fully conscious one left and I had the wind knocked out of me. My vision cleared as I fought back as hard as I could but I was no match for Tom. It was like he had been bitten by a radioactive animal or fell into a pit of human strength because I seemed to do absolutely nothing. Tom continued to drag me as if I was a limp stuffed animal.

"Hurry up before they gain their strength back." Serenity huffed, tossing Rayn like a rag doll, letting her head hit against the cement.

"Do it." Tom hissed. "It's time we prove ourselves to the elders once and for all."

Once I was inside the blood red circle, Tom shoved his knee into my chest. I squirmed beneath him, kicking my legs and thrashing as hard as I could. I nearly knocked Tom off of me once but he regained his balance quickly. Clearly, these two psychopaths had been training for this moment for who knew how long.

I trembled with fear. I could barely breathe. I was terrified, not only for myself but for the other girls. Rose should have let me come into this basement alone. I couldn't bear the thought of Rose getting hurt let alone losing her life trying to help me.

Serenity grabbed my wrist, digging her fingernails into my skin. She pulled out a large, silver-hilted blade and pressed it hard against my arm. I shrieked as the knife sliced my skin. Serenity didn't seem to care how deep she cut or how much noise I made crying out. It was clear that no one was coming.

"Mit! Brooke!" I screamed as loud as I could, but my voice bounced off of the stone walls. The room must have been soundproofed somehow.

I was an idiot for thinking I could run in here with nothing but my naïve outlook, grab Rayn and walk out. There was so much about magic I had left to learn.

Serenity moved to Rayn and Rose, cutting a gash in each of their arms as well. Our blood dripped down like a leaking faucet and pooled onto the concrete, mixing together.

"We already have Rose's blood," Tom said to Serenity as she towered above us. "Why are you wasting time cutting her?"

"Payback," Serenity growled.

The realization hit me like a ton of bricks. Tom and Serenity put the curse on Rose. They sent the shadow to attack Brooke. They were what caused Lauren's unexplainable cut on her arm. They had been planning this since my family arrived in Rifton.

Tom went to a metal shelving unit where a small altar had been set up. He grabbed a golden chalice that sat next to four dimly-lit candles and rushed back to the circle before I could attempt another escape.

"Rise from the darkness! Once more from the realm of the shadows!" Tom said in a deep and foreboding voice that boomed through the small basement.

Serenity backed up slowly, her eyes wide with excitement. Whatever Tom was trying to accomplish, Serenity was thrilled to see the result. Neither of them had their hands on me and I was finally able to breathe again. I took my opportunity and grabbed my groggy sister, dragging her out of the circle as Tom reached out and poured a thick, black sludge from the chalice over the puddle of mixed blood. The black sludge glopped down onto the concrete like old oil, bubbling as it touched the thick red mixture.

Once I had Rayn out of the circle, I went back for Rose. I didn't care that warm blood still gushed from my stinging wound. I could barely feel the pain, I was so rushed with adrenaline and sheer will to survive the horrid séance we had been dragged into.

As I grabbed underneath Rose's shoulders and pulled, the concrete below us began to rattle. An earthquake shook the entire basement, causing Serenity to squeal with pleasure.

"We did it!" Her voice bellowed through the room.

I yanked on Rose harder and the moment I pulled her from the circle, the concrete cracked. A bright, silver light beamed through the gaps in the floor as it opened wider and wider. I used all my strength and pulled Rose as hard as I could to keep us both from falling through the floor and into Hell.

"Rose, wake up." I shook her desperately. "Please, wake up!"

Finally, the cracks in the floor stopped growing and I sighed with relief, until a black-taloned paw reached out from the depths and pulled itself into the land of the living. A shadow crept out from under the floor and hissed as it surfaced, showing sharp, black teeth.

"Holy shit," Rayn mumbled and grabbed my arm in fear.

Shadow after shadow came crawling up behind the first one. It was like a small army of terror. A shadow slithered toward us, its claws tapping against the concrete with every step, its fangs flashing with malicious intent. This was a demon, a fully formed shadow. It closed in on us, shoulders bobbing up and down like a prowling lion.

Rayn screamed and scrambled backward. My eyes grew in disbelief. The shadow I had seen outside my window was frightening but the black beast staring me down was the true definition of fear. My heart stopped beating, causing my blood to run cold.

I lashed out impulsively and kicked my legs forward in an attempt to get the shadow away from me. As I kicked my leg out, my foot went right through its face. The structure of the creature's outline wisped about in a cloud of smoke.

"We have to get out of here," I told Rayn, inching closer to the staircase.

"We can't let them leave!" Tom's voice bellowed as we moved toward the stairs.

Tom loomed over us, holding out his hands which I could only assume brought hostile magic with them. I was infuriated. I was dripping with terror but I shoved past the fear. Tom and Serenity may be powerful, but they were no Elemental and I was not going to allow them to wreak any more havoc on my generation. I was stronger than this. I was not going to allow us to be taken advantage of any longer.

As Tom came closer, I held up my hands and imagined the entire room filling with water, drowning both Tom and Serenity and the shadows along with them. I furrowed my brow in deep concentration as my hands trembled in front of me.

At first, Tom looked at me pathetically, like I was a child attempting to play a game for the first time until he began to choke. Tom fell to his knees quickly with his hands around his throat as he coughed up water. It was only a mouthful at first, before water poured out of his body. Water gushed from his mouth, his nose, and his ears. His eyes bulged as he fell to the ground and convulsed like a fish out of water until his body went limp.

I stared at Tom's dead body until my vision grew speckled again and I fell over, dizzy and exhausted. Blood dripped from my nose and into my mouth, the metallic tinge coating my tongue. I looked past Tom's limp body to search for Serenity as another, much larger figure rose from the cracked concrete.

The figure hunched over and slowly rose before it collapsed on its side, weak and frail. A boney, bloody hand reached toward us, inching closer and closer as it trembled. Two red eyes flew open and peered right at me with such intensity and hatred that all the warmth was stripped from my body.

The moment my eyes locked with the creature before me, I knew I'd seen him before in a previous life. He knew when he looked at me that we had battled before. He wanted nothing more than to rip my beating heart from my chest. The figure before me was none other than Erebus returned from the dead.

The last thing I remember before my eyelids collapsed in fatigue was an ear-shattering screech and the entire room erupting into flames.

CHAPTER TWENTY-FIVE
THE BEGINNING

"Whitney? I think she's started to wake up." A distant voice woke me. The voice was underwater, far away. Or I was. "Whitney, honey?"

"Mom?"

My eyes fluttered open but I closed them quickly. My head pounded. My muscles and joints ached. I felt like I had been hit by a truck.

I groaned and tried to move but that only made it worse.

"Brooke, get me white willow bark. Quickly."

Amilia.

I couldn't be dead if Amilia was here. I opened my eyes once more and my vision became clearer as I adjusted to my surroundings. I looked up at the ceiling of the cottage, a pillow supported my head and a blanket came up to my waist. I was lying in a bed.

"Rayn." I groaned and tried to sit up but Amilia put her hands on my shoulders and eased me back down gently.

"No, Whitney, don't get up. Rayn is fine. You're all fine." Amilia reassured me but I didn't believe her. I wouldn't believe another word until I saw my sister and the other girls with my own eyes. "You need rest in order to heal. Take this."

"Rose," I muttered.

"Rose is all right. You are all here and alive." Amilia spoke in a warm voice, holding a cup to my lips.

The aching was almost unbearable, but whatever tonic Amilia gave me instantly began to ease my suffering. She truly was a remarkable healer.

I remembered back to our confrontation with Tom and Serenity where we had gotten pummeled. We lost. But the fire...the flames that took out those shadows saved us.

"Rayn," I muttered again.

"I'm right here." Her hand was warm in mine.

I turned toward the sound of Rayn's voice lying beside me. The fire had to have been from her.

"Where's everyone else?" I asked, looking around to see only Amilia and Brooke.

"Rose is in the next room. Lauren and Dmitri are in the living room," Amilia explained. "Brooke, go get them, please."

"I'm so glad you're awake." Brooke gave my other hand a quick squeeze before leaving the bedroom.

"Thank god." Dmitri rushed to our bedside as he stepped into the room. "I was afraid you'd never wake up."

"I feel so stupid. I am so tired of getting screwed over," Rayn said quietly with her eyes shut tight. "First Jon and now this? Am I really that naïve to not see that these were bad guys?" Tears formed in her eyes, and one fell down her cheek slowly. I put my arm around her and held her close.

"Tom went out of his way to play his part, he made damn sure that no one would suspect him." Dmitri put his hand on Rayn's arm for comfort. "He fooled all of us."

"I should have known," Rayn whispered.

"You never saw the mark on his wrist?" I asked. "Didn't he ever take his shirt off?"

"He did," Rayn paused, looking away from us. "But he always had the lights off when we were together like that. I figured he was just self conscious."

I sighed. "I'm so sorry, Ray."

It took every bit of me not to cry when I saw Rayn's black eye and the cuts on her face. I didn't want to know what I looked like.

Brooke rushed back into the room. "Rose won't stay in bed."

"I'm fine!" Rose shouted. She came up behind Brooke and pushed past her. "I haven't slept since we got here, I'm not tired. Are you two okay?"

Rose had a nasty bruise on the side of her face and cuts on her arms, but all in all, she looked okay considering she had been thrown into a wall and knocked unconscious.

I looked down at my own skin where Serenity's giant blade had sliced me open. All that remained was a bright red scar with no stitches or dried blood. It looked as if I had received the scar weeks earlier rather than only hours before.

"Brooke's handy work," Amilia replied full of pride as she noticed me running my fingers over the scar. "She truly has a gift."

"Gabriel wrote in the book that the more you heal, the easier it becomes. You have to use your own health but it replenishes in time. The trick is to make sure you fully recover each time." Brooke grinned. Clearly, she had been doing more reading than I realized. "I'm going to take the scar away, too."

"Thank you, Brooke, but I think I'm going to keep it." I ran my fingers along the damaged tissue. "I'm sore, but I'm fine. I can't believe we all got out of there alive."

I couldn't feel relieved. I couldn't feel like we had been victorious. Our encounter with death had been too close of a call. We all should have seen it coming from miles away.

"We almost didn't," Rose replied, sitting down on the edge of the bed.

"What was that thing...that thing they brought up from the floor? All I remember was the shadows that came with it." Rayn sat up in the bed and looked around the room, making sure none of them followed us here.

"Erebus." I answered. "He's back."

"I have feared this moment for many years. Erebus has been revived from the depths of darkness. He was the vilest witch to ever live, and now he walks amongst us." Amilia tightened her arms across her chest. I could almost see tears forming. I had yet to see true fear in her eyes until that moment. I knew the girls and I were in deep trouble for the part we played.

"What does that mean exactly?" I asked, a bit confused.

"All I know is the last time that creature walked the earth, it was the end of generations for centuries," Amilia replied with a somber tone.

I turned to look at my sister. "Rayn, how did you light the whole place up after you had been hurt so badly?"

"What do you mean?" Rayn looked confused.

"The fire...the fire you lit that burned Dragonfly down."

Rayn still looked clueless. "I didn't light a fire, Whitney."

Rose filled my missing gaps. "When I woke up in the back parking lot, the entire place was engulfed. It had to be you, Rayn. Only a pyro could have lit the place up that quickly."

"Did you feel Rayn use her powers when the fire began?" Amilia questioned, a concerned look on her face.

I thought hard for a moment, trying to replay every detail of the horrors we had witnessed. But no matter how many times I thought back, I couldn't remember feeling Rayn's powers.

"No," I whispered quietly. "No, I don't think so."

Amilia put her hand over her heart in disbelief.

"That Abe kid is probably dead. Rayn's psycho ex is dead. You almost died and we would have been next." Lauren spoke from the doorway of the bedroom. Her arms crossed against her chest. "Everything was fine until you two showed up."

"Are you serious right now?" Rayn's voice was hoarse. "Tom is only dead because Whitney killed him."

Whitney killed him.

Her words echoed in my head. I never thought I could take someone's life but there I was, a murderer. It was self-defense, I had no other choice. The excuses repeated over and over in my head but I still saw his blood when I looked down at my hands. The image of Tom's eyes bulging from his head was forever imprinted in my memory.

Everyone else in the room was talking but all I could hear was Tom choking on my water, gasping for air. My stomach churned and I gagged. I clenched my teeth but the bile rose up in my throat like an open floodgate, and there was no force that could stop it.

Amilia grabbed a bowl and held it in my lap. She rubbed my back gently as I emptied my stomach, sobs catching in my throat in between heaves. Amilia sat patiently, waiting until the sobs turned into heavy breaths and I had nothing left in my stomach before she took the bowl and silently left the room. Brooke handed me a damp cloth, helping me to press it against my face.

Lauren was stewing in the corner, finally unleashing her anger in all directions. "We were staying away from each other and nothing bad was happening to us. Nothing like this would have happened if you two never came here. You brought this with you from wherever you came from."

"Wow," Rayn's eyes widened in disbelief. "Lauren, Tom would have targeted any of us."

"But he didn't. He targeted you." Lauren pointed at Rayn. "I can't do this anymore. I won't do this and I don't want to. We are in way over our heads and I want out." Lauren's voice shook as she spoke.

"You're gonna walk away?" Brooke dropped her jaw in shock. "How could you do that after what happened?"

"Especially after what happened!" Lauren shouted back. "This isn't over, and I don't want to be around when the next person gets dragged off to be slaughtered. Do you think I'm going to allow myself to be next? Or my parents?"

"What about your bracelet?" Rayn asked.

"Take it." Lauren ripped off her bracelet and threw it on the ground. "I don't want it anymore. I never wanted any of this in the first place. This is your battle and I won't fight it." Without hesitation, Lauren turned around and left the room. The front door slammed behind her.

"She'll be back. She has to be." Brooke picked the bracelet up off the floor.

I'd be shocked if I ever saw Lauren Thaner come near us again and she didn't witness the atrocity Rayn, Rose, and I went through.

Rayn threw back the blanket and struggled to get out of bed.

"Ray, lay back down," Dmitri insisted but Rayn threw her hand up at him.

"I need to walk." Rayn replied. "If you want to help, come walk with me. I want to be by the fireplace."

Dmitri rushed to her side and helped her hobble into the living room.

"What a fucking mess," I muttered and fell back on the bed. The impact of hitting the soft cushion felt like pins and needles. I let out a groan of pain and frustration.

"That's not all." Hesitation filled Rose's soft voice. "Can I talk to Whitney alone for a moment?"

"Of course," Amilia put her hand on Brooke's shoulders and led her from the room.

"What's going on?" I asked with concern.

Rose looked guilty. "My brother is on his way here."

"What? Bryan's coming here?" I sat up as quickly as my brittle bones would allow and swung my legs off the side of the bed.

"I called him about fifteen minutes ago," Rose admitted. "Whitney, it's time he knows the truth."

She stood up and walked across the room, shaking her hands.

"No, no it's not." I fought back but the decision had already been made. I did my best to remember that the choice wasn't mine to make in the first place.

"Rose?" Bryan's deep voice bellowed through the entire cottage. I attempted to swallow the giant lump in my throat.

Bryan stormed through the open door. It was the first time I had seen him in days. He looked as radiant as always, except for the terrified look in his eyes.

"Rosie?" Bryan walked straight to her side. I wasn't sure he had seen me.

"Hey, Byn." She looked down at the floor.

"What happened?" Bryan asked, pushing some of Rose's brown hair out of her face and examining the cut on her forehead. Guilt flooded my entire body as I felt his panic. "What happened to you?"

"I...I don't know where to start." Rose couldn't look at him. "There's something I need to tell you. Something *we* need to tell you."

Bryan turned to look at me. "Whitney...what are you doing here? Are you alright?" Bryan's eyes widened with confusion, moving a strand of hair from my face to further examine my injuries. His thumb was gentle against my cheek. "How do you two know each other?"

"I-" The words lodged in my throat. I wanted to say something, but I didn't know what. I never wanted to tell Bryan about our powers.

"Whitney, what's going on?" He looked into my eyes. I froze, meeting that gorgeous gaze. He saw it too, he could see me getting lost in him.

"Rose, I can't do this." I left Bryan's eyes as quickly as I could.

"How are we going to cover this one up? I'm good, but I'm not this good." Rose replied, quietly, meeting my eyes. "Like I said, it's time."

"One of you needs to tell me what the hell is going on." Bryan's voice shook with concern.

"Byn, you know I'm different." Rose began. "You always tell me how different I am." Here we go.

"What are you getting at?" Bryan's heart pulsed throughout his entire body, anxiety overwhelming his nervous system.

"I'm a witch." Rose announced. "Whitney and I are both witches."

There it was out in the open and there was no traveling through time to put those words back in her mouth. Not exactly the way I would have worded it to him, but it was the truth. Short, sweet, and honest.

The gears that had been turning in his head ground to a halt. After a moment of silence, he put a hand on Rose's shoulder. "How hard did you hit your head?"

"It's true," I told him. "We have abilities."

"What kind of abilities?" Bryan asked, his nerves kicking back in. His face fell, looking back and forth between Rose and I.

My heart pounded so hard in my throat my stomach churned. I couldn't look Bryan in the eyes when he turned to me for answers. I couldn't do anything but listen as Rose tried to explain the unexplainable to her brother. I scanned the room, desperately looking for anything to ground myself as the wave of conflicting emotions came over Bryan and I. I settled on the panels on the door. One. Two. Three. Four.

"A group of five witches, like us, is called a generation. We each have a specific element that we have the ability to control and create. Whitney can control water and I can control-"

"Stop." Bryan held up his hands, interrupting her. "Back up. When did you get into witchcraft?"

"We didn't *get into* it. I've had my powers since I was five," I replied, counting the panels again.

"You're saying you've had magical powers your whole life and I never knew about them," Bryan said to his sister.

"Until now," Rose agreed. "Remember that time we went to the coast for a week and Mom's fern was dead when we came back? And the next day it was green and Mom said it was because she watered it and put that special food? It wasn't. It was me."

"You bring plants back to life?" Bryan asked, lines appeared on his forehead from his indented brow.

"That's part of it," Rose explained.

"With what?"

"Magic."

Bryan took a deep breath and cleared his throat, but didn't look at me. I sat there, small and worthless in the corner watching my secret exposed, not knowing what to say about it. I bit the side of my mouth and watched him pace back and forth in the small room.

"Byn, I know it sounds absolutely ridiculous to you, but think about it. You know weird things have happened that give you evidence to support it," Rose said.

I hated this. I wanted to go home.

"And where do you play into this?" Bryan asked, turning his attention to me.

"Like Rose said, there are five witches in a generation. Rose and I happen to be two of those five. That's why our necklaces are so similar." I kept my eyes on the ground, still counting the knots in the hardwood. I had never sat down and told someone about the powers like this, someone who wasn't already involved somehow.

"Is that why you got involved with me?" Bryan took a step toward me as I felt his heart crack inside his chest. "Because you needed to get closer to my sister?"

"No!" I shouted. "No, of course not. I didn't know you and Rose were related until after the bonfire. How could you think that?"

"How could I not?" Bryan ran his fingers through his hair. "You've been so hit or miss the entire time. Then you come over for a booty call in the middle of the night and I haven't heard back from you since."

"Byn, I told Whitney to stop talking to you," Rose admitted softly.

A feeling I'd never experienced with Bryan before washed over him. Anger. "What?" he snapped.

"I didn't want you to get hurt, because this magic is a dangerous thing. I didn't want-"

"That's not up to you. What compelled you to think you could interfere in my relationship like that?"

"Byn, I-"

"You crossed a line, Rose. It's not okay."

Rose sighed. "Well, now you know the truth about both of us."

Cold tears ran down my face, I reached up to wipe them away before it was too obvious that I was beginning to cry. I tried to swallow it down, but I was only half successful.

"Whitney, please don't cry." Bryan knelt down in front of me, resting his hands on my knees. I still couldn't look at him. "Baby, it's okay."

"You're thinking with the wrong head, Bryan, you're not listening to me." Rose jumped up and walked over to one of the potted plants in the corner of the room. "If words won't convince you, this will."

"What are you doing?" Bryan inquired apprehensively, his hands warm against my legs.

She scooped up a handful of dirt and held it gently as she closed her eyes. Before I could speak up to stop her, the tingle of Rose's powers rushed over me. I wanted to scratch at my arms and make it stop. I didn't want this, any of this.

"Rose, what are you doing?" Bryan asked again, but Rose was deep in concentration.

A small green leaf sprouted up from the soil inside of Rose's hands as long, stringy white roots pushed their way through her fingers. The leaf was limp and stood no longer than an inch tall. Rose was exhausted and she and I both knew that was all she could muster, but that was enough for now. A droplet of crimson blood fell from her nostril.

"Rose, I get it." Bryan's voice shook. His heart pounded against his ribcage, as did mine. "Please, stop before you hurt yourself."

Rose put her tiny green stem back into the dirt and turned to face her brother, "Do you believe me now?"

Bryan took a long, deep breath. "Okay...so you two are witches. Who hurt you? What happened?"

"Because," Rose took a deep breath and looked at me. "They took Rayn, we had to go after her. It's magic, Byn… there are good witches like us, and bad witches, too. "

"Bad witches? What is this the Wizard of fucking Oz? How long has this been going on?"

"A couple months, give or take," Rose whispered. "Please understand."

"I'm trying," Bryan admitted. He shook his head and went back to pacing the room. He was going to wear marks on Amilia's flooring. "I'm trying to wrap my head around why it took you eighteen years to tell me the truth, Rose."

"I thought it was the right thing to do," Rose whispered, her voice small and broken.

"Neither of you have been honest with me." Bryan glanced at me.

"You want the truth? I moved to Rifton from Kansas because Rayn's ex found out about our powers and he told everyone. We were outcasted. It was hard enough living in that town with people threatening Dmitri for being gay, but magical powers too? We weren't safe. They…they tried to light my sister on fire, Bryan. The only way for us to stay safe is to stay hidden." I took a deep breath and ran my fingers through my hair. I continued my story more collected, though the lump remained in my throat. "Coming here was supposed to make our lives better, but it didn't. I'm sorry, but what was I supposed to say to you? Everyone back there treated us like we were less than human when they found out what we are. I wanted this to be our new home so badly."

Bryan didn't say anything. He listened intently to our words but shock didn't pulse through his veins like I imagined. He wasn't floored hearing that magic existed and that real witches lived in Rifton. That all the stories weren't ghost stories but true tales. Sure, he was taken back by Rose and I having powers, but he wasn't surprised by the magic itself.

"You aren't surprised," I announced aloud, meeting Bryan's gaze.

"What?" he asked, confused.

"We just told you that we're witches and that magic is real and you aren't surprised. You watched Rose's powers for the first time and you weren't surprised. Like you already knew," I explained further. Bryan shrunk down a size and Rose's shoulders fell.

"How do you know that?" Rose asked me, denial washing over her.

"I can feel his emotions," I admitted. "I've been able to since we first met."

"Wait, what?" Bryan's voice raised in surprise. "What do you mean you can feel my emotions?"

"Did you already know about our powers?" I demanded, ignoring the question.

"No," Bryan answered. "I had no idea you two were like this until now."

You two. His choice of words was not lost on me.

"But you knew witches in Rifton existed?" Rose asked, her face pale. As if everything she had been trying to protect him from, the entire facade she had created in her head came crashing down.

Bryan gave a silent nod. "Yeah, I knew."

"How?" Tears streamed down Rose's red cheeks. She didn't bother to wipe them away, she left her hurt lying bare for him to see.

"I can't...I can't say. I promised. I'm sorry." Bryan wouldn't look either of us in the eye.

My brain rattled over who he could have possibly known that had powers. Not only that, but someone who would have trusted him enough to share their deepest secret when his own sister kept her true self locked away.

"The Drakes," I announced. "It was Emma wasn't it?"

"No," Bryan answered truthfully.

My heart collapsed into my stomach. "Serenity."

The side-eyed glance he gave me answered my question without Bryan needing to speak a word.

"You knew Serenity Drake is a witch this whole time!" Rose barked with a sob caught in her throat. "You knew and never said a word?"

"I promised," he defended himself. "She told me before she changed, back when we were all still friends. Back when she and Emma were actually sisters."

"Is Emma a witch?" I demanded, needing to know the truth once and for all.

"No," Bryan answered. "Emma has nothing to do with it. I don't have a lot of answers but I know Emma would never do anything to hurt either of you."

"How do I know you're not lying to protect them?" I demanded. I knew he wasn't lying, I could feel it in my bones, but the hurt and jealousy of his connection to the Drake sisters overwhelmed me.

Bryan's shoulders fell as he absorbed my accusation. "I would never lie to you, Whitney."

"But Serenity told you all her secrets?" Rose was still trying to put the pieces together.

Bryan turned to his sister. "In case you've forgotten, Serenity used to be one of my best friends."

"Well, your best friend did a number on me." I held up my arm so Bryan could get a good look at the massive scar that took up most of my forearm.

His heart fell into his stomach and I swore I saw his eyes gloss over. "Serenity did that to you?"

"If Serenity had her way, we would both be dead, Bryan. How could you protect that psychopath all these years?" Rose demanded.

Bryan dodged the question. "You should have told me, Rose."

"I was trying to protect you!" Rose matched his anger.

"The fuck do I need protection from? I've known about the truth of this town for six years and nothing has happened to me yet, Rose. There's nothing for you to protect me from." Bryan admitted. "How am I supposed to keep you safe if I'm wearing a blindfold?"

"I'm not the one who needs to be protected, Byn, you are," Rose said.

"Have you looked at yourself in the mirror?" Bryan let out an irritated sigh. "I'm fine, you're the one with a black eye."

"Fuck around and find out." I muttered under my breath, causing both of them to look at me.

"What?" Bryan asked, furrowing his brow.

I glanced up to meet his gaze. "That's what they said when I told Serenity and Tom that they wouldn't touch you. He said fuck around and find out."

Bryan shook his head. "She hasn't done anything yet."

"Not yet. That was before the five of us found each other. We opened a can of worms last night. Everything has changed now. Byn, I never told you because I can't stand the thought of you getting hurt. I'm doing this now to protect you," Rose explained, desperately. "I don't know what I'd do if someone came after you like they did to Rayn last night. We don't fully understand what's happening and anyone could be next. I can't risk you like that."

Her words woke me up out of the daze I had been in since Bryan first walked into the Corner Cup. Rose was right. She had been right all along. I wouldn't have accepted it if the night before never happened. Bryan and I being together was more than him knowing about the powers. I was putting him in danger.

You're reckless and you're going to get him killed.

I glanced down at my hands, blood dripping down from my fingers onto the floor. I gasped and closed my eyes, opening them back to bruised but clean skin. My heart lodged itself in my throat as I did my best to breathe. I took a life, something I never felt capable of. Tom may have been Renati but his blood stained my hands. I was a murderer, tainted.

Do you actually think someone could love an Elemental?

Bryan didn't deserve any of this.

"I don't care about that. I want to keep you safe, both of you. I don't quite understand what this all means," Bryan raised his eyes to meet mine. "But I know that I care about you. I meant what I said."

I released a deep breath and with it, a tear fell down my cheek. "Bryan, you and I can't be together."

"Wh-what?" he stammered. "What do you mean?"

"Something dark and evil is in this forest and the Renati will want revenge after what happened last night. You need to stay as far away from me as possible. You don't want to be with me, not in the long run. It can't work. I have too much baggage and you deserve better than that." I put on a brave face and pretended my words weren't breaking my heart, like they weren't tearing my soul apart.

"Whitney, that's not true." Bryan's voice was small, his eyes sincere. "I want us. I want you."

My voice trembled and my heart cracked into pieces. Tears streamed down my face as the lie left my mouth. "But I don't want you."

The knife Serenity held against my arm hurt much less than this.

"Rosie, can you give us a minute?" Bryan asked Rose but his eyes remained locked on me. "Wait for me in the living room."

Rose slid off the bed and watched my face carefully as she left the bedroom, leaving Bryan and I alone for the first time since I was fumbling for my clothes in his bedroom. The air was different than it was that night, heavy and thick with uncovered secrets and hurt feelings. My eyes never left the floor, afraid that if I peered into him I would be sucked back in.

"Whitney, look at me."

"No. It's not up for discussion. I said what I said." I stiffened my upper lip and hardened my feelings, building the thick concrete wall up around myself once again.

"You're a terrible liar."

"Bryan, I mean it. I don't want to be with you."

"Okay, I get it. You're ending this, but I'm worried about you. I can't walk out of here without knowing you're going to be okay. I actually meant everything I said the other night. I can't just walk away, Whitney."

He actually meant it. Like I didn't. Like this had all been a game to me. Like I wasn't doing this because of how much I cared about him.

"Are you going to be okay?" he asked again when I didn't respond.

"I've been through worse," I answered through my teeth.

He shifted his weight. "That's not what I asked you."

"I will be fine. I'm always fine. You know who isn't fine? Your sister. She has been agonizing over how to tell you about all of this and you're letting whatever this is between us eclipse her right now and you can't do that. You can't do that to her after everything she went through last night. Forget about me and go take care of your little sister and I'm going to take care of mine." I hardened myself, depriving myself of any emotion whatsoever. I became a shell of myself. It was the only way I'd be able to let him walk away.

"I will but you-"

"You should go." I cut him off. "You need to go, Bryan."

He sighed. "If that's what you want."

"It is."

He turned to the door but stopped after a few steps, looking back over his shoulder. "If you ever need anything, or if you ever change your mind. Well, you know where to find me."

"I won't." I didn't recognize my own voice, cold and hard as a steel beam.

"Take care of yourself, Whiney." He walked away.

I stayed firmly planted on the hardwood floor until I heard the front door of the cottage open and close. Not until I knew Bryan had walked out of my life for good did I allow myself to feel the crack in my heart deep inside my chest. A wound that time itself would never be able to mend. Something I'd have to live with for the rest of my life.

"Are you okay?" Dmitri came into view and slowly made his way into the bedroom. "Whit? Are you okay?"

"Yeah," I lied. "I'm fine."

I always had to be okay. If I wasn't okay, then my brother and sister wouldn't be okay. I was responsible for protecting them. I felt responsible for protecting my generation and I had failed miserably. I couldn't let this happen again. I had to stay strong if I was going to piece this back together.

"Come on." Dmitri reached out and took my hand in his.

We walked into the living room together and sat in front of the fire with Rayn. It was too warm for my taste, but it was comforting to be with my family. I still had Rayn, Dmitri, Brooke, and Amilia with me. I realized the days of facing these trials alone were over.

I reached out to Brooke, silently inviting her to sit by the fire with us. Brooke knelt down on the floor next to me and rested her head on my shoulder.

"This has been the worst day of my life," Rayn muttered, a tear slowly trickled down her cheek.

I looked down at the thick scar on my arm and ran my fingers along the cut.

"Hang in there, guys," I replied with a stiff upper lip. "This is only the beginning."

ABOUT AUTHOR

Meg Lynn is a debut author who has been writing for most of her life. She wrote her first short story in third grade and has been creating fantasy worlds in her mind ever since. Meg is a Northern California girl married to her high school sweetheart, they have three beautiful children and three cuddly cats. She received a bachelor's degree in Social Science from CSU Sacramento and loves coffee, books, and witchcraft. When Meg isn't writing, editing, or marketing you can find her binge-watching TV, playing BioWare games, or shuffling a tarot deck.

www.meglynnbooks.com

@meglynnwrites

Acknowledgments

Dave, my sweet husband, thank you for always believing in my voice, even when I didn't believe in myself. Thank you for making sure I had the resources and support to make my dream a reality. Thank you for keeping the kids occupied so I had silence to focus on writing and for being my biggest hype man.

Kerry, my best friend and sister. This story, Rayn and Whit's story, would not exist without you. You've been through every step of writing this book with me and your support has made all the difference. Thank you for having my back and keeping me alive for the past sixteen years.

Mom and Dad, thank you for passing on your love of books and fostering my curiosity in writing. Thank you for always supporting me in everything that I do.

My beautiful and loving friends who have hyped me up and supported me along the way, thank you for promoting Tidal Wave from the very beginning and making me feel like a genuine author.

My fantastic editor, Sydney. You put your entire heart into editing this book and I'm forever grateful. Thank you for treating my book baby with respect and for loving it too.

Bianca at Moonpress Design, thank you for bringing my scattered vision of a book cover to a beautiful reality. I couldn't have asked for more perfect, eye-catching artwork.

My beta readers, thank you for taking on this story in one of it's rawest forms and helping me make the best book I could produce. Every word of encouragement gave me so much validation and every bit of constructive criticism gave me a new perspective on things. You guys were the fresh eyes I needed.

And you, the reader, thank you for taking a chance on a newbie like me. I wouldn't be here without you.

Lastly, this book would not have been possible without the two loves of my life: Starbucks and Taylor Swift. Thank you for the motivation and inspiration in fiction and reality.